PERFECT POISON

PERFECT POISON

JOYCE AND JIM LAVENE

WHEELER
CHIVERS

This Large Print edition is published by Wheeler Publishing, Waterville, Maine, USA and by BBC Audiobooks Ltd, Bath, England.
Wheeler Publishing, a part of Gale, Cengage Learning.
Copyright © 2008 by Joyce Lavene and Jim Lavene.
The moral right of the author has been asserted.
A Peggy Lee Garden Mystery.

The text of this Large Print edition is unabridged.
Other aspects of the book may vary from the original edition.
Set in 16 pt. Plantin.
Printed on permanent paper.

LIBRARY OF CONGRESS CATALOGING-IN-PUBLICATION DATA

Lavene, Joyce.
  Perfect poison / by Joyce Lavene and Jim Lavene.
    p. cm. — (A Peggy Lee garden mystery) (Wheeler
  Publishing large print cozy mystery)
  ISBN-13: 978-1-59722-826-8 (pbk. : alk. paper)
  ISBN-10: 1-59722-826-5 (pbk. : alk. paper)
    1. Lee, Peggy (Fictitious character)—Fiction.
  2. Botanists—Fiction. 3. Charlotte (N.C.)—Fiction. 4. Drowning
  victims—Fiction. 5. Large type books I. Lavene, James. II. Title.
  PS3562.A8479P47 2008
  813'.54—dc22   2008028079

BRITISH LIBRARY CATALOGUING-IN-PUBLICATION DATA AVAILABLE

Published in 2008 in the U.S. by arrangement with The Berkley Publishing Group, a member of Penguin Group (USA) Inc.
Published in 2009 in the U.K. by arrangement with The Berkley Publishing Group, a member of Penguin Group (USA) Inc.

U.K. Hardcover: 978 1 408 42127 7 (Chivers Large Print)
U.K. Softcover: 978 1 408 42128 4 (Camden Large Print)

LT-M

Printed in the United States of America
1 2 3 4 5 6 7 8 9 10 11 12 13

PERFECT POISON

1

Trout Lily
Botanical: *Erythronium americanum*
Ants pollinate the trout lily or dogtooth
violet. After a seed is planted, it may take
seven years to make a mature plant and
then, only plants with two leaves will
flower. The lily opens each morning and
closes each night, and during the heat of
the day, the sepals appear to be curved
backwards. The plant grows from a deep
rootstock or corm, which is three to five
inches underground.

"You will all die!"

A few people attending the funeral service
for Mayor Jim Garrett were jolted out of
their sorrow and reverie with the preacher's
avid declaration. One or two, who had never
been to a fundamentalist Baptist service,
looked shocked and confused as well.

The tall, gaunt scarecrow of a minister

squeezed one eye shut and pointed his skeletal finger at each member of the congregation. The other eye glared at them. "The living know that they shall die, but the dead know nothing. Their hatred and their love is now perished."

Peggy Lee had almost been asleep in the drowsy heat of the afternoon service. She pushed her worn black hat back on her white/red hair. It was too hot in July for black, but her Liz Claiborne suit and hat were as funereal as her summer wardrobe allowed. People shouldn't die in the summer. She fussed with her pocketbook, looking for something to do. It was too hot and too easy to go to sleep during a memorial service.

She looked at her son, Paul, who sat beside her. They had both known the former mayor of Badin since Paul was a baby. It was proper that they should be there even if it was inconvenient. But dying had a way of being difficult.

Paul looked over at her and smiled back. He took her hand, his green eyes so like hers clouded with memories of another funeral. His father, Peggy's husband, John, had died only two years before. His funeral had been crowded like this one, but instead of hundreds of civilians, there had been hundreds of police officers from all over the state.

"Jim Garrett was a good man," the preacher intoned. "But every man is guilty of sin. Every man will suffer this life in sorrow until he is reunited with our Lord."

Peggy definitely agreed with him, especially when it came to this funeral service. She was definitely suffering without air-conditioning. The doors and windows to the little white wooden church were thrown open to the oppressive heat. Many of the mourners stood in the doorway and on the steps. She supposed they were in even worse shape than she was; at least she was sitting down.

She looked at her friend, Tom Harrison, the present mayor of Badin, who sat beside her. The heat was getting to him as well. He was nodding off, his chin almost resting on his chest. She pushed her elbow into his side. He snorted a little and opened his eyes. She smiled at him as he shook his head to clear it, and the preacher rattled on about death and salvation.

"If I could stay awake through this," Tom whispered, "I'm sure I'd be scared enough not to do anything bad again."

"I think I've been awake," she whispered back. "It doesn't matter. We're all going to suffer and die. There's no help for it."

He would've laughed but caught himself in time. It was a good thing. He had a big, booming laugh that could be heard easily in a crowd during the annual Badin Festival. At this point in the lengthy memorial service with half of the congregation asleep, there might have been a few heart attacks if his laugh had boomed over the crowd.

The organ music came up, and the preacher opened his eyes after his final prayer. "Go with God," he blessed the group of mourners. "But remember, your day is at hand."

They filed out of the musty old church and into the sunlight filtering through the trees on Morrow Mountain, one of Badin's tourist attractions. The air was refreshing even though it was superhot. The shade offered a little relief, but no breeze stirred the old oak trees that surrounded the church.

"He was a fine man." The man who spoke looked to be at least one hundred. "He did a lot for this town. He always believed in it, even when things looked bad."

"We're gonna miss him." Lora Jeon, the woman beside him in a dark brown crepe dress, agreed. She was a perennial council member. "How are you, Peggy? I haven't seen you in an age. What have you been up to?"

Peggy took off her black hat. She couldn't stand it a minute longer. She fluffed her mostly white hair with an impatient hand and hoped it didn't look like a goose had been squatting on it. "I'm doing fine, Lora Jean. I was out here a few months ago. Paul was fishing. Tom loaned us his boat. I think he said you were in Atlanta with your daughter."

"That's right. Where's my mind?" The other woman tapped her forehead. "It's a lot for Tom to fill Jim's shoes as mayor, but I think he'll do a good job."

Mayor Harrison put his arm around his friend's shoulders. "And she's not a bit prejudiced."

She laughed. "No! Not at all. You all are coming to the house for something to eat, right?" Then as Peggy began to make her excuses, Lora Jean interrupted. "I won't hear of you going all the way back to Charlotte without something to eat and drink. You know where we live. I expect to see you. And I want to hear about your garden shop. How's that coming along?"

"The Potting Shed is hanging in there," Peggy answered. "You'll have to come to Charlotte and let me give you a tour."

"I just might do that. I've been looking for some nice blueberry bushes to plant."

11

Lora Jean wiped the sweat from her brow. "But right now, let's get to the house and out of the sun."

Paul shook his head as the mayor and Lora Jean walked away. "Smooth, Mom. I guess we're going to get something to eat. Why does every funeral have to have food?"

"I'm not sure. It's tradition. I'm glad I brought that banana pudding now. It's not good to go to one of these things and not take food."

"So *that's* what the ice chest is for!"

"Always be prepared." She opened the door to her truck and glanced over at the recently dug grave that was covered with flowers. "Jim worked hard his whole life to get this town on its feet. If anyone deserves to rest in peace, it's him."

There was a wait getting out of the church parking lot. Even on Christmas day, the tiny church probably only saw a fraction of the number of cars that were here today for the service. The road that curved up and down the mountain was more like a parking lot. It took time to get the cars and pickups going.

"I hope we aren't sorry we brought your truck." Paul tried to see across his mother to the gauge that said how much of a charge was left in the batteries that filled the back of the electric pickup. "How far does this thing go before you have to plug it in?"

"Don't worry," she defended her modified Ford Ranger. "It will make the trip without a problem. I was out here a few months ago making sure all the sunflowers were safe, remember? Everything was fine."

"Except for your competition opening up in Founders Hall, we both had a good month until this. I guess it was too much to hope for nothing bad to happen."

Paul didn't have to remind her that Smith & Hawken had already hung their shingle in the busy mall area in Charlotte Center City. She'd watched them every step of the way from rumor to reality.

The Potting Shed was a short walk away in Brevard Court. She did a good business there with eager condominium buyers who wanted to spruce up their balconies and window space with plants. But part of her market was the same type of outdoor furniture that Smith & Hawken sold. Her store was much smaller and couldn't hold as many pieces. There was no doubt many of her customers would buy plants from her and the pricier garden items from her competitor.

This came at a time when Peggy had embarked on a second retirement from teaching botany at Queens University. The

Potting Shed was doing well, and the Charlotte-Mecklenburg Police Department had offered her a contract position as a forensic botanist. She'd hoped that would get her through. She'd mortgaged everything and spent John's pension to open her shop; *their* shop, the one they'd dreamed about for years before John was killed.

"We'll be fine." She presented an assured face to Paul, but inside she was worried. She was a worrier by nature, so that wasn't surprising. She wasn't sure how often the police would need a contract forensic botanist. So far she hadn't done any work for them. The Potting Shed was doing all right, holding its own between the landscape business and the shop itself. Thank goodness Charlotte's downtown housing boom had come along so she had someone to buy her garden supplies.

It was a short ride down the mountain in the blessed air-conditioned environment of the truck. Too short, she realized, when she saw the dinner was being held outside in Tom Harrison's yard. Two large white tents had been erected to handle most of Badin plus friends of the mayor from out of town. It was going to be a sultry memorial dinner.

She parked where she could find space on

one of Badin's old, twisted streets. One thing she'd always loved about the town was its French flavor. It was left over from the French engineers who'd built the town at the turn of the last century when mining aluminum and harnessing the great falls of the Yadkin River for power seemed like the best thing to do.

Despite losing interest during the First World War, the village continued to grow under the ownership of United Metals. The corporation still maintained its stranglehold on the community, alternately giving with one hand while taking away with the other. The aluminum smelting plant was all but closed down now, a symbol of Badin's problems coping with the twenty-first century.

But the sweet charm of the streets with their stone storm water channels and French-design houses overlooking beautiful Badin Lake, and the Uwharrie Mountains rising in the mists, never failed to delight her. She, John, and Paul had spent many pleasant afternoons on the lake. Jim spent many of those long summer days with them. Men died, she considered, but the beauty and power of the land went on.

"I'll get the banana pudding," Paul offered. "Do you think anyone will mind if I leave my suit coat here in the truck?"

"Good Lord, no! It must be one hundred degrees out here! I'm sure most of the men will lose their jackets and ties somewhere between the church and here. If it's any consolation, Jim would've been the first one to take it off."

"Yeah. He was a character. Remember that time he taught me how to make balloon animals? I think I drove you and Dad crazy for a couple weeks after that."

"A *couple* weeks?" She looked at her hat on the seat in the truck and decided to leave it there. Women had as much right as men to be comfortable. "I think your father sent Jim a package of balloons for Christmas that year to thank him."

Paul laughed. "Yeah, but just think, last year that skill came in handy at the Children's Hospital benefit. How many other rookies can make sheep out of balloons?"

"I don't want to think about that." She locked the truck. Charlotte habits didn't go away because she was in a small town. "I pretended I didn't know who you were."

Lora Jean greeted them as they walked under the first big tent. Long tables were covered with white tablecloths and filled with casseroles, pies, cakes, and fried chicken. "It's like a banquet, I know. I'm

16

sure Jim would've been proud at this turn-out."

"I'm sure you're right." Peggy handed her the banana pudding. "He would've sampled most of this food, too."

"Oh, you didn't have to bring this." Lora Jean took the dish and set it on one of the long tables. "But you're right. Jim could eat more chicken than any man I ever knew. He had a hunger for life, and that's the God's honest truth."

Peggy and Lora Jean hugged, then another family showed up with a big bowl of potato salad. Lora Jean went with them to find a place on the table for it.

"Wouldn't be fried chicken without potato salad," Mayor Harrison said as he circulated through the crowd. "What did you bring, Peggy?"

"Banana pudding. It's the one over there in the white bowl."

"Is it vegetarian?"

"No. I always put ham in it instead of bananas."

He laughed. "Just checking. You still don't eat meat, huh?"

"No. Your fried chicken is safe with me."

"And why is that?" He continued teasing her. "You love plants. Why are you willing to eat *them* but not cows?"

17

"I never met a plant with a mother." She shrugged. "If I do, I might change my mind."

Paul was already moving down the long table with a plate in one hand when Mayor Harrison turned away to greet a member of the town council. Peggy grabbed a plate and followed Paul. She noticed the sudden sway of the tablecloths and glanced up at the sky. Dark clouds hovering over Morrow Mountain were starting to move closer to the lake. She hoped the weather would hold for a little while longer.

It was fun visiting with so many people she knew from the past. She didn't get out to Badin as much as she wanted to. Between the shop and the rest of her hectic life, she was lucky she could find time to take a shower every day. Some of the faces she recognized but couldn't put names to. Others she recalled right away. They usually warranted hugs and long, sometimes tearful, hellos.

Whitecaps developed on the lake. The wind scattered the gulls that usually rode the buoys that marked the swimming areas. Children and their parents still played in the water, trying to ignore the storm that was brewing. Screams of happiness drifted across the lake along with the smell of roasting hot dogs.

Peggy found herself sandwiched between a city councilman who had gone to school with John and a woman from the Historic Badin Commission. They were arguing about United Metals, always a subject that came up here. Half the town thought the corporation was like an evil overlord, while the other half still looked to them for salvation. The argument grew heated when a congressman sitting close by put down his chicken leg to add his opinion.

Not having enough information on the subject to voice an opinion, Peggy made her excuses and drifted away from the table with a glass of sweet tea in her hand. She watched the clouds grow darker and heard the growl of thunder come across the ancient Uwharries. She knew they might all be scattering for shelter quickly, whatever their opinions on United Metals.

"Peggy!" A petite woman with a shock of silver hair approached her. "I didn't think you'd be out here today. I haven't seen you since you attended my forensic seminar in Raleigh."

"Ruth! You know me. I can't resist a lot of food and politics at a funeral. I saw you finally got the funding for the new underwater forensic school at the University of

North Carolina at Charlotte. Congratulations!"

"I guess I was tougher than they figured. How is your work with the CMPD going?"

"Slow right now. I haven't had a chance to use my newfound status as a contract forensic botanist yet. How are you doing?"

Ruth Sargent shrugged. "We're out for the summer, but it's such a perfect time for diving that I decided to take a few students out. Last week we were doing some recovery work at Lake Tillery. I still have a house there."

"That's a beautiful area." Peggy smiled at Ruth. She barely came to Peggy's chest and probably only weighed eighty pounds. But she had a mighty intellect when it came to explaining how a forensic investigation should be done underwater. Her plain words and graphic slides were almost too much right after lunch during the seminar in Raleigh.

"Did you know Mayor Garrett well?" Ruth sipped some lemonade from a plastic cup.

"We were friends for years. How about you?"

"We'd only known each other a short time. I respected him. He'll be missed."

"It looks like this weather is agreeing with

you." Peggy watched shards of lightning pierce the darkening sky. "I think we're going to have to take this inside."

"I think you're right. It's good to see you. We need to have lunch and catch up." Ruth smiled at her. "I'm going to see if I can help move some things."

Peggy watched Ruth walk away, her tiny purple suit lightweight yet very appropriate. She didn't recognize the design but knew quality when she saw it. She looked out at the lake that was whipped into angry froths. Coming up from the water, orange trumpet creepers gave some color to the green grass and a colorful little trout lily poked its head through some pine straw. She was surprised they hadn't been cut down with the shorter grass, but that was the beauty of wildflowers; they survived through almost everything man could throw at them.

She turned back to help everyone as they busily moved plates, pots, and chairs into the mayor's house. A few raindrops had already fallen, leaving shimmering trails on the surface of the large white tents. She looked for Paul and saw him deep in conversation with a very pretty brunette. No reason he should help with the food. Almost all of it was already gone. It was more important for him to take an interest in a

21

woman his age again. Since his disastrous relationship with the assistant medical examiner, Mai Sato, Peggy had all but given up on seeing grandchildren in her lifetime.

"Let me give you a hand with that, Mom," Paul said when he saw her struggling with her banana pudding and an ice chest.

"That's all right. I can take care of it. You go on with what you're doing."

He took the ice chest from her. "I was just talking to Stephanie. She's a student at UNCC."

"Hi. Nice to meet you." Stephanie walked with them toward the house.

"Sorry." Paul grinned, and his face turned red. "Stephanie Nichols, this is my mother, Dr. Peggy Lee. Mom, this is Stephanie. She's studying something to do with water at UNCC."

Was this her son, blushing and stammering? It was a good sign. Peggy shook hands with Stephanie. "Nice to meet you. You wouldn't by any chance be studying under-water forensics with Professor Sargent?"

"That's right!" Stephanie grinned, her blue eyes lighting up. "How did you know? Is there something about me that gives it away?"

Peggy laughed. "Of course not. I saw Ruth here. I've known her for years. I took her seminar in Raleigh."

"Please don't get my mom started on describing plants that grow on dead people," Paul said to Stephanie.

"In that case, you wouldn't want to hear what I have to say about algae that grow on dead people." Stephanie smiled at him in the time-honored way that meant she was interested in him.

Another very good sign. "I'm sure we could have an interesting conversation," Peggy told her as they entered the mayor's house. "But I'm going over here with the old folks. You two talk about something besides dead people. Maybe babies."

Paul's green eyes were like emeralds as he flashed a look that could kill. "Thanks, Mom. Maybe you should pull out those pictures of me with my underwear on my head."

"Not recent ones, I hope," Stephanie teased.

"No. He hasn't tried that since he was about seven, I think." Peggy laughed off her son's embarrassment. "Excuse me. I see someone I have to talk to."

She left the two young people alone by the door as she waded through the crowd packed into the house. The breeze coming off the lake brought some relief from the

23

heat, but the storm that accompanied it was bearing down with a terrible intensity.

"Better batten down the hatches, eh Peggy?" Mayor Harrison joked. "Don't look so worried. This house was built in 1911. It's weathered two hurricanes, a flood, and a landslide. The worst that ever happened was finding those rattlesnakes in the attic."

"Spare me the horror stories." She held up her hand. "I've heard all the Badin stories from Jim a hundred times over."

"But did he tell you about the black racers chasing him around the lake?"

A huge clap of thunder shook the midsize brick house and momentarily caught everyone's attention. Conversations lapsed midsentence.

"I think that's the devil coming to get you for those lies." Peggy laughed at him. "I hope you have some hatches to batten down. This could get bad."

"We have all of the fire department and rescue squad here. How bad could it be?"

As soon as the words were out of his mouth, the front door blew open, and two men in rescue uniforms searched the room with frantic eyes. "Chief Morrison?" One of them called to the head of the rescue squad. "We have a problem, sir."

Peggy migrated across the room with Tom

as he joined the growing group at the door. Chief Morrison, a stocky, middle-aged man with a buzz cut, was nodding as he listened to what his men had to tell him. "The diver sent in to check out the dam isn't responding to hails. We think he might be in trouble."

"Why are you telling me?" Morrison was decisive. "Get somebody down there after him."

"That's the problem, sir. We don't have anybody with that kind of training out here right now."

"What about Stevens? He's a sport diver."

"On vacation."

"What about Jolly?"

"Can't get in touch with him. His wife says he's off somewhere fishing."

"Let's not stand here arguing, son. That man could be drowning." Morrison called his men together. "Get the rescue boats. We might need to call in the county squad."

"If I could make a suggestion." Peggy stepped out from behind Tom. "There's an experienced forensic diver here. I don't know if she has her gear, but maybe she could help."

Morrison looked at her like she'd jumped off of a spaceship and landed right there in the mayor's house. "What are you talking

25

about? What do you mean an *expensive* diver anyway? Any man who wouldn't volunteer his time for this isn't worth a crap anyway."

Somehow, Ruth had managed to slide between the tight-knit group of men. "I think she said *forensic* diver, Chief. I've got my gear in the van. Can I help?"

At first, Chief Morrison had a hard time even finding the top of Ruth's silver head. When he finally located her, he stared then nodded. "Okay. Let's get down there. We'll have to take the service road that leads to the dam."

"Who's down there this year, Chief?" one of the rescue workers asked.

"I don't know. They don't tell me who United Metals wants to send in or when they send him in. Let's worry about that after we find him."

Ruth turned to Peggy. "Will you come, too? If something bad has happened, it might be good to have a second opinion."

"I don't know a thing about underwater rescue, Ruth. But I'll come along if you want me to be there."

"I'll come too, Professor," Stephanie volunteered. "Paul is a Charlotte police officer. Maybe he could help, too."

The chief nodded. "The more the merrier. Let's get out of here. That man can't hold his breath all day. You two, go with Healy. You," he pointed to Ruth, "let's get your gear. You can ride with me."

"I've got my diving gear, too," Stephanie said. "It will only take me a minute to get it."

2

Muskgrass
Botanical: *Chara spp.*
Often called skunkweed because of its musty, garliclike aroma, muskgrass is a grayish green alga that is many times confused with flowering water plants. But muskgrass doesn't flower and can't live above the surface of the water. Muskgrass, though considered useless by humans, is consumed by many species of ducks.

After retrieving the women's gear, they rode in a convoy of fire and rescue trucks to the service road that ran up to the dam. The road was surrounded by lush vegetation on one side and a pine forest on the other. It was only a dirt road used irregularly by EPA experts and divers hired by United Metals, who checked the dam structure several times a year.

"Does anyone know what time the diver

got here?" Chief Morrison asked the driver.

"All I could get from those boys at United was that he was out here, and they couldn't contact him." The young rescue worker winked at Stephanie in his rearview mirror. "They didn't even know his name."

"But of course they knew who to contact when things went wrong." Chief Morrison shook his head. "Somebody should've told us this was going on. We should've had someone out here."

"How were the people from United keeping in touch with the diver?" Ruth asked.

"I'm not sure, ma'am," the driver replied. "You'd have to ask them about that."

Ruth looked at Peggy and Stephanie. "They were probably monitoring the dive with a remote camera that fed to their computers."

"So that's how they know he's in trouble." Peggy nodded.

"He should've had a partner," Stephanie added. "No one is supposed to dive alone."

"It would be nice if the real world was like what we teach in school." Ruth put her hand through her thick, silver hair. "But nobody wants to pay two divers if they can get one to do it."

They finally reached the site where the diver entered the water. His green pickup was still parked on the road. The rescue vehicles stopped when they saw it. A crowd of people jumped out and began to take a look at the situation.

"Help me suit up," Ruth said to Stephanie. "I'll let you know if I need you down there."

"But I'm here," the girl protested. "Let me help you."

"You're a first-year student. Let me sum up the situation. If it isn't too bad or I need help, I'll call you."

Ruth's gaze met Peggy's, and they understood each other. Peggy squeezed Stephanie's shoulder. "I'm sure you'll have your hands full keeping everyone calm up here. You can help us understand what's going on, since we won't have a camera."

"Looks like there's some kind of guide rope down here." Paul crouched beside the truck. "Should I pull it in?"

"No," Ruth advised. "Not yet. Let me see what's going on. No one should touch anything until we know what's happened. I shouldn't have to tell *you* that, Paul."

Stephanie helped Ruth get on her wet suit, air tank, mouthpiece, and goggles. They checked the gear carefully before Ruth started into the lake. "I hope this doesn't take much time," Stephanie said to Peggy.

"We were out in Lake Tillery this morning, so she doesn't have a lot of air left."

"It gets pretty deep right by the dam," the rescue driver advised. "That's where you'll find those big white catfish, too. My brother caught one a few years back. Ten feet long. Weighed at least a hundred pounds."

"Some fish story," Paul said. "That's about as good as the bells ringing on the church that's underwater in Lake Lure."

The driver sized him up with a cocky smile. "You don't live around here, Officer. There's a lot more strange stuff out here than most folks know."

Stephanie didn't seem impressed. "Anyone who dives hears strange stories. Most of them are myths. I took a year of marine biology. A catfish doesn't get that big."

"I'll be glad to take you out one night on my boat, sugar, and show you the sights."

Paul rolled his eyes and returned to the pickup abandoned by the diver. "Maybe we should call the sheriff and let him know there's a problem. Someone should look through the truck and find out who the diver is."

"We'll do that in good time, son," Chief Morrison said. "No point bringing in the sheriff until we know for sure there's a problem."

Stephanie glanced at her watch and looked out over the rough water. "She's already been under for five minutes."

A loud clap of thunder punctuated her words before heavy rain started falling on them. The chief and two of his men took to their truck to watch the proceedings from a drier vantage point. High winds buffeted the heavy trees around them, bending branches and blowing loose leaves across the road.

Peggy looked up at the top of the impressive dam structure that rose like a giant holding back the heavy water of the Yadkin River. Forks of lightning lit up the dark sky behind the dam. The portals were closed, no water escaping, probably in deference to the diver in the water below the dam. The sight made Peggy shiver. She was already soaked and uncomfortable but she was not willing to hide when there was so much at stake. She didn't know what she could do to help, but she didn't want to miss the opportunity if she was needed.

Mayor Harrison drove down to join them. He ran out of his pickup and stood beside Peggy and Stephanie, his gaze on the lake like everyone else's. "Have you heard anything yet?"

"Not yet." Peggy looked up at him. "You

should've brought an umbrella."

"You're right. Actually, I thought I had one in the truck, but by the time I realized I didn't, I was already here." He laughed and looked up into the full, driving force of the rain. "My mama always told us kids rain was good for us anyway. I guess she thought if it made flowers grow, why not kids?"

"Look!" Stephanie pointed at the lake. "I see someone surfacing. I hope it's Professor Sargent. She can't have much air left."

Another truck joined them on the road that was rapidly turning into orange mud. The name on the side told them the corporation had decided to find out what was going on. Chief Morrison jumped out of his truck, despite the storm, when he saw the Badin chief of police with a local United Metals representative. They stood off out of earshot from the rest of the group, obviously discussing the situation.

"Here comes trouble," Mayor Harrison promised.

Stephanie ran to the edge of the water. Rain had long since plastered her dark hair to her head and pressed her pretty suit to her thin body.

Peggy couldn't help noticing most of the men's eyes, including her son's, were riveted on the young woman as she stood waiting for word from her teacher. She supposed, despite any horrific situation, sex would always take a front seat.

The group gathered closer to the shoreline, ignoring the fast-paced lightning strikes close by and intense wind pushing at their bodies. Ruth dragged herself up out of the water. Stephanie rushed out into the lake to help her. "He's dead," Ruth pronounced as soon as she took off her mouthpiece. "I found him wedged into the intake bulkhead gate at the base of the dam. It looks like he was sucked in. He didn't have a chance."

Her voice was strained, and her gaze wandered uneasily across the crowd. Stephanie started crying and hugged her. The police chief nodded and pulled out his radio to call for help. The United representative took out his cell phone to relay the information to his superiors.

"I guess that's it then." Mayor Harrison stared at the dam. "How many times are we going to lose divers like this?"

"What do you mean?" Peggy asked.

"This is two that I know of. That dam is a menace. Something should be done about it before they send anyone else down there."

"Careful with your words, Tom," the police chief warned. "You aren't *only* a citizen anymore."

"Yes I am. And it's about time someone spoke out about it."

"Now's not the time for politics." Ruth's steady but darker voice rode over the sound of the storm and the conversation around her. "We have to get the body up. The scene has to be processed, and his family has to be notified."

"Processed?" The chief of police seemed surprised at her words. "No crime took place here, ma'am. I think we need to send someone down for the body and get on with notifying his kin."

"It doesn't matter if the circumstances seem suspicious or not," Ruth argued. "I'm a forensic underwater expert. This is what I do. This is the scene of a questionable death. It has to be processed."

There was intense debate as to what was the right thing to do. It stopped abruptly when the United rep put away his cell phone and joined the group. "We have nothing to hide here. The diver's death was an unfortunate accident, but we welcome processing the scene for future safety issues that could be addressed."

Mayor Harrison mustered a wry smile. "Well, that says it all, doesn't it? I guess we know what we're doing now."

■ ■ ■ ■

The storm hung over Badin while they waited for another group of rescue workers and the Stanly County sheriff. Peggy helped Ruth go over everything in her kit that she might need when she got down there to process the scene around the body.

"I wish they'd get here," Ruth said for the tenth time. "I'd like to get this over with."

"You've done your part," Peggy assured her. "I don't think anyone would think less of you if you decide to leave this for someone else."

Ruth's head shot up. "You heard them. This will be just another drowning accident if I don't stay and take care of it. This is a new day for underwater investigations. But most people don't realize it."

"I'm sure this man's family will appreciate whatever you can do for him." Peggy wasn't surprised by her friend's anxiety. She knew Ruth had given up doing the real-life job to teach because she'd seen too much.

"Thanks. I'm glad you're here. I guess I need the moral support." Ruth glanced at Stephanie, who was standing outside the truck talking to Paul. "She's a smart girl. Good student. She's just too eager. And she's not ready for actually seeing a drowning victim."

Peggy wasn't sure if *she* was ready for that either, but she didn't mention it to Ruth. Her friend was upset enough as it was. "Is there anything I can do that could make this easier for you?"

"Not really. I appreciate you being here. And I'd like your thoughts after I get the body out. I think it might be difficult to make them let us have some time to look it over, but we'll do the best we can."

With six weeks of forensic training behind her, Peggy didn't want to point out that this was her first case as an examiner. She understood her role, grisly as it might be. She'd be looking for anything botanical on or in the diver's body that could help explain why and how he died.

There was no way of knowing what she'd be looking for, if anything. She remembered distinctly attending Ruth's seminar where the underwater expert spoke of how to tell what kind of fish had bitten flesh that had been underwater and different ways of deciding how long a drowning victim had been down. It wasn't the most pleasant of conversations, but she had to admit to a certain morbid fascination with the subject.

Fortunately, this poor man, bless his soul,

hadn't been underwater for very long, and he was wearing a wet suit. The body probably wouldn't be that bad.

Ruth took a deep breath and let it out slowly. "I think the storm is over. I might as well get on with it."

The second rescue crew, this time equipped with boats, nets, and terrible large hooks that Peggy didn't want to speculate about, came up behind them with a sheriff's car at the rear. A dozen or so men got slowly out of their vehicles. Apparently, word had already filtered down that there was no rush, no life to save.

There were introductions all around. The deputy sheriff asked Ruth a few questions. Then she was hooked up to Stephanie's air tank that contained a better supply of air. Ruth nodded, ready to go down again. This time she had her processing kit and several plastic zip top bags with her.

"Want to take one of these grapplers with you to haul him back?" one of the rescue workers asked her.

The look on her face should have been answer enough, but she added, "No, thanks. I can handle it. I don't want to damage his suit. There could be evidence inside."

The man snorted rudely. "Evidence of what? The man drowned. What are you expecting to find?"

"I'm not expecting to find anything," Ruth assured him. "But I don't want to miss anything either."

Peggy watched as Ruth turned her back on him and started walking into the water. The rescue worker rolled his eyes and shook his head, indicating what he thought of the process. No one else was as open with their opinions, but the general feeling was that Ruth was wasting their time.

"Does she think the diver's death is questionable?" Paul asked when Ruth's head disappeared under the lake's murky water.

"I don't know," Peggy admitted. "She's very nervous about it. I don't think she'd do this unless she really believed it was important."

"It's not always a question of whether or not a crime has been committed," Stephanie said and then reiterated the position on correct procedure. "It's more like any other investigation. The police wouldn't let a run-of-the-mill car accident go without asking some questions. That's all this is. But for some reason, people think it's okay to let a drowning victim get dragged up and taken away without any investigation."

Another car pulled up behind the sheriff's car at the back of the line of vehicles taking up most of the service road at the dam. Two deputies moved in fast to tell the driver to pull back out, but before they could stop them, a woman and a teenage girl jumped out of the late-model Toyota Tundra and started running toward the lakeshore.

"Is he all right?" the older woman screamed out as she ran. "Have you brought him up?"

"Hold on there!" The Badin police chief put his bulky form in front of her frenzied flight. "This is off limits. You'll have to leave."

"That's my husband down there!" the woman said. "Channel 14 News called to talk to me about the accident. You told *them* before you told me."

The chief looked at the deputy sheriff, who stared at the United rep, who was talking on his cell phone and didn't notice the chain of information that ended with him.

"Let's settle down here and get some information about your husband and what he was doing in the lake today." The deputy sheriff finally took charge of the situation.

"Not before you tell me what's going on. Where's Gerry? How long has he been down?"

"I'll need your husband's full name and Social Security number," the deputy sheriff persisted.

"Get out of my way!" The diver's wife stalked past him, daring him to stop her. The teenager glanced at the deputy sheriff as she walked by, but kept walking.

The diver's wife and daughter paused when they reached Peggy, Paul, and Stephanie standing on the shore. "Do any of you know if Gerry's okay? Has anyone been in touch with him?"

Peggy put her hand on the woman's shoulder. "Another diver was sent down there. I'm sorry. She said it appears he was sucked into the intake bulkhead gate. She's bringing him back now."

Tears gathered in the woman's wild eyes. "You mean he's dead? That's not possible. He's been diving in this lake all his life. It's his third dive for United. He knows the dam. It can't be true."

"Maybe it was the storm," a young rescue worker, barely out of his teens, said. "It was pretty bad."

Peggy didn't add anything to his words. Maybe it *was* the storm. It was certainly raining and windy before the rescue workers came to the mayor's house for Chief Morrison. She didn't see how the weather above the water could affect someone under it, but she certainly wasn't an expert.

"That's stupid!" the diver's wife told him. "That shouldn't have made any difference. Where are the two men who always monitor the dive? They should know what happened." She looked through the group, and her gaze settled on the only man in a suit and tie; the United Metals rep. "I'll see what's going on. Stay here, Mandy. Let me know if you see anything."

Mandy was a very plain young woman who looked like she was wearing her older brother's clothes. She glanced at Peggy, sniffed, then wiped her eyes on the back of her shirtsleeve. She stared out at the lake, which was rapidly calming, as if she was expecting a miracle to change the news she and her mother had been given.

Peggy felt bad for her. She knew there was no chance her father was coming back alive. She supposed this was one of the things Ruth was worried about. What was it going to be like dragging the dead diver to shore under the eyes of his watchful relatives?

She slipped her arm around the girl's shoulders and hugged her. "It shouldn't be long now. I'm sorry I didn't know your father. Was he a professional diver?"

Mandy didn't respond at first. She kept her eyes on the water, shifting away from Peggy. "He's been a diver his whole life. He taught me to dive. We were going to go to the coast next week to do some diving in the shipwrecks off Hatteras. I can't believe this. He's always so careful."

Peggy wrapped her arms across her chest. "No matter how careful you are, things happen. I wish it wasn't so, but it's a part of life we all have to live with."

"I hate suits!" Mandy's mother rejoined them. "They don't know what's going on. Gerry's out there alone. I'm standing here. He probably needs someone."

They all saw Ruth surface at the same time. It was enough to quiet all the conversation as every eye turned to watch her bring Gerald Capshaw's body back to shore. Mandy's mother paced and swore, but she was sobbing at the same time. Mandy stood beside her as much as she could. Large tears poured down her face, leaving streaks on her dark skin.

As they watched, it suddenly must have occurred to the rescue workers they could be doing more than staring at Ruth. Two of them jumped in a boat and started the small motor. It was only a matter of minutes before they reached her and brought both divers into the boat. They turned the boat around and came straight back to shore.

The heat came back with the vengeance

of a South American jungle. The sun heated up the moist air, making it difficult to breathe with the high humidity. The area hadn't been cordoned off yet. Several boats filled with laughing families raced toward the dam. They slowed down when they saw something was happening, people pointing and staring at the rescue workers. They parked their boats and watched to see what was going to happen next.

The rescue workers ignored them. Peggy supposed it didn't matter what the onlookers did as long as they kept their distance. The boat bearing Ruth and the dead diver kept coming closer until two other rescue workers were able to wade into the lake and bring the boat to shore. They helped Ruth out and then carefully lifted the dead man even though nothing they did now would make a difference. They put him down in the back of Chief Morrison's truck, where the temporary forensic office was set up.

Ruth walked immediately to Peggy and handed her two bags containing evidence. She took off her breathing apparatus with Stephanie's help, not looking at the mother and daughter who hugged each other. "Do either of these plants look familiar to you?" she asked, gesturing toward the bags.

Peggy walked with her to the back of the

truck. "I recognize both of them. One is duckweed. The other is muskgrass. They aren't uncommon to find in North Carolina lakes."

Ruth kept her focus on the back of the truck, ignoring the diver's wife and daughter. "I hate it when it's like this. It's what I was talking about. I have a job to do, and a crying audience won't help."

Together they went over the man's body, first with the wet suit on and then with it off. The assistant medical examiner joined them. Peggy was surprised he didn't protest that Ruth had begun to process the scene before he got there. She took notes while the two seasoned professionals marked everything about the body from head to toe. There was some bruising and a few abrasions but nothing else outward that could have had anything to do with his death.

"I appreciate your help, Dr. Sargent," the assistant ME said when they had finished the exam. "I'll take over now."

3

Bougainvillea

Botanical: *Bougainvillea spectabilis*
Admiral Louis-Antoine de Bougainville began his long journey to the Pacific Ocean in 1768, discovering a beautiful vine in Brazil that now bears his name. Today it is one of the most popular tropical flowers. These plants are members of the four-o'clock family and can be trained to grow as potted plants or in hanging baskets. Unlike most flowering vines, the vibrant color comes from the bracts that surround each flower rather than the flower itself.

"So what happened after that?" Sam Ollson, Peggy's landscape manager, asked when she was back at the Potting Shed recounting the event. "How was your first job as a forensic botanist?"

"Shh! Let her finish telling about it," Selena Rogers, her shop assistant, interrupted. "You're always so impatient."

Selena's pale blue eyes clashed with Sam's darker blue gaze as she flipped her summer blond-streaked hair out of her face. The two liked to squabble. It was always good-natured but sometimes, like now, it was irritating.

Peggy waited for them to realize they had *both* interrupted before she resumed her story. The late afternoon shop traffic was slow. Charlotte's Center City gardeners had already purchased most of their supplies for the summer. The hot weather was notorious for driving customers out of garden shops around the area. Business would pick back up in September for fall planting.

"I can tell you one thing; my six weeks' training in Chapel Hill didn't really prepare me for examining a dead body."

"I bet it was super nasty being there with that dead dude, huh?" Selena ventured an opinion.

"Peggy's seen so many dead people by now," Sam's assistant landscaper, Keeley Prinz added, "I'm surprised it bothers her anymore."

"I don't think it works like that." Peggy shook her head at her best friend's daughter. Keeley was so like her mother, Lenore, in more ways than her striking, dark-chocolate good looks. There seemed to be a pragmatic streak that ran through the family. "At least it doesn't seem to work that way for *me*. I don't think I'll ever get used to seeing a dead person in or out of a coffin."

"Who was he?" Hunter Ollson, Sam's older sister, who was a lawyer, asked as she munched on peanuts.

"His name was Gerald Capshaw. The people from United Metals had hired him to check the dam like they do a couple of times every year. Something happened that no one could explain, and he drowned in the intake gate. It was terrible." Peggy sighed as she continued checking her order for garden supplies.

"Did it look like an accident?" Hunter asked again. She looked up from her peanuts and found three pairs of eyes fixed on her. "Okay! Someone's probably going to sue United Metals and maybe the town of Badin for this. I'm a lawyer. It could be me. Think of this man's grieving family. Imagine if he was really killed by a tragic but avoidable mistake that's happened before."

"And imagine Hunter being able to make some money for that poor, grieving family," Selena began.

"And coincidentally for herself." Sam

flashed his even, white-toothed smile that stood out against the dark tan of his face framed by golden blond hair.

"There's nothing wrong with trying to protect the public from unscrupulous corporations who'd take advantage of them." Hunter sniffed and took a sip of her Mountain Dew. "I recently read John Edwards's biography. He did the same thing; then he became a multimillionaire and ran for president."

"Are you seeing yourself as presidential material?" Sam laughed. "I think you need to pay your electric bills on time before you think about running for the White House."

"Anyway." Peggy stopped the discussion and brought the conversation back to where it had been. "It was fascinating watching Ruth process the scene. I helped a little with some water plants I recognized. I don't know if it made any difference. Whether Mr. Capshaw's family sues United Metals or not, it was a terrible accident."

A customer wandered in from Brevard Court, where the afternoon heat rose off the brick walkway like steam from a new loaf of bread. She seemed surprised to find them all standing around the counter near the front door. She smiled, clutched her pocketbook a little closer to her white linen skirt, and fled back out into the heat.

"What was that all about?" Sam wondered. "I'm glad I don't work in the shop all the time. Landscape customers are weird, but shoppers are really strange."

"I don't know," Peggy said. "Maybe there's a storm headed our way. They say people can feel things like that."

"I think it was more us staring at her." Selena picked up a butterfly that had fallen from the summer display that included living and artificial plants. She adjusted the rocking chair that was always part of the scene. A shower of rose petals fell from the rose tree above her. "Great. I was afraid it wasn't going to get enough light from the windows. We'll have to replace it."

"Not right now," Peggy corrected. "We'll have to cut a few corners over the summer. You know how slow things get. I told Brenda and Dawn I'm giving them the summer off. We don't need to be open extra hours. I'll bring them back in September."

"How worried are we about the competition?" Sam asked.

Peggy looked at the Smith & Hawken grand opening sale spread across a whole page of the *Charlotte Observer*. "I don't know. We aren't totally dependent on furniture and accessory sales, but they make up

50

a fair amount of our business."

Keeley shook her head. "Peggy, you should run for political office, because I don't have any idea if you answered Sam's question or not."

"Sorry." Peggy smiled. "It won't be good for us. I don't know how bad it will be until the store is open for a while."

"That I can understand. Is there anything I can do to help?" Keeley asked. "I just got my grant to go back to school this fall. I was kind of planning on the money I make here to take me through."

"I don't think you have anything to worry about," Peggy answered. "The landscaping part of our business is very strong. We get new clients every day because you two do such a good job. We can always landscape the areas around Smith & Hawken furniture in people's yards."

Keeley laughed, but Selena didn't like that answer. "Does that mean *my* job is in trouble? Because I've worked at Wal-Mart, and believe me, it was bad. Not to mention I signed a new lease on my apartment, an apartment I took *because* it's close to the Potting Shed."

Peggy squeezed Selena's shoulder. "I think the Potting Shed is going to be fine. We'll see."

"That sounds good," Hunter said. "Because I might be looking for a job."

"*You?*" Keeley laughed. "Sorry. But you aren't exactly the outdoor type."

"I'm very well-educated," Hunter reminded her. "I'm sure I could do what you and my brother do every day. It isn't exactly rocket science."

Sam rubbed his hands together. "Do I smell a bet coming on? Are you telling me you think you could keep up with me and Keeley for a whole day?"

Hunter raised her chin. "I'm sure I could find intelligent solutions to work harder and faster than either of you in *any* field."

"Hunter, is that wise?" Peggy asked, but it was too late.

"Done!" Sam hooted. "I get to pick the day. You can decide how you're going to do the work, but it has to be to *my* specifications. Don't forget; I'm the boss. Right, Peggy?"

"Right, Sam. But if I hear you've given her *too* hard a time, I'll have to come down on *you*." Peggy gave him an evil look. "You never know when you might need a good lawyer."

Sam's reply was a massive grin. He picked up two fifty-pound bags of fertilizer, his tan, muscled arms bulging. "I'm taking this over to the Fosters' on my way home. Don't forget you promised Jane Mysen you'd be at her place tomorrow morning before we start work."

"I remember," Peggy told him. "I'll be there by seven. Good night, Selena, Keeley. Thanks for your help. I'll see you tomorrow."

"See you, Peggy." Selena waved on her way out with Keeley, who said her good-byes while talking on her cell phone.

"I'll be there at six. But it's okay for you to sleep in," Sam added.

She laughed and turned off her computer. "That's why I pay you the big bucks."

"That's right. I almost forgot."

"I'm going to wait for you out in the truck, Sam." Hunter answered her cell phone and went out the back door. "Don't forget about me this time. And the mechanic closes at six. Sorry, Peggy."

When they were alone, Peggy smiled at Sam, who had come to be a friend and very near a son to her since the Potting Shed opened. "How's summer school going? Do you need any more help to fit your classes in around the landscaping schedule?"

He looked lost for words, not a usual occurrence for the handsome, blond giant.

"You aren't going, are you?"

"Peggy —"

"Sam, I promised your parents you'd have time to catch up with the classes you need help on. You're never going to be a doctor like this."

He put down the bags of fertilizer on the old heart-of-pine floor. "It's not that there isn't time. I decided to take a break."

"I think you took a break last quarter. That's why you need these credits." She put her hand on his arm. "You wanted to be a surgeon more than anything in the world when I first met you. What happened?"

He shrugged. "I don't know. It's not that I don't want to go to med school anymore. I don't know what the problem is. I need a breather. Not everyone starts college and goes through without stopping. It doesn't mean I won't go back for the spring session."

"Your father is going to have a fit."

"He doesn't have to know."

"He might get suspicious if UNCC returns your tuition." She sighed and hugged him. "You should tell him up front. *I'd* want to know."

"I wouldn't have told *you* either." He hugged her back until she groaned. "But you're so nosy, I suppose you were bound to find out."

"It's not anything else, is it?" She looked into his clear eyes. "Your father and you are all right?"

"We're fine." Sam bent down and picked up the two bags of fertilizer again. "Well, as fine as we can be, considering I'm not wonderful like Hunter, and I'm gay."

Peggy knew Sam's parents had only recently learned that their son was gay. She'd played a small part in his reluctant outing. She wouldn't have given him away on purpose for anything, but she believed it was better for his family to know.

Hunter honked the horn on the truck behind the Potting Shed several times. Peggy might have said more, but it was already 5:30, and traffic was going to be terrible getting out of Center City. "Okay. I'll see you tomorrow. We'll talk."

"I have no doubt." He rolled his eyes as she opened the back door to the loading dock. "See you at seven."

Peggy watched him load the truck with the fertilizer and a spreader, then pull out into the traffic on College Street. She closed the back door and locked it. Thinking about Sam quitting school would make for a restless night. How many times had she considered how great it would be if Sam was her partner? She knew from the beginning that wouldn't happen. She wasn't even sure why she ever thought about it. Now it was like a nightmare coming true.

She walked around the Potting Shed, making sure the shelves were tidy. Unfortunately, they were *too* tidy. Not enough people coming in to mess things up. There wasn't much to do about it. Summer was hot and slow. It had been like that both years she'd been in business and was the same for every other garden shop. She couldn't blame this on Smith & Hawken.

It was still bright and sunny outside in Brevard Court, where eight other small shops nestled at the back door of historic Latta Arcade. She waved to the nice lady at the travel shop whose name she could never remember. The other woman waved back as she finished her cigarette. Wonderful smells came from the French restaurant across the courtyard and from Anthony's Caribbean Café.

She moved away from the door and the beautiful bougainvillea that was blooming in front of her shop before Sofia and Emil Balducci could see her. Her neighbors at the Kozy Kettle were good-hearted but tended to be long-winded and intent on matchmaking. There was something about a single woman that seemed to bring that out in people. Emil and Sofia took it to the extreme.

Closing the heavy wooden door that was set between two large plate glass windows, she locked it and pulled the shade. Despite bringing in many Center City dwellers, there weren't many late-night or weekend shoppers. She did her best business during lunchtime when all the office workers stepped out of their cubicles for some fresh air and lunch.

She kissed John's picture she kept by the door. This was all his doing. The Potting Shed, an urban gardener's paradise, was his brainchild. They'd started talking about it when Paul, their only child, was in high school, and the question of retirement came up. She and John were both garden lovers, although his choice of profession, law enforcement, took him as far away from green and growing things as possible. He'd always loved to come home and work in the yard.

Being a botanist, gardening was a more natural extension for Peggy and should have been for John, too. He'd loved to watch her dabble with plants in the basement and create new species in their backyard. If he'd chosen to work as a botanist instead of becoming a homicide detective with the

Charlotte-Mecklenburg Police Department, he might still be alive. He might have lived to see his dream come to life in this turn-of-the-century shop.

Instead, he was killed by the man he was arresting after answering a domestic disturbance call. He'd been dead for more than two years. They had been the longest two years of Peggy's life.

Not that she hadn't tried to fill them up. She'd cashed in John's retirement and gone back to work for Queens University teaching botany to freshmen while she found the perfect place to open the Potting Shed. At the time, anger and fear drove her. She could hardly rest with the need to do something that might give some meaning to John's life. She'd pushed herself brutally building the business, teaching, and lecturing on her specialty, botanical poisons.

She wasn't complaining. It got her through the last two years, and the Potting Shed was thriving. It might take a hit from Smith & Hawken, but she believed her diverse services would weather the storm. They had branched out to plant maintenance as well as landscaping and putting in temporary garden areas, as they were doing for Jane Mysen's wedding party tomorrow. And she had more tricks up her sleeve. Somehow she would find a way to compete with Smith & Hawken. She wouldn't let John down.

She finished closing up by putting the day's receipts into a bank bag and picking up her pocketbook. She looked around the store one last time as she always did, listening to the swish of cool air coming down from the ceiling. She loved this shop. She couldn't imagine she'd have loved it more because John was there, but she wished she could've tried. He would have spent as much time here as she did usually, rocking in the display rocking chair, sipping peach tea while looking through a seed catalog.

But not tonight. She'd been away all day and there were other things she had to take care of. One of them was her 140-pound Great Dane, Shakespeare, an accident that had turned into an unexpected friendship. There were also experimental plants in her basement on Queens Road to tend, and if she was lucky, there was a hungry veterinarian waiting for her.

The phone rang as she got in the pickup. She knew who it was. "I hope you have takeout for dinner."

"Hello to you, too! How are you? I hope the funeral wasn't too bad. Why didn't you call me when you got done?"

She smiled at the sound of Steve's voice.

59

He was even more unexpected than Shakespeare. Between them, they had rounded out the life she'd made so hectic. They'd made her want to have time to breathe again. "I think I'm hungry. Memorial luncheons never quite hit the spot."

"Maybe I can help with that. Though I should remind you it was your turn to get takeout."

"You're right. I'm just leaving the Potting Shed, so I can still stop."

"That's okay. Come home. I want to see you more than I want to eat. Besides, I can call Papa John's from here."

"You're an inventive, clever man."

"That must be why you love me."

"That's definitely one of the reasons, although I can think of a few more."

"Okay. I know traffic is bad out there. I don't want to keep you on the phone. I'll see you in a few minutes."

Peggy negotiated the narrow streets between the Potting Shed, in the middle of Center City, and her home a few blocks from Queens University. Traffic was terrible, as usual. She was getting a little concerned about how much power her batteries still had after coming back from Badin. She hoped it would be enough to get her home. After that, the truck she dubbed Sparky

60

would have a nice long rest. Most of the time, she rode her bicycle around the city. It was hard to be a botanist and not worry about clean air.

It only took about thirty minutes to reach what had once been her quiet neighborhood. Queens Road traffic was almost as bad as Center City now. When she'd first come here with John, fresh out of college, she could hear the wind blow through the old oak trees that lined the street. Now she was lucky if she could hear the radio in the house. Last year, a drunk driver had plowed into the oak in front of her house. She and a city tree maintenance chief had managed to save the tree, but it was only a matter of time before the cars won out.

Maybe she'd move to Badin before then. She didn't want to see the neighborhood lose any more of its charm. Most of the houses were still there from the turn of the twentieth century. The house she and John had moved into had been in his family since it was built in the 1920s. It had passed to John but would not pass to their son, Paul. John's nephew would be the lucky recipient of the beautiful old house, with its twenty-five rooms and the exceptional garden she and John had created.

She parked her truck in the old garage

beside the 1940 Rolls-Royce, ghostly in the twilight under its perennial tarp. Despite the sounds of traffic, she could hear her neighbor Clarice calling to her pet poodle, Poopsie, who was no doubt dyed to match the color of the month. What surprised her was hearing the sound of Steve's deep voice talking to the woman.

"Oh, Peggy! I'm so glad you're here!" Her neighbor, Clarice, sobbed into her lacy yellow handkerchief.

Peggy hoped the dog wasn't the same color but was destined for disappointment. The yellow poodle came running around the corner of the fence that separated their two yards. "What's wrong?"

Steve smiled, his eyes focused on Peggy's face. He slipped his arm around her, but Peggy took a step back. "Poopsie had a run-in with a stray cat today. Clarice was worried he might be rabid."

"I hope you reassured her." Peggy smiled despite herself. She wasn't ready to announce her relationship with Steve to the neighbors. Especially *this* neighbor, who couldn't keep her mouth shut.

"I did. The cat actually belongs to another neighbor who assures me he has his shots."

"It was terrible." Clarice continued to sob. "I didn't know what to do. Thank God

Steve was here checking on that big horse of a dog you own. Sometimes I think his barking is going to shatter my grandmother's crystal."

Peggy was too tired and too hungry to stand there and listen to the woman whine. She tried to think of some way to get away from her and into the house. Hopefully a plan that included Steve being with her. She was about to say something polite but effective to get them both out of the yard when a car pulled up into her driveway. "I'm sorry I can't stay and chat. It looks like Paul is here. I'm glad Poopsie is okay. Steve, Shakespeare has that thing you need to look at before that big surgery at your clinic tonight."

"Oh, what kind of surgery?" Clarice pressed.

If Peggy didn't know Steve so well, she might have missed the laughter in his voice when he answered, "I'm removing a cancerous lump from a hermit crab."

"Really? I didn't know they got cancer." Clarice stopped sobbing. "Of course, they're so cheap, you'd think someone would throw it away and get another one. They don't live very long, do they?"

Peggy drew in a deep, exasperated breath. Couldn't the woman take a hint?

63

"They can live for hundreds of years as long as they don't get cancer," Steve answered, tongue in cheek.

Paul joined them after getting out of his squad car. "I have to talk to you, Mom."

"Good night, Clarice." Peggy left her neighbor gratefully.

Turning to her son she said, "I'm glad you came up. We weren't having any luck getting away from her."

Steve walked quickly away with them. "Hi, Paul. Is something wrong?"

"Something happened I thought Mom might want to know about." He shook Steve's hand. "It seems Professor Sargent had a secret of her own tucked away about the dead guy at the dam."

Peggy hugged her son. "Hello to you, too. What terrible secret is Ruth hiding about Gerald Capshaw?"

"She had an affair with him, according to his wife. Mrs. Capshaw has stirred up a hornet's nest about her husband's death. She claims Professor Sargent murdered him."

4

Pumpkin
Botanical: *Cucurbita*
Pumpkins are native to North America, growing from a trailing vine. The flowers are pollinated by the native squash bee, whose numbers have declined due to pesticide usage. Honeybees now pollinate flowers, with some hand pollination used as well. Pumpkins are grown more for decoration today than for food, with secret growing techniques used by growers who want to produce the biggest pumpkins.

Steve paid the Papa John's pizza delivery driver and they split the cheese pizza with Paul, who was on his dinner break. Peggy felt alternately angry and guilty after learning Ruth had an affair with Gerald Capshaw. Why hadn't Ruth said anything?

"I'm sure the murder accusation was because her husband had an affair with

Professor Sargent." Paul helped himself to pizza, avoiding the salad Steve had made. "Mrs. Capshaw probably wanted to get even. I don't know how seriously the sheriff out there is taking her statement."

"You'd think she'd want to just sue United Metals." Peggy fumed as she ate her salad. Knowing the way Paul ate, she'd decided to sacrifice her pizza for him. "An affair with Ruth didn't contribute to his death."

Steve put some slightly stale donuts on the table before he sat down beside Peggy. He knew Paul's eating habits belied his tall, slender frame, too. "You didn't do anything wrong, so there's nothing to worry about. There was no way for you to know about your friend and the dead man."

"I know," she said. "I guess I feel a little guilty because I'm so new at this. What if we missed something? What if his death wasn't an accident?"

"I don't see how it could've been anything else." Paul managed to keep the conversation going around mouthfuls of pizza. "I was there, too, Mom. People drown. Even professional people. Maybe them more than others because they're so cocky most of the time."

"What do you mean?" Steve wondered.

"It's like you, for instance. Someone who

66

wasn't a vet would be less likely to tackle a job alone or without the proper safeguards resulting in injury or even death."

Peggy smiled at her son's matter-of-fact turn of phrase. He sounded like he'd been lecturing on the subject all of his life. "For instance, I'd be more likely to wander out into a swamp looking for plants."

Paul nodded. "Exactly. Steve wouldn't think anything of going out alone to pick up a sick dog. That dog could be rabid and bite him."

"That happens to me all the time," Steve agreed. "Especially with skunks and possums. People are always calling me to pick up their sick, wild animals."

Paul took a large swig from his Coke. "You're laughing, but it *could* happen. And you'd go without thinking about it. It happens to everyone. That diver was alone and obviously hadn't followed correct protocol, whatever that is for divers. Most accidents happen that way."

"You'd better go ahead and give up that uniform now." Peggy glanced at her son's dark blue CMPD uniform. "Your mistakes would be deadlier than most."

"That's what happened to Dad. He didn't take the domestic disturbance call seriously, even though he knew there were shots fired.

He walked in there without waiting for backup and got himself killed."

A long silence followed his words. Peggy didn't know if she should be relieved that Paul finally had a palatable explanation for what happened to his father or if she should feel he was slighting John's memory. Either way, it disturbed her, even though she had hoped for closure for Paul. She had believed from the beginning that Paul's sudden urge to become a police officer was more out of vengeance than commitment. Up until that point, he was determined to be an architect. John's death changed that. She'd worried her son might be killed trying to find the man who'd killed John and gotten away.

"I'm sorry." Paul looked at her apologetically. "I didn't mean to get carried away."

Peggy touched his hand. "It's okay. I know what you meant. And you're right. I don't know anything to do about it. One way or another, we're all in the same boat."

"Last piece of pizza." Steve tried to ease the heavy tension.

"You have it." Paul smiled. "I'd rather eat the donuts."

Steve brought the topic back to the original subject. "The burden of proof will be on the diver's wife. She'll have to prove your friend did something wrong."

Peggy got up from the table and put her salad plate in the dishwasher. "I feel like the weakest link in this chain. Everyone else there had plenty of experience. This is essentially the first time I've worked as a forensic botanist."

"You'll be fine, Mom." Paul glanced at his watch. "I have to go back on duty. Would you like me to stop by later, spend the night or something?"

Peggy kept herself from glancing at Steve. "I'll be fine. By the way, what happened between you and Stephanie?"

"I got her phone number!" He grinned. "I'm hoping to see her this weekend. She lives in Charlotte on Sharon Road. That's convenient."

"Sounds promising!" Peggy hugged her son. "I'll talk to you tomorrow."

"See you, Steve," Paul said. "Take it easy."

After he was gone, Steve helped Peggy stack the dishwasher and clean off the table. "Thank God those donuts are gone," he said. "They were starting to scare me."

"It's hard to keep food fresh when there's only one person eating it." She shrugged as she called for Shakespeare. The big, fawn-colored Great Dane ran into the kitchen, skidding across the hardwood floor on one of the flowered throw rugs. "You must have the same problem."

He put his arms around her waist and drew her close. "Neither one of us should have that problem anymore." He kissed her gently. "There's no reason not to share the day-old donuts."

Peggy kissed him back, and a few minutes passed until Shakespeare's whining got their attention. "I think I should take him out."

"You should've done that when you first found him."

She laughed. "You know what I mean."

"I'll come with you."

They walked around the back of the house together, the dog not pulling as hard on his leash as he had before his obedience classes. The overcast sky hung heavy with unshed rain, making the scent of honeysuckle and roses stronger from the garden. A small sliver of moon and two stars struggled valiantly to shine through the cloud layer, but it was a difficult endeavor.

"Why are you still embarrassed about us being together?" Steve asked as they walked through the humid darkness.

"I'm not embarrassed. I'm careful."

He laughed, a rich sound in the midst of crickets and traffic. "Keep telling yourself that, but you're not fooling anyone. You're embarrassed for people to know we're to-gether."

For that, read sleeping together, Peggy thought. Their relationship already stunned her by existing, and it had taken an even more unexpected turn when they'd started sharing each other's beds. She didn't think of herself as a prude. After all, sex was biological. There was nothing to be ashamed of. It was perfectly natural. A botanist would know that better than most people. Part of her training had to do with pollenization and fertilization. She and Steve were no dif-ferent than the plants in her garden.

But no matter how much she tried to shake her proper, Southern upbringing, she found herself wanting to handle the relation-ship quietly, even though she didn't want to admit that to herself.

"I got over that months ago," she scoffed.

"Then why the brush-off when we were talking to Clarice?"

"There was no brush-off. I was hot." It was plain Steve wasn't from the South. No *Southern gentleman* would press a lady this way.

He hugged her and kissed the side of her neck, while Shakespeare explored some of Peggy's purple mushrooms he'd found under one of the 200-year-old oak trees.

71

"Yes, you are. I think about it all the time."

She laughed. "You know what I mean. I didn't want to make either of us uncomfortable."

"That is by far the lamest excuse I've ever heard. Why not own up to it? You're embarrassed we're having sex. You don't want people to know."

"I wouldn't share that information with Clarice anyway.

"Or your son. Or your friends. Or your family. I'm not even sure Shakespeare would know if he wasn't around all the time."

Peggy stopped and glared at him in the pale glow of the streetlight. "What do you want me to do? Put an ad in the *Observer*? I'm a widow with a grown son. I'm sleeping with a man seven years younger than me. I'm defying all the traditional morals that I grew up with. I don't know if I can do any more than that."

"You could move in with me. Or I could move in with you. This sneaking back and forth thing was fun in a teenage kind of way to begin with. Now I'd kind of like to leave my toothbrush in one place."

She took a deep breath and stared up into his face, wondering how she ever thought he was plain because he had brown hair and brown eyes. The light picked out streaks of gold and red in the subtle shades of his hair. His eyes were flecked with green and gold. He was passionate, intelligent, and funny. She wasn't looking for someone to ever be in her life again, but if she had to choose a person, it would be Steve.

"I love you. You know that, but I don't know if I can make that commitment right now." She kissed his cheek. "I hope you understand."

He sighed. "I don't. But that's okay. Half of the time, I'm running behind you trying to catch up. This must be the only thing I'm out in front on. As long as the possibility exists, I guess my toothbrush will be with yours, wherever that is."

Shakespeare looked at the two of them as though he was trying to figure out what they were talking about. Peggy laughed and pointed out his inquisitive look, one side flopping up on his uncropped ears. She'd only had him for about nine months, and she couldn't bring herself to have his ears cut. Maybe if he was a puppy . . . but no, probably not even then.

They walked into the house through the French doors in the basement. In what had become a routine for them, Steve took off Shakespeare's leash while Peggy checked and logged her botanical experiments. Some of them were even more complicated; over long weekends, they were journaled and watched every few minutes. Steve, who cared for all types of animals in his clinic, understood the concept if not the exact content of what she was doing with the plants.

The basement, which ran the entire space of the house, wasn't air-conditioned, so the air was close and muggy. Steve watched as Peggy sat on the edge of her pond and counted things in the water, recording everything she found. "Are those fish?"

"Not exactly. They're a new type of potato that has the potential to grow in water. Underwater, actually."

"Why would anyone want a potato to grow underwater?"

"Because it's possible the aquatic atmosphere could reduce the number of diseases potato crops are subject to. It's only a theory right now. I'm testing it for a friend who teaches at Berkeley."

"How does anyone think of these things?" He walked around the dimly lit room. "Do botanists always think about different ways to grow crops?"

"Not always." She recorded more data on her potato plants. "I choose not to be involved in genetic research. I like the old-fashioned way. I guess you could say I'm an organic girl at heart."

"What about this thing?" He studied a pumpkin vine with several pumpkins growing on it.

"That's *Curcurbita pepo,* basically a pumpkin. It's prized because it produces both jack-o'-lantern-quality pumpkins plus an abundance of pumpkin seeds. The seeds are good for people to eat, and that's why Dr. Abin of the Royal Institute of Botany is trying to grow them in a desertlike atmosphere."

Steve smiled. "It's not exactly desertlike in here. If it was any more humid, it would rain."

"That's why it's in the box." She tapped the sturdy Plexiglas that housed the drier, more desertlike atmosphere. "Next month, Dr. Abin and a team from the institute will take a thousand of these pumpkins to Africa for field trials. They've done very well. I'm a control on the project."

"All this, and you still grow tasty tomatoes, too." He picked a ripe tomato from a thick vine that received plenty of morning sunshine from the French doors.

"Well, it wouldn't be as much fun if it was all science and nothing to eat."

75

Steve's cell phone rang, and he took it out of his pocket. The reception in the basement was bad, so he walked outside to talk. Peggy watched him, biting her lip. She could pretend their earlier conversation didn't bother her, but she'd be lying to herself.

She wanted to be with Steve, but she was nervous. The whole idea of living together seemed unrealistic. She wouldn't be willing to give up her house. Certainly he wouldn't be willing to give up the house his uncle left him. Besides, how could they have her botanical experiments and Steve's clinic in one house? There was no way that would ever work.

And part of her wasn't keen to live with him without marriage. Yes, they were sleeping together. But proclaiming to the world that it was a regular occurrence made her Southern roots shake. Her mother would no doubt have palpitations, and she was moving up to Charlotte as soon as the family farm outside Charleston was sold. How could she face her with Steve living in her house?

On the other hand, she didn't want to lose Steve. She didn't even want to stop sleeping with him. She loved him and loved being with him. He reminded her that she was still more than just someone's mother, daughter, botanist, and erstwhile crime solver. She liked that feeling. It had been gone, sleeping, she supposed, since John died.

Peggy stopped vacantly staring at Steve's back as he put away his cell phone and turned to come inside. Feeling stupid for staring at him, she busied herself with watching and counting the fire ants in her makeshift ant community. It was another project, this time with a new fungus that the University of North Carolina was experimenting with. They hoped it might be the answer to the ever-increasing population of the stinging insects.

"Sorry. There's an emergency. Mrs. Walter's Chihuahua apparently didn't mate with the Chihuahua she'd hoped, and the puppies are too big. Maybe it won't take too long."

She put down her journal and put her arms around him. "I'll see you later then."

He kissed her and winked. "Count on it. Don't stay down here in the heat for too long."

"You forget I grew up in Charleston. We laugh at this mild summer weather. Sometimes I think I might need a coat to get through it."

"Okay. Since I grew up in Ohio, and this

place feels like a sauna to me, I'll make sure the air conditioner is on full blast in the Vue. I'll see you later."

Peggy listened to his footsteps as he went up the stairs. The sound of the door closing when he went outside seemed very lonely. The big, old house was quiet around her. The summer humidity was good for it and seemed to quiet the creaks and groans prominent in winter, or so she imagined as she turned off the extra light downstairs and went up to the ground floor of the house.

Shakespeare was on his way back down after seeing Steve out the door. She patted his large head, and he licked her hand then whined at the kitchen door Steve had gone through. "You miss him, too, don't you? We're a pretty pair. Mooning over Steve when he isn't here. I think we should make some popcorn and chocolate mint tea and find ourselves a silly romantic movie to watch. What do you think?"

Shakespeare barked, the sound echoing through the big house. He pushed himself up against her and almost knocked her on the floor. "You don't realize your own strength," she reprimanded as she went into the kitchen and took out her popcorn maker. "Or I don't realize how weak I am."

As the popcorn popped, she watched the

news and steeped her tea. Nothing much new ever seemed to happen. Two men were shot and killed in Charlotte, and a drunk driver was going the wrong way down I-485. There was a brief mention of Gerald Capshaw's death in Badin. The news crew, who weren't on the scene until after the body had been taken away, made it sound like it was a routine drowning incident. They didn't mention anything about Gerald being an experienced diver.

The news anchor ended up telling the audience that Mrs. Capshaw had accused Ruth of sleeping with her husband. There was also some question about what happened at the scene. "We don't know at this time if the widow is planning to sue the rescue workers."

"That makes her sound like an ungrateful victim," Peggy said to Shakespeare.

The doorbell chimed from the front as her tea was ready. The popcorn was popping. It would be fine without her for a few seconds. She glanced at the clock on the stove. It was almost ten p.m. Who'd be calling at this time of night?

Thinking about all the stories she'd read about home break-ins, she looked through the peephole before opening the heavy oak door. It was Ruth. Now she was even more curious.

Peggy took off the latch and opened the door. "Hi. Imagine seeing you twice in one day. Is everything all right?"

"I'm sorry to bother you," Ruth said. "I wouldn't have come if I could think of anyone else to talk to about this."

"Why don't you come in and tell me what's wrong." She opened the door wide into the foyer. "I have some tea and popcorn ready in the kitchen."

Ruth stepped into the house, her eyes immediately taking in the thirty-two-foot blue spruce with the wide, marble staircase circling up behind it. "Wow! I always forget how stunning that tree is."

Peggy laughed. "I suppose so. You know, I planted it when I moved here right out of college. I cheated, really, because it was at least five feet already."

"It makes a terrific first impression. I can see why everyone calls you the plant lady."

"I don't mind. They could call me something a lot worse." Peggy closed the door behind her.

Ruth smiled. "I hope I'm not interrupting anything. I would've called first, but I couldn't find your phone number. I wasn't sure how often you check your email. That seems to be the only way I talk to people anymore."

"At least my address is easy to find." Peggy led the way to the kitchen. "You know I'd rather someone know my phone number than my address. What's the worst they could do? Breathe heavy?"

"I suppose that's true. Unfortunately, no one gives us a choice, do they? Are you still living here alone?"

"Yes." Shakespeare whined and pushed against her. "I'm sorry. No, I don't live alone anymore. Ruth, this is Shakespeare."

Ruth patted his head. "Nice to meet you. I have a cat that lives with me, Mr. Buttons. I'll bet he'll be smelling me all night when I get home, wondering who the dog was."

The popcorn was ready when Peggy checked the popper. She poured two cups of tea and set them on the old wooden table that had seen so many meals with John, Paul, and her sitting around it. Peggy put the popcorn in a bowl between them then sat down opposite her friend.

"This is good." Ruth sipped her tea. "I thought it was hot chocolate to begin with, but it's not, is it?"

"It's made from chocolate mint, the plant. It has a strong hot chocolate smell with none of the dairy." Peggy drank some of her tea and waited for her guest to tell her why she was there.

"You have a beautiful house." Ruth glanced around the kitchen. "I don't know if I could live in something this big, even if I could afford it. Not alone anyway."

"It doesn't really belong to me." Peggy explained about John's family. "I don't want to be rude, although usually that statement prefaces someone being *quite* rude, but why are you here? I know you didn't come to admire my house again or have tea this late."

Ruth smiled and bowed her head over her teacup. "It's not rude at all. I don't know where to start now that I'm here. It seemed like a good idea when I left my house. Now I don't know what to say."

"If it's about what happened between you and Mrs. Capshaw —"

"It is." She looked up at Peggy. "I'm sorry I didn't tell you. You can't imagine how surprised I was to find Gerald's body in Badin Lake. I didn't mean for you to get involved in my personal problems. But I guess it's too late for that."

5

Dahlia

Botanical: *Dahlia imperialis*
Dahlia is the national flower of Mexico, the home of the dahlia's ancestors, taken from the mountains by Spanish soldiers in the sixteenth century. Growers were more interested in using dahlias as a food source when they were first brought to Europe, but by 1810, dahlias had become gardeners' favorites as gorgeous double blooms that are still popular today.

"I'm sorry your personal life has come into play with this," Peggy said. "But I don't think you allowed it to influence your work. Were you still seeing Gerald?"

Ruth got to her feet and paced the wooden floor, reminding Peggy of herself when she was trying to think. "No. I broke it off a long time ago. It was stupid. I should've known better. I guess I was lonely."

"It could happen to anyone." Peggy thought about her relationship with Steve. At least she wasn't breaking up a family being with him. She would never know if she would've made the same mistake Ruth had.

"I appreciate your faith in me. I think we both did a good job processing the scene. It was hard. I've never had to do my job with someone I cared about. I don't know what to think about his wife's ranting that Gerald was murdered. It looked like a drowning to me."

"That's what it looked like to me, too. The medical examiner seemed to agree as well. Any professional can make a mistake," Peggy reminded her. "No matter how good you are, your mind can be on something else and then something terrible happens."

"I know what you mean. I've known divers who were careless just that one time. I know it happens. Did you notice some kind of glitch between United calling the rescue squad and us actually finding Gerald's body? That bothers me."

"I agree there was some kind of negligence that Mrs. Capshaw was right to point out. Whoever heard of rescue workers going to get their boss before going to save someone in distress? Is that what you're talking about?"

"Yes!" Ruth's eyes gleamed in the kitchen light as she sat down at the table again. "Maybe there's something wrong with the dam that United doesn't want anyone to know about. Maybe Gerald found something he wasn't supposed to find."

Peggy frowned. "They didn't seem too surprised by what happened. It seemed like a lot of damage control. Didn't someone say other divers have died there?"

"Exactly." Ruth took a crumpled piece of paper from her pocket. "I looked it up on the Internet. Two other divers have died there in the last ten years. Both at the intake bulkhead gate they keep replacing."

"Anyone who looks at this might see a case for OSHA to investigate, but I'd hardly call it a murder. I think Mrs. Capshaw is overwrought. It's not surprising."

Ruth ran her hand through her spiky silver hair. "I know. I feel so bad about it. I can't really imagine what she's going through. I don't know if I wouldn't do the same thing."

Peggy tried to put her thoughts as delicately as possible. "How long has it been since you broke up with him?"

"It's been three years. We met teaching a diving class in Florida. I knew he was married, but being recently divorced at the time,

I was in a vulnerable place. I knew it wouldn't ever be anything serious. Not that he was devoted to his family or anything." She smiled. "Gerald wasn't like that. If he was devoted to anything, it was diving. He lived for it."

Peggy patted her hand. "John told me victims' families go over and over what they know about what happened to their loved one. He even made me promise if it ever happened to him that I wouldn't do the same thing. But I did when he was killed. I wanted it to make sense. I'm sure that's all that's going on in Badin right now. Paul told me he didn't think the sheriff would take it that seriously."

Ruth sniffed, and Peggy handed her a tissue. "I feel terrible having it come out like this. I'm on every news show in the area. Maybe I should've backed out when I saw it was Gerald. I just thought I could do the job that needed to be done."

"I think you did the best you could. I'm sorry about the press, but you never know what they'll dig up."

"You're right. I don't know. I don't trust my instincts, if that's what you call them, right now. I guess I needed to say it out loud to someone, you know?"

"I do. I live alone, too. Sometimes, I say it

86

out loud to Shakespeare before I tell anyone else."

Ruth got slowly to her feet. "Thanks for hearing me out. I appreciate it. I'm up for tenure at the college, and you know how that can be. I hope this doesn't affect my standing."

"Don't worry about it." Peggy walked with her to the door. "But let me know what happens. I'll let you know if I hear anything about the case."

"Thanks for the tea and sympathy. Good night, Peggy." She stopped at the door and smiled. "Let's do lunch sometime, just the two of us."

"I'd love to. Good night, Ruth."

"She told me how she felt about Gerald's death." Peggy clipped a turquoise necklace around her throat as she spoke. "I can't believe this happened on my first case. Everyone will be going over everything with a fine-tooth comb."

It was morning, and according to the weatherman on the radio, it was already hot and humid. Sunshine coursed through her large bedroom windows that overlooked Queens Road. She was running late to meet Sam and Jane Mysen for the garden wedding additions. Shakespeare yawned on her bed, stretching his long legs and nodding his head as she spoke.

"You'll be fine. You did a good job." Steve walked out of the bathroom, tucking his shirt into his pants.

"I hope so. I really think Mrs. Capshaw is looking for revenge. It had to be terrible seeing her husband's mistress processing his body. And Ruth *did* bring him up from the lake. I don't know what I'd think."

"Aren't the police looking into it anyway as a matter of course, since he didn't die in his bed of old age?"

"I'm sure they are." Peggy glanced at the clock again. "I'm sorry I can't have breakfast with you this morning. I was supposed to be somewhere ten minutes ago."

"That's okay." He kissed her. "At least I get to see you this morning."

"You should've woken me up last night when you got here." She smoothed her hand across a loose hair on his shoulder.

"You were sleeping so beautifully, I didn't have the heart." He pulled her close and nuzzled her neck. "You smell good. Is there anything less than a week old to eat in the house?"

"Maybe. I'm sure there's something edible."

"That means I should explore the deli-bakery at Harris Teeter, right?"

She laughed as she opened the bedroom door. "That's probably the wisest course if you're looking for fresh food."

Shakespeare barked, wagging his tail as he sped past Peggy, almost knocking her down. Steve stepped toward her to help, and they stood together, framed in the doorway as Paul yelled a cheerful, "Good morning!" up from the ground floor. He looked at the two of them, a large bowl in his hands. "Steve! What a surprise. Is this a personal or professional call?"

Steve looked at Peggy, then smiled at her son. "I had to go out early this morning, so I stopped by to see if I could buy your mother breakfast."

Paul smiled. "Not a problem. I'm off this morning, so I came over to make breakfast for Mom. I'll add a little more flour to the pancake batter."

"Will you let Shakespeare out in the backyard, please?" Peggy tried to sound normal. She didn't want to break the news to Paul that she and Steve were sleeping together yet.

"Okay?" Steve whispered.

"It's fine." She smiled and kissed him again. "I don't think I've done so much sneaking around since high school."

He laughed. "Fun, isn't it?"

"Yeah. A blast." She hurried down the long circular stairs to get her pocketbook and car keys. "I can't stay for breakfast, Paul. I'm late meeting Sam. But you and Steve stay and eat something. I'll see you later."

Paul looked at her carefully. "Did Steve spend the night?"

"Of course not." She laughed. "Don't be silly."

He continued stirring the pancake batter in the bowl. "I guess that *would* be kind of crazy. I didn't mean to sound like you'd do something like that."

She kissed his cheek. "I'm very late. I'll talk to you sometime today."

Steve was coming into the kitchen as she was walking out the door. He and Paul began to discuss crispy pancakes and summer football camp. She shut the door behind her, glad she didn't have to sit down to breakfast with her son that morning.

He was going to have to know the truth sometime. She wasn't promiscuous by any means. She had nothing to be ashamed of, except for her mother's voice inside her head reminding her that nice girls didn't share a bed with a man unless they were married.

She took her bike out of the shed and told herself how yesterday that was. It wasn't necessary to be married to a man to sleep with him. Not that she and Steve only had a sexual affair going on. They enjoyed many other things. The sex had come in as a natural part of their growing relationship.

Hooey.

Peggy was glad she had the bike ride to clear her mind as she made her way through Myers Park to Dilworth, where the Mysens lived. When she was with Steve and they were alone, she didn't think twice about their relationship. It was hard for her to believe at her age that she gave a petunia's pistil what other people thought. But she'd be lying to herself if she didn't acknowledge her feelings. Steve was right. She was embarrassed by their relationship. It might be old-fashioned, but it was a real problem for her.

Sam and Keeley already had half of the all-white floral design set up in the tasteful garden behind the old, renovated stone house. The wedding colors were black and white. There was nothing they could do about all the greenery, so they tied black ribbons and bunting on everything. It was a little odd looking, particularly for an outdoor, summer wedding in an otherwise lush garden.

Jane Mysen greeted Peggy with worried eyes. She was a petite, older woman with flowing, gray-streaked black hair and a habit of wearing clothes that matched it. "Do you think it's too much? I mean really. Deanna had us cut off all the roses because they were red and pink."

"They'll grow back," Peggy consoled her. "I think the garden looks very formal, very different. It should set off Deanna's black-and-white theme perfectly."

"That's exactly what I was telling her." A tall, gaunt, young man with a very bad haircut joined them. "I'm Warren, the wedding planner. I'm glad you agree with my decision to cut the roses."

Peggy shook his hand, looking beyond him for Sam or Keeley. "I'm sure it will be very lovely." She *wasn't* so sure, but it was too late to be negative. "Excuse me. I'm looking for my assistants."

Warren pointed toward the east side of the house. "I believe Sam's over there. He's a very good worker. I hope you appreciate how hard he works for you. He's very talented, isn't he? He said he's going to school. Is he studying something to do with gardens?"

"He *is* very special," Peggy agreed. Anything else Warren was going to have to get from Sam. There were too many admirers, male and female, for her to chat about him, even if she would. "Excuse me, please."

She walked around the side of the house, scooting between workers getting set up for the event. She found Sam and Keeley standing over a large pond, arguing. "What's wrong with the two of you? Sam, this isn't Selena, and you don't have time to disagree. We went over this plan a dozen times."

"Yeah." Keeley glanced around to see who was listening. "But no one said *anything* about killing the poor fish."

"What are you talking about?" Peggy waved and smiled at Jane. The woman was paying them a fortune to set this up. It wasn't a good time to fall apart.

"She's crying over a bunch of goldfish." Sam crouched down beside the pond, already decorated with white lilies and trillium. "Mrs. Mysen wants us to take the gold koi out and put the white and black koi in."

"We're not doing it. Right, Peggy?" Keeley demanded. "We aren't assassins. We don't kill fish for a living."

Jane looked up, a worried expression on her thin face. Why was it people always seemed to know when something wasn't working right? Peggy faced the girl. "You're right, of course, Keeley. We aren't fish killers. In this case, though, we could be fish *movers.* There's no reason we can't transfer the fish into something else until after the party. I'm sure Jane will want her old koi back again."

But Peggy was in for an unpleasant surprise when Jane joined them a few minutes later. "Is there a problem? The band is already here. I need the pond to be finished."

Sam explained the situation, and Jane nodded. "I have a trash bag right over there. Put the gold koi in it. You can drop it off at the dump the next time you go. Or use them as fertilizer. Didn't the Native Americans do that when Columbus found them?"

"Only the ones living in Japan," Keeley growled.

"Excuse me?" Jane looked confused.

Peggy stepped in. "You go see to everything else, Jane. I'll take care of the fish."

"Please do. I'll never hear the end of this from my daughter if it's not perfect."

After she left, Keeley stomped her booted foot. "I won't let you kill those fish! They can't help it they aren't white and black!"

"They're just fish!" Sam argued. "You eat fish. What's the difference?"

"Never mind," Peggy interrupted them. "Sam, let's scoop the fish out. Keeley, you get the other fish ready to go in. Too bad you already ripped open the containers. We could have used them. We won't kill any of them, I promise. I don't eat fish, and I certainly don't plan to kill any today. I'm sure we can find another way."

She looked around for something that would hold the fish and some water. She spied a large silver punch bowl with elegant handles and ran for it before the caterer could grab it. Keeley grinned when she saw what she was thinking and rushed to help her. Sam started scooping the gold fish out of the pond while Peggy held the punch bowl. When two of the caterer's assistants started looking for the bowl, Keeley draped herself artistically around it so they wouldn't see what they were doing.

"Is that all?" Peggy whispered as Sam dug through the depths of the shallow pond.

"Looks like it. Did you bring your truck?"

"No. But you could sneak it out to your truck, and Keeley and I will finish up here."

"Sure. Why not?"

"We saved them!" Keeley enthused as they put the ten or so white and black koi in the pond.

"Without ruining our reputation." Peggy

95

glanced at Jane, who was trying to help the caterer find his missing punch bowl.

"We have to draw the line somewhere," Keeley reminded her. "We're gardeners, not fish killers or turtle movers or dog walkers. People are always asking us to do weird stuff. I think we should lay it on the line."

"This job paid ten thousand dollars plus plant costs." Peggy smiled. "You two were out here a couple of hours. I think we could move a few fish for that."

Keeley considered that angle. "I suppose we could. But not kill them. I'm not a fish killer."

"Not today. Let's go."

"So what are we going to do with the fish?" Sam asked when they got to Peggy's house. Peggy had thrown her bike in the back of the truck and ridden over with them while Keeley sat in the back to keep the fish safe. "I'm not letting them live in the back of my truck."

"I suppose we could let them go in the lake at Freedom Park," Keeley suggested, her dark eyes glued on Peggy for help.

"I think we can put them in my pond in the basement," Peggy decided. "I have a few already. A few more probably won't hurt. Then we'll send the punch bowl back where it belongs."

Sam and Keeley took the fish around to the back of the basement. Peggy held the French doors open, and the orphaned koi made it to their new home. The humans stood watching the fish as they swam around the pond for a few minutes.

"I guess that's it," Sam decided. "I'll see you tomorrow."

"Can I get a ride back to the shop?" Keeley asked him.

"I don't know. I had to come all this way to save these stupid fish because of you."

"Never mind," Peggy told her. "I'm going over to the Potting Shed myself. You can ride with me."

Keeley bit her lip. "Not to complain, but can we take the truck? I don't fit well on handlebars."

Sam burst out laughing at that. "I'll take you over. I was only kidding. You two can't take a joke."

"Thanks," Keeley said. "Peggy, you could ride over, too. Your bike is still in Sam's truck."

"I'll do that and ride back on my bike after I close up," Peggy decided. "Are you sure you don't mind riding in the back?"

"Not compared to being a passenger on your bike," Keeley quipped.

They went back out, Keeley and Sam exclaiming over the lushness of Peggy's backyard. "I don't think I've ever seen dahlias this big." Sam knelt down beside one of the big, red flowers. "What are you using on them, and why aren't we using it at the shop?"

"Nothing special," Peggy said. "Well, I take that back. I've been mixing a special blend of fertilizer that seems to be working really well. I think the colors are brighter, too."

Sam got up. "Has it occurred to you that this could be your edge against Smith & Hawken?"

She laughed. "I don't see how this could sell furniture."

"Come on! You read gardening magazines! Special mix fertilizer is one of the hot sales items. We get plenty of promo around town from our projects. If we could produce flowers like this in our yards and places like the Atrium, we could make a fortune."

"That sounds a little outrageous," she protested.

"No, he's right," Keeley agreed with Sam. "Look around your yard. Who wouldn't want flowers like these? I haven't seen anything like it."

"It's not like some secret experiment

you're doing for a university somewhere, is it?" Sam asked.

"No. It's something Dad and I were fooling around with while he was here. It's not really anything that special."

"Good!" Sam declared. "The simpler it is, the cheaper to make. Write down the recipe, and we'll start using it on the next job. We could make a hundred times what we make on furniture with Peggy's Special Blend."

"No," Keeley said. "I don't like that name. Let's call it Potting Shed Special Blend."

Peggy wasn't crazy about either name and thought there would probably be more to marketing your own fertilizer than coming up with a cute name. "I think we'd better check into the logistics of doing this before we get started."

Sam opened the truck door for her as Keeley climbed in the back. "Maybe we should call it Peggy's Potting Shed Blend."

"Or Plant Lady's Blend," Keeley yelled out as they started down the drive to Queens Road.

Peggy's two assistants traded fertilizer names back and forth until they got to the Potting Shed. Selena was glad to see them there early, since she had a hot date. Sam and Keeley immediately got her involved with the fertilizer. Then the three of them tried to come up with names, until Peggy pushed them all out the door as she was getting ready to close up.

She was glad to see them go. It was always interesting working with college students. Sometimes it was *too* interesting.

The day's receipts weren't any better than they had been yesterday. She sat down in the oak rocker and had a cup of peach tea. Maybe Sam was right. She needed something to carry her through these slow times. She had relied on furniture, which could be purchased all year long. But maybe fertilizer would be better. People used a lot of it, even during the summer when planting was slow. Gardeners had to keep all those plants blooming.

It seemed like the perfect solution. And it might be, but not until she did her homework. She'd seen too many business owners do stupid things that got them in trouble with the state or federal government. Nothing could shut a business down faster than getting on the wrong side of the EPA or some other organization that could conceivably regulate fertilizer.

Peggy looked around her shop, loving every little corner of it from the glass pond frogs to the purple iris wind chimes that tinkled in the breeze from the air conditioner. She loved the smell and feel of the older building, the way it settled around her like a cozy corner safe from the storm. She knew she would do whatever she could to save it from closing down. She'd worked too hard, invested too many of her and John's dreams, not to mention his pension, to lose it.

Her cell phone rang in her pocket. She looked at the number displayed on the screen. It was Detective Al McDonald, John's old partner. "Hi, Al. How are you? How's Mary? I hope you've called because we have a date for that dinner in the garden."

"I wish it was something that easy, Peggy," Al said. "I hope you're ready to do some contract forensic botany for us. I'm afraid we have a questionable death you might be able to help with. Can you meet me out at SouthPark?"

6

Duckweed
Botanical: *Lemna minor*
Duckweed is a tiny green aquatic plant with one or more fronds that come from a single root growing from each frond. It grows in large colonies in the water preferring not to be disturbed. Duckweed is an aggressive species that can deplete oxygen levels in the water and is banned in some areas where wildlife officials destroy it.

Peggy met Al and Captain Jonas Rimer at one of the large houses on Sharon Road near SouthPark mall on the south side of Charlotte. The area was growing rapidly around what was once only a prestigious neighborhood where the Duke Mansion was located. Cars swarmed like angry bees through the narrow, tree-lined streets as commuters came home to elegant houses that continued to multiply.

The house was one of those typical southern white-washed, redbrick two-stories popular in Peggy's hometown of Charleston. The upper windows were shuttered against the noise and fumes of the city traffic. The bottom drapes covered large downstairs windows, keeping the family's secrets intact.

Peggy left her bike beside Al's SUV, not sure what the protocol was for parking. There were several squad cars, Captain Rimer's car, and the crime scene van all parked in the long driveway. She was a little nervous about her first real case, even though she had technically been working with the police on forensic botanical issues for some time. She wasn't sure how far the scene of the crime extended or if there was a crime.

A questionable death meant Al wasn't sure if there was a crime or not. It might be up to her and what she could find to make that determination. That idea raised her level of nervousness to slightly less than panic.

"Peggy!" Al greeted her like he'd been keeping watch for her. His plain black face and tall, portly frame were almost as familiar to her as her own. He had been coming to her house for dinner since he and John joined the force. He'd gone to high school with John and been the best man at her wedding.

She hugged him back. "Good to see you. I talked to Mary on the way over here. She told me you've been moonlighting. Is anything wrong?"

"Can't a man want to make a little extra money without people wondering what's wrong with him?"

"I suppose." She was surprised by his response. "Mary was a little upset about it, especially since you didn't tell her. I agree with her that it's unusual for a man facing retirement to suddenly decide he wants to do security work on the side."

Al took Peggy's arm as they started walking slowly around the side of the house. "I didn't want to tell Mary because this isn't a normal security guard position. I'm doing some side work with a federal agency. When John was alive, we did a few things with the same agency. They contacted me about a case John and I worked on, and I wanted to help out."

"The CIA?"

Al looked around at the uniformed officers who were walking past them toward their cars. "Not so loud, huh? I don't want the whole world to know about this. I'm only telling you because I know John told

104

you this stuff. I never told Mary. I was afraid she'd make me stop."

Peggy bit back her laughter. Mary was formidable at five foot nothing, ninety pounds. "I can see why you'd want to keep it secret." She thought about her Internet contact who claimed to be an ex-CIA agent who'd worked with John. Was Al working with Nightflyer?

"You can laugh, but she'd bust me up side the head if she knew. I'm too old to go out and look for somebody else. I'm not as flexible as you."

She wanted to ask him about his CIA contact. She hadn't heard from Nightflyer in a month or so. Al disparaged him when Nightflyer gave her information on cases in the past. She kept her mouth closed as they rounded the back of the house and came to a huge pool.

Police photographers were snapping hundreds of pictures of the woman floating in the clear blue water. Crime scene techs were checking along the edges of the pool for any details they might need. It was controlled chaos while the CMPD tried to decide if this questionable death was an accident or something far worse.

"The victim is Marsha Hatley, age thirty-six, married, two children. She's lived here for five years. She's a research nurse, and her husband is a bond trader. The pool boy found her a couple of hours ago. We've been waiting to move the body until you got here, so we didn't disturb anything. The ME hasn't examined her yet, so we don't know time of death."

"Why am I looking at her first?" Peggy asked with none of the trepidation she felt in her voice.

"The Captain saw some stuff on the body he wants you to check out. He was afraid it would wash away if we tried to move her."

"What kind of stuff?"

"Plant stuff, I guess."

"Peggy!" Captain Jonas Rimer greeted her from across the pool. He was a compact man, trim and spare, with short brown hair and a chiseled face. "I'm glad you could join us. I guess this is your first official case. You don't know how happy it makes me to have you working *for* us instead of against us."

"Hello, Jonas. I don't think I've ever worked *against* you."

Harold Ramsey, the Mecklenburg County ME, laughed. He was a tall man with heavy, black-rimmed glasses. "Not against perhaps, but you've made poor Jonas look like a monkey's behind a few times. That's what

106

he means."

Rimer took offense with that. "I said what I meant, Harold. It's good to have you here, Peggy. I hope you can help us solve this little problem."

Peggy really took a good look at the body in the pool. She hadn't seen a lot of bodies outside of coffins, but it seemed to happen a lot in the last year. It started with finding Mark Warner dead in the Potting Shed and continued here today looking at Marsha Hatley's floating form.

She didn't see anything out of the ordinary. She looked at the young, Latino pool boy who was being questioned by two other detectives. He was wearing the skimpiest red bathing suit she'd ever seen. It was little more than a rubber band and a patch. She didn't have a pool, but if she did, her pool boy (*What a ridiculous title for a grown man!*) would wear a normal bathing suit or shorts. Was Mrs. Hatley expecting him to look like that? Did he know she'd be here?

She supposed the police detectives were asking him those same questions. She focused on her part of the investigation; whatever the "plant stuff" was Jonas saw on the body.

"Our theory," Jonas came closer to her as he spoke, "is that she had a little too much to drink and drowned." He pointed to a chaise lounge and umbrella beside the pool. "I don't think the pool boy had anything to do with it. She was probably partying before he got here, although we'll check that out."

"And the plant stuff?" Peggy asked.

Jonas walked her to the edge of the pool closest to where the body was floating. She realized it was tethered now to the side of the pool by the ladder. The police hadn't wanted to move Mrs. Hatley, and they didn't want to go in the pool after her yet.

"You can see some of it here." Jonas pointed to the green matter on the side of the pool. "There's some on her as well."

Harold crouched beside them and kept his voice low. "We think the plant may be something she picked up in the yard and walked over here. No big deal. We only need you to verify that."

Peggy looked around the yard. It was close-cut fescue, expensive and well kept. There were one or two big oak trees. The rest were shrubs and ornamentals. Virtually no wild plant life to be seen. It was probably poisoned or pulled out long ago. The house and grounds were at least fifty years old. There was no wild growing kudzu or honeysuckle as there was in many other yards.

Ignoring the two men watching her, Peggy knelt down beside the woman's body. Bless her soul, Mrs. Hatley worked hard to keep that body in the pink underwear in good shape. What a shame to end up this way. She hoped her children weren't too young. No one should have to lose their mother before they became adults.

The green matter was instantly recognizable to her. It grew in almost every pond, swamp, lake, and river in North Carolina. It was the same plant they found on Gerald Capshaw's body: duckweed.

It shouldn't be there. This was not a pond. As far as she knew, duckweed wouldn't grow in a chlorine pool. The scent of pool chemical filled the air around them. The duckweed was in Mrs. Hatley's hair as well. How did it get there? On Gerald Capshaw, it was an expected occurrence. Here it made the slightly questionable death even more so. Harold and Jonas weren't going to like it, unless . . .

"I'm going to have to inspect the bottom of the pool." She explained about the duckweed. "The only way this would make sense is if the drain has some in it. I don't see how it could grow in the water, but since pools are rarely emptied here, it's possible it could be growing up in the drain."

"You can't go in there without a wet suit," Harold said. "The water is contaminated. There are fluids expelled when a person drowns, you know, like the contents of the stomach. I'm sure you wouldn't want to swim around in all that."

"That's fine. Whatever it takes."

Jonas smiled. "Have you ever done any diving?"

"No. But I have a friend who could be what we're looking for." Peggy pulled out her cell phone and called Ruth at UNCC. "She's got forensic diving experience. She'll know what to do."

Ruth told Peggy she'd be happy to come out and take a look. Peggy thanked her, gave her the address, then closed her cell phone. "There. You see? That's not such a problem."

"Except that we have to pay her." Jonas ran a hand around the collar of his white shirt. "I was already going to have to put in for extra expenses for you."

Peggy looked around at the group of officers surrounding the pool. "No one else seems to have a wet suit, Jonas. One way or another, if you want an answer about this duckweed, someone will have to check the drain."

"Let's say the dickweed —"

Peggy cut Harold off mid-thought. "*Duck-weed.*"

"Sorry. Duckweed." He cleared his throat and adjusted his glasses. "Let's say the duckweed *isn't* growing in the drain at the bottom of the pool. What would that mean?"

"It would mean she went swimming in another body of water before getting in the pool, although, quite frankly, I can't imagine she wouldn't notice having duckweed in her hair. She looks like a fastidious kind of woman to me."

Al laughed. "What makes you say that?"

"Look," she pointed, "no tan lines. And no roots showing, although clearly that's not a natural hair color. She's also very trim and muscled. I'd say she works out regularly and takes care of herself."

"Good observation," Harold agreed. "I guess the duckweed is important."

"Has anyone wondered where Mrs. Hatley's children are?" Peggy glanced at her watch. It was a little after seven p.m. "Obviously she's not old enough to have grown children."

Jonas looked at Al. "Do we know where her kids are?"

"Not here." Al shrugged. "We tried to contact Mr. Hatley at Beldon and Dean. We haven't been able to get in touch with him.

But we haven't given anything to the press yet until we hear from him."

"The brokerage." Jonas's radio squawked a warning that a minivan had pulled up in the drive. "Great," the captain growled. "This is probably a soccer dad with both kids in tow."

"Someone has to stop him," Peggy stated the obvious. "You can't let the children see their mother this way."

Al started around the house to speak to the father, telling the officer in the front to hold the man and children in their vehicle until he got there.

Ruth called Peggy on her cell phone to let her know she was out front, too. Peggy excused herself from the group and went down the drive to meet her. She didn't want to see the look on the father's face when Al told him his wife was dead. She really didn't want to see the looks of question and fear on the two children's faces.

She had no choice. Mr. Hatley was with Al by the time she walked around the side of the house. The two children, a boy about ten and a girl about seven, stared out the window of the minivan as their father dropped to his knees on the perfectly mani-cured green lawn. They didn't know yet exactly what was wrong, but with the terrible wisdom of youth, they already suspected.

"Peggy?" Ruth hailed her from the white UNCC van. "I could use a hand lugging some of this up that hill. What happened here?"

Peggy explained, seeing Al put his big hand on Mr. Hatley's shoulder out of the corner of her eye. She'd been a mother for too long. All she wanted to do was run to the minivan and comfort those poor children. What could she say to them? What could anyone say?

The only thing she could do was make sure what happened to their mother was an accident. She picked up the box of gear Ruth gave her, and they started back toward the house.

"So, you need me to check out the drain for the same plant we found on Gerald." Ruth shook her head. "It's a weird world, isn't it?"

"Yes, it is," Peggy agreed. "I don't think we're going to find anything down there. But there's no point in explaining to the police that duckweed only grows in open water. That's going to set off an investigation they don't want. If Mrs. Hatley didn't drown here, where did she die?"

Ruth introduced herself to Jonas and

Harold. She'd brought her underwater forensic credentials in case there was some question of her being up to the task. She presented them to Jonas as the officer in charge of the investigation. He took them and briefly perused them before folding the paper and putting it in his pocket.

Peggy helped Ruth get ready for the dive, such as it was. The pool was barely ten feet at the deep end. Not exactly Badin Lake or even the Catawba River. "Won't you need an air tank?"

"I'll be fine. It's not much of a dive, and either the duckweed will be in the drain or it won't. Either way, I'll come right back up. Don't worry. I won't take in any water."

They all stood back while Ruth slid into the crystal blue water. The ripples made Mrs. Hatley's body slap lightly against the side of the pool. Two crime scene techs held her in place with gloved hands.

Al came around the side of the house with Mr. Hatley and both children. The boy and girl were silent and subdued, walking beside their father.

Jonas frowned when he saw them. "What the . . . ?"

"Mr. Hatley insisted he and his children had a right to be here," Al informed him. "Besides, he brought up a good point. We have no ID for the victim. He can ID her."

"That's ridiculous!" Peggy hissed. She didn't care if it was her place or not to say it. "Those children have no business being back here."

Mr. Hatley, blond hair spiked on his head, probably no tan lines either, stared at her. "They deserve the truth. Life isn't always pleasant."

Peggy made a noise somewhere between *pshaw* and *pfft* then grabbed each of the children by the hand, taking them away from their father and starting toward the house.

"You can't do that!" Their father took a step forward to stop her. "They should be here, too. I'll file charges."

Al stepped in front of him. "I believe you said you could ID this woman, Mr. Hatley. Is this your wife or not?"

Peggy ignored them both and took the children into the kitchen through the open glass doors that faced the pool. Their small hands were icy despite the heat of the evening, and their traumatized faces were devoid of color. She didn't have to be a doctor to see they were in shock. What on earth was that man thinking bringing them back there? He might be a stockbroker, but he was obviously a moron as well.

She sat each of the children on a tall bar-stool, grunting a little as she lifted the ten-year-old, even though he was thin. They both looked straight ahead without moving or speaking.

Not exactly sure what she could do or say, if anything, to lessen what they had seen, she turned on the little flat screen TV in the corner. She didn't want to make light of what had happened, but they needed to get their minds away from their mother for a time.

"I think I'll make some tea. That always helps me." She looked in the cabinets but couldn't find any tea. "On the other hand, you're probably hungry. You must have had soccer practice or something after school. My son played soccer in school. It's a great game. I played a little in school, too."

She knew she was rambling, but the girl blinked a few times. Maybe she was headed in the right direction.

"We usually have milkshakes," the girl said. "Mom always makes us milkshakes."

Peggy smiled, relieved, and opened the freezer. Thank God! There was chocolate ice cream! She found a gallon of milk in the refrigerator and looked around for the blender.

"It comes up out of the cabinet," the boy

told her.

"Isn't that ingenious?" Peggy looked where he pointed. "Do you know how it does that?"

That brought both children off their stools and over to the cabinet. In less than five minutes, she had them dipping ice cream into the blender and pushing buttons to make the milkshake whirl around. She learned their names, Blade and Kenya, where they went to school and, most importantly, their grandmother's phone number. She stayed away from the subject of what had happened outside.

While Blade and Kenya watched Sponge-Bob Square Pants, Peggy called Marsha's mother and told her she was needed at the house. She told her there had been an accident and left it at that. Being a contract forensic botanist didn't pay enough for her to tell a woman her daughter was dead. Being a mother, she knew the woman would keep herself together for the children. And, hopefully, reprimand her son-in-law.

Only a moment later, an older woman peeked around the corner of the kitchen. Peggy was astounded that Mrs. Hatley's mother had gotten there so quickly until the woman introduced herself as being from the Department of Social Services. She smiled at the children, who barely looked up from their cartoon and milkshakes. "I'll take it from here," she told Peggy. "They'll be fine."

Peggy explained she'd called the children's grandmother, then left through the glass doors without looking back. She wasn't sure she could leave if she'd looked at their sad little faces again. By now, Ruth should've surfaced, and they'd all know if it was a simple drowning or something more.

Ruth was packing up her gear as Peggy went back outside. The evening was finally cooling with twilight falling on the city. The incessant sound of traffic from Sharon Road made Peggy wonder why anyone would pay so much to live here. She thought Queens Road was bad, but it was nothing like this.

"What did you find?" Peggy asked.

"Some hair and some other colored fibers, probably from clothes. No duckweed." Ruth zipped her soiled wet suit into a large plastic bag then looked up. "Sorry."

Peggy shrugged. "It was a long shot. I thought it was unlikely, but you never know." She watched Al and Jonas talking to Mr. Hatley, who, besides the scantily clad pool boy, could become a suspect in what might be a homicide investigation. "Thanks for coming, anyway."

"No problem." Ruth smiled at her. "It's funny how we can have normal conversations around something like this, isn't it? That's why I started teaching. Ten years bringing up bodies was enough for me."

"I can understand that."

"I got a call from the Badin police today. They asked me nicely to come out for a chat."

Peggy's cinnamon brows raised. "Are they are taking Mrs. Capshaw seriously?"

"I suppose they're only doing their job. But I feel kind of like a suspect." Ruth nodded toward Mr. Hatley. "Like him."

"I'm sure it's nothing of the kind. I think they know what happened out there. They only need to go through the motions."

"Maybe."

Al joined them. "Peggy, Rimer wants to talk to you. I'll help Dr. Sargent to her car."

Peggy said good-bye to Ruth again then walked around the edge of the pool. The lights had come on in and around the water. Mrs. Hatley's body was gone. She didn't notice the morgue team there until she looked up. Mr. Hatley glared at her as he walked by with an officer at his side.

"I suppose this means Mrs. Hatley didn't drink too much and accidentally drown." Jonas put away his notebook.

119

"Probably not. Not unless she went swimming in a lake or river before she went in the pool," Peggy replied. "I'm sure an autopsy will tell us more."

Harold put his hands behind his back and rocked on his heels. "I think they're playing my song."

7

Oxalis

Botanical: *Oxalis acetosella*

Oxalis is easily confused with clover, especially as a pest growing in cultivated lawns. The colorful flowers of oxalis tell a different story, distinguishing itself from clover even if it doesn't win any points in our hearts as it emerges in our grass. Native Americans liked the taste of the plant, but the flavor is oxalic acid, which can cause digestive disturbances.

They didn't need her for the autopsy, a fact that made Peggy happy. She got on her bike and started for home through the evening traffic. A few large SUVs almost ran her off the road, and she lamented the lack of bicycle paths through the city. She'd been too busy to hound the city council about it recently, but she decided to put it on her calendar for next month. If Charlotte wanted people to think of it as a metropolitan city, it had better start acting like one.

She could smell something cooking in her kitchen as she put her bike in the garage. The lights were on in the house, a welcome sight after what she'd seen at the Hatley home. It might be awkward at her age having an almost live-in boyfriend, but it was very nice.

"I thought it might be you." She kissed Steve as he handed her the mail and stirred whatever concoction he had in the oversized skillet. "Whatever that is smells delicious."

He smiled. "I call this 'what I found in Peggy's refrigerator plus a few Bojangles biscuits I saved from lunch.' Where have you been? I tried your cell phone a few times, and it went to voice mail. I was getting worried."

She told him about the Hatley incident. "It was terrible. That poor woman was probably murdered."

"Isn't there some stricture about discussing police cases with people outside the department?" He took the biscuits out of the microwave. "I don't want you to get in trouble on your first official case."

"I'm not worried about you going to Channel 9 News and blabbing." She took out two plates and two glasses then fished around in the dishwasher until she found two forks. "John used to tell me about his cases. I'm not even officially with the department. Of course, if you'd rather me not tell you . . ."

"Like that would stop you." He put some of the goulash-type food on the plates. "Just kidding. I'm glad they hired you so they can keep you out of trouble, at least until your dad moves up here."

"Don't start." She got some napkins, poured each of them some sweet tea, and sat down. "I don't get into trouble. I investigate and try to help people."

Steve took a seat opposite her. "And once in a while confront killers, lunatics, and Internet stalkers."

"This is really good." She changed the subject. "You can raid my refrigerator whenever you like."

"In other words," he translated, "shut up and eat your dinner."

"Did you have anything interesting happen to you today?" Peggy went farther along the road of changing the subject from her to him.

"Well, I had to tell a woman her Pekingese has brain cancer. I delivered a litter of kittens C-section. I examined a pregnant goldfish who isn't late but isn't ready to

123

deliver either. And I agreed to start taking care of some horses at a ranch in Cabarrus County."

Peggy raised her eyebrows. "You *were* busy! That's great about the horses. Your business has really picked up since you got here last year."

"Thanks. I'm really glad it did, because I don't know how to do much of anything else, and I really want to stay here."

"Oh?" She smiled at him. "Any particular reason you want to stay in Charlotte especially?"

"One important one with red hair and beautiful green eyes."

"That could be anyone," she teased.

He took her hand and kissed her fingers. "Not for me."

The phone rang, and Steve buttered a biscuit while Peggy answered it. It was Mai Sato from the medical examiner's office. Harold Ramsey was requesting her presence.

"I have to go out," Peggy told Steve after she hung up. "I guess they discovered something new in the Hatley case and want me to have a look at it."

"Okay. I'll watch a movie or surf the Internet until you get back. All my patients are tucked in for the night."

"I shouldn't be long. I can't imagine what can't wait until morning."

"Well, imagine this." Steve produced a small cake from the refrigerator. "Me here waiting for you with a triple chocolate fudge cake for two."

"I'll make sure it's even shorter than I thought." She kissed him as she picked up her pocketbook. "At least there won't be as much traffic this time."

"Hurry back."

Peggy brought her bike into the Center City medical examiner's office. It wasn't a good place to leave anything unchained for long, despite the large police presence. She decided to mention getting a bike rack to Harold and locked the chain on her bike.

Mai was waiting for her near the front door. "Peggy! It's good to see you!"

"Even though it means you have to work late?"

"I work late when he works late, and around here, that's almost every night. How have you been?"

"I'm fine. You're looking very good, too. Are things going well for you?"

"Very well. I bought a small house in Myers Park. Nothing like yours, of course, but it's a good investment, and it's comfortable for one . . . or two people."

"Anyone in particular you have in mind?"

"Not yet. I'm still working on that part." Mai handed her a white lab coat. "This is for you. And here's your ID badge. It'll get you in the door without anyone being here to get you past the front desk."

"Thanks. I feel so official now. No more sneaking in and out of the morgue for us, huh?"

Mai laughed but looked around. "Let's keep that *our* little secret. How's Paul doing?"

Peggy glanced at her as she put the lab coat on. Mai dated Paul for a short while. Maybe there was still a spark of interest there. "He's fine. Still alone. He recovered from that shoulder wound quickly, so he's back on duty."

"That's good." Mai pushed her shiny black hair out of her face after leaning over to run her ID card through the scanner to open the door into the lab. "I'm glad he's okay again."

"I'm sure he still misses you." Peggy watched Mai's beautiful Asian face for any sign of emotion, but her dark eyes gave nothing away. "I'm sure he'd like it if you gave him a call."

"I don't have any hard feelings against

him anymore," Mai answered carefully. "But I don't have any romantic feelings toward him either. Sorry."

"That's all right." Peggy followed Mai into the brightly lit lab. "I really didn't want grandchildren in my lifetime anyway. I'm sure it would only make me feel old."

"You're a big fake, Peggy Lee!" Mai giggled. "But I don't think grandchildren are a possibility, at least not from me and Paul."

"I hope I'm not interrupting your important social life." Harold loomed up suddenly from the hall. "Because if I am, I can go out and get something for dinner. I'm not doing anything important here besides trying to solve what could be a murder of the mother of two children."

"Good evening, Harold." Peggy wasn't fazed by his manner. She was used to it by now. "If you're going out, I'll take a large mocha. Decaf, please. This time of night I get a little wired from caffeine."

"Of course!" He took a pad of paper out of his jacket pocket. "Ms. Sato, would you like something?"

"A bagel would be nice. I missed dinner, and I'm starving."

He glared at her. "I don't care. And none of us are leaving this lab until we have a few more answers about Mrs. Hatley's death. Send out for pizza or something. Stop whining!"

Peggy rolled her eyes, amazed the girl fell for Harold's pretense. The man was impossible. She didn't know how Mai worked so closely with him every day. "Exactly what is it you wanted me to see?"

"I finished the autopsy on Mrs. Hatley despite the fact that I have six dead gang members who are waiting for me in the cooler. The mayor wants to know what happened to our esteemed mother who lived in his neighborhood before we know if the gang members were really killed by that drive-by shooting that left them full of bullets."

"And you needed me for . . . ?" Peggy prompted.

"There's something you should see. Being the botanical expert on this case, I thought you might like to have dinner with me on Thursday night. I have tickets to the symphony. We could go there after we eat. I was thinking maybe Morton's. I enjoy a large steak and a good glass of red wine. You might want to make a note of that."

Peggy stared at him. "Did you ask me to come over here so you could ask me out?"

"It really just came up in conversation."

"You were talking about why you need me to see something you found in a dead woman's body," she reminded him. "How do the two go together?"

"Everything goes with food and wine." He led the way to the autopsy area. "So it's a date?"

"You know I'm seeing someone." She took a deep breath and got ready to view the body that had been autopsied. It wasn't going to be a pleasant sight, and she didn't think she could consider steak and wine at the same time.

"That vet fellow? Is he still around?"

"Yes. And no, I can't go out to dinner with you. Thank you for the invitation."

He stopped at the door plastered with warning signs that separated the autopsy area from the rest of the lab. "Are you sure? Once I ask someone else, it will be too late."

Mai hid a smile behind her clipboard as Peggy answered, "I'm sure. Thanks anyway."

"Maybe next time." He threw back the door and presented the body for her consideration. "She's been dead more than twenty-four hours. I found something unusual in her lungs and throat. It goes along with your supposition that Mrs. Hatley did not in fact die in her pool."

Peggy glanced quickly at the body that was

recently dissected. "And that is?"

"Ms. Sato?" Harold stared at his assistant. "Phytoplankton."

"Well done, Ms. Sato. I'll commend your efforts to the mayor." He looked around the room. "Have you ordered that pizza yet?"

"Sir?" Mai's beautifully shaped brows came together in confusion.

"Pizza. It's a big, round pie sort of food with tomato sauce and pepperoni."

"You want me to order pizza?"

"I believe we all agreed we're hungry, Ms. Sato. What's keeping you?"

Peggy exchanged looks of frustration with Mai before she left the autopsy area. She knew the girl had hopes of someday being the county medical examiner, but she was paying a high price for it under Harold Ramsey's dominance.

"Whenever you're ready, Dr. Lee." Harold tapped his pen on his hand.

"Ready for what?" Peggy asked.

"I'd like you to take a look at the phytoplankton and tell me where it came from. That should identify our POD."

"And that is?"

"Place of death. That's where we'll find more clues as to what happened to Mrs. Hatley." Harold finally put the pen in his pocket.

"I'll be glad to take a look at it, but without comparison samples, I won't be able to tell you where it came from."

"I thought that was part of being a *local* botanist."

"I don't keep samples of phytoplankton from lakes and rivers in the area, if that's what you mean."

Harold took out a slide and set it up for her. "We brought a microscope over here especially for you. Could you tell us where it came from with comparison samples?"

"Yes. But it could require samples from any body of water large enough to drown a human. I don't know how long that would take —"

"Good." He turned away and started walking across the lab. "Let me know when you've found it."

She looked up from the microscope. "A project like that could take months! There must be some other way."

He waved to her as he kept walking. "If there is, I'm sure you'll find it. Welcome to the world of contract forensic botany, Dr. Lee. Good luck."

She stared at him until he disappeared around a corner of the large lab office. There were several other people working on various projects around her. She took a quick glance back at the hall that separated her from what was left of Marsha Hatley then applied herself to the microscope.

There was nothing special about the phytoplankton. It truly could have been from any lake, river, or stream, possibly in the whole state. If Mrs. Hatley had been killed more than a day ago, she could have died anywhere.

According to what she'd overheard from the police, Mrs. Hatley had been out of town. She was last seen leaving work the day before she died. Her husband had seen the children off to school that morning but hadn't spoken to his wife since the day before.

Peggy noticed Mrs. Hatley's file on the table beside the microscope. She picked it up, glancing around the room to see if anyone noticed. It was silly, of course. She was working with the ME and the police. She could have access to the file.

Frankly, she wished the pool boy's alibi wasn't so good. He had names and destinations of every house and every pool he'd been to that day. Mr. Hatley had a good alibi as well. He was either with the children or at work during the time Harold believed his wife was killed.

Without having any frame of reference

besides the phytoplankton, it was going to be a tough search. Each body of water would lend its own particular structure to the individual phytoplankton. But searching every place a woman could drown would be impossible. She supposed they would have to start with the closest places then move out if those didn't match. It would have to be an isolated area. It would be too hard to drown someone in the lake at Freedom Park.

"Find anything interesting?" Harold's booming voice made her jump as he came back into the lab.

She closed the file abruptly then opened it again after reminding herself that she wasn't doing anything wrong. "I was trying to work out where the closest place to drown someone would be."

He smiled, closed his eyes, and put his hand to his heart. "You are the perfect woman. If you won't let me take you out for dinner and the symphony, will you marry me?"

The sound of a pizza box hitting the tile floor brought both their heads up. Mai scrambled to pick up the box and her purse while juggling another pizza box. Peggy closed her eyes and sighed. This was already out of hand.

"Ah! Pizza!" Harold took the boxes from Mai and opened them on an empty desk. The sight was almost enough to make Peggy lose her dinner.

Mai put her purse down next to where Peggy was sitting at the microscope. She pretended to be organizing her things. "You aren't *serious* about Dr. Ramsey, are you?"

"I'm seeing Steve," Peggy rebutted. "What do *you* think?"

"Thank God!"

"I'm sure he's not so bad." Peggy thought a moment then retracted her statement. "I take it back. I'm sure he's much worse than I've seen."

Mai nodded. "You've got that right. I can't tell you how many times I've thought about quitting since I got promoted. I wanted this position for so long, I can't believe it's so awful I dread coming into work every day."

"I'm sure you'll find a way around it. You're a bright, capable young woman. There's always an answer."

"Thanks." She looked at the closed file. "Did you see anything that seemed out of the ordinary?"

"No, not really. You?"

"I thought the duckweed was a little over the top." Mai looked at her. "If you were going to kill someone and you went to all the trouble of drowning them somewhere else and trying to make it look like they drowned in their pool, wouldn't you have taken a minute to get that weed off of them?"

Peggy considered her point. "You may be right. If the killer wasn't sloppy or pressed for time before the pool boy got there, there's a chance he or she wanted everyone to know it was a setup."

"Like maybe we would suspect someone."

"My money would be on the husband. He was as cold as ice." She told Mai about the incident with the children.

"That should be enough to have him locked up whether he murdered his wife or not."

"He seems to have a good alibi. I guess I'll have to give the police some time to figure it out."

"We're on the same side now, remember?"

"Of course. Besides, I'm going to have my hands full searching for this phytoplankton. I wonder if Jonas would like to lend me a few able-bodied officers."

"That's funny. It's a good thing to develop a sense of humor when you're thinking about manpower or money from the police department." Mai laughed. "You might as well get used to it."

"It never hurts to ask." Peggy packed up her things and got ready to go. "If not, I have a friend who might be willing to help. We'll see."

They said good-bye at the lab door. Peggy smiled as she hung her lab coat on the rack by the door. Her new ID badge shone in the bright fluorescent lights. It was a sharp curve from where she had been. She wondered what John would have thought of her taking this job. Certainly they never discussed using her knowledge of plant life to solve a murder. As far as she knew, John had never used a botanist to help with a case.

She tucked her ID badge into her pocketbook before she got on her bike for the ride home. It was still warm outside with a faint hint of rain she didn't remember seeing in the forecast. She pedaled past a large display of orange and yellow daylilies, looking for a sign that said who the gardener was. Without one, she supposed it was city maintenance. Lucky for them, daylilies were easy to grow and hard to kill. They made a lovely addition to the otherwise austere building.

The ride home was fast, with almost no traffic. She waved back to some young joggers she recognized but couldn't name. She remembered Sam planting yellow roses in their garden beside some gorgeous golden dinner plate asters. She even recalled the tiny clumps of oxalis growing in their yard around ornamental rocks. But she couldn't remember the names of the people.

Selective memory loss, she decided. SML. Someone should do research on it. She rode her bike down Third Street to Providence then across to Queens. She knew before she reached the garage that Steve was gone. His green Saturn Vue was absent from her drive. It must be another emergency.

Shakespeare met her in the kitchen to tell her all about it. He was like having a small child who ran to the door to tell his mother everything that happened that day. He couldn't talk as well as a two-year-old, but he tried, making growling, mewling sounds in the back of his throat. She laughed. "You sound like Scooby-Doo more every day. I wonder what you'd be willing to do for a Scooby Snack."

She patted his head, and he settled down as she locked the kitchen door behind her and set the exterior alarm. There was a note on the kitchen table from Steve. She was right. There was an animal emergency. He reminded her that there was cake in the refrigerator and that he would be back as soon as he could.

"Between the two of us, it's a wonder we have time for a relationship." She yawned, put her pocketbook on the foyer table, then headed upstairs. Shakespeare padded after her, following her into the bedroom.

Her computer was chiming, which meant she had a new message. She yawned again. It was probably the Swedish botanist who'd contacted her earlier in the month looking for help with growing some warm weather plants in his experimental garden. She looked at her bed, where Shakespeare had already taken up residence, then kicked off her shoes.

"I suppose I can answer a few emails," she said to the room in general. "If they don't put me to sleep." Shakespeare yawned, and she laughed. "Exactly. You know what I mean. I love to work with plants, but sometimes the discussions can be boring. Well, if they are, I'll just shut it down."

The new message was from Nightflyer. *Good evening, Nightrose.*

8

Partridge Pea
Botanical: *Cassia fasciculata*
Partridge pea is a native legume that springs up in old fields or open wooded areas. It grows upright and has bright yellow flowers during the warm summer months. The plant has pods like pea pods that burst open, allowing the seeds to spread the plant. The leaves are sensitive to touch and will close when disturbed. The plant is poisonous to cattle but not to deer.

It's been a while, Peggy typed. *Why is it I only hear from you when I'm investigating someone's death?*

Believe me; I'm not aware of any investigation right now. I apologize. I would've contacted you after you couldn't meet me in the park. Unfortunately, I've been in the hospital.

Peggy felt bad that she'd been hard on

him. It was difficult to know what to say to a man she'd never met, only conversed with online. Not that it wasn't the case in many of her professional relationships. She'd met many other botanists online that she might never meet in person.

Nightflyer was different. He claimed to know so much about her life and had given her valid, if vague, answers to some of her problems with other investigations. *Not that I had other investigations exactly,* she backtracked in her thoughts. She may have helped the police a few times, but she wouldn't really call those investigations.

Her mysterious online visitor had made more than one romantic overture that she'd ignored. The last one had almost cost Peggy her relationship with Steve. She wouldn't let that happen again.

I hope you're feeling better, she typed on the screen.

I am. Thank you. It was only a mild heart attack. I've had worse, but this was life-changing. I'm a new man.

Peggy raised her eyebrows and considered what to say. It was unusual for them to chat so much. They normally played chess. *I hope that's a good thing. Would you like to play chess somewhere?*

Not tonight, Peggy. As I said, I am a changed

man. I want to meet you.

She considered their last attempt at a meeting. It was scheduled for midnight in Myers Park. Steve followed her there, and Nightflyer left a package for her but didn't hang around to meet her. Steve said at the time it was ill-advised to meet a man she'd only talked to on the Internet, alone, in a park in the middle of the night.

Peggy agreed with him now. *I would be happy to play chess with you face-to-face. But no more midnight meetings. I think we're both too old and hopefully, too wise to do something like that.*

That's fine. Name your time and place.

She was surprised by his answer. *No more secrets?*

Not anymore. I told you, I'm a changed man. I quit the group I was with. I don't have any more ties to the Company. I'm free to live my life the way I want. One of those ways includes you, Nightrose.

Peggy's heart fluttered a little, and her hands were trembling. Not that she'd do anything to hurt Steve. It was only vanity. Whoever thought she'd have two men who wanted her at *her* age? Her mother would be scandalized. *I don't know what to say. You know enough about me to know I'm with someone.*

Dr. Steve Newsome. I know. All I'm asking for is a chance to meet you, talk with you, and perhaps, give him a run for his money. I've waited all of my life for a woman like you. I won't let you go without a fight.

She *really* didn't know what to say now. She didn't want to encourage him. She was in love with Steve. Their relationship was perfect. There was nothing Nightflyer could say or do to persuade her to leave Steve. Still, there *was* that little thrill she couldn't deny.

Hadn't Steve accused her of harboring those feelings for Nightflyer? She'd denied it, of course, but they were there whether she wanted them to be there or not. Her mother always said she had a contrary nature that went with her red hair and temper. Peggy believed she must be right.

I'll be glad to meet with you and play chess with you. That's all I can promise.

That's all I ask. When and where would you like to meet?

She thought about asking him to her home. He'd sent gifts to her. He knew where she lived. But that seemed too personal, knowing how he claimed to feel about her. She considered meeting him at the Potting Shed, but she didn't want to deal with giggly college students who might run back to Steve with news of the meeting. She definitely was *not* telling Steve about the event.

Let's meet at the main branch of the library. Say, 2 tomorrow?

That's fine. I'll bring the chessboard.

I look forward to finally meeting you. It wasn't anything remarkable. She ended conversations with colleagues that way all the time.

Shakespeare barked, not the deep, booming sound he made when someone unusual pulled into the drive but the tail-wagging, higher octave he reserved for Sam, Paul, or Steve. At this time of night, it was probably Steve.

Guilty of everything except something substantial, she turned off her computer, pushed her chair under her desk, took off her slippers, and jumped into bed. She lay there listening to the now-familiar sounds of Steve letting himself into the house, closing the door, and rearming the alarm system. She could picture him putting his keys on the foyer table beside her pocketbook then coming up the stairs with his lengthy strides.

"I thought you'd be asleep by now," he said, entering the bedroom. "You must be planning something."

143

He knew her too well. "I'm not planning anything. I was thinking about everything that happened today, especially tonight." She told him about what she'd done at the ME's office and the task Harold had assigned her.

"That doesn't seem like too much for what they're paying you." He took off his shirt and walked into the bathroom. "Search every body of water someone could drown in. Maybe you should start with the water fountain at the Atrium."

Peggy took a deep breath as she heard him brushing his teeth. She'd managed to distract him. She was lucky this time.

Not that she was really doing *anything*. It wasn't like Nightflyer was hiding under the bed like the lover in some 1940s movie. There was actually nothing to distract Steve from. It was only her overdeveloped sense of guilt. She could thank her mother for that, too.

Steve turned out the light and got in bed beside her, pulling her close to him. "You were busy today. What's on tap for tomorrow?"

"Nothing much," she lied, almost able to feel her mother's switch against her legs for the act. "I'm sure it will be an ordinary day."

Peggy had breakfast with Steve before riding over to the Potting Shed. Sam and Keeley had already been there and gone. They tried to get as much yard work done in the morning as they could before the hot part of the day dragged in.

She had barely opened the door to the shop when Sofia and Emil Balducci hurried over from the Kozy Kettle. They came with fresh blueberry bagels and her favorite peach tea, so she could hardly complain when they stayed around to talk.

"How is business, Peggy?" Sofia looked at Emil in a significant way. She shook her head, her thick, dark hair moving from side to side.

"Good. How are you two doing?" Peggy knew something was coming. Emil and his wife never came over to simply discuss business.

"Fine. Good." Emil thumped his large chest. His heavy black mustache that curled on the ends quivered. "We only think of you over here going slowly out of business because of those greedy Smithy and Hawk people. If this were my homeland, I would take my seven brothers, and we would

145

avenge you."

"The store is fine, really." Peggy almost laughed. "And it's Smith & Hawken, Emil."

"Never mind." Sofia moved closer to her. "I have just the thing to take care of this. We don't need Emil's stupid brothers. My great-aunt Persephona is a witch. She taught me a curse to get rid of unwelcome intruders. I am going to give that curse to you."

Sofia held out her hands, her dark eyes glowing with joy for what she was about to do. Peggy didn't feel quite the same way. She knew Sofia meant well, but she could have anything from a dead bat to a potion of some sort. She wasn't sure she wanted to take it from her even if she was only going to throw it in the trash.

Not that she didn't believe in magic. They had plenty of magic in the Low Country where she was from. Her grandmother did magic spells; there was the spell before you kill a chicken (one of the reasons Peggy was a vegetarian), the spell before the full moon for good corn, and lots of other spells for everything from childbearing to headaches.

Her great-great-grandmother was part Gullah, the descendant of slaves brought to South Carolina to work the plantations. You couldn't tell by looking at her, since she'd had a full head of bright red hair, but she laid claim to the colorful heritage.

Peggy finally worked up to taking what Sofia offered. The woman would stand there all day if she didn't. She kept her eyes open as she held out her hand and tried not to cringe.

Sofia placed a silver cloth bag in her palm. It was tied shut with a piece of brown jute. "This will take care of it. It is very powerful. Just take it to Smithy and Hawk and drop it on the floor after you open it. They won't last a week."

"Thank you." Peggy put the bag on the counter behind her with all the deference she could muster. After all, it might be the real thing and ruin her business if she dropped it. "I'll go over there this afternoon."

Sofia winked elaborately, her heavy fake eyelashes almost weighing down her eyelids. "I know you would like to know what's inside. I wish I could tell you. But Persephona told me to tell no one."

That was just as well for Peggy. She smiled and waved good-bye to the Balduccis. Sofia was almost out of the Potting Shed before she turned back to whisper, "There is a little raw meat inside. If you have to wait, you might want to put it in the refrigerator. It works best when it is fresh."

Peggy put the curse bag into the mini-fridge behind the counter under Sofia's watchful eye. The Sicilian woman smiled and nodded then crossed the courtyard to her coffee shop.

Feeling like she should draw a deep breath and cross herself three times, Peggy set up the cash register and computer for the day. Selena was coming in late since she'd closed the shop so often recently. Peggy wasn't expecting a lot of traffic, but she made sure everything was stacked neatly on the shelves and filled up the seed rack near the door.

A shipment of fall bulbs had come in. She found Sam's note about it in his broad, scrawling handwriting on top of the case. It seemed too hot outside to think about the cooler autumn breezes, but she knew they would be here. Her store needed to be ready for customers who were thinking ahead, or they would go somewhere else.

She remembered a case of clay pots she'd ordered a month before from a local woman who made them in her basement. They were adorable, sporting faces the woman sculpted in the clay of everyone from Richard Nixon to Marilyn Monroe. They were comical poses that exaggerated the attributes but left the viewer in no doubt as to who the pot was supposed to resemble.

Peggy lined the pots up along the wide sills of the old windows that faced the courtyard. She put a few bulbs in each one, added a few pairs of new gloves, and some of the new ergonomic trowels they just got in, and the Potting Shed was getting ready for fall.

The phone rang, and Peggy answered it. It was Harold Ramsey wanting to know how much progress she'd made toward identifying the mysterious phytoplankton. "Can I expect to see a report on my desk soon?"

She almost laughed. "This is going to take some time, Harold. I'm going to call my friend from UNCC, but no matter what, there are a lot of possibilities. I'll do the best I can."

"I hope that's good enough." The phone at the other end of the wire clicked in her ear.

"You are such a charmer." She put the phone down and called Ruth on her cell phone. As she thought, the other woman was delighted at the chance to work with her on the case. They arranged to meet at McAlpine Creek at 10 a.m., figuring it was as good a place to start as any.

A few customers straggled into the store as Peggy was looking at a map of Charlotte for possible drowning locations for Mrs. Hatley. They weren't part of her usual lunchtime office crowd, just a few stay-at-home moms shopping before the day got hot.

"I'm looking for something red that will perk up the flower box that sits on my terrace," a young woman with a crying baby in her backpack told Peggy. "I've got a lot of green and yellow. I thought some red might be nice to break it up."

Peggy showed her some bright red Gerber daisies and took the baby out of the backpack for her so she could look around. The little girl had sweet blond curls and huge blue eyes. She stared at Peggy as the rocking chair in the summer display swished back and forth.

"I love this birdbath." The mother brought the birdbath up to the counter with an armful of other gardening items. "I don't think I can take it back with me. Do you deliver?"

Peggy said she would be glad to help out and ran the woman's credit card after counting up her purchases. "I think you'll be happy with those daisies. They're very good in a box. They like full sun."

"That's what I love about coming here." The mother looked around the Potting Shed and smiled. "You guys always have such interesting things, and you're such a big help. I bought a new swing from Smith & Hawken yesterday. They were all right, I guess. Just not very personal, you know?"

It was already beginning, Peggy thought as she bagged up the purchases. The inevitable comparisons. Maybe she should take Sofia's curse bag over there and save herself some headaches. Not that she carried any outdoor swings, but she could have ordered one.

The mother and baby left the store, headed toward the Kozy Kettle. The other customer was looking at the few pieces of outdoor furniture she carried. One was an unusual fireplace pit made by a local man who worked with wrought iron. It was a little pricey, but Peggy liked the way it looked, and she enjoyed selling products made by hometown people whenever she could.

"I like this," the older woman told her. "Do you know the man who made it?"

"Yes. His name is on the tag." Peggy pulled it out and turned it over to show her. She did a double take when she saw the woman's Smith & Hawken name tag. "Are you looking for something for yourself or for the store?"

"Maybe both," the woman admitted,

straightening up. She held out her hand. "My name is Nancy Dwight. I'm the manager at the new Smith & Hawken store over in Founders Hall. If your boss isn't what you'd like him to be, give me a call. I'm always looking for new employees." She handed Peggy a card with her name on it.

What red was left in Peggy's hair set her temper on fire and made her tap her foot in impatience. "I have a very good working relationship with my boss. I'm Peggy Lee. I *own* the Potting Shed."

Nancy Dwight stared at her, then frowned. "I'm sorry. I wasn't expecting to find the owner here. You have a very nice place, but I'm afraid we'll be competing for a similar market. No offense, but you can't compete with our store."

Peggy laughed. "None taken. And you can't compete with our service or the fact that we sell living things as well as outdoor furniture."

"None taken." Nancy glanced around the shop and smiled. "This place is very sweet. I hope you'll be able to stay open. Nice meeting you, Peggy."

She was walking out the door that led to the courtyard as Nathan Allen, Peggy's summer student, was walking into the shop.

Every summer Peggy "adopted" a botany student who was working on a project and could use her advice. Nathan was cataloguing North Carolina wild plants that would become part of his thesis for graduation. He was a second-year botany student who showed unusual interest in the study.

"Who was that?" he asked after the door closed behind Nancy. "She must really like garden stuff."

"Why do you say that?" Peggy was already reprimanding herself for losing her temper. It wouldn't help the situation. But Nancy had been so smug, she couldn't help herself.

"She looked so happy." He shrugged and took out his portfolio. "Look what I found yesterday."

Peggy moved over to the counter to look at Nathan's work. He was not only extremely observant but a very gifted artist. His plan was to collect one of each species, catalog it, then draw it in his book. It was ambitious, since there were hundreds of thousands of wild plants in the state, but she appreciated his enthusiasm and ambition.

"I found it yesterday out in Matthews. Know what it is?"

"I'd say a partridge pea. Is that right?"

He laughed. "You know everything."

153

"Not quite. But I've been doing this a long time." She smiled at his work. "It helps to look at the drawings of such an accomplished artist as well."

"Not as good as my great-great-grandfather. I'm glad I have his journals, but the comparisons are harsh."

Peggy knew that Nathan wished he'd been around 200 years before to accompany his little-known but important ancestor on his historic journey of mapping all living things in the Carolinas. "I'm sure he'd be very proud of you. I wish I could draw half as well as you. Your work belongs in a museum."

A few more customers came in, mostly just browsing. The hot summer weather drove pedestrians inside to escape the sun. Sometimes they bought, but mostly they looked around and thanked her before they left.

In this case, one of them bought one of the new clay pots in the window, complete with bulbs and potting soil. The pots would definitely be the hit she'd imagined when she first saw them at a flea market in Pineville. She'd have to call and order more. Fall would be coming and hopefully an end to the Potting Shed's slump with it.

"This is a great place," Nathan told her

after walking around while she was busy. "I can imagine owning a place like this. It looks like you, Professor."

"Please. Call me Peggy. I'm not going to be a professor much anymore."

Selena burst into the store, slinging her backpack behind the counter as she came. "You aren't going to believe what I saw on my way over here." She pushed her summer-gilded hair out of her sweaty face then stopped abruptly when she saw Nathan.

Peggy looked between the two attractive young people. She wasn't too old to see the sparks flying. "Selena, this is my summer student, Nathan Allen. Nathan, this is Selena Rogers. She runs the Potting Shed. I only help out."

"Hi." Nathan ran his fingers through his thick, dark hair and smiled.

"Hi." Selena wet her lips with her tongue and smiled back.

Ruth picked that moment to come into the shop. "Peggy, I thought I'd swing by on my way across town and pick you up. I have three of my students with me. I thought I might as well make this a learning experience."

"That's great." Peggy glanced at Nathan, who was supposed to accompany her on the trip to McAlpine Creek to test the water.

"Would you like to stay here?"

Nathan looked at her like he'd forgotten she was there. "Yes!" He glanced at Selena. "I mean, I said I'd go with you. I'm ready to start working on water plants. This would be a good opportunity. I'll go."

Peggy nodded. "Selena, this place has been really quiet. I shouldn't be gone too long. If you need any help, let me know."

"Not a problem." Selena didn't even brush a glance at Nathan. "I've got other stuff to do between customers. Don't worry about me."

"All right. I guess we're ready to go." Peggy gathered up her supplies, freshly arrived only a few weeks before from the ME's office. Her evidence kit had been waiting for this moment.

They were about to walk out the door when Selena called Peggy back. Ruth and Nathan continued into the courtyard without her. "What is it?" Peggy asked.

"You know how you were talking about hiring someone else to help out in the shop?"

"Yes."

Selena looked out the window at Nathan's retreating back. "The person you hire could look like him. That would make my time fly by."

Peggy laughed. "I'll think about it. Thanks for the suggestion."

9

Trillium

Botanical: *Trillium undulatum*

Trilliums, also known by other names such as wake robin and toad shade trillium, are wild spring flowers that continue to flower into early summer if they are located in a shady area. They have three leaves radiating from the top of a tall stalk with three-petal flowers and smaller leaves attached with the petals. The colors are variable and may change with age.

Peggy put on her latex gloves before she began testing the creek water. Because she needed her sample as well as a control sample, Ruth was taking samples also. Her students took water samples, too, when they weren't too busy flirting with Nathan. Some things didn't change.

Steve had called her an hour ago to tell her he was going to be late tonight. One of the house farms he'd agreed to work with was having a problem with three sick horses. Because the farm was outside the city, he didn't know how long it would take him to get there and back. He said he'd grab something for dinner and meet her later at the house.

She was surprised and pleased. If she decided to have dinner with Nightflyer after their 2 p.m. meeting, she wouldn't have to explain it to Steve. Not that she *wouldn't* tell him, she considered, capping the bottle she'd just dipped into the creek water. She wrote the time and location on the side then sealed it. She certainly planned to tell Steve everything . . . after it was over. He tended to get a little bent out of shape when they talked about Nightflyer.

"So our dead woman had to drown somewhere and be transported back to the pool." Ruth put her sample into Peggy's case. "That means there should be other corroborating evidence, right? I mean, the body had to be in the trunk of a car or the back of a truck or something. No one would throw someone in the backseat all wet and full of duckweed."

Peggy sat back on her heels. "I suppose that's true. Although I think you have to remember whoever did this wasn't in their right mind."

"That's probably true." Ruth watched her students as they sat next to Nathan while he was sketching. "But not all killers are crazy. Some of them have a reason to kill, I suppose. At least in their own minds."

"I'm sure you're right." Peggy glanced at her watch. It was almost one p.m. She needed to get back home and take a shower before she went to the library to meet Nightflyer. She might wear that new turquoise skirt and flirty little top she wasn't sure about buying. Maybe this would be a good time to try it out.

She got up from the squishy mud on the side of the creek. She was covered in dirty water, plant material, and mud. Probably sunburned a little and windblown, too. She was glad they'd come in Ruth's old van. "Whoever killed Mrs. Hatley took the mother from those two children. I hope he or she considered that. I'd like to help catch that person and give them a long time to think about it in jail."

Ruth gathered up her evidence kit and wiped perspiration from her brow with the back of her arm. "It doesn't seem to me like it's always that black and white, Peggy. Not that I don't think we should catch this person and take him or her off the street.

But there have been times when I've wished something would happen to someone."

"Like Gerald Capshaw?"

"Yes." Ruth smiled grimly. "I know. I was stupid. I should've known better. He was up-front with me about our time together. But you know, it's not that easy to turn it on and off."

"I don't think you're alone in that," Peggy consoled her. "Things happen sometimes. We don't always like them, and maybe we wish we could do something about them."

"I guess that's the difference between a killer and someone who wishes they *could* kill someone. Come on. I don't know about you, but I need a shower before I plead my case to the funding board."

"Problems?"

"You know how academic life is. One day, you're the best thing since sliced bread, and the next day, you're old news. They want to cut my funding. I have good student numbers but not good enough. Apparently, they think the market for underwater forensics is limited."

"Well, maybe your work on this will help. I'll be glad to write an endorsement for you if you think that will make a difference."

"I'm thinking about trying to get a grant to start a small, private school," Ruth

161

explained. "Maybe set it up on one of the lakes around here. Maybe at my house on Lake Tillery."

"That would be great. I'm sure you could find the students."

"So maybe I could take a rain check on that endorsement until I'm ready to look for some grants." Ruth laughed. "If you can't live with them, join them."

Peggy laughed, too, and they parted company as Ruth went to round up her students and she went to find Nathan. He was sitting beside a nice trillium as he sketched it on the edge of the water. She looked over his shoulder. "That's very lifelike."

"You think so?" He flexed his hand. "I don't know. There's something about the petals that doesn't look right." He carefully put the sketch away with the sample of the plant. "Did you find what you were looking for?"

"I won't know for a while." She explained about the phytoplankton as they walked back to the van. "This is my first real job for the police. I'm not sure if what I'm doing is going to be helpful."

"Yeah. I get a lot of that. Especially from my parents. They're both super math oriented. They really don't get me studying plants. Maybe I could tell them about your work with forensic botany. My dad might get that. He's the DA for two counties."

"Really? I can see where that would be difficult." Peggy held the sliding side door to the van while Nathan helped load her evidence kit. He sat down in one of the seats to look at the work he'd done. Stephanie Nichols sat close beside him, studying the plants with him while Ruth's other students sat farther back.

Peggy closed the door and climbed in the front with Ruth. So much for Paul's romance with Stephanie. She either liked Nathan better or wasn't ready to settle down yet. At her age, she wouldn't blame her.

Paul was too serious for that kind of relationship, although there *was* the brief fling with a stripper. His father had been the same way. He'd wanted to get married and start a family right away. It was all Peggy could do to put her foot down and finish her education. Paul had scared Mai off that way. She was ready to be serious, but not as serious as Paul.

Peggy glanced at her watch a few times as Ruth regaled her with stories of past investigations and her ideas for the underwater forensic school. "Badin might be a good place for it," she said. "Property values aren't as high out there as they are around the other lakes."

"That's true," Peggy agreed. "That might be the best place for it. I'm sure you could make a go of it."

It was 1:30 before they reached Queens Road and unloaded Peggy's supplies. She thanked Ruth, who offered to give Nathan a ride back to the Potting Shed to retrieve his bike.

Peggy knew the samples she'd collected from McAlpine Creek were going to have to be dropped off at the lab. She couldn't leave them lying around without risking the possible evidence being seen as tainted. She wasn't going to have as much time to put on her makeup and give long thoughts to what she would wear for her first face-to-face with Nightflyer.

She ran through her bedroom, throwing off her clothes as she raced for the shower. Shakespeare watched with one lazy brown eye open. Peggy tried to decide if she could do anything with her hair if she washed it, but one look in the mirror told her she had no choice.

Out of the shower in less than seven minutes, a towel around her hair, she quickly applied some eye makeup, hoping the light sunburn on her face would make up for not using foundation or powder. She dried her hair with the blow dryer and looked at it critically. It looked a lot like she'd been driving a convertible with the top down. But she didn't have time for anything else.

Glad it was summer so she didn't have to wear stockings and could slide her feet into sandals, she wrapped a towel around her and rushed into the bedroom.

She looked up when she ran headfirst into Steve. "What are *you* doing here?"

He smiled and kissed her. "I'm glad to see you, too."

"No. Really." She started again, trying to get her thoughts together. "I thought you were going to be out at the horse ranch."

"I thought I was." He sat down on the side of the bed. "Is something wrong?"

She glanced at the clock. "No. Why do you ask?"

"For one thing, you keep looking at the clock. Are you late?"

Her eyes narrowed. He couldn't *possibly* know. She just had to be pleasant and get out of there. "I'm afraid so. It took so long getting those samples, I couldn't take them in since I was full of mud, but now I'm late for a . . . staff meeting."

"Sorry. I didn't mean to throw you off."

165

He got to his feet and took out his car keys. "I was going past the house and saw your truck was still here."

She looked at the clock again. "That's okay. I'm sorry I'm so distracted. Can I make it up to you over dinner? My treat."

He smiled. "I guess so. My ego is kind of bruised. No one likes to be ignored by a half-naked woman."

Peggy realized she was going to have to mend this fence before she left. Even if it meant missing Nightflyer at the library. She stepped forward and wrapped her arms around Steve. "I'm sorry. Really." She kissed him slowly and smiled. "Can you forgive me? I was so surprised to see you."

Steve studied her face for a moment. "Any more of *that* kind of sucking up, and I'll think you're up to something." He shook his head. "You're not up to anything, are you?"

"Anything I would be up to now would be perfectly legal, since I'm part of the investigation," she reminded him.

"That's true, I suppose." He looked at her again. "Still . . ."

Peggy kissed him and ran to the closet. "You're going to have to trust me. I have water samples from a creek where that poor woman could've drowned. They have to go to the lab right away. Then I have the . . . meeting. I'll be back as soon as that's over."

"All right. I'm going to check on my patients and see if anything else is going on."

She looked back at him from the closet. "What else would be going on?"

"I don't know. That's what I'm going to find out." He kissed her and left.

Peggy grabbed the first thing she could find in the closet. It wasn't the cute skirt and top she'd thought about, but the green sundress was elegant and cool. Steve had told her it matched her eyes.

She looked at the closed bedroom door. Guilt made her wonder if what she was doing was wrong. Excitement told her it wasn't. Steve wouldn't understand why she wanted to meet Nightflyer. That's the *only* reason she was keeping it a secret.

She shooed Shakespeare out of her bedroom when she was finished and hurried downstairs. Grabbing her truck keys, she ran out the side door, only to run back and set the alarm. She started up the truck and backed quickly out of the drive.

Half expecting to see Steve's green Saturn Vue behind her, she looked in the rearview mirror. She wasn't going to make the same mistake twice. The last time at the park was bad timing, but she didn't have to let it happen again.

Peggy had to wait for a parking space at the lab, tapping her fingers impatiently on the steering wheel. Honestly, they *could* make the parking lot bigger. She locked the truck after taking out her evidence kit then had to run back when she realized she'd forgotten her ID badge.

Breathless by the time she reached the lab, she forced herself to take the time to catalog her samples. It would be terrible to botch things up on her first job.

"Hot date, Dr. Lee?" Harold asked, watching her.

"No." She rescued a sample she'd almost dropped. "Why do you ask?"

"You're looking particularly fetching in that green dress with all that red in your cheeks."

Great! This wasn't the time or the place. "Thank you. But the red is sunburn from being outside for hours, and the dress is the first thing I could find to wear."

He nodded and adjusted his glasses. "I see. I don't want you to get the wrong idea and file some kind of charges against me for sexual harassment or anything, but if you ever change your mind about your veterinary friend, don't hesitate to call."

Peggy couldn't imagine going out on a date with Harold, but she didn't have the heart to be unkind. "I'll do that," she promised as she finished up her samples. "Excuse me. I have to go."

"Of course. I assume you'll be back later to study these samples?"

"Of course." She glanced at her watch. "I'm sorry. I really have to go."

She realized she hadn't put on her white lab coat when she saw it hanging by the door as she left. *Oh well.* She'd only been there for a short time. It was 1:50 when she reached the door of her truck in the parking lot. Plenty of time to get to the library by two.

"Excuse me," a woman's voice called from behind the truck. "Aren't you one of the witnesses who was out at Badin Lake when my husband drowned?"

Peggy opened the door to the truck, thinking she could get in and leave despite the fact that the woman was standing behind her. It was rude and went against her upbringing not to answer her. But there was bound to be a lengthy conversation involved. It was hot, and she didn't want to be sweaty when she met Nightflyer. There were many more reasons to turn away than there were to acknowledge the other woman, but one

169

glance at her, and she couldn't leave without speaking to her.

"I'm sorry to bother you." The woman walked around the truck bed. "I'm Benita Capshaw. I remember seeing you out there. I just came from talking to the police. No one will help me."

Peggy could see she'd been crying. She was a plain, heavyset woman with dull blue eyes and sandy-colored hair. Her clothes were wrinkled and old. Her hand, when she held it out to Peggy, was callused. "I remember you, Mrs. Capshaw. I'm so sorry for your loss."

Benita looked back at the large brick building behind them. "No one cares about what happened to Gerald. It doesn't make any sense, him dying that way. But no one will listen to me."

Peggy would've given anything to have been raised without her southern sense of duty and good manners. No southern lady could leave a widow crying in a parking lot on such a hot day. She looked longingly in the direction of the main library on Seventh and Tryon Streets. She mentally apologized to Nightflyer for missing the opportunity to meet him then smiled at Benita Capshaw. "Let's have some frozen lemonade and sit in the shade for a while."

Peggy was rewarded for her sacrifice when the other woman smiled through her tears. "Thank you. You'll never know what this means to me."

Benita had no money, so Peggy bought them both frozen lemonade from a corner vendor. There was a small, shady area under some large oak trees near the bus stop. The two women sat down together as traffic raced by in the street and the sound of rap music boomed from CD players as two skaters went by.

"Why did you come to Charlotte about your husband's death?" Peggy asked.

"Because the sheriff and the police out in Badin aren't going to do anything. They're calling it an accident. I know it wasn't any such thing."

"Why did you think Charlotte police would help you out of their jurisdiction?"

"Because *she* lives here, I thought they could arrest her here."

Peggy knew who she was talking about. "I know what happened between your husband and Dr. Sargent was wrong, but that doesn't mean she killed him."

Benita's plain face grew animated. "You don't understand. That witch made his life miserable. She wouldn't break it off with him. She followed him around and threatened him like that woman in that movie with Michael Douglas. She wouldn't let him alone. She thought because he slept with her, they were going to be together."

"It happened before with him and someone else?"

"Yeah." Benita ate some of her frozen lemonade. "It happened all the time. He was a good-looking man. Always was. We'd walk into a restaurant, and all of the waitresses would stop what they were doing to wait on him. I understood. I was lucky to be with him. Look at me. I'm no prize. But he loved me, in his way, and he loved Mandy. He fooled around, but he would never leave. *She* couldn't take that."

It was difficult for Peggy to imagine Ruth as a crazed stalker trying to take Gerald Capshaw away from his family. But she didn't say that. "Let's think about this like the police do. My husband was a detective for many years. He always thought about what could make someone kill a person before he started the investigation."

Benita's eyes grew wide. "You mean he was like Jim Rockford or Spencer for Hire?"

Peggy smiled. "Not exactly. He was a homicide detective with the Charlotte police."

"He's gone, huh? Was he killed?"

"Yes." Peggy briefly explained how John died.

"The good ones always go out fighting for justice. That's all I'm asking for Gerry. I want justice for him. If someone would only check to make sure she didn't kill him, even though I'm sure she did, I'd feel a lot better."

"All right," Peggy agreed, sure she would be sorry later. "Let's start by me asking you why you think Gerald's death wasn't an accident."

Benita shifted uncomfortably on the bench. "He was too good a diver to die that way. And look at where she brought him out of. There was no flags marking where he was diving. And he never would've gone out like that."

Peggy took out a small notebook she used for ordering plants for her customers. She turned over the last page that contained six dozen salmon-colored geraniums and started a new page. "So Gerald was very careful. What if he was in a hurry? Did you know he was diving that day?"

"Yeah. He told me. I had to take Mandy to horse camp out in Midland, or I would've been there with him. He told me it was okay. He'd done that job for United before. I was supposed to meet him out there. Then

I heard about him drowning."

"What about the other divers who died the same way by the dam? Couldn't Gerald have been pulled in like that?"

Benita waved her hand. "*Please!* He was too familiar with that old dam. He's the one who caught that old eighty-pound catfish that lived out there for so long. Those other divers weren't from around here. They didn't understand the tricks that dam pulls. Gerry did. Something else happened."

"What did the autopsy find?"

"What autopsy?" Benita spat out. "There isn't going to be one. They say the county shouldn't waste its money on an accident."

Peggy was surprised by that. It was a questionable death. Even though other divers had died at the same spot, they still should have performed an autopsy. "Have they released his body to you yet?"

"That's another thing." Benita started crying again. "They say they aren't doing any more tests, but they won't give me his body. Gerry wanted to be buried by his family in the church cemetery. If nothing's wrong, why won't they let me bury him?"

10

Prickly Pear
Botanical: *Opuntia*
The prickly pear cactus is probably one of the most recognized of all the desert species. It has flat, fleshy pads that appear to be large leaves but are really modified branches that store water, create photosynthesis, and initiate flower production. The fruits of most prickly pears are edible. The pads can also be cooked and eaten as a vegetable.

Peggy walked Benita to her car, promising to find some way to help her. She wasn't sure what she was going to do, but she found herself empathizing with her. Benita was probably close to her age, despite the fact that she still had a teenager living at home. Peggy knew what it was like to lose a loved one and have no ready answers. Maybe what happened to Gerald *was* an accident as the sheriff in Stanly County claimed. Or maybe there was more to it as Benita believed.

Peggy didn't believe Ruth was responsible. The other woman was candid about her relationship with Gerald. But she could understand how Benita's feelings of hurt and betrayal could color her perception and lead her to believe Ruth was stalking Gerald.

It was pathetic but touching to hear Benita describe how fortunate she was to have such a good-looking husband and how this could justify his philandering. Peggy couldn't empathize with that kind of personal self-degradation, but she'd known many women of all ages and levels of education who'd suffered from the same disease.

Peggy glanced at her watch once Benita was driving out of the parking lot. It was a little after two p.m. Maybe it was possible Nightflyer had waited a few minutes for her. She'd certainly wait to meet him. If she started over there now, she could be there by a quarter after, give or take a few minutes. At least she could say she tried to get there.

She was in her truck about to turn on Tryon to get to the parking deck on Seventh Street when her cell phone rang. She looked

176

at the number; it was the Potting Shed. Selena probably needed to ask her something. Possibly something minor that could wait until she met Nightflyer. Or not.

She picked up on the last ring before the call went to voice mail. *This had better be good.* "Hello, Selena."

"Not Selena." Sam's usually calm voice was gruff. "But close enough. We have an emergency. A water pipe broke, and the store is flooded. Can you get over here superfast?"

"I'm only a few minutes away." She turned away from the library. Nightflyer would have to wait.

As Peggy parked in the lot behind Brevard Court, she saw Sam, Selena, Keeley, and Emil were taking seed racks, bags of potting soil, and other items out of the Potting Shed and stacking them in the back storage area. She stopped Sam to ask what happened.

"I'm not sure. I've been a lot of things in this job, but never a plumber. I came in with Keeley to pick up some supplies for tomorrow, and Selena was freaking out. Water was gushing everywhere, and all I could think about was getting everything out."

"It's a water line," Emil told her with surety. "It happened to us once. We almost lost everything in the flood. I had to pull Sofia to safety."

Not particularly in the mood for another one of Emil's tall tales, Peggy walked into the shop. It wasn't a flood, but there was about an inch of water everywhere. Selena hugged her, almost in tears. "I'm so sorry. This couldn't come at a worse time. Here we are racking our brains to find ways to keep the Potting Shed open with Smith & Hawken coming into town, and now this. I wish I could've stopped it. I didn't know what to do after I ran out of paper towels."

Peggy looked at the floor. There were hundreds of brown paper towels floating in the water. She wondered if there was a class Selena could take that would've prepared her for the emergency. *Bless her heart.* "Don't worry. This isn't great, but it's not the end of the world. You can't get to be my age without dealing with a few plumbing emergencies. Did I ever tell you about the time Paul flushed one of his teddy bears, and the water came through the ceiling into the dining room? Trust me. This won't shut us down, but we have to call for help."

While Sam and the others hauled everything out of the shop that could move, Peggy got on the phone with the rental agent for Brevard Court and Mint Condition Janitorial Service. She knew Jack and Marcy Saumby well. They'd weathered a few emergencies together since she'd opened the shop. They were sympathetic and fast-acting, promising help with the cleanup right away. Peggy also called her insurance agent.

When she was done, she looked around the shop, assessing the probable damage. They couldn't take out the wooden counter, and it might warp if the water was there too long. The floor might have to be replaced, though she winced at what heart-of-pine would cost to replace. Smaller items like some seeds and bulbs might be damaged. Mostly the question would be how long the cleanup and replacement would take. The Potting Shed would have to be closed for that time, however long it was.

As times went, now was a better time for this to happen than spring or fall. If she had to be closed, a slow season like summer meant less loss of revenue. But she would have to push to get the shop reopened for the fall planting season.

She put out the Closed sign that faced Brevard Court and saw Nancy Dwight with a smug smile on her face. The Smith & Hawken manager was not making any friends. The woman had a terrible attitude problem.

"I think we got everything out that we could," Sam said. "Everything else is nailed down."

Peggy turned away from her nemesis. "Thank you for acting so quickly. I don't know what Selena would've done once she ran out of paper towels."

He smiled, white teeth against his golden tanned skin. "That's why I get the big bucks."

"That must be it," she agreed, wading across the floor.

"What now?" He put his hands in the pockets of his faded jean shorts.

"Now we wait for help cleaning up." She told him who she called. "We'll keep everything in back until we get this taken care of. No more shipments except for landscape supplies for now."

"I'm sorry, Peggy. Will we be okay?"

She surveyed the almost empty shop, remembering what it had looked like the first time she'd seen it. She'd been alone; John had been dead only a few weeks. Everyone told her the plan to open the shop that she and John had always wanted was crazy. But she'd known when she saw it that this was the place. The rent was steeper than she'd hoped for, but she put her money down and started to work, throwing her dreams before her like a magic carpet out of her sorrow. "We'll be fine. This is a minor setback. You'll see."

Peggy didn't bother trying to get to the library by the time she left the Potting Shed. She'd called Steve to let him know what happened and then waited for everyone from her insurance agent to the rental agent to come and take a look. The only people she didn't have to wait for were the cleanup crew. Once again, Mint Condition came through.

Surveying the damage was terrible. The rental agent argued with the insurance agent. Neither one could decide on the best course of action. There would have to be estimates and contractors contacted, supplies and workers. It sounded like it could be months before the shop would reopen.

Heavy-hearted despite her upbeat words to Sam, Peggy drove home, worried about the impact of the store being closed. There was nowhere else in the Center City area to buy many of the things she carried. At this time of year, people could buy cheap plants at the farmers' market down on Seventh Street. Many residents were involved in the community garden and would take home plants from there, too.

She sat in her truck in the garage for a few minutes, trying to gauge the damage and put a positive spin on it. There was a way this would all work out. It didn't look promising at the moment, but she wasn't kidding when she'd said she'd weathered other storms.

There was a faint knock on the driver's side window. She rolled it down and smiled at Steve. "Are you coming in tonight or staying out here?" He opened the door for her.

"I don't know," she joked. "It's lovely in the garage this time of year."

"I know. I've thought that many times as I walked by. But Shakespeare and I are hungry. We thought maybe you could come inside and eat dinner. Then you could always come back out here again."

"I could do that. What would you and Shakespeare like to eat?"

"We were thinking about some Thai food. How about you?"

"Thai would be lovely." Steve held out his arms, and she hugged him. "Thanks for rescuing me."

Shakespeare barked and wagged his tail. Peggy commended him as well. "I think he sees himself as the hero in this," Steve told her. "But I think he sees himself as the hero in most things, especially if you're involved. It's a good thing I'm very secure, or I'd be finding ways to get him out of your bed."

She laughed. "I don't think you have anything to worry about. He won't ever take your place."

They walked into the house together, and Peggy's cell phone rang. It was her insurance agent calling about the Potting Shed. Steve took the Thai food out of the containers and put it on the good china. He poured them both a glass of Noble red wine from their last trip to Uwharrie Vineyards.

Peggy was fussing with an aloe she kept in the kitchen window for burns as she spoke to the insurance agent. He was assuring her that her policy would cover the flood in the shop, but they would try to recoup some of the money from the rental group. Peggy was thinking about transplanting the overgrown aloe with some new potting soil and fertilizer as he spoke.

As he finished, her cell phone beeped. She glanced at her caller ID. It was an unknown number. *Nightflyer.*

She looked back at Steve as he was lighting a little tea candle on the table. She couldn't call Nightflyer back right now. The whole series of events that kept them from meeting that day was unfortunate, but things would have to stay as they were for tonight. She'd done all she could do for one day. She put her cell phone in her pocketbook and sat down to dinner.

Peggy and Steve sat around watching an old movie and talking until after midnight. They went up to bed, but Peggy was too wound up to sleep. She explained that she needed some time alone with her plants and went down to the basement with Shakespeare behind her.

Checking her plants and the progress of her botanical experiments took her mind off of the flood and Benita Capshaw. She even forgot about Nightflyer for a while as she transplanted her aloe. There were plenty of babies to be shared with others. Tomorrow was her garden club day. She could give some to her members and one to Emil and Sofia. Thank goodness she'd always held those meetings at the Kozy Kettle. At least they could go on through this disaster.

She paused as she got out ten tiny pots to transport the aloe shoots and suddenly recalled a devastating storm that hit her parents' farm when she was a child.

Usually they were far enough away from the ocean that they didn't experience problems with hurricanes ravaging Charleston. But one year, Hurricane Cecile came farther inland than anyone had expected. It shot off twelve tornadoes as it came. Heavy rain, hail, and winds of more than 150 miles per hour hit their house and land.

When they could come out of the root cellar under the house and assess the damage, their barn, with all the hay they'd harvested for their livestock, was gone as though it had never been there. All of the corn they'd planted for their money crop was wiped clean off the sandy land. Amazingly, there was no damage to the house, and all of the livestock, except for a few chickens they never found, survived.

Peggy, barely eight, started crying when she saw what had happened. Her mother shushed her, telling her it wasn't right to cry when so much had been spared. Her father took her up on his shoulder as he walked across the land where the barn had been. There were only a few scattered tools and pieces of wood to mark its passing.

"As long as we're still here," her father said, "we can build it all back again. The good Lord never meant us to stand still, so he sends these little reminders from time to time. That's all this was, Margaret Anne. Just a little reminder that things need to change."

Peggy sat down, leaving most of her little

aloes unpotted. Why hadn't she seen it before? Just like that hurricane made her father build a bigger and better barn, this was an opportunity to strengthen what she had with the Potting Shed. She could remake it. Smith & Hawken might be strong in furniture sales, but she had strengths, too. She had to make the most of them.

She looked up and surveyed her basement. There was the pond with her water plant experiments and the rescued koi. She had divisions of various plantings laid out according to how much sun they required and how long the experiments would last.

For the last two years, the heart of the Potting Shed had been her seasonal display. It was only an idea she'd had when she first got started. But suppose she built a pond and used the water feature to be the first thing customers saw as they walked into the shop?

She jumped up and found the first piece of paper she could lay her hands on and a pencil she got from the Southern Living Show last year. She began a rough drawing of the interior of the new Potting Shed on the brown paper.

Water plants and features were one of her hottest sales items. Everyone wanted a pond of one size or another. She made a note to talk to Sam about finding a contractor who would outsource putting in larger water features for customers at their homes.

What was her other strength? Living plants. She drew some new shelving that could incorporate grow lights, so she could actually have plants growing beside the seeds and bulbs to illustrate what she was selling. There were plenty of overhead beams where they could put up hanging baskets.

And what about using some hydroponics? Everyone enjoyed seeing the root systems as plants grew. She could put in some hydroponics and even give classes on the subject.

She continued drawing and planning until she noticed it wasn't dark outside her windows anymore. She'd lost the night, but she'd gained so much perspective, and she felt much better, despite being a little tired. The adrenaline was still coursing through her when she finished potting her aloes and then went upstairs to tell Steve everything that had happened.

The bedroom was still dark and shadowy, since it faced west and got the afternoon sunlight. Her computer was chiming a message as she opened the door.

She looked at Steve, curled up in the bed asleep. Maybe her news could keep for a few minutes as she checked her email. She owed Nightflyer an explanation.

Tiptoeing across the hundred-year-old hardwood floor was tricky, but she'd done it long enough to know how to avoid the squeaks. She sat down carefully in her desk chair and opened her email.

She was right. There were several messages from Nightflyer. All of them asked what had happened, where she had been. Why didn't she call him? She didn't chance waking Steve with a phone call, instead settling for a message.

I'm sorry I missed you. I had an emergency at the Potting Shed. Nothing life-threatening but something I had to deal with. Can we try again? I'm going out to look for some answers about Gerald Capshaw's death this morning but will be back in town this afternoon. How about the library at four?

Peggy clicked Send, and the message went out. She glanced at Steve again as the morning began to lighten behind the heavy blinds and drapes she used to keep out the hot sun. She felt guilty, of course, but she would make it up to Steve.

She sat on the side of the bed and kissed him. He murmured in his sleep and turned over to hold her. "Are you just coming to bed?"

"I'm afraid there is truly no rest for the wicked," she said. "It's almost six. I'm just here in place of the alarm."

"You're much better-looking, and you smell like plants, dirt, and water." He nuzzled her neck and kissed her ear.

She laughed. "I probably don't look all that great, either, after being up all night and having all that dirt and water on me."

"I think it smells sexy." He rolled over with her across the bed. "Like growing, earthy stuff."

Peggy kissed him, loving him so much it almost hurt to think about it. How could anyone be any more perfect for her? Then a giant tongue licked the side of her face, and Shakespeare jumped up into bed with them to participate in their new game. His huge paws were wet from being in the basement with her, and his tail beat a tattoo on the mattress.

Steve groaned and rolled away before the tongue could get him, too. "There's nothing like a big, wet dog to spoil the mood."

Peggy wiped her face with the sheet she was going to have to wash. "I guess he's letting us know it's too late to fool around."

Steve smiled, his face barely visible in the morning light. "Okay. Race you to the shower."

"I think we should just meander in there together like civilized folks," she replied. "Then I can tell you about my new plan for the Potting Shed."

Steve was impressed with the makeshift drawings they looked at over breakfast. Sam stopped in at the house to be sure Peggy was all right, and they sat over the plans for another thirty minutes after Steve went to check on his patients.

"I really like this," Sam told her. "It's a sweet idea. The water feature would attract attention when you first walk in. Do you think the insurance money will pay for the upgrades?"

"I'm not sure, but if not, I'll foot the bill for whatever else is needed." Peggy's green eyes glowed with satisfaction. "We can come back stronger and better able to fight Smith & Hawken this way."

"Are you totally abandoning the furniture aspect?"

"Except for catalog special order. We'll see about that, but we won't rely on it. If we do this right, the Potting Shed will do as much to enhance what Smith & Hawken sells as their products will enhance ours."

Sam hugged her, picking her up and dancing around the room. "You're a genius,

Peggy. I think this is going to be hotter than last summer."

She considered his words as she drove her truck back out to Stanly County. Coffee had taken the place of adrenaline, but she tried to put her newfound plans and excitement behind her so she could find some way to help Benita.

She parked her truck in the small parking lot attached to the Stanly County Sheriff's Office in Albemarle. The office was tiny compared to Mecklenburg County, but since the two counties were so much different in size, she supposed it wasn't surprising.

A deputy was stationed at the desk where she walked in. There was a nice prickly pear garden near the front window that got good light, and she silently commended whoever chose to put it there. It didn't take much effort to keep something like that alive.

"I'm here for some information on Gerald Capshaw's death," Peggy told the deputy. She'd rehearsed what she was going to say all the way from Charlotte.

"Deputy Hall is handling that case, ma'am." The young woman didn't look up. "That information isn't available to the public as yet."

"Of course not. I'm Dr. Margaret Lee.

I'm with the Charlotte-Mecklenburg Police Department. Deputy Hall is expecting me."

11

Magnolia

Botanical: *Magnolia acuminata*

Early U.S. settlers chewed the bark of the magnolia to replace tobacco when trying to kick the habit. The tree was named in honor of Pierre Magnol, a French botanist in the early eighteenth century. The bark has an aromatic quality that most people find pleasing. The wood is nicely grained but not durable.

It was only a mild deception, Peggy told herself as she followed Deputy Phillip Hall to his office. He hadn't looked at her credentials very closely (good thing, because it was only her ID badge from the lab) before extending his hand to her and welcoming her to Albemarle. He was a young man, tall and a little on the gangly side, with dark hair and large brown eyes.

"Actually I'm glad to see you." He ushered

her into his tiny office and closed the door. "We're about to close this out, and it would be nice to have some intercounty co-operation. Not that there's any problem . . ."

". . . except for Mrs. Capshaw."

He smiled and sat behind his cluttered desk as Peggy sat in the only chair. "I guess she's been up there talking to you all, huh?"

"She believes her husband was murdered." Peggy looked for a place to put her pocketbook on the floor. Not finding one, she held it on her lap. "She thought we might be able to help."

Deputy Hall searched around on his desk until he found the right file. "Take a look for yourself, Dr. Lee. We don't have anything to hide. It's just a simple drowning. Tragic, but not murder."

Peggy looked slowly through the slim file. There were only a few documents in it. "I see you did an autopsy on Mr. Capshaw. His wife seemed to think you weren't going to do that."

"We may be out a'ways from Charlotte," Hall bristled, "but that doesn't make us yokels. The man's death was questionable. We did an autopsy."

She smiled. "Of course you did."

"As you can see, everything is in order. We went by the book on this one. The

194

sheriff is still worried Mrs. Capshaw might sue. That's why it'd be good to have you in on this. It would show we went to extra lengths to look at everything."

She continued to study the file. The photographs were grucsome, but she tried not to appear upset. She might have nightmares for days. It seemed so much worse to see the intimate photographs than it had been to be there. She flipped through the pages of the autopsy. At first, she didn't see anything unusual. There was nothing that stood out like it did in Marsha Hatley's death.

Then she noticed a faint notation in the margin of the blood test. Aconite. Trace amounts of aconite were found in Gerald's system. It might not mean anything, but she had to ask. "What about this aconite notation?"

Deputy Hall pulled down the other side of the file and craned his neck to try to see what she was talking about. "I don't know. The ME said there was nothing questionable. I guess that includes . . ."

". . . aconite?"

"Yeah." He nodded. "I guess that normally occurs in the body."

"I'm not really sure about that." Peggy's heart was racing. Had she discovered something that might prove Benita was right? On the other hand, she was a botanist, not a specialist in what could or could not be in the human body. She knew there were traces of arsenic and other toxins. Maybe aconite was there as well. If no one asked, they might never know. What was the worst that could happen; she would somehow give away her disguise?

"I don't know either, but I guess the ME knows." Deputy Hall handed her a pen. "If you could initial that line at the bottom and write down your title, we'll be done here."

Peggy looked at the pen. "I can't do that until I know if this aconite is naturally occurring or was introduced into his system."

Deputy Hall sat down hard on his chair. "Well, if that don't beat all. I was happy to see you because I thought you were the end of this thing. Instead, you're here to cause more trouble."

"Don't you want to know what happened? Don't you want to know the truth?"

"I'd really like this off my desk, ma'am," he admitted. "But since you aren't happy with that idea unless you ask your question, let's go see Doc."

Peggy hung back after he picked up his flat-brimmed hat and opened the door. "I'd like to use the restroom before we go, if that's all right?"

"Sure." He pointed the way to a tiny door at the end of the hall. "I'll be waiting outside for you."

She smiled and hurried to the bathroom, where she locked the door and took out her cell phone. This might not be necessary. Maybe she could've told Deputy Hall she needed to talk to the Mecklenburg County ME without blowing her cover. Funny, she had been a detective's wife for so many years without wondering what was going on.

Her cell phone was searching for service. *Great.* She looked up at the notebook-sized window at the top of the wall and held the cell phone that way. She got about half a bar with the exercise. *Okay.* She climbed up on the toilet and held the phone up. One bar. If she could take it outside, she'd probably be all right.

It would have to do. She punched in the lab number then waited as the hesitant ring tried to go through. Finally, someone picked up the phone and she managed to get across that she wanted to speak to Harold.

Waiting impatiently, someone knocked on the bathroom door. "Just a minute," she called out.

Harold picked up. "Who is this?"

"It's Peggy," she whispered. "I have a question."

"What? Speak up! It's a federal offense to call a police lab without authorization."

Whoever was at the door knocked again. "I need to get in there sometime today."

"It's Peggy," she said to Harold. "I need your help."

"Ah! Dr. Lee. What can I do for you?"

Peggy tried to find a way to ask about the aconite without telling him what she was doing. He didn't understand, and she finally blurted out, "How much aconite does a normal body have in it?"

"A normal *living* human body doesn't have any aconite in it," he responded. "Why do you ask?"

"That's all I need to know. Thanks."

"When are you coming in to take care of your samples? I can't stand things lying around the lab unfinished."

Peggy clicked off on her phone. At least she had something to go on. She opened the bathroom door, smiled at the young woman who was waiting outside, then hurried to find Deputy Hall.

He was leaning against a brown sheriff's car. There was a stunning magnolia tree silhouetted against a pale blue sky behind him. Peggy's eye caught the scene and made

198

her wish she had a camera.

"So, are you ready to go?" he asked. "Or can we get rid of this thing here?"

"I think we'll have to see the medical examiner. I hate to leave loose ends, don't you?"

"Yes, ma'am."

They drove to Stanly Regional Medical Center where the morgue was located.

The medical examiner for the county was a short, serious man whose hair curled a little in the damp air-conditioning. Deputy Hall introduced them then explained why they were there. "I want to get this over with, Doc. Can you answer her questions?"

Brandon "Doc" Williamson offered Peggy his hand. "Dr. Lee! I've read some of your work on botanical poisons. It's a pleasure to meet you. How can I help you?"

"I have some concerns about this autopsy." She showed him his notation in the margin. "I don't think aconite should be here."

"It wasn't much," he said. "Not enough to kill him, if that's what you're thinking. Mr. Capshaw drowned."

"That wasn't what I was thinking, actually. I was thinking more of how the properties of aconite affect someone. Even a small amount can cause dizziness, difficulty breathing, and fainting. All of these things would be very bad if you were underwater at the time when the poison kicked in."

Doc agreed. "I didn't consider that. From that aspect, I suppose it could be as deadly as a sleeping pill in the same situation."

"Exactly." *Why isn't Harold this easy to get along with? Maybe Stanly County needs a contract forensic botanist.* "I don't know how you'd tell if he was affected by the aconite except that he drowned and he was an experienced diver. I believe that's something Mrs. Capshaw had a problem with."

"It's possible," Doc admitted. "We'd have to know when and where he came to ingest the aconite, if that's what happened. Do you have any ideas on that score?"

Peggy shook her head. "It could be administered almost any way. There would be no sensation of burning or illness in a small dose, yet it could be enough to make him experience those symptoms that could be deadly in this situation."

Doc turned to Deputy Hall. "We'll have to reopen the investigation to satisfy this question. The body can't be released yet. I need my team to go over Mr. Capshaw's pickup again. We need to know what he did before he arrived at the dam."

Feeling validated by her discovery, Peggy

was ready to call it a day and head back for Charlotte. She'd done what she could to help Benita.

But the ME had other ideas. "I'll need to go back over everything. I hope I can count on your help, Dr. Lee."

She wanted to say no. She'd done her part, and she wasn't a pathologist. On the other hand, she didn't want the whole thing to blow up in her face. It could mean they wouldn't even start investigating again if they realized she was only contract help. Swallowing revulsion at seeing another autopsy victim, she agreed to do what she could. "But my strength is in botany, as I'm sure you can appreciate. And I have to leave by two p.m."

Doc's eyes lit up. "I can't tell you how happy I am to have someone else to give me a hand with this. Thank you, Dr. Lee."

A few hours later, Peggy's eyes were too tired to focus on the slides in the microscope. She sat back in her chair and covered them with her hands.

"You should probably take a break," Doc Williamson told her. "It's one-thirty, and we haven't had lunch."

Peggy's stomach groaned as he reminded her. She glanced at him, hoping he was too polite to say anything about it. He was right. It seemed like yesterday that she got up and had breakfast with Steve. "Maybe we should order something in."

"Not unless you want Domino's. That's about the extent of our take-out menu around here. You aren't in Charlotte anymore."

She smiled. "What do you suggest?"

"I know a little place that has great food, and it shouldn't be too crowded by now."

"All right." She glanced at her watch, even though she knew what time it was. She'd said two p.m., but maybe she could stretch to three p.m. if she didn't stop to change clothes. Four had seemed late when she'd emailed Nightflyer about meeting. Now she'd be lucky to make it back by then.

They walked to a small greasy spoon a few blocks up. The exercise was good, even though Peggy was a little dubious about finding anything vegetarian to eat at the café. They talked about the case until they were seated in the high-backed booth, and the waitress asked if they were ready to order.

Peggy glanced at her menu, surprised to find a veggie burger and fries on the list. She ordered, with Doc putting in an order for a bacon cheeseburger after her.

"Are you a vegetarian or just health conscious?" he asked when the waitress was gone.

"I've been a vegetarian most of my life. I was raised on a farm outside Charleston. We ate everything from crawdads to squirrel brains. I think that might have influenced my decision."

He laughed. "I know what you mean. I probably wouldn't eat meat if I had to see it alive or kill it. We live in a plastic-wrapped society. I suppose I'm a victim of my times."

Peggy pushed her straw up and down in her glass of sweet tea. "You know, it doesn't make any sense that Gerald Capshaw would have aconite in his system. Especially since we can't seem to find out where it came from."

"We may never know. It doesn't mean it's not there. If he was poisoned, it could've happened during the time that's unaccounted for between lunch and when he got to the dam."

"You're right. I really believe this aconite is tincture of monkshood. It would be very powerful in a small dose and not leave a lot of residue."

"Let's consider that." He sat back in the seat, his gray tie falling to one side of his blue shirt. "To use something like that would require specialized knowledge, wouldn't it?"

"Not really. I could name you a dozen farmers like my father who grew up on the land and know it intimately. They know the roots and herbs. I'm sure anyone around here with that type of background could use monkshood. It's not hard to distill."

"That makes it a lot tougher. Like I said, we may never know who did this."

The waitress brought their burgers and refills on their drinks. Peggy was amazed at how good her veggie burger was. She wouldn't have stopped here to eat, because the place looked kind of run down. Who knew they'd make the world's best veggie burger?

"I don't know where to go from here," Doc confessed around a mouthful of burger. "If anyone could make this stuff, we might have a hard time picking out a suspect."

"Not that we have anyone in mind."

"What about that woman in Charlotte I read about? The diver who brought Mr. Capshaw up."

"I suppose it's possible she could have that knowledge, although it seems unlikely to me. She's kind of a city girl. I think Benita is grasping at straws to prove her point, although Ruth *did* have an affair with Mr.

Capshaw."

Doc shrugged his thin shoulders. "Of course you know the rule of thumb about dead bodies."

"If that's the case, I'm a killer a few times over." Peggy exaggerated a little but was thinking about finding Mark Warner dead in the Potting Shed. "I believe something is wrong with the way Mr. Capshaw died, but I don't think Ruth was involved."

"That leaves us out in the cold." He slurped some coffee and called the waitress over for a refill.

"I'm afraid so."

"Maybe there's something else I'm missing. If you'd help me go over the other forensic evidence, we might be able to come up with something."

It was two p.m. on the chicken clock above the grill. Peggy wasn't sure she had time to do anything else except head back to Charlotte. On the other hand, she hated to leave this unsolved. It was in her nature to see things through. Besides, she was incurably curious. "I suppose I can stay a while longer."

He grinned broadly, showing two gold-capped teeth. "Great! Working with you has made my day."

They finished their burgers, and Peggy

told the cook how wonderful his veggie burger was. He was a round, blustery-looking man with thinning black hair swept forward under his white hat, but he blushed red as a cherry at her compliment.

The sun was at its hottest, reflecting off the pavement and sidewalks as they walked back to the lab. A wind was rising from the west, scattering dust from the dry ground but not cooling the temperature.

"It feels like rain." She looked up at the fast-moving clouds in the sky. The trip back to Charlotte would be even longer in the rain.

"You're welcome to stay the night if it gets late." Doc held the door open for her. "My wife and I have some extra room or I'm sure the sheriff wouldn't mind compensating you with a hotel room for your work out here."

Peggy laughed, thinking about how that would work. There might be a few questions raised about her position with CMPD if she asked for money. "I wish I could stay, but I have to be back, or my Great Dane will eat my house."

He laughed with her. They put on lab coats and gloves and went back into the lab. As much as she wanted to know the truth about what happened, Peggy was dreading this part. She wanted to help Benita and

206

clear Ruth of any wrongdoing. But actually working with a dead body was very different than collecting water samples or checking plant DNA.

"I have samples from everything I took out of Mr. Capshaw." Doc approached a large refrigerator. "That might be a good place to start."

Peggy was horrified to see Tupperware containers and cans of Coke in the refrigerator next to organs and other body tissue. She looked away quickly.

"I still have the stomach contents, although I couldn't find a significant amount of aconite there," Doc said, holding up a large jar. "I have the water we took from his lungs, too. But that probably wouldn't be helpful."

Peggy told him about the other case she was working on in Charlotte, as though it were indeed her case. "I'd like to take a look at that. It could save me a trip out here to test Badin Lake if we run out of bodies of water in Charlotte."

"Be my guest." He handed her another jar. "This is *great!* I'm going over the stomach contents again anyway. I may have missed something."

She took the jar of lung contents and sat down at a microscope. She was glad she had her gloves on. This was worse than working in the yard. She used an eyedropper to get a sample of the water in the jar and slid the slide under the microscope.

Immediately, she noticed the phytoplankton. It was incredible. How could it be possible unless Marsha Hatley drowned in Badin Lake as well? It seemed so unlikely that both drownings, probably murders, happened here so close together. She frowned as she checked the slide again. This didn't look good for Ruth, although how they were tied together was difficult to imagine. Did Marsha know Gerald, too?

There was no doubt about it. The phytoplankton was identical. She'd need a sample from the lake for comparison, although she knew Gerald died there. Her mind raced ahead at what this was going to mean. Benita was going to declare hunting season on Ruth's head.

She called Doc over to take a look at what she'd found. "What exactly am I looking at?" he asked. "Is there something unusual that might've killed him? Did he breathe in the aconite through the water? People around here have been complaining for years about the chemicals United has left behind."

"No." She explained about the identical

aquatic plant. "This means my victim and yours both drowned in Badin Lake. I'll have to get a control sample to be sure, but that's the way it looks to me right now."

"That's quite a coincidence." He shook his head. "And I don't put much stock in coincidence."

She looked at her watch. She would never make it back to Charlotte in time to meet Nightflyer. Not that she knew for sure he would be there, since she hadn't heard from him. It might be that she'd go back for nothing anyway.

Her mind rationalized all kinds of excuses, but it came down to the fact that she had to know. Once she tested the lake sample, she could say conclusively that Marsha Hatley drowned in Badin Lake.

Doc offered to drive her to the lake in the county ME's vehicle. She took him up on it, and they left Albemarle, heading out on the main road to Badin. Their intense conversation revolved around how the two deaths could be linked. Neither had any idea how that was possible, but it seemed plausible.

"Maybe Mr. Capshaw, being a ladies' man and all, had an affair with Mrs. Hatley," Doc hypothesized. "Badin isn't *that* far out."

"I suppose so." Peggy saw the large expanse of lake surrounded by mountains come into view. A coincidence like that would set Benita off again about Ruth. She'd already told the police that Ruth stalked Gerald after he tried to break up with her. What would she do if she knew he'd taken up with someone else?

12

Night-blooming Jasmine
Botanical: *Cestrum*
This is one of the most popular poisonous plants, second only to angel's trumpet in planting. The white yellow flowers are open at night and are extremely fragrant but not as beautiful as many other perfumed species. The scent has been used to create perfumes across the world and has been used in some religious ceremonies.

It was after six by the time Peggy got back with the water sample from the lake and had tested it three times. "This can't be right."

Doc removed his glasses and rubbed his tired eyes. "Do you need another sample?"

"No." She sat back in her chair. "There's no doubt. The phytoplankton match in both victims, but it didn't come from Badin Lake."

"Maybe we need to get samples from various parts of the lake," he suggested. "Or maybe the sample we got wasn't from deep enough in the lake."

"I'd like to think that's the case, but it would be present all through the system. Neither of our victims drowned in that lake, but they both drowned in the same place."

"That's truly astonishing!"

Peggy agreed, although she was almost too tired to care. She wanted answers, not more questions. It didn't look like it was going to be that simple. "I have to report this to the Captain. I'm not sure what we're supposed to do from here, but I assume there'll be some kind of joint investigation."

"I can't say I'm unhappy about that," Doc enthused. "I've enjoyed working with you, and I'm sure together we can crack this case. Was there any sign of aconite in your victim?"

"I don't know. I'll have to ask our ME and get back to you." She got up and took off her lab coat. "I have to go home and report this. I'm sure we'll be in touch."

"I'm sure. Are you sure you won't stay the night? We could get a fresh, early start in the morning."

"I have to go home, Doc. But thanks anyway." She glanced at her cell phone. There were ten calls she'd missed while it had been on silent mode. "I hope my house is still in one piece. I'll see you or call you tomorrow."

She picked up her pocketbook and started out the door, but a barrage of cameras and reporters were waiting for her on the other side. They started yelling out questions as soon as they saw her. She closed the door and went back inside.

"Did you change your mind?"

"Not exactly." She told him about the media. "How did they find out?"

"I don't know. Let's go talk to the sheriff."

They drove down to the sheriff's office and found him in his office taking a phone call. He held up one finger for them to wait as he finished the call. He put the phone down and smiled grimly at both of them. "We haven't met. I'm Sheriff Dick Barbee. You must be the big city detective I've heard so much about."

Peggy shook his hand, immediately disliking the man in the uniform with his military haircut and chiseled face. "I'm Dr. Margaret Lee."

Barbee clasped her hand tight enough to make her want to squirm. "A doctor, huh?

They're getting pretty fancy out there in Charlotte."

"Dr. Lee," Doc said with great pride in his voice, "is a well-known poison expert as well as a homicide detective. Any law enforcement group would be lucky to have her."

"I'm not actually a detective," she protested.

"I'm sure we couldn't afford a detective with letters after her name out here, Doc, so just settle down," Sheriff Barbee said.

Doc shrugged his shoulders and was quiet.

"I've been talking to your Captain Rimer, and he tells me we may be looking at a double homicide."

Peggy's green eyes narrowed. "How did you know what we were working on?"

"That's my job, Detective. Just like it's my job to bring in suspects. Captain Rimer is looking for Dr. Ruth Sargent right now. I think we'd both like to have a word with her." The sheriff leaned forward with his hands on his desk. "I understand she's a colleague of yours."

"She is." Peggy didn't bother denying her status as a detective a second time. She had the feeling this man would choose to ignore her no matter what she said. He seemed to have his own version of the world, and nothing could shake it. "She's been helping me with our case in Charlotte. I think you shouldn't be influenced by hearsay."

His lazy smile disappeared. "Excuse me?"

"Just because Benita Capshaw *thinks* Dr. Sargent is responsible for her husband's death doesn't mean it's true. The woman is grieving for her husband. She doesn't realize what she's saying."

"I think she does, ma'am." The sheriff's tone was dismissive. "I appreciate your help, but you eggheads stick to what you know, and I'll take care of business."

That tone and his easy acceptance of Benita's accusations with no real proof made Peggy's temper flare. "We have no idea where the two victims drowned or how," she reminded him. "And there's the little matter of the aconite poisoning. I believe you might want to investigate a little further before you jump the gun."

"And I appreciate your opinion." He smiled then looked down at the paperwork on his desk. "That's all."

"Listen to me, you big —"

Doc pulled Peggy out of the sheriff's office before she could finish the sentence. "He's not a good man to rile up. Let's stick to what we know."

"Part of that is making sure innocent

215

people don't get blamed for things they didn't do," she said, still hot.

"Are you so sure she's innocent? She *did* bring the body up from the lake, and it happened to be her ex-lover. That's awfully coincidental, don't you think?"

"He was already dead when we got there. We were called to the scene by whoever found him in the first place. That rule of thumb doesn't apply."

"But there's still the matter of her being Gerald Capshaw's lover."

"Not recently," Peggy argued. "I *know* Ruth, Doc. She's a good person. She didn't do this."

"I guess that's why there's an investigation." He shrugged, defeated by her fierce defense of her friend.

"I guess so." She pushed open the outside door again. "And thank goodness, we don't have lynchings anymore."

A young woman with a large television camera on her shoulder pushed to the front of the group of reporters. "Is it true the Charlotte Police have Dr. Sargent in custody and are bringing her out here for questioning?"

Doc laughed and helped Peggy get around the camera. "Jennifer, you know we can't say much about an ongoing investigation.

We'll update you as we can. We're very fortunate to have Charlotte homicide detective and poison specialist, Dr. Margaret Lee, working on this with us."

This immediately changed the focus of the newspaper and television reporters who turned around as Peggy was getting in her truck. They were an instant too late to stop her from leaving the parking lot.

Relieved to be out of there, Peggy got on the highway headed toward home. She returned a few of the calls on her cell phone. Selena wanted to tell her she didn't expect to be paid while the shop was closed. Hunter called to offer legal advice about the flood in the shop and complain about her brother's harsh treatment while she worked with him and Keeley that day. Steve called twice, but his phone was going back to voice mail when she tried to call him. Probably an emergency.

Paul called to tell her he was making dinner at the house. He had someone special with him. That sounded promising. He'd asked if she could be back by 7:30 for dinner. She called him to let him know she was on her way.

"I noticed your change in rank," he said. "You're all over News 14. I don't think Jennifer Moxley liked you ducking out on her like that."

"I'll explain when I get there." She sighed. "It's been a long day."

He laughed. "And a busy one. I can't wait to hear the story. I hope it's good, 'cause I'm sure Rimer is gonna want to hear it in the morning."

"I know. Never mind. I should be there in a few minutes." She closed her cell phone and turned her truck onto Queens Road.

Peggy could smell the night-blooming jasmine as she walked from the garage to the house. Steve called again as she opened the kitchen door. He explained that he was going to have to spend the night at the horse farm waiting for one of the mares to foal. "I'm sure you can find plenty of things to do without me . . . like go to another county and solve their murders."

"Good grief! Has everyone been watching the news?"

"Probably only all the people who know you, *Detective* Lee. I'm sure Paul will get a laugh out of that."

"I'm sure he will when he comes up for air." She was watching Paul kiss Stephanie Nichols by the kitchen sink. "I'll see you tomorrow."

"Don't have too much fun without me.

Love you."

"Love you, too. See you tomorrow." She closed her cell phone and put down her pocketbook, clearing her throat loudly before the couple in the kitchen separated. "I hope dinner is ready, because I'm starving."

Paul smiled, but his face was as red as Stephanie's tank top. It might have been bigger, too. "There you are! Back from a hard day of solving crime in Stanly County. You remember Stephanie."

"Of course." She smiled at the girl. "Nice to see you again." She'd been happy at first to see Paul with someone besides Mai after their breakup. But after seeing Stephanie with Nathan, she wasn't so sure.

Paul and Stephanie put the spaghetti and salad on the table after Paul turned on the little TV on the cabinet to show his mother what the scene was like when she left the sheriff's office.

"You won't believe what's happened." Peggy wasn't embarrassed by her exploits. As far as them referring to her as a homicide detective, she'd tried to tell that big, stupid sheriff the truth. He wouldn't listen.

She explained about the link she and Doc had found between the two victims. "There might be something more yet. The ME out there found traces of aconite in Gerald Capshaw's body."

Paul glanced at Stephanie's face and tactfully changed the conversation. "Stephanie grew up right here in Myers Park. We probably went to some of the same schools, but we never met."

"That's very interesting." Peggy took some salad on her plate as she took the hint. Not everyone wanted to talk about dead people while they ate. "Where do your parents live, Stephanie?"

"They live in Switzerland right now, Mrs. Lee." Stephanie looked at Paul and ran her hand across his cheek as she spoke. "My father is a geologist. He travels around the world. But I want to make Charlotte my home."

"Call me Peggy, please. That must be an interesting profession. Do you plan on underwater forensics for your career?"

"I'm not sure yet." Stephanie looked around the kitchen. "This is a beautiful house. Did you grow up here, Paul?"

"Not only did he grow up here," Peggy said. "He still has some gum stuck on the underside of this table."

They all laughed, and Paul explained about the house being part of the family estate. Peggy thought Stephanie's blue eyes got a little rounder and larger as he spoke. She hastily added, "Unfortunately, Paul won't inherit it. It will pass to his cousin when I leave."

Stephanie blinked almost comically and focused on Peggy. "You know, if you need to go somewhere, Paul and I could house sit until you get back. That way his cousin won't get it. I don't know how you can bear to part with it."

Peggy smiled. "I meant when I die, dear, bless your heart. I'm sure they'll have to carry me out feet-first before anyone else lives here. I've spent most of my life here."

The disappointed look on the girl's face *was* comical this time. "Oh."

Paul gave his mother *the* look and picked up Stephanie's manicured hand. "After we finish eating, I'll give you a tour. Mom has a botanical paradise in the basement."

"That's interesting," Stephanie said with far less enthusiasm.

At that moment, News 14 came back with the breaking story of Gerald Capshaw's death and the link to Charlotte. Jennifer Moxley looked pale in the bright light she was directing on herself as she told the story.

"The sheriff is bringing in Dr. Ruth Sargent as we speak. You can see her going into the sheriff's office behind me. They will be questioning her about this new information that might change Gerald Capshaw's death from an accident to a homicide. We'll have more information on this story as it continues to break."

"Here it is." Paul pointed out as Ms. Moxley told the backstory and showed Peggy leaving the parking lot in her truck after Doc Williamson told the media about her. "Nice going, Mom. I can't believe you could find a way to get in trouble on your first assignment for CMPD."

"They're arresting Dr. Sargent?" Stephanie sounded bewildered. "Do they think she killed Gerry Capshaw?"

Peggy explained about Benita's accusations against Ruth. "It may be ridiculous, but if the police can put Gerald and Marsha Hatley together in some way, she could be accused of a double homicide."

"I knew Dr. Sargent and Gerry saw each other for a while." Stephanie bit her lip. "I didn't consider anything else. I mean, when would she have killed him that day? I was with her the whole time." She paused. "Except for when she dropped me off at the funeral and went to the store. You don't think she killed him then instead of picking up some cinnamon rolls for the funeral because she forgot to bring food, do you?"

"No, dear. I don't," Peggy said in a conciliatory tone. "I don't think she killed him at all. I think it's possible Mr. Capshaw was seeing someone else, someone more recent. That person may be who took care of him."

"Of course you said there isn't a link yet between Capshaw and Hatley except for forensic evidence, right?" Paul poured himself another glass of sweet tea. "Someone will have to establish that link."

"But in the meantime, they like Ruth for Capshaw's death," Peggy reminded him.

"Oh! It's just *too* gruesome!" Stephanie jumped to her feet, tears in her eyes, and ran toward the bathroom.

"I tried to change the subject." Paul sat back in his chair. "Not everyone can talk about stomach contents over the dinner table."

"It was the contents of their *lungs*, sweetie." Peggy picked up her plate and his to load in the dishwasher. "And if she plans on working in the field of forensics of any type, she better get over it."

"Not everyone is as tough as we are." He picked up the rest of the tableware. "We listened to Dad's stories for years before getting into this ourselves. I'm sure she'll be able to cope with it better after a while. But isn't she great?"

Peggy wasn't sure how to reply to that question. She fell back on her answer from when he was a child. "She's wonderful. I'm glad you like her."

Stephanie appeared in the doorway as Peggy turned on the dishwasher. "I'm sorry I acted so silly. I guess I'm not used to this kind of thing. I'd like to see the house now."

They walked through the dining room with the massive table and chairs that had been passed down from Paul's great-grandmother who lived in Savannah. Stephanie remarked on the fourteen-carat gold rims of the china in the cabinet and the Edwardian anniversary clock that had been a gift from Winston Churchill to Peggy's great-aunt.

Paul led the way into the basement from there. Peggy went into limited detail on her experiments as she showed them around. There was no point in wearing out the poor girl's brain. "Paul used to grow herbs down here when he was in school. I still have some of them growing in the kitchen window."

"I liked to cook when I was in high school," he admitted. "I grew some parsley and a little pot of lemon balm for spaghetti."

Stephanie smiled at him. "Not lemon balm. You didn't use that in spaghetti, did you? Don't you mean oregano or basil?"

"You know herbs?" Peggy asked in surprise.

"I remember my mom saying that lemon balm was a weed in the yard." The girl shrugged. "That's about all. I was surprised to know you could use it in food."

Paul laughed. "You're right. I was thinking of oregano and saying lemon balm. I don't really know much about herbs."

They went on to tour the rest of the house. Peggy excused herself from the remainder of the tour to change clothes and journal her experiments. She could hear Stephanie giggling through the house.

She shook her head and kept her mouth closed. Paul was going to marry whomever he chose. She would have to make up her mind to get along with anyone, even Stephanie. After all, it was Mai that broke up with him. Too bad about that. At least she didn't simper and giggle.

Overall, her experiments were doing fine. The pumpkins were growing steadily larger each day. She hoped the toy nets she was using to hold them would be enough. She made some notes and entered some data into her computer to share with her colleagues. After finishing in the basement, she went upstairs to do more planning on her changes for the Potting Shed. She opened her bedroom door, surprised to find it closed, and Shakespeare lunged out, barking and jumping like a wild thing.

"You scared the liver right out of me," she told the dog, who joyfully licked her face after almost knocking her down. "Don't tell me you got stuck in there all day. I thought for sure you were downstairs with Steve when I left."

The dog looked up suddenly and his floppy, uncropped ears went straight back. He barked and ran for the spiral stairs, flying down them like he was being chased by the devil.

Peggy ran after him, calling him back, but it was too late. She heard Stephanie cry out as Shakespeare reached her and knocked her down on the hardwood floor in the foyer, growling like she was a prowler.

"Get him off! Get him off!" Stephanie yelled, kicking her feet, the only part of her she could move under the dog's weight.

"Get down, Shakespeare!" Paul yelled trying to wrestle the dog away from his date. He saw Peggy and said, "That's why I had him locked up! We had an issue when we first got here. Call him off, Mom."

Peggy tried, but Shakespeare wouldn't listen. She found it ironic that the dog didn't like Stephanie any more than she did.

He looked up at her as she called his name as though to ask why she'd want him to let the girl go. She finally got his leash and pulled him off Stephanie, who was almost hysterical by that time.

In all fairness, he *was* a big dog. Stephanie probably *was* afraid. But after Paul half carried her from the house with an angry look over his shoulder, Peggy smiled and patted Shakespeare's head. "Bad boy! You shouldn't maul guests. Even stupid guests we'd rather not have. Now, if you outlive me, that woman could be married to Paul, and they won't take you in. You'll be bound for the pound for sure."

Shakespeare barked and licked her hand enthusiastically, the sound echoing through the big old house, reminding Peggy she'd be alone that night. "We'd better go out for a walk before we lock up. I hope you didn't leave me any surprises in my bedroom. Not that it would be your fault, since Paul locked you in there."

She couldn't wait to tell Steve about her day and called his cell phone, but there was no answer. He was probably too busy, literally having his hands full delivering the foal. She remembered when her family had horses when she was a child. She never saw one of them born, though there were many foals. Her mother didn't think it was proper for her to see something like that. Lilla Hughes would be truly upset if she understood what kinds of things her little girl was looking at now.

It was pleasantly cool in the yard, and Shakespeare was very good at walking on his leash, thanks to his training. They walked through the backyard under the hundred-year-old oaks, listening to the sound of an owl up in the branches above them. The combination of honeysuckle, jasmine, and roses made an indescribable perfume on the night air. Peggy took a deep breath and closed her eyes as she enjoyed the moment.

She wished she could bring this to the Potting Shed, but that wasn't possible. However, the changes she had in mind would create a different atmosphere she hoped her customers would enjoy. It would be far less like a catalog environment and more like a living, growing spot, an oasis in the city.

Shakespeare was done in the yard. She was glad they went out when they did. He didn't have many accidents, but they were memorable when they happened.

Her cell phone rang in her pocket. She took it out and looked at it before answering. The number was unknown, and her heart did a little dance. *Nightflyer.*

13

Larkspur

Botanical: *Delphinium Spp.*

Shakespeare called the plant lark's heel, perhaps because of its connotation with the Trojan War and the death of Achilles (slain by an arrow in his heel). The first blue larkspur was said to grow out of the blood of Ajax, Achilles' companion, who took his own life after his friend was killed. Gardeners enjoy its versatility and brilliant colors.

"I've sent you some flowers." His voice was deep and raspy. "You should have them tomorrow. I suppose it's rather corny in this day and age. But I know how much you like flowers."

She'd talked to this man every way except in person. She wasn't sure why that mattered. She had many friends and associates from around the world that she'd never met.

But in her mind right now Nightflyer was a combination of Cary Grant, Robert Wagner, and Rock Hudson. He was a self-professed master spy who had given up the job but still kept his finger on the pulse of the world.

"Nightrose, are you there?"

She didn't know why she was so tongue-tied. It wasn't like her. "What kind of flowers did you send?"

"Baby's breath for happiness, forget-me-not for memories, pink heather for good luck, and larkspur for an open heart. Is that right?"

"That's right. You're a fast learner. I'm sorry I stood you up at the library. Things got . . . complicated."

"I'm sure they were."

"But we could still meet somewhere. You could come here. I brew a mean pot of tea." She forgot about her own misgivings regarding inviting him to her home.

"I wish I could. Getting away from everything I've done in my life hasn't been as easy as I thought it would be. I may be a new man, but life has remained the same."

"What do you mean?"

"I'm leaving. I can't tell you where I'm going or if you'll ever hear from me again. I couldn't pass up the opportunity to talk to you. I hope you'll forgive me."

She laughed nervously. "Forgive you? I'm glad you called. It's not really good-bye anyway. I'm sure we'll talk again."

"I wish I could ask you to leave everything you love and come with me. But my future is too uncertain at this point. I'll try to get back in touch. In the meantime, stay safe and well."

"Take care of yourself . . . Do you want to tell me your real name? I hate to say good-bye to a handle."

"My name is Daniel. I can't tell you my last name. Not now. Good-bye, Peggy."

The cell phone went dead. He was gone. *Daniel* was gone. At least she'd learned something about her mysterious friend. She didn't know what to make of him telling her he wanted to ask her to leave with him. That probably needed to be filed away for another time when she could think about it.

Peggy, feeling chilled, hurried back inside, pulling on Shakespeare's leash as she went. The phone rang as she closed the French door. *Was Nightflyer calling back again?*

It was her father, calling to tell her he'd seen her name on the Internet on News 14. "That sounds like an interesting case you're working on, sweet pea. I can't wait to get up there and help you with your investigations."

"Thanks, Dad, but this hasn't gone exactly the way I'd planned." She explained about both deaths and the flood in the shop. "Now *that* I could use your help with. Not that you haven't already been a big help with it."

"How's that?"

She told him what she'd recalled from those moments after the hurricane swept through their farm. "That's when I decided to redo the Potting Shed."

"Great! It could be like one of those makeover shows your mother likes so much on cable. Maybe we could all get in there with sledgehammers and pressure washers."

She laughed. "That's not exactly what I had in mind."

For the next half hour, they talked about the improvements she planned to make to the shop. Her father was very enthused about the project . . . but not as excited about remodeling as he was about finding killers.

"I promise to have an investigation going on when you get up here," she said. "How's that going?"

"That's why I called you. We closed on the sale today. We still have all that packing to do, but we should be in Charlotte by fall at the latest."

"Not so much packing as your father imagines," her mother added from another phone. "Most of this old junk is staying right here, either in someone else's house or the Goodwill."

"That sounds like a tough sell," Peggy told her. "Not even one rusty railroad spike?"

"Not even one, Margaret Anne." Her mother laughed. "New life, new rules. We don't keep anything we don't use. That includes horse blankets, totem poles, and pig troughs."

Peggy could imagine the discussions going on between her parents. Her mother was a firm believer in getting rid of things that weren't useful. Her father was an inveterate pack rat. "Have you looked at any houses up here?"

"We've looked, but we haven't seen anything we like yet."

"In other words," her father added, "nothing small enough to keep junk out of."

"How's my favorite grandson doing?" Lilla asked. "I hope he's dating someone who's interested in settling down. I'm not getting any younger. I'd like to see at least one great-grandchild before I die."

Peggy smiled. Paul was going to enjoy having his grandparents living close by. "Not really someone serious, I'd say. I think he's more interested in playing the field."

Her father whooped in appreciation and told them both to leave Paul alone. "He doesn't need any meddling women telling him what to do. He's a free spirit. A man about town. That's the way it should be at his age."

"What are you saying, Ranson?" her mother demanded. "We were married and buying this farm when you were his age."

"If you two would like to argue about this in private, I can get off the line," Peggy offered.

"Never mind," her mother said. "How's Steve doing? Are you two planning on getting married?"

"Not really, Mom. We like things just the way they are for right now."

"See?" Ranson interjected. "Peggy's a woman about town! She's living her life the way she sees fit."

"That's ridiculous," her mother argued. "She's a middle-aged widow with a grown son. She's not anything about town. But you *do* need to consider appearances, Margaret. I hope you're using some discretion."

"Always." Peggy said the word, but she knew Steve spending the night at her house wouldn't keep up appearances to her mother. They'd have to watch it when her parents got up there. "I have to go. I love you, and I can't wait until I see you."

"We're looking forward to seeing more of you and Paul," her mother said. "Good night, Margaret. We'll talk to you later."

Peggy hung up the phone and turned out the lights in the basement. She walked upstairs with Shakespeare, turning out lights as she went. It was almost three a.m. She yawned as she put on shorts and a tank top to go to sleep.

She tried not to think about Nightflyer. *Daniel.* He was a strange, disturbing presence in her life. She loved Steve. He was everything she needed him to be. She didn't want to fantasize about some middle-aged ex-spy who played a good game of chess and had worked so long for the CIA he couldn't speak straight anymore.

But there was something sad and darkly romantic about Nightflyer that captured her imagination, much like Humphrey Bogart in *Casablanca.*

Shakespeare climbed up on the bed beside her and settled down. When Steve was there, the dog slept on a rug on her side of the bed. He'd adapted better than she had to sharing her life, house, and bed.

She stared up at the ceiling for a very long

time. She thought about John. What would he think of all of this going on in their house? She frequently wondered how he'd feel about Steve sharing their bed. She didn't think she could sleep in Steve's dead wife's bed, if he'd ever had a wife.

It was all nonsense. John didn't feel any way about Steve. He was dead. She was alive. He wouldn't want her to be alone. She wouldn't have wanted that for him either if she'd been the first one to pass. If you really loved someone, you wanted what was best for them, regardless of your feelings on the subject.

Peggy got up and pulled on her robe. She turned on the light by her computer. There was no use wasting time lying in bed asking herself silly questions. She might as well get up, answer some emails, and ask a few questions that made sense.

She consulted a disk she'd been working on for the last few years compiling information about poisonous plants from the Southeast. She went to monkshood and looked at the photos she'd put in there along with the information, both factual and anecdotal. The plant had a long, interesting history.

Aconite poisoning was one of the first types to be used in the Carolinas. She had accounts of its use going back to the sixteen hundreds when the first settlers came from Europe. Of course the plant had been used medicinally for possibly a thousand years before recorded history, but even the last few hundred years had given it a colorful reputation.

She checked out the basic information on the plant's toxicity, wondering if she'd missed something that might help her investigation. Surely Marsha Hatley and Gerald Capshaw didn't both have traces of aconite in their systems without it having some meaning.

There was no evidence of them having ingested the plant. A tea would still have been in their stomach contents. If they were poisoned, what was the mode?

She took out her disk and got on the Internet. She typed in Marsha Hatley's name and found some basic information about her. She typed in Gerald's name and compared the two profiles, both from their obituaries. If there was some common denominator, she couldn't see it at first glance.

She was going to have to go out and ask more questions. Mr. Hatley had been slightly obnoxious, but she was going to have to speak with him again.

She was afraid to say anything else to Benita. Talking with her had already caused Ruth enough trouble. Peggy felt responsible for the position Ruth was in. She was just going to have to get her out of it.

Steve didn't get back to Charlotte until late the next morning. He pulled up into the back parking area of the Potting Shed as Sam and Keeley got there. "Is she in there?"

Sam slapped him on the shoulder. "You should know better than to ask me. I called her, but she didn't answer at home or her cell phone. I had to stop here for supplies anyway."

"I tried the same thing." Steve yawned. "I just got in from delivering a healthy foal who put up a whale of a fight not to come out into the cold, cruel world."

"You know she's here." Keeley took the back stairs two at a time. "She's planning the new shop. Where else would she be?"

Sam shrugged and followed her in with Steve right behind him. Peggy was sitting in the middle of the now dry shop floor with a measuring tape, pencil, and notebook. They watched her for a minute or so before she noticed they were there.

"Sorry." She grinned. "Did I miss a group meeting memo?"

Sam laughed. "You were right, Keeley."

"How's the new shop coming along, Peggy?" Keeley walked around looking at the crude drawings laid out on the floor.

"This looks great." Sam followed her. "When do you think you can reopen?"

"I'm not sure yet. I'll need the insurance money, and apparently there's some question of my insurance paying off before our rental agent's insurance. I'll know more later today."

"What's this?" Steve looked at the drawing in the middle of the floor.

"It's going to be what's commonly known as a water feature," she explained.

"Translate that to mean 'large pond,' " Sam told him. "You won't recognize the Potting Shed when it reopens. Right, Peggy?"

"That's right. We're going to have to come up with a crowd-drawing diversion. Maybe a grand reopening party. We can send out invitations to all of our customers and put an ad in the paper."

"I have a friend who works for WSOC," Keeley volunteered. "Maybe we can get some coverage: 'Local Store Rises from the Ashes.' What do you think?"

Sam tilted his head to consider the concept. "Not bad, except that's a whole other element. This would be more like 'Local

240

Store Floats Despite Flood.' "

"Both very good ideas," Peggy agreed. "If you can get us some media coverage, Keeley, please do."

"Oh yeah," Sam said. "I might have found us a water feature dude. He's been putting in ponds and fountains for about a year. He hasn't built up much business yet, but he has some supergood stuff. I've seen his work at some of the houses we've done. He's brilliant. I talked to him about subbing for us. He seemed like he thought it was a good idea."

"Great!" Peggy got up off the floor. "We're on the move here, lady and gentlemen. This flood is going to be the foundation for a new and improved Potting Shed."

"It could be even greater if you'd let me do something with your fertilizer mix." Sam told Steve about Peggy's creation and the remarkable job it did. "It could make a fortune."

"It sounds good, Peggy," Steve said. "I don't know anything about fertilizer, but if I could market my own brand of pet food, I'd be rich."

"That's the same idea!" Sam replied. "She won't tell me exactly what's in it, but I've seen the results. It's Peggy's Miracle Fertilizer for sure."

"I think it would be too expensive to create commercially," she warned. "I have nothing against you taking a look at it, Sam. If it worked out, I think it would be fine."

"All right! Email me a recipe, and let's get cooking." Sam laughed. "I'd like to be a millionaire this time next year. In the meantime, Keeley and I better hit the road. I'll talk to you later."

"See you later, Sam," Peggy said. "You two take it easy out there today. They said we could break a heat record before the day is out."

When Sam and Keeley were gone, Steve moved closer to Peggy, taking her measuring tape and pencil then putting his arms around her. "I missed you last night. I hope you got some sleep."

"A little. How did the birth go?"

"Excuse me?"

She blinked and looked up into his warm, brown eyes. "What? Did I miss something?"

"Me, I hope." He kissed her chin. "I said I missed you last night, despite catching your face on the late night news. I don't think I heard a reciprocal statement."

Peggy rose up on her toes and kissed him passionately. "I missed you so much; I almost had to drive out to that horse ranch to be with you. Shakespeare was miserable, too. He has a big, sloppy wet kiss waiting for you."

"That doesn't sound too appetizing. But it's nice to know you thought about me between murder investigations. How did you get involved with that second investigation?"

"It's a long story."

"You can tell me about it over breakfast."

They walked across the courtyard to the Kozy Kettle despite Peggy's reluctance to see Sofia and Emil before her garden club meeting at ten. Steve refused to take offense at the Sicilian couple's constant remarks about the two of them not being suitable for one another, not to mention their endless attempts to hook Peggy up with one or another of their male relatives.

"They're just fooling around," Steve said as they walked into the shop that was still quiet at that time of the morning. The coffee shop would get more crowded as the day went on, one of the reasons Emil offered Peggy the use of his place for her garden club on Thursday mornings. "You take them too seriously."

"Whatever." She walked up to the counter to order breakfast, the smell of vanilla coffee and baking cinnamon rolls making her stomach groan. "We can eat here, but we have to sit in the courtyard. That way they won't have enough time to come out and talk to us."

He laughed. "That's fine. What sounds good?"

Emil's booming voice and huge grin beneath his large black mustache greeted them. "Peggy! You bring your friend! I have some wonderful food for you. I hope you are both hungry."

Sofia, hearing Peggy's name, hustled out of the kitchen, wiping her floury hands off on a pristine white towel. "Look who it is! It's Peggy and her friend. It's good to see you! We have a surprise for you, don't we, Emil?"

"We do," her husband agreed. "You won't believe who flew in from Paris last night."

Peggy darted a glance at Steve, hoping he was taking it all in. "Who's the surprise?"

"She is Emil's great-aunt Tunia. We asked her here to help you out. She came at great personal expense because Emil once saved her life," Sofia explained.

"It's true." Emil crossed his heart in his broad chest as he always did to show verity. "Tunia was trapped in a fire when her father tried to burn her alive for being a witch. I was only a boy at the time, but they say I had the courage of a lion, rushing into the flames to drag Tunia out."

Sofia nodded. "And since then, no matter how busy she is, she comes when Emil calls her."

Emil agreed. "And she's very busy, you know. She recently matched the crown prince of Denmark with his future bride. She was going to Egypt next, but she came here for you instead, Peggy."

Peggy raised a single cinnamon-colored brow, knowing what was coming but wanting Steve to clearly understand what the other couple was up to. "Matched?"

"She's a matchmaker," Sofia explained. "She's coming to find you the perfect husband. I am so excited I could fall on the floor."

"I'm already in a relationship," Peggy told them for the hundredth time. "Steve and I are together." She looked at Steve, who seemed oblivious to the conversation. "Isn't that right, Steve?"

"Uh — sure. I'd like the egg and cheese on a bagel, toasted, and a large coffee." He smiled at Peggy. "What would you like?"

"*Matchmaker,* Steve." She glanced at the couple behind the register. "Emil and Sofia want me to meet their *matchmaking* relative, so she can find me the perfect husband."

"Really?" He smiled pleasantly at Sofia

and Emil. "I didn't know anyone did that anymore."

Peggy rolled her eyes as Sofia and Emil launched into an explanation and history of matchmaking in their country, following it through to America, and ending with a splendid recommendation of Tunia for all of Peggy's matrimonial needs.

Steve sipped the coffee Sofia had managed to give him between matchmaker stories. "That sounds fascinating. But if Peggy is going to marry anyone, it'll be me."

Both Emil and Sofia were struck silent with the declaration. Steve smiled at Peggy and asked again what she wanted to eat. She mumbled something about peach tea and a croissant. *What did he just say?*

Without another word about Great-aunt Tunia, Sofia and Emil made their food and gave it to them, refusing to take a dime. Emil shook Steve's hand and apologized for any misunderstanding they might have had.

"I don't understand," Peggy said when they sat down outside on the patio furniture. "I've told them at least a hundred times that we're together. You say it once, and they stop talking about it. What's up with that?"

Steve shrugged as he chewed the first bite of his bagel sandwich. "I guess it's all in the way you say it. You were going to tell me

how you got involved with two murder investigations . . ."

14

Monkshood

Botanical: *Aconitum*

Monkshood has been the source of hundreds of stories of witchcraft down through the generations. That may be because of the medicine women who used the herb to help a vast array of diseases. It has been used to poison arrows and enemies for centuries. The blossoms are entirely pollinated by bumblebees. The two long spears that hold the plant's nectar are only reachable by the bumblebee's long tongue.

Peggy thought about Steve's concern for her well-being as she rode to the police lab. He'd been patient and asked intelligent questions as she'd explained about the two deaths and how she believed they could be linked.

She loved talking to Steve, but she frequently wished he wouldn't worry so much about her. She'd managed to survive for a long time. His concern about her being spread too thin was nice but a little irritating. She could handle what needed to be done.

She refused to allow herself to think about what Steve had said about marriage. It wasn't like they'd talked about it. She didn't know if she was ready for that step yet.

After Steve had left her at Brevard Court, she'd met with a contractor about the changes she wanted to make to the Potting Shed. He was a very nice young man with imagination enough to envision what she was talking about from her drawings on the shop floor. He'd added a few of his own ideas that complemented hers then wrote everything down in his notebook and promised to get back with her with his bid by the end of the day.

She finished up there, locked up, and headed back to the Kozy Kettle for her garden club meeting. Since it was so nice outside, she'd decided to hold the meeting on the patio. She noticed a few passersby who stopped to listen for a while. It was free publicity to her; something good in the long run.

"Today we'll be talking about common

house plant insects. You see this lovely jade plant. It looks strong and healthy except for this white waxy material that almost looks like spiderweb on it. Of course it's not a spiderweb." She passed the plant around to the fifteen attendees, mostly from Myers Park and Center City condos. "This is a sign that the plant has mealy bugs."

Some of the women gasped, and the one holding the jade plant dropped it on the ground. Thankfully, the pot was plastic, and nothing was damaged. She picked it up with profuse apologies and handed it carefully back to Peggy.

"Mealy bugs suck plant sap and excrete honeydew," Peggy explained. "They will stunt your plant's growth and could eventually kill even a healthy specimen like this one."

"They aren't dangerous to humans, are they?" Cynthia Chappelle asked with her hand waving rapidly in the air.

"Of course not, Cindy," her mother, Florine told her. "They can't sting or bite."

"That's true," Peggy agreed with her. "The only thing a mealy bug can hurt is your plant. The best thing to do if you see an infestation like this one on one of your plants is to get some insecticidal soap like this." She held up the bottle. "Take a cotton ball like this. Put on some gloves and soak the cotton ball with the soap. Rub the white stuff off the plant with the soap and the cotton ball. That will help the plant and kill the mealy bugs."

The women nodded and some wrote quickly in notebooks. The sun was warm, but there was a cool breeze that weather forecasters said was bringing in some much-needed rain. Ice tinkled in glasses of sweet tea, and food odors mingled in the courtyard from the French restaurant and Anthony's Caribbean Café.

"Now here we have some mites on this fern. These are not really insects but are closely related to spiders. You can't see their handiwork like you can the mealy bugs, but they're busy trying to kill this plant."

Flossie McKnab gasped in the front row closest to Peggy. "That's just awful. Why are they so spiteful?"

Peggy smiled at her. "It's their nature to try to survive just like the rest of us. Unfortunately, they picked an indoor plant to survive on. You'd never notice them outside."

Flossie smiled and tossed her long blond hair. She was the fourth wife under the age of twenty-five to be married to a local investment banker over fifty looking for his lost youth. The first three young wives made the mistake of getting pregnant. There was even money among the people who knew the couple that Flossie would make the same fatal mistake.

"Plant damage, in this case light-colored speckling on the upper surface of the leaves, is usually the first sign that you have a mite problem. If you don't take care of it, the next step will be yellow leaves that fall off, and the plant will die. Insecticidal soap works for mites as well."

"Is there anything we can do to protect our plants from infestation?" Cynthia asked.

"Not really." Peggy put aside her infested fern. "Usually you pick them up bringing in new plants from the store. You can try keeping a new plant isolated for a few weeks in hopes that any bugs on it will show themselves before you put the plant in with any others. Otherwise you'll have to do catch-up work after the fact."

"What about aphids?" a new woman Peggy didn't know asked.

"You can follow the same advice, except pick the aphids off and dispose of them when you see them."

"Peggy, when will the Potting Shed re-open?" Cynthia asked.

"I hope to have it open again by Labor

Day." She told them about the flood and a few of her ideas for the new shop. "I hope you'll all come for the grand reopening party."

All of the women promised they would come, and the meeting adjourned itself to the inside of the Kozy Kettle for lunch and snacks. Peggy stood outside in the courtyard talking with a few of the women she'd known for the last two years. They wanted to know more about Marsha Hatley's murder.

"That must be awful for you." Jane Hayes put her hand on Peggy's shoulder. "I don't know how you can look at something like that."

Cynthia added, "It's a good thing she can! She's solved a few crimes around here that the police didn't get."

"Yes," Jane agreed. "But I couldn't do it. Peggy, what's your secret?"

Peggy smiled. "I don't think I have one. Except maybe I'm a detective's widow, and I've heard so much down through the years. I guess, too, it's like a puzzle, but a puzzle that can make a difference to the people who are left behind. That's what keeps me going. I want these people to have some closure."

Florine laughed, her smooth face belying

her age. "And she wants to catch the bad guys, too, right?"

"That's right." Peggy glanced at her watch as her cell phone rang. "And that's the medical examiner wondering why I'm not at the meeting he called this morning. I have to go. It was good to see all of you. Take care."

The ride to the lab wasn't long enough. She knew Jonas and Harold were going to be angry about her helping the ME in Stanly County. She wished she had some excuse but couldn't imagine what it would be besides curiosity. That was her only defense. And if they decided they didn't want her to work with them anymore, it was probably what she deserved.

She locked her bike chain and rushed inside, holding out her ID to the man at the front desk. She was going to get her lab coat, but Mai forestalled her at the door. "Peggy! I was *wondering* where you were. Everyone is wondering where you are. They held the meeting for *you*."

Mai hustled her into the conference room where Harold, Jonas, Al, and Sheriff Barbee from Stanly County sat beside Doc Williamson. They all looked up as she and Mai walked into the room.

"Nice of you to find time for us in your

busy schedule," Harold began the assault. "I think we all know each other by now, so we'll skip the formalities."

Sheriff Barbee leaned forward with his fingers meshed together on the table. His smile reminded Peggy of a possum she'd once found in her garbage can. "Dr. Lee. Or is that *Detective* Lee?"

"She never claimed to be a detective." Doc stood up for her. "It's something we assumed. Not that it matters. She found out enough to link these two cases together when we were about to call it quits on Mr. Capshaw."

"In all fairness," Al said, "he's correct. We wouldn't be here today working together if it wasn't for Peggy. I think she deserves some credit on that front."

Sheriff Barbee slammed his hand on the conference table. "Well let's just give her a medal! Gentlemen, the woman perpetrated a fraud on the Stanly County Sheriff's Department. We think she should at least be suspended."

Jonas rolled his eyes. "She can't be suspended, Sheriff. I already told you that. She doesn't *officially* work for CMPD. She's a contract worker, an independent. We pay her to give us ideas on her specialty, botany, in this case."

"Does that mean she can do whatever she pleases?" the sheriff persisted.

"No, sir." Jonas looked at Peggy. "It means she's good at what she does, although she tends to bend the rules a little from time to time. I'll speak with her about that. But in the meantime, I believe we have a double homicide here to resolve. I think we'll need her help. Unless you have another forensic botanist up your sleeve."

"I put a call in to the state forensic botanist." The sheriff's face was hard. "Unfortunately, he can't help us out until at least October. I guess we'll have to play by your bent rules, Dr. Lee."

Peggy had waited impatiently for them to stop discussing her like she wasn't there. She wanted to say something conciliatory, but the words didn't want to come out. "Sheriff Barbee, I'm sorry you got the wrong impression, but my 'bent' rules are the only things you have to carry this case with right now. You may not like what I do, but you're not required to. I stand on my results."

Mai sat down hard on the chair next to where Peggy was standing. She looked around the room, wondering what was going to happen next.

"As I said, shall we get started with this

meeting?" Harold looked up at Peggy. "Dr. Lee, if you'll take a seat and catch all of us up on where we need to be with this thing? And please, tell us more about monkshood."

Peggy told them everything she knew. She could tell the sheriff wasn't impressed. When she'd finished, he leaned back in his chair, his stomach pressing out on the brown material of his uniform. "I don't see why any of this is really necessary," he said. "We have the killer. She's sitting in my jail."

"She hasn't been charged," Jonas reminded him. "And we have nothing of any substance to link her with our killing. We know the two deaths are linked in some way, but as far as we can tell, there's no connection between Capshaw and Mrs. Hatley."

"It's only formality we haven't charged her," the sheriff proclaimed. "She's not going anywhere. We know she was sleeping around with Capshaw until his wife told him he better cut it out. Dr. Sargent didn't want the affair to end, and when she saw she couldn't influence the deceased anymore, she killed him."

"Excuse me, Sheriff," Peggy interrupted. "But exactly *how* did she kill him?"

"She poisoned him with that stuff Doc told me about."

"Did he also tell you the forensic evidence won't support that theory? He had a modest amount of aconite in his system. It could've led to his death because he was underwater. But we don't know how it was introduced into his system. Until we know that, the longest you can hold Dr. Sargent is forty-eight hours."

"Now listen here, ma'am —"

Doc Williamson interrupted. "She's right, Sheriff. We have more work to do before we can prove anyone is guilty."

"Well, I'll be." The sheriff puffed out his cheeks. "My own man turned against me."

Peggy rolled her eyes at the drama. Doc assured the sheriff he hadn't turned against him, but he wanted to make any charges stick. Jonas added his opinion that the two medical examiners should work together until it was clear exactly what had happened.

"That's fine with me," Doc said, a big grin on his face. "Is that okay with you, Peggy?"

Harold cleared his throat. "I'm afraid *I'm* actually the medical examiner of Mecklenburg County." He looked around the table. "But that's fine with me."

"Peggy *did* find this evidence that's brought all of you to this point," Mai said.

"I think she should be included on this team."

"I don't know." The sheriff sat back and rocked in his chair. "She also caused a lot of trouble, and she's friends with our prime suspect. I kind of think she should withdraw from the case."

Doc shook with anger. "I won't work without her. She understands what we're doing. No offense, Dr. Ramsey."

"None taken." Harold nodded. "I concur with Dr. Williamson. Dr. Lee has a good grasp of both cases. She's actually more like a liaison between the two counties. Besides, she's already tested a lot of water."

"And we don't yet know where both victims drowned," Peggy spoke up. It was amazing how people could talk around you. "That's as important as the aconite."

Nodding in agreement, Jonas and Sheriff Barbee shook hands then stood in one corner of the room talking quietly. Mai smiled at Peggy as the two medical examiners shook hands. Al stood awkwardly by himself, looking out the window.

"What's next?" Both MEs looked at Peggy. Jonas and the sheriff looked up.

She felt like the old commercials where everyone stopped talking to get brokerage advice. Only this time, it was information

259

about what killed two people. "I think the next thing is to continue the water testing. We need to know where both of them drowned."

Jonas ran his hand around his neck in agitation. "That could take some doing now that we know Stanly County is involved, too. Cabarrus County is between them. Saying our killer thinks linearly, we might only have those three counties to check. Otherwise anywhere would be fair game."

Al took down a map of North Carolina that was hanging on the wall in the conference room. "We used to do this thing where you use a compass to make a circle around a search area on a map. There's probably a computer program for that now, but let's say we could look at it that way for now."

"I have a compass." Harold offered it from his pocket protector.

"I don't think I want to know why he has that," Mai whispered to Peggy.

"Ears!" Harold shouted. "I have ears, Ms. Sato!"

He didn't elaborate or try to answer Mai's question. Peggy thought it was just as well. She didn't want to know what he did with a compass.

"All right." Al put the point of the compass halfway between Badin and Charlotte. "If we figure a reasonable amount of time to drown someone, say half an hour —"

"It only takes a few minutes to drown," Sheriff Barbee reminded him.

"It would take a little longer to get someone to go, get them in the water and hold them down, then get them out of the water and load them up in a truck or something," Doc added his opinion.

"Dr. Sargent has a big old van," the sheriff told them.

"Anyway." Doc frowned at him. "It would take a good thirty minutes."

Al cleared his throat and started again. "If you look at the map, the area would extend through Cabarrus County, but we could restrict our water testing to this area in the circle. I don't know how many lakes or rivers are out that way —"

"A hell of a lot." The sheriff grimaced. "It would take an army to check all that water."

Peggy looked at the scenario they were creating. "You know, you don't need a large body of water to kill somebody. It only takes a teaspoon of water to drown. Just because the water has certain characteristics doesn't mean it didn't come from a smaller place where it was being stored."

The room fell silent around her.

"Are you saying we won't ever find out

where this happened?" Jonas asked in a voice tight with exasperation.

"Not exactly. But it might be impossible to find the place by looking at specific bodies of water in the area." She didn't want to complicate matters, but it was a daunting prospect.

"Maybe we can find some volunteers," Doc Williamson suggested. "We could get some law students who understand handling evidence. That would make it go quickly."

That wasn't what Peggy meant, and she could see the meeting was beginning to go around in circles. "If you'll excuse me, I have an appointment."

"We need you here to do research," Jonas said with a glance at Harold. "Right, Dr. Ramsey?"

"I have my cell phone," she replied. "Call me if you need me. Don't forget I'm not salaried. You're paying me by the hour."

Jonas understood that, and she left the conference room with his blessing. Mai went out with her. "You're up to something. I want to come along."

"I'm going out to talk to Mr. Hatley. I don't think we're going to gain anything by getting a bunch of college students to bring in test samples of water. We need to know what happened to these people and how the same thing happened to both of them. There has to be a common denominator."

Mai smiled. "Sounds good to me. Can we stop at Starbucks on the way? I haven't had coffee yet."

"Since *you're* driving, you can stop wherever you like."

"You tricked me into this, didn't you?"

"Not really. I could ride home and get my truck. This way would be faster."

Mai grabbed her pocketbook and took off her lab coat. "I need some fresh air. Let's go."

They took Mai's new Subaru and drove to Sharon Road with a stop at Starbucks along the way. Peggy had just finished her iced mocha when they pulled up in the Hatleys' driveway. There was still yellow crime scene tape around the back and side of the house. Mr. Hatley's SUV was in the yard.

He wasn't happy to see them when he opened the door to the house and saw Peggy. "What do you want now? You've got her body. What else do you need?"

"Information." Peggy could be as plain-spoken as the next person if it called for it. "We think your wife was having an affair with another man found dead in similar circumstances."

Hatley took a step back from the doorway.

"Having an affair? Do you know this for certain?"

Peggy grabbed Mai's hand as she pushed into the house. She glanced into the living room. Mr. Hatley was not as tough as he sounded. "Why don't we come in here and sit down. Are your children here?"

"No." He sat down on an emerald green leather sofa with a dazed look on his face. "I sent them to stay with their grandmother. I was supposed to be at work today. I thought it would be best for them."

"Did you think your wife was having an affair?"

"If she was, I didn't know about it. As far as I know, our relationship was good. The police were joking about the pool boy. Marsha and I joked about Julio, too, sometimes. I can't believe she was with someone else."

"We don't have any proof of that yet." Peggy felt sorry for him. "The man in Stanly County who died in similar circumstances was known to fool around. I thought that could be the link between them."

"I hope not." He shuddered. "This has been bad enough without that."

"You said she worked for the bio lab in Kannapolis. Was she a researcher?"

"Yes. She'd started as a nurse then took some classes. Before you ask, I don't know what she was working on."

"Do you have any idea if she worked with poisons?" Peggy watched him closely.

"I don't know. I don't know what qualifies as a biohazard." He took out his wallet and gave her a business card with Marsha Hatley's office and cell phone numbers on it. "You should probably ask her supervisor out there. We didn't talk much about our work at home."

"Had she ever gone scuba diving? Or taken scuba lessons?"

"I don't think so. Not since I met her anyway. Marsha wasn't exactly afraid of the water, but she didn't go swimming or enjoy boat rides. I don't think she'd purposely go underwater."

Peggy sighed. This seemed to be going nowhere. She stood up and thanked him for his time. "I'm sorry to have to ask you these questions. We're just trying to figure out what happened to your wife."

He began crying, tears flowing heavily down his face. "I think she would have fought hard if someone tried to kill her. Marsha was a fighter. She wouldn't have left Blade and Kenya without a knock-down, drag-out fight."

15

Sweet Shrub
Botanical: *Calycanthus floridus*
Known as Carolina allspice and strawberry shrub as well as its even more common name, sweet shrub, the dark red flowers on this plant are attractive and unusual. But it is the scent of the plant that has made it most memorable. A gentle brush against it causes a cloud of fragrance to arise. Along with its other names, it is also called the bubby bush in parts of the southern U.S.

Mai hurried out of the Hatleys' home after Peggy. "Do you think Mr. Hatley had something to do with his wife's death despite his alibi? Like maybe he had her killed by someone else?"

"No. I was simply trying to think through what the two victims could possibly have in common besides the same phytoplankton in their lungs." Peggy brushed up against what her mother called a sweet shrub. It was really Carolina allspice, a common, native bush. The scent followed her as she walked away. It was an unusual, old-fashioned shrub to have in that modern setting.

"Did you find out anything new talking to him? Because I couldn't tell if there was anything there."

"No, not really." Peggy sighed as she got into Mai's car. "There's one thing I just thought of. I don't know why I didn't think about it before."

Peggy got out her cell phone and called a colleague from UCLA, Dr. Nystrom, who was tops in her field of toxicology. Peggy had met her at a conference a few years back and kept in touch. Now she verified what Peggy was thinking about monkshood. "Thank you very much, Dr. Nystrom. Please let me know about that case you're working on. It sounds very interesting."

"Well?" Mai asked when Peggy was off the phone.

"It's as I thought. Monkshood is one of the few poisons that can be administered topically. That could account for our victims having aconite in their systems. If they absorbed it through the skin, there would be no trace in the stomach."

267

"Good going!" Mai turned the car into the lab parking lot. "How do we test for that?"

"Dr. Nystrom said we have to swab an area of the skin and check for aconite there. If it's topical, there could be a heavier concentration of poison there rather than internally."

Peggy and Mai met Harold at the entrance to the lab. His angry gaze skewered Mai from behind his heavy, dark-rimmed glasses. "There you are, Ms. Sato. I was wondering what happened to you. Did someone authorize a field trip for the two of you?"

"I asked Mai to come with me." Peggy was anxious to tell him what she'd discovered.

"And since you're the head of the lab, Ms. Sato was able to leave without getting permission from anyone else. Does that sum it up?"

Mai bowed her head, the hot sun shining on her inky black hair. "I'm sorry, Dr. Ramsey. I didn't think to say something to you before I left."

"We'll talk about this later, Ms. Sato," Harold dismissed her and turned to Peggy.

Peggy didn't want to cause trouble. Goodness knew she'd been accused of it often enough. But she couldn't abide him treating her friend like a third-class citizen for one more minute. She waited until Mai was inside the lab, then she squared her shoulders and faced Harold. "How dare you talk to that young woman in that tone? She's nothing but loyal, helpful, and hardworking. She's taken more crap from you than I would've, Harold. You've got to cut her some slack."

He feigned a comical mask of distress. "Please, Dr. Lee, be gentle with me."

"Don't make this into one of your unfunny jokes. I want to see you treat her with more respect. There's no reason for your obvious disdain."

"Except for the fact that Ms. Sato *chose* to work directly for me, despite knowing how unfunny I am, I might agree with you, Dr. Lee. But I'm still the chief medical examiner in these here parts. I'll deal with my subordinates the way I see fit. It may not seem to you as though I have a method to my training, but I've taught hundreds of medical examiners around the country. Can *you* say the same?"

"You're a heavy-handed bully, Harold," she informed him as other lab workers passed them on the hot concrete steps going into the building. "No excuse of using those techniques for teaching is going to wash with me. You forget I've taught for more than twenty years myself. I know a thing or two about method."

He leaned down slightly. "Then we are at an impasse, ma'am. I suggest we both do our jobs and allow that we do them differently. Unless of course you want to become the medical examiner and take over the lab."

Peggy's Irish temper flared, and she tossed her head. "You're impossible, Dr. Ramsey. You deserve to have Mai quit her position."

"I've been called worse before. And if Ms. Sato chooses to leave, I have a list of twenty students waiting to take her place."

There was no getting around him, so Peggy left him standing there without another word. She supposed she could influence him to treat Mai differently, but she couldn't demand it of him. She stormed into the air-conditioned building with a sigh of relief. It was too hot to argue on the steps and not a bit ladylike. She knew what her mother would have to say about that.

"What were you saying to Dr. Ramsey?" Mai asked anxiously when Peggy picked up her lab coat. "You didn't get me fired, did you?"

"Of course not!" Peggy answered. "I wouldn't do such a thing. But really, sweetie, he treats you so badly. You *should* leave."

"I've worked hard to get here, Peggy. You know that. I don't mind what he says. You have to leave this alone. *Please!* For my sake."

"All right. You know best." They both looked away as Harold walked into the lab. "I'll keep it to myself."

Harold bellowed, "Ms. Sato!" and Mai scurried to answer him after thanking Peggy.

The girl clearly undervalued herself, Peggy thought as she went back to her microscope to begin checking some of the water samples she and Ruth had gathered.

"I told Dr. Ramsey about your theory," Mai said when she came back a few minutes later. "Maybe you should explain further, Peggy."

Harold looked expectantly from one woman to the other. "Is this one of those things best shared over a Lifetime movie and hot chocolate?"

Peggy ground her teeth but managed to present a pleasant face when she turned from the microscope. She told Dr. Ramsey her suspicion about the delivery of the aconite.

"This sounds promising, Dr. Lee. We should get those skin samples. Call your friend in Stanly County and then join me in the autopsy room." Ramsey barked his order then turned away and left them alone.

"He really likes you, Peggy," Mai told her.

"How can you tell?"

"Because he takes your suggestions so easily. Dr. Ramsey is one of the top medical examiners in the state. He doesn't pay attention to just anyone."

Peggy's cell phone rang. "I feel so honored," she lied. "Could you tell Harold I'll be there in a minute after I take this call?"

"Sure. It's really wonderful to work with two people like you and Dr. Ramsey," Mai gushed. "You're both so professional and talented."

"Please," Peggy frowned. "You don't have to suck up to me, sweetie, and I wish you wouldn't treat me like you treat him. I may get an ulcer or something from it."

Mai laughed. "At least you know I'm not after your job."

"Thank goodness!"

Peggy answered her cell phone. It was Ruth. "I'm finally on my way back to Charlotte. The sheriff told me it was partially your help that made them let me go. Thanks, Peggy."

"I'm so sorry, Ruth. I'm glad they released you, but I feel responsible for them harassing you in the first place."

"Not at all. It was my own poor judgment

in dating a married man. I've learned my lesson."

"I've learned some interesting things since I saw you last. We'll have dinner, and I'll fill you in. You might be able to give me some insight."

"I'll do what I can, but it will have to be on a personal level," Ruth told her. "Sheriff Barbee made sure I understood I'm not clear on this yet. They couldn't hold me, but I think they still believe I had something to do with it."

"That sounds like police mumbo jumbo to me. But I don't want you to risk anything else. We'll keep this between ourselves."

"Thanks. I appreciate your faith in me. I don't know how this could've happened. I hope you can figure it out."

"Don't worry about that," Peggy assured her. "I'll get to the bottom of it."

"Well, I'm headed home for a hot shower and some sleep. I might cross Stanly County off my list of friendly places. I'll talk to you tomorrow."

Peggy said good-bye and then put away her phone. She followed Mai and Harold into the autopsy room after donning gloves, mask, and a cap. She wasn't looking forward to seeing them work on poor Mrs. Hatley, but she supposed it was necessary.

"Glad you decided to join us," Harold said as she stepped up to the table. "I've just taken some skin and hair samples. Ms. Sato will process those with your help, checking for aconite levels. We have several alternate test sites on the body to compare samples. Let's hope this gives us some idea of what went on. Have you contacted Dr. Williamson yet?"

"No." Peggy glanced away from the body. "I'll call him as soon as I get out of here."

"Good. I hope we aren't interrupting your private life, Dr. Lee."

"Don't worry, Harold. I'll let you know if that happens." She stared at him across the table, not flinching from his comment. He might treat Mai like his private doormat, but she wouldn't put up with it.

She thought she heard him chuckle but couldn't be sure since he was wearing a mask. She didn't like to think she was only indulging his warped sense of humor, but she would do whatever was necessary to get the job done while maintaining her dignity. After all, she never planned to take his place as the medical examiner like Mai did.

While Mai and Harold finished collecting the skin and hair samples, Peggy pretended she was somewhere else — maybe in a beautiful walled garden in Charleston. Or with Steve. Or in a garden with Steve. Anything rather than being in that wretched room with that pitiful dead woman.

"We're ready," Mai told her. "Are you okay?"

"I'm fine," she said. "Let's go."

It took hours to carefully mount the skin samples on slides and put each one into vials to test individually for the aconite. Steve called twice, but Peggy ignored her phone, wanting to get the job done. They wouldn't be able to test until the next day, but they would be ready to go.

Doc Williamson asked her to join him in Albemarle for the tests and was disappointed when she told him she couldn't leave the Charlotte lab. He still agreed to do exactly the same tests on Mr. Capshaw as they were doing on Mrs. Hatley.

Peggy hoped the tests would prove her theory correct. It wouldn't be the end of the case, but it might offer some insight into how the couple was killed.

She thought about whether or not she believed the two victims were actually a couple in the romantic sense of the word while she worked with her aconite samples. It didn't sound like they had anything in common, though that didn't prove anything.

Many lovers had nothing besides their relationship that kept them together.

Take her and Steve. Steve knew a lot about animals. Until she adopted Shakespeare, she'd never had a pet. She knew a lot about plants. Steve only knew what he'd learned from her and how to cut his grass. They were an unlikely pair, yet they were together. If something similar happened to them, would anyone make the correlation?

She supposed that's where forensic investigation left them empty. As John would have said, knocking on doors and asking the right questions was the backbone of all police work. Science couldn't do what a detective with good instincts could do, but science could back up those instincts and make a stronger case.

"I guess that's it for tonight." Mai sat back and glanced at the watch on her slender wrist. "I think I'll grab some Mexican food on the way home. Want to join me?"

"No, thanks. Steve is waiting with dinner for me. We've been out of town a lot lately on separate trips, and I hate to pass up the opportunity to see him."

Mai took off her lab coat and dropped it in the biohazard garment bin. "How's Paul doing? I haven't seen him around much lately."

"He's fine. Dating." Peggy smiled at her. "How about you?"

"Like I have time to date."

"I think that's part of his problem, too."

"Yeah. That happens a lot. I think it has something to do with why we broke up. Not enough hours in the day."

"I know what you mean." Peggy pushed open the door into the parking lot. "I'll see you bright and early tomorrow morning."

"Enjoy your dinner with Steve."

"You know I will."

But the intimate dinner she'd envisioned didn't materialize. Paul was there with Stephanie again. The girl was managing to keep Steve and Paul in a good mood while they were waiting for Peggy to get home.

Somehow, Peggy thought Stephanie wouldn't come back again after her last run-in with Shakespeare. She was doomed to disappointment. Steve facilitated the visit by putting Shakespeare in the backyard.

"He seemed to have a problem with her," Steve said. "I don't know what was wrong with him. He's been so well-mannered with everyone else."

"Maybe it's my perfume." Stephanie giggled. "It's called *Animal Instinct.* Maybe he got overpowered by it."

Peggy rolled her eyes but managed to keep

her mouth shut as they sat down to dinner. No one asked about the flowers on the table. She knew they were from Nightflyer. Steve probably thought Paul had bought them. Paul and Steve had made a nice gazpacho with some crusty bread from the Panera Bread Company, and there was a chilled bottle of Moonlight Magnolia from Duplin Winery.

Stephanie only had time for one joke before Peggy's cell phone rang. She walked into the other room to answer it with a measure of gratitude. Why was it that men of all ages found women like Stephanie so enthralling?

Peggy answered the phone, but it went dead in her hand. She pushed Talk and the number on the view screen, and a woman answered, "Best Buy, where our everyday prices can save you money. This is Sandra. How may I help you?"

Peggy managed to get it across to the overeager salesgirl that she'd dialed a wrong number. She stood looking at the phone for a moment or two, wondering what it was all about before Steve pushed open the door. "Is everything all right?" He glanced around the shadowed room as though expecting to find someone else lurking there. Or maybe that was just Peggy's imagination.

"Everything's fine," she answered. The phone rang again. This time it was the contractor she'd talked to about the work to be done at the Potting Shed. "This will only take a minute."

Steve looked around the room again. "Okay. Hurry. Your gazpacho is getting warm."

The contractor came back with a surprisingly good bid on the project. She accepted right away and asked him when he could get started. "I could start tomorrow, if you like," he said with a smile in his voice.

"That would be great! I'm looking forward to working with you."

There were no more excuses to keep her out of the kitchen. Stephanie was telling another joke, and Peggy decided she was going to have to ignore it as she sat down to eat her dinner.

A knock at the kitchen door brought her to her feet again. She didn't make it all the way across the floor before Mai popped her head around the door. "I know you said you didn't want Mexican, but I thought we could eat together anyway. I don't have anyone waiting at home for me." She stopped, too late, when she saw Paul and Stephanie at the table. "I'm sorry. You have company. I'll go."

Peggy grabbed her arm. "Don't be silly. There's no reason you can't eat with us. Let me introduce you to Stephanie. She's one of Ruth's students."

Stephanie slid her arm through Paul's and smiled at Mai. "It's wonderful to meet you. I understand you and Paul were good friends when you were children."

Mai was taken aback by the other woman for an instant, but she regained her composure quickly. "It hasn't been *that* long since we were house hunting together, has it, Paul?"

Paul, caught between the two young women, smiled and blushed almost as red as his hair. "Mai is the assistant medical examiner in the county, Stephanie."

"How nice for you." Stephanie brushed Mai aside when she realized she couldn't score off of her. She resumed telling her ridiculous story as Mai took a seat at the table next to Peggy.

"Try some of this gazpacho," Steve said picking up a bowl. "It should go well with your taco."

Peggy ate some bread and soup in silence as Stephanie entertained Steve and Paul with her antics. She could tell Mai felt the same way about the other woman. She wished again that Stephanie wasn't there with Paul. He and Mai were so good together. It was so unfair.

"I was working with Dr. Sargent, looking for the phytoplankton Peggy needs, when we realized we had switched samples!" Stephanie laughed heartily. "Can you imagine how hard that was to straighten out?"

"It seems to me that if you're serious about entering the field of forensic research, you'd better take your work more seriously." Mai said the words with a straight face and a small smile. "Your work could save or ruin someone else's life."

Stephanie laughed again and looked at Paul. "Is she for real? No wonder you stopped house hunting with her. Who'd want to come home to that poker face every night?"

No one laughed, and the statement hung in the air between them like a foul stench.

"Actually, it was Mai who threw me out of her life," Paul told her quietly. "I was too serious for her."

"You weren't that serious," Mai replied. "I wasn't ready to make that kind of commitment. I thought we were fooling around. I think I've grown up some since then."

Mai's and Paul's gazes locked hungrily across the dinner table. Stephanie didn't pretend not to notice. "You're here with *me* now, Paul."

He tore his gaze from Mai's. "I guess we should finish eating."

Stephanie got to her feet. "Are you brushing me off? I can't believe you'd prefer *her* to me."

"Why don't we all finish our tea on the terrace?" Peggy suggested.

"I don't think so." Stephanie slid her chair into the side of the table with enough force to jar all their teeth. "I've had better times than this sleeping. And that's no joke." She stormed out the side door and squealed her tires as she left the drive.

The four who remained didn't say anything for a moment, then Steve got to his feet. "I think I'll take you up on that offer of tea on the terrace."

Peggy smiled at Mai and Paul. "You two come along when you're ready. I'm sure you don't need a chaperone."

"Do you think they'll get back together?" Steve asked quietly as they walked through the French doors into the soft summer night.

"Anything is possible." Peggy sat down in her favorite flowered chaise. "Now that I've had a taste of someone Paul could be with, I'll be rooting for Mai."

Steve laughed, sitting beside her and taking her hand. "Stephanie wasn't *that* bad."

"Not if you don't mind brainless comedians." Peggy saw a shooting star and closed her eyes to utter a whispered wish. "I don't understand what Ruth sees in her. But I suppose there's more to her than her personality."

Her cell phone rang again in her pocket. She wanted to ignore it, but after it finished one set of rings, it went on to another. "I'm sorry. I should've left this in the house."

Steve sipped his tea. "Neither one of us has that privilege most of the time. I'll call Shakespeare in. I'm sure he's dug up enough of your plants for one night."

"Thanks." She answered the phone as he left her. "Dr. Williamson? I hope this is important."

"Only as important as learning that your theory is correct, at least as far as Gerald Capshaw is concerned. The amount of aconite on his hand was off the charts."

283

16

Sago Palm
Botanical: *Cycas revoluta*
The sago palm belongs to one of the oldest living group of plants still found on earth today: the cycads. The order has been unchanged for millions of years and probably originated in East Africa. When sago palms have sexually matured, the female sagos begin to flower, producing a basketball-like circle. The male sago then produces a long, thick structure with which to propagate.

Doc Williamson joined Peggy, Harold, and Mai the next morning to compare notes on their respective victims. Peggy was running late because she first had a meeting at the Potting Shed with the contractor, who was ready to start work on the improvements.

She hoped to get Mai alone for a moment to ask, politely, of course, if anything was different between her and Paul. Paul had left last night without saying anything about what had happened, and Peggy was dying to know if the two were back together.

But there had been little opportunity to talk to Mai privately since she'd arrived with everyone waiting for her. The case took precedence, but Mai and Paul's relationship was at the forefront of Peggy's mind.

"I think there's no doubt Dr. Lee is correct about how the aconite was introduced into the two bodies," Harold said, acknowledging her part in the investigation. "The question is: Where did the aconite come from? Did it need special preparation? Perhaps we can narrow the field of suspects by knowing those answers."

"As I told Dr. Williamson," Peggy answered, "anyone could get monkshood and create a tincture capable of having this effect. It's usually sold at herb stores and grows wild in this state."

"Then anyone could be responsible." Harold sat back in his chair.

"Well, we don't really have a field of suspects," Doc reminded them. "We have a woman who dated Mr. Capshaw and was violently jealous of his relationship with his wife. It stands to reason she would be even worse with *another* lover in his life."

"I assume you're speaking of Dr. Sargent." Peggy got up and paced the tile floor as she spoke. "If she was so violently jealous of Benita Capshaw, why didn't she try to hurt her instead of waiting for Gerald's *next* lover? And I should point out that Gerald had more than one affair. It could as easily be Mrs. Capshaw getting fed up with her husband's philandering."

"But Mrs. Capshaw said Dr. Sargent was stalking her husband," Harold said.

"Yes. But no one has been able to put Gerald with Marsha Hatley as yet," Peggy reminded him. "Her husband firmly denies she was having an affair."

"But spouses mostly say that," Doc added.

"I don't know if anyone has spoken with Mrs. Hatley's friends or coworkers," Mai began timidly, "but her parents and sister said she wasn't the type to fool around."

"This is far too much of a coincidence: the two were killed at close to the same time, probably by the same person," Harold stated. "I think we should go with that hypothesis and find ways to support it forensically."

"I've had a lot of luck with victims' clothing," Doc said. "Maybe we could get some of their clothing and check them for semen or other fluids. We might be able to put them together that way."

"Good idea! I'll call Captain Rimer and see if he can make that happen." Harold picked up the phone.

"I'll speak with Sheriff Barbee." Doc mimicked his actions.

"Well, I guess that puts us going out to where Mrs. Hatley worked," Peggy told Mai. "I wanted to go out there anyway. We know she worked with biohazards. It's possible she could've been infected there without anyone knowing about it."

Harold nodded, on hold for Rimer. "That's brilliant, Dr. Lee. If we can put her in bed with Capshaw, that would explain the aconite at least. She could've transferred it to him."

"It wouldn't explain both of them having the same phytoplankton in their lungs," Doc said, on hold for Sheriff Barbee, "but it would be a start."

Peggy and Mai took off their lab coats and ID badges and walked outside together. Peggy was about to ask her coworker about what happened with her son, but before she could ask the question, she saw Paul waiting in the parking lot. She couldn't help but smile and say a little prayer of thanks.

Mai looked at Peggy nervously. "I don't know what he's doing here. He must be here to see you or something."

Peggy laughed. "I'm sure that's it. He stops by *every* day to see me."

"You're being sarcastic, right?"

"Yep. I think he's here to see you."

"Maybe." Mai bit her lip and smiled a little. "I think he still likes me."

"I think so, too."

Paul wasn't afraid of his mother knowing why he was there. He walked up to Mai and kissed her lightly on the lips. "Good morning. I had to drop off some samples. I have a friend who works in the lab. He said you might be leaving soon."

"I'm glad you waited." Mai took his hand and kissed his cheek. "It's good to see you."

Paul looked up as though just noticing his mother's presence. "Hi, Mom. Where are you two off to?"

"The new bioscience lab in Kannapolis." Peggy's smile was as wide as both of theirs. "But I could go by myself. Maybe the two of you could have coffee or something."

"I couldn't do that," Mai protested. "It's my job, too."

"I wouldn't ask you to," Paul reassured her. "You be careful out there."

"You, too." Mai kissed him again. "I'll call you when we get back to Charlotte."

"Okay." He reluctantly let go of her hand.

"I'm off at two this afternoon."

Peggy got in Mai's car and let the two of them gush for a few minutes. She was tickled to death to see them together again. They were so right for each other. Maybe this time they could make it all the way to grandchildren. Now, that would be a bio accomplishment!

Mai finally joined her in the car. "You aren't going to ask me about every little thing, are you?" She started the engine. "This is all happening really fast again. I don't know what to tell you about where it's going or where it will end up. I'm hopeful that something will work out for us, but it's hard to say. I have very strong feelings for Paul. I hope he has them for me, too."

Peggy didn't say a word, letting the younger woman ramble on about all the little things she supposedly didn't want to talk about. There was no need to ask any questions of her.

By the time they got to Kannapolis, a small town about thirty minutes away down Interstate 85, Mai was talked out. They got on a secondary road that led into the downtown area where an old textile facility had been torn down to make room for the huge complex that grew into the bio lab.

"I always forget how big this is." Peggy

filled in the silence. "It's odd to think about all the years Charles Cannon ran this place with an iron hand. I wonder how he'd feel about losing all the textiles and gaining a bio research lab."

"I'd think he'd be happy people out here have jobs again." Mai turned into the main parking lot of the lab building. "From what I've heard, there wasn't much going on when they started building this."

"The jobs are certainly better anyway," Peggy remarked. "People around here used to call the textile workers lint heads because they were covered in cotton after they'd worked a shift."

"Let's hope what they're doing out here now isn't as hazardous to their health as cotton used to be." Mai opened her door and stretched her legs. "I can't believe there are people in Charlotte who work out here. This drive would kill me if I had to make it every day."

"You're such a city girl." Peggy got out and shut her car door. "The first job I had was at UNCC. I had to drive over there every day until there was an opening at Queens. We drove much farther to go to Charleston when I was a kid."

"Was that back in the day when you had to hitch up the horse first?" Mai teased.

"You are such a minx!" Peggy laughed. "I don't know how you keep from giving Harold a hard time at the lab."

"I know my place and my plan. I can manage to keep a civil tongue in my head, as my mother calls it."

"To answer your question, we *did* have horses and even a couple of buggies. But we took our old Studebaker to town when we went."

"Is that a kind of horse?" Mai looked at her curiously.

"You really don't know what a Studebaker is?" Peggy asked as she opened the door to the multimillion-dollar facility.

"I really don't. Is it a car farmers used?"

Peggy would have explained, but they were immediately joined by a tall, thin woman with dark red hair. "I'm Sarah James. You must be Dr. Lee. We've been expecting you."

"Nice to meet you." Peggy shook her hand. "What gave me away?"

"I'd know you anywhere, Dr. Lee. I had you for botany at Queens. That was too many years ago to remember. I'm the liaison for the lab."

"If it was too many years ago for *you* to remember, I certainly don't want to try." Peggy turned to Mai. "This is Assistant Medical Examiner Mai Sato. I suppose you already know why we're here."

Sarah started them walking down the long, ultraclean hall with all the speed and push of a White House tour guide. Her voice was carefully modulated, probably to avoid the echo in the building with high ceilings, or at least that's what Peggy imagined. "Yes. Captain Rimer called the director to let him know you were coming. I hope we can be of some assistance in this matter. Mrs. Hatley's death was a terrible blow to us all."

"Tell me, Sarah," Peggy wasted no time getting to the reason she was there, "did you ever see Mrs. Hatley with a man who wasn't her husband?"

"This man." Mai held out a picture of Gerald Capshaw.

"I'm afraid our offices were on different floors." Sarah looked at the picture. "Is this the man from Stanly County who died?"

"Yes, it is." Mai put the photograph away. "We were wondering if there was any possible connection between the two of them."

"I'd like to help you, Ms. Sato," Sarah said. "But I don't know. I can check the visitors log and see if he ever signed in."

"That would be nice," Peggy said. "We'd appreciate any help we can get on this."

Sarah stopped walking in front of an office with closed double doors. "This is Director Finley's office. He'll want to see you for a few minutes, then I'll be back to take you to Mrs. Hatley's office."

Peggy thanked Sarah, then she and Mai walked into the office. It was very plush with thick, sound-deadening carpet underfoot and a huge chandelier hanging from the ceiling. It was as sumptuous as the outer hall and lobby had been sparse.

A short woman in a no-nonsense gray business suit got up from behind a French Provincial desk and hurried over to them. "You must be Dr. Lee. I'm Mr. Finley's assistant. He's expecting you. Please go in."

Mr. Finley rose from behind his large mahogany desk as Mai and Peggy came through the door. His handshake was as overly enthusiastic as his greeting. "I'm very glad there's something we can do to help find out what happened to Marsha Hatley. She's been with us since the beginning. We'll all miss her."

Peggy wondered if he'd recognize the woman if she showed him a photograph. Up here, in his luxury suite, it didn't seem as though he mingled much with the masses. "Thank you, sir. We have a few questions about Mrs. Hatley's work."

"Of course! Of course! Sit down, please.

Would you like some coffee or a soda?"

Both women smiled and told him they were fine. Mai took out a tape recorder and started to push the Record button.

"Is that necessary?" Finley looked at the device as though Mai were about to shoot him with pepper spray from it. "I've told you, as I told your captain, I'd be happy to tell you anything about Mrs. Hatley and her work here."

Mai didn't turn off the recorder. "How long did Mrs. Hatley work here?"

"As I said, she was one of our first recruits. The lab has been open for two years, so I suppose that's how long she's been here. She came to us very highly recommended from Carolinas Regional Medical Center."

"And you knew her well?" Mai glanced up at him.

"I've spoken with her several times. She was a staff manager, so we attended meetings together. I can't say I knew her beyond the workplace, but she was very competent and an excellent manager."

Peggy noticed Marsha's employee file on the desk in front of Finley. She wasn't convinced he knew her at all. "Did you ever meet her husband?"

"Not that I recall," he hedged. "I probably met him, but I don't really know anything about him."

"Did you notice anything peculiar in Mrs. Hatley's attendance or attitude recently?" Mai asked.

Finley frowned. "No. She seemed fine. Her performance was still very good in the last three months."

"Because that's what her file says?" Peggy pinned him down.

"I beg your pardon?"

"You've been reading Mrs. Hatley's file." Peggy tapped the folder with her finger. "Did you really know her at all?"

"I don't know what you're intimating." He cleared his throat and adjusted his tie. "I've worked very closely with her in the last two years."

"So you knew about her struggle with cancer." Peggy watched as his eyes darted to the folder and back. He started to grab it, but she put her hand on top of it. "If you worked closely with Marsha, you should know about something as big as that without looking."

"You're right." He smiled nervously then glanced back and forth between the two women. "It was a terrible struggle for her. We spoke of it often. We all did what we could to help her and her family."

Peggy sat back in her chair. "Marsha Hatley didn't have cancer."

He was dumbfounded. "Then why did you *say* she did?"

"Mr. Finley, we need to talk with the people she *really* worked with," Peggy explained. "They're the only ones who have the answers we need."

Finley shuffled the papers on his desk. "We normally don't allow those types of interviews. I had a meeting with Mrs. Hatley's direct supervisor, and he assures me everything was fine."

Mai sat forward. "You can give us access to the employees who worked with Mrs. Hatley, or we can get a court order and News 14 splashes it all over the evening news."

"I suppose something can be arranged." Finley called in his assistant. "Anna, get Sarah back down here." He turned to Peggy and Mai. "Sarah will take you to her department. I must insist that she sits in on the meetings in case any sensitive material is discussed."

"That's fine." Mai got to her feet. "Thank you, sir. We'll let you know if we need to speak to you again."

Mai and Peggy waited in the hall for Sarah James after Mr. Finley gushed his good-byes and promised to help wherever possible.

"How did you know he wasn't being sincere?" Mai wondered. "I thought he really knew the woman."

Peggy smiled. "I'd like to tell you it's some dark secret, but really it's a combination of working with people for so long and seeing Marsha's file on his desk."

"I suppose after years of listening to students' excuses for everything, you learn to figure out who's telling the truth and who's lying."

"Exactly. Don't forget I raised a teenager, too."

"You mean I have to have a child to learn to read people better?" Mai groaned.

"Not necessarily," Peggy said. "But it helps."

Sarah James joined them again, apologizing for the time it took to get back to them. "This is a huge complex. It's hard to stay on top of everything. And by the way, I checked the register. Gerald Capshaw hasn't been here."

"Has there ever been a breach in security?" Peggy asked her.

"No, of course not. We have state-of-the-art digital surveillance twenty-four/seven. Nothing goes in or out without us knowing about it."

"Have you ever done any work with an

aconite compound?" Peggy pursued the subject.

"I'm not privy to the details of *all* the biological experiments," Sarah answered carefully. "Each group is responsible for each project, and there are hundreds of small groups studying various media at any given time."

"Could you find out if any experimentation with aconite has been done here in the last few months?" Mai smiled. "It would save us having to get a search warrant."

Sarah appeared shaken. "I can check into that. It will take me a while, but I'll do the best I can." She stopped outside a double door that said Lab #3. "There are five other members of Mrs. Hatley's team. They're all here today. They should be inside."

The lab on the other side of the security door was painfully clean and neat. Peggy wondered if it always looked that way, even when they were working, or if the team in Lab #3 had been alerted before their arrival. The police medical lab wasn't that clean, she considered, noticing she could see herself in the mirrorlike finish on the floor.

The only thing that wasn't black, white, or silver was a huge Sago palm by the window. Peggy was struck by the anomaly of having the most ancient of plants in the most modern of settings. The deep green leaves were stately and welcome in the austere room.

"This is Donna Patterson, Zeke Whitley, Joe Gillette, Mary Von Cannon, and Frances Phillips. Ladies and gentlemen, this is Mai Sato and Dr. Peggy Lee of the CMPD medical examiner's office." Sarah introduced everyone and invited them to sit down at one of the long tables. "Ms. Sato and Dr. Lee have some questions for you about Marsha Hatley."

The five, white-coated workers waited for their questions. Mai glanced at her notebook, hands trembling, as she tried to decide what to ask first.

Peggy jumped in. "How many of you knew Mrs. Hatley well enough to know if she was having an affair?"

The lab partners looked at each other then back at Peggy. Zeke Whitley stepped forward first. "I think we all knew her that well. We've worked together as a single unit for two years. We know a lot about each other."

"And was she having an affair?" Mai got her feet wet.

"No." Donna Patterson responded with nods from her coworkers. "Marsha and her husband were happy together. They lived a kind of hopped-up life, but I think she loved him and her children."

"Hopped-up?" Mai looked up from her notes. "What do you mean by that?"

"You know, fast-paced, on edge. Her husband wasn't doing as well financially in the past year as he had been. They had some financial worries with the kids in private school and the upper-level lifestyle."

Frances Phillips agreed. "They were doing okay, but things were tight for them. Marsha worked a lot of overtime trying to make up the difference. But we don't make the kind of money bond traders make. She'd been worried about that recently."

Peggy absorbed the information and wondered how it fit together. Certainly Gerald didn't have any money to offer Marsha. She supposed stress could push Marsha into an affair with him. "Did anything seem unusual the day she died?"

The five people opposite Mai, Peggy, and Sarah talked among themselves for a few seconds. Zeke Whitley finally spoke for them. "Now that you mention it, Marsha was supposed to be here for a staff meeting that day. She called in sick at the last minute. She never missed staff meetings."

"The weird thing was that I was running late that day," Mary Von Cannon said. "I saw her at the UPS store on Highway Two-eighteen in Mint Hill. I live out that way. She was carrying a large package inside. She seemed kind of nervous, looking around and just kind of agitated. After I got into the lab and found out she'd called in sick, I thought that was why. But now I wonder if it had something to do with her being killed."

"What makes you think that?" Mai asked. "People go to the UPS store all the time. Maybe she took the time off to catch up on some errands."

"Maybe." Mary shrugged. "I guess knowing she was killed just sent my imagination over the edge. Maybe I watch too much *CSI* on TV."

"Do you remember if there were any markings on the box?" Peggy asked.

"No. Not really." Mary thought back to that moment. "I remember she wasn't driving her car. It was an older pickup, kind of rusty."

"What kind of truck was it?" Mai questioned.

"It was an old green truck. Kind of in bad shape with some kind of tank in the back. Marsha drove a new red Honda when she didn't have the SUV. I couldn't believe she'd be caught dead in something like that." Mary put her hand to her mouth. "I didn't mean it that way."

"And you say this UPS store is in Mint Hill?" Mai continued writing.

"Yes. It's a little place in a print shop. I've sent things from there myself."

"One more question," Peggy added. "Have any of your recent projects involved any kind of aconite solutions?"

The five workers spoke together again in furious undertones. Zeke Whitley finally nodded. "As a matter of fact, they have. We've been working with an aconite compound that is —"

"I think that answers Dr. Lee's question, Mr. Whitley." Sarah James stared at Peggy. "Is there anything else?"

17

Anthurium

Botanical: *Anthurium*

Anthuriums were first planted under citrus trees. They were often destroyed during the harvesting of fruit, particularly tangerines. Interest in the unusual plant grew, and cultivation began in the 1940s. They are mostly grown in Hawaii and are heavily used by florists for their color and longevity.

"So we're two for two," Mai said as she and Peggy walked out of the bio lab. "We know Marsha knew Gerald Capshaw, since that was obviously his truck, right? And we know they were working with aconite. We don't have to know what they were doing with it, right?"

Peggy got in Mai's Subaru on the passenger side and looked back at the imposing structure of the lab. "It *could've* been his truck from the description, although without some kind of positive ID, there's no way to know for sure. There are a lot of green pickups in the area. As for the aconite, I don't know exactly where to go with that. I don't feel much better now than I did when we went in."

Mai climbed behind the steering wheel and fastened her seat belt. "Geez, Peggy. You could've let me feel good about this for a while before letting the truth get in the way."

"Sorry." Peggy smiled. "I can't see what's going on. It's plain as anything that these two people were involved in some way. It could've been romantic from Gerald's past record, even though Marsha's coworkers sounded as though they'd rather cut off their right arms than admit anything was wrong with Marsha's marriage."

"Where does that leave us?" Mai asked as she started out of the parking lot, heading back toward Charlotte.

"I think we should visit the UPS store in Mint Hill," Peggy told her. "When you do research and you hit a dead end, you always look for another way around the problem. That's what we have to do."

"Didn't you think it was weird that Mary Von Cannon thought seeing Marsha at the

UPS store had something to do with her death?"

"I don't know about weird, but maybe we should check her out. She may have been involved."

"You have a devious way of looking at things," Mai told her.

"That's why I'm here, I guess. The question is: Did the UPS shipment have anything to do with Marsha's death? And if so, what does Mary know that we don't know?"

They drove down Interstate 485 to Mint Hill, a small town on the east side of Mecklenburg County. Traffic was less here as there were more houses and fewer businesses than in Kannapolis. Mint Hill was more a bedroom community for Charlotte than a major player.

The UPS delivery store was located in a small print shop, just as Mary had said. It was easy to understand why Marsha was so visible, since the parking area was right on the road. A line of prickly lettuce caught Peggy's eye. Someone wasn't too handy with a Weed Eater. She was glad. She loved to see native plants thrive, especially in urban areas.

Mai and Peggy introduced themselves to the store manager and asked him about packages sent the day of Marsha's death.

The manager only had ten packages shipped through his location that day. Eight of them were sent by men. The other two were women, but neither was in Marsha's name.

Peggy looked at Mai. "Mary said she was running late for work. The shipment had to be in the morning."

The manager looked at his shipping book again. "One of those was sent at about nine thirty," he told them. "The shipper's name wasn't Hatley though, it was Goins. You know it's illegal to ship something with a fraudulent name."

"Where was that package sent?" Peggy asked him.

"It was sent to Badin. The name is Gerald Capshaw."

Mai showed the manager a picture of Marsha. He wasn't sure if it was her. "Thank you anyway, sir."

"I'm not in any kind of trouble am I?" he asked.

"Not at all," Peggy assured him. "Just for the record, what did Ms. Goins list as the contents of the package?"

"She listed it as fragile and took out extra insurance on it." He looked up from his computer. "I hope that helps."

Mai and Peggy thanked him and went

back outside where the hot, dry sun beat down on them. "Are you thinking what I'm thinking?" Mai asked Peggy.

"First we have to know that Marsha Goins is really Marsha Hatley," Peggy responded, picking up her cell phone as she got into the car. "I'm betting it's her maiden name."

"Should we drive out to that address in Badin?" Mai backed the car out of the parking lot.

"I don't know yet. Let's find out if this is the same person, and then ask Captain Rimer what he wants to do."

"He'll want someone in Badin to get it. All our legwork and someone else will get the credit for it."

"If it means we don't have to go all the way out there, that's okay with me." Peggy cut herself short as a police lab tech answered the phone. He transferred her to Harold's office, and she asked him to look at Marsha's file to see if Goins was her maiden name.

"Bingo!" She nodded at Mai then filled Harold in on what they'd discovered.

"Do you have any indication that Mrs. Hatley sent some kind of aconite poison to Mr. Capshaw?" Harold asked.

"Not for sure," she replied. "But it sounds

like it could be possible. She may have contaminated herself with the compound then sent it to Gerald, who did the same."

"But what would be the point?" Harold speculated on the subject.

"I guess we'll know if we find the package." Peggy waited for him to decide what they should do. "Do you want us to go to Badin and check it out?"

"No. Come back to the lab. The Captain will call the sheriff out there. They'll probably send out a biohazard team." Harold checked the address one more time with her. "I'll see you when you get back. Good work, Dr. Lee. Tell Ms. Sato I'm starting to feel her presence on the team."

Peggy thanked him and closed her phone before she related the conversation to Mai. "I guess we're on the right track."

"The only thing about it that doesn't make sense is the bodies were found so far apart. Someone had to move them after they were dead."

"That's a good point," Peggy agreed. "There's still apparent third-person intervention with the drownings. If they'd just poisoned themselves, it would be different. But in Marsha's case, someone drowned her and brought her home, possibly from outside the county. There must be another person out there who knows what happened."

They got back to the police lab after lunch. Harold was tied up in a meeting with Jonas and a few department heads. No one was sure when he'd be back.

Mai showed Peggy the negative water test results run by a few of the techs while they were gone. "Still no sign of that phytoplankton. It's like looking for a needle in a haystack."

Peggy glanced at her watch. "I'm going to take lunch and go over to the Potting Shed to see what's going on. Call me if you need me or if anything else breaks in the case."

"You already sound like you've been on the job for years."

"In a way, I guess I have been. What do you think John and I talked about when we weren't talking about plants?"

Peggy left Mai at the lab, contemplating which vending machine item she wanted for lunch. She rode through the heavy pedestrian lunch traffic to the Potting Shed. Seeing the big buildings empty out on the sunny day put a pang in her heart. She missed her little shop, talking about plants with her customers, and even listening to Sofia and Emil's stories over peach tea and a croissant. Her life had made an abrupt change as she took on this new and unfamiliar role of working with the police.

She parked her bike at the back of the shop and went inside, not sure what she expected to find so soon after hiring the contractor. He'd only been on the job since that morning. She hoped she didn't scare him away when she nosed around to see what he was doing.

She walked past the bags of fertilizer and potting soil. The back door was open, and music was coming from the shop. She crept inside, promising herself just a quick look then out for lunch. The poor man didn't need her looking over his shoulder.

But Peggy couldn't hold her tongue when she walked into the shop. "Wow!"

"Mrs. Lee!" The young man she'd hired to remodel the shop looked up from where he was working on the water feature area in the heart of the Potting Shed. "I wasn't expecting you back so soon. I ran into a few problems getting the old water lines to run to the center for the pond you want to put in, but I think it's going okay."

"Okay?" She couldn't believe her eyes. He'd already done more than she'd expected in a month. "You're very fast."

"I don't mess around, ma'am. But I do a good job. Being good at what you do doesn't mean you have to be slow."

"I never thought it did." She walked around the shop, admiring the new shelves he'd started and thinking how perfect it was going to be. "It's amazing how something terrible can turn into something wonderful if you let it."

"Yes, ma'am." He stood there looking like he wasn't sure what to do.

"Don't let me interrupt you. Everything looks great. I appreciate how hard you've worked already on it. We may be open again before the end of the summer after all."

"Thanks. If I have anything to do with it, you'll be up and running before you know it." He scratched his chin as if deciding whether or not to continue. The look on his face told Peggy he was nervous about what he said next, "Do you have anyone lined up to put in your water feature?"

"My associate knows someone he plans to ask," she answered. "Why?"

"It's something I've messed around with." He took off his hard hat and safety glasses. "I made my mama and grandma each a pond a couple of years back. I wanted to get into creating water features with land-scapers, but I couldn't seem to find the right person. You telling me about your plans made me think about it again."

Peggy wasn't sure what to say. She was embarrassed to admit it, but she couldn't even remember the young man's name. To cover for that oversight, she offered to buy him lunch at Anthony's next door. "That way, we can talk about it." *And I can look at your business card in my pocketbook without you knowing.*

"I guess that would be all right," he agreed. "I haven't had lunch. But I don't want you to think I'm taking up all your time."

"I don't think you have to worry about that." She smiled. "Let's go."

Anthony had done a makeover on his Caribbean restaurant a few months before. It was still colorful, but now there were touches of neon lighting. Flamingos danced on the walls and a large parrot greeted patrons by the door. He had a small fountain his customers threw coins into.

At the entrance, there were two anthurium plants that were bright red. Peggy picked off a few dead leaves and blooms. She'd put them in for Anthony and didn't want them to look bad.

"Peggy!" Anthony saw her and came across the crowded restaurant to greet her. "You haven't been here for so long, I almost forgot what you look like." He smiled at the young man with her. "And this is your new fellow, right? I remember. Welcome to Anthony's!" He shook the contractor's hand.

"It's good to see you, too!" Peggy hugged him back. "But this isn't Steve." She was embarrassed to think Anthony thought she was dating a man in his twenties. "This man is working on the shop for me. We came over for lunch, but I don't think you have an empty table."

"Business is good!" Anthony laughed loud and hearty, his black face glistening with steam from the kitchen. "But I can always find room for a friend. Come in the back with me. I was sitting down to lunch myself."

They talked about what had happened to the Potting Shed, Anthony empathizing with her dilemma and encouraging her inventiveness in remodeling the shop. "That's what everyone should do when they're faced with tragedy. Make it new!"

Peggy stole a glance at the contractor's business card in her pocketbook as he went to wash up for lunch. How humiliating not to be able to introduce him to Anthony by his name. She read his name, Jasper Wheeler, then slipped the card into her pocket. That's what came of doing too much and not paying enough attention to things.

"My red beans are primo today," Anthony told her. "And you won't want to miss dessert."

"I'll wait until Jasper comes back to order." She sat down in the middle of the busy kitchen with the back door open. People bustled around turning out spicy luncheon favorites, and she was afraid she might be in the way. But the talented ballet that Anthony and his workers put on kept things whirling around the kitchen without anyone even looking her way.

"Peggy? Is that you?" Stephanie smiled and looked around the kitchen. "I thought I saw you head back this way. I was on my way in for lunch. You have the best seat in the house."

Peggy wanted to send the girl away, but every polite southern bone in her body screamed in outrage. "Why don't you join us?"

"Us?" Stephanie looked around. "Are you having lunch with someone?"

Jasper returned to the table at that moment and nodded at Stephanie before he sat down. "Ma'am."

"I see you *aren't* alone." Stephanie smiled and stared at Jasper as though he were the last man on earth.

"Stephanie, this is Jasper." Peggy introduced them but privately swore to herself that if Jasper started acting like Paul and Nathan, he was *never* going to build her water feature. "Jasper, this is Stephanie."

Jasper shook Stephanie's hand in a disinterested kind of way then turned to Peggy and began talking about his ideas for the large garden pond she wanted to put in her shop.

Anthony came to bring them mango-flavored tea and their first course, a lively fruit salad with spicy chutney. He introduced himself to Stephanie and Jasper but couldn't sit down with them.

Peggy was amazed when Jasper completely ignored Stephanie and focused in on highlighting his qualifications and everything else he could think of to win her over. She wasn't upset by his promotional efforts, but she was surprised when he continued to try to convince her that he was right for the job.

Stephanie did everything *she* could, including butting into the conversation, to tell them about her shopping excursion that morning and standing up a few times on the pretext of straightening her bright green tank top and short shorts.

The man had to be made of stone, Peggy

thought as he glanced at Stephanie then turned back to continue his pitch to create the water garden. Paul would certainly be panting on the table by this time. If staying focused on what you were doing was a reason to hire this young man, she'd certainly have to discuss it with Sam.

"Will you consider me for the job?" Jasper had the most sincere look on his tanned face.

She hated to put him off, but she wouldn't do that to Sam. "I'll have to talk it over with my associate. Please don't feel bad about it. You have the job in my book. But I always discuss this kind of thing with Sam before I do it."

They were just finishing their salad, and Jasper nodded. "I understand. I'll be happy to talk with him, too." He glanced up at the big clock on the kitchen wall. "I guess I better get back to work. Thanks for lunch."

Peggy shook her head when he took out his wallet. "Put that away. Lunch is on me. Are you sure you won't stay for the main course?"

"I have a certain amount of work I expect to get done each day. I still have a few hours to go." He smiled at Peggy and Stephanie. "It was nice having lunch with you ladies."

Stephanie huffed as he walked away.

"What's with him?"

"What do you mean?"

"I mean, why did he leave? He didn't pay much attention to anything, did he?"

By anything, read Stephanie's attempts to draw him in like she did Steve and Paul, Peggy thought. But she was stuck with the girl for lunch, and she knew she was going to have to make the best of it. "Have you had much class disruption with everything Professor Sargent has been through the past few days?"

"Not too much." The girl shrugged. "I think the professor should be a little more discreet with her affairs. That was embarrassing for the class."

"She has a right to live her life outside of class," Peggy defended. "Besides, she didn't do anything wrong. She was simply in the wrong place at the wrong time."

"I've dated married men before, Peggy. You can't let them get to you like Ruth did." Stephanie laughed lightly. "You have to keep the upper hand."

"I'm sure you're very experienced."

"I am. There's more to life than underwater forensics, you know."

Peggy wished she could get away as easily as Jasper, but she didn't want to hurt Anthony's feelings. Stephanie told her about

317

several of her adventures with married men. Peggy didn't know if she believed the girl or not, and she didn't really care. It was becoming a matter of urgency that she get away from Stephanie.

Finally her phone rang. "Excuse me. I'll have to take this." She'd already decided she was using this call as a way of escape when she saw the police lab phone number come up on her display.

Stephanie immediately switched audiences, ensnaring Anthony as she asked him about his famous salad dressing. Peggy rolled her eyes. *Better him than me.*

"Peggy? It's Mai. I wanted to tell you the sheriff in Stanly County found the address where the package was delivered. He called in a hazmat team, and they're looking for any clues to the aconite. But the address it was delivered to is an abandoned building in Badin. They're also bringing Gerald's wife in for questioning."

"That hardly makes any sense." Peggy watched the traffic outside Anthony's back door. "Benita probably wasn't involved. Whatever was going on seems to be between Marsha Hatley and Gerald. Have they found any evidence that links them together yet?"

"Not that I've heard," Mai responded.

"That's all that's new, but I thought you'd like to know."

"I appreciate it." Peggy made a firm decision to turn around and tell Stephanie she couldn't stay. Goodness knows she'd gone beyond the bounds of polite conversation. She said good-bye to Mai then turned around to find the kitchen table empty.

On one hand, it was a relief. On the other, it had to be one of the rudest events of her life. She put her cell phone away, kissed Anthony's cheek, and told him she had to go. He packed her a small bag full of leftovers and told her to come back sooner next time.

"You know I would if I could." She laughed. "I couldn't eat like this all the time, or I wouldn't fit on my bike."

"Who's that friend of yours? She was quite the looker."

"She's a friend of a friend," she explained. "Did you see her leave?"

"She sneaked off while you were on the phone." He shrugged. "A girl like that doesn't have much time for women, you know what I mean?"

Peggy humored him by pretending she knew what he was talking about and then left the café and headed back to the Potting Shed. It surprised her to see Sam there, talking to Jasper as he worked. "There you are. I suppose you've already introduced yourself."

"You know me." Sam shrugged his broad shoulders in his green Potting Shed T-shirt. "Actually, I know Jasper from school. Sort of."

"What he means is that I dropped out last year," Jasper said. "I needed to make some money. Besides, this is what I want to do. They don't teach this in college."

Peggy didn't argue the point. There was room in the world for all kinds of people. "Maybe we should tell Sam about your idea."

"Been there, done that." Sam grinned. "Get out more, Peggy."

She laughed. "I forgot. You can't spend more than five minutes with someone without knowing their life history." She smiled at Jasper, whose face was bright pink. "So what do you think of Jasper doing the water garden?"

"I think it's a great idea," Sam enthused, surprising her.

"What about the other landscaper you thought we should use?" She waited, but there was no response. She glanced over at her friend. "Sam?"

"Oh. Sorry." He shifted his focus back to

her. "He was just a suggestion. I think I could work with Jasper. I mean, Jasper and I would be good together. Gardening. Doing the water garden."

Peggy decided to ignore his sudden inability to speak. If Sam felt like Jasper would do a good job, she trusted his judgment. "Okay. We'll do it. Jasper, you're on!"

Jasper smiled at Sam then at her. "Thank you, Peggy. You won't be sorry. People will come from all over when this is finished."

18

Hydrangea
Botanical: *Hydrangea macrophylla*
Cultivated since 1730 in England, hydrangeas were brought to the West from Japan, where they were treasured for the beauty of the flowers and also used as an herb that was made into a sweet tea. Lacecap hydrangea has grown to be one of the most popular forms of the species, replacing even the *serrata* that came from Japan. Their remarkable range of colors and delicacy has captivated growers for generations.

"That seems like too much coincidence to me," Steve said that night over dinner. "Both people were poisoned by aconite, and Marsha Hatley worked with it. Do you think she sent some to Gerald Capshaw?"

Peggy passed the salad. "It would make sense. My question would be why?"

"Maybe she wanted to poison him and accidentally poisoned herself."

"See, that's the thing. Neither one of them died from it. If they hadn't been in the water somewhere, they'd both still be alive. This wasn't a fatal poisoning, except for the circumstances."

"But at least you know now that they knew each other." Steve passed the potatoes. "Now all you have to find out is who killed both of them."

Peggy sighed. This was the first dinner they'd had alone in days. She really wanted to talk about something else besides dead people and poison. But Steve was keen to learn all the details about the case. "I think I'll leave that to the police. I helped get them this far. They need to figure out the rest on their own."

Steve raised his glass of red wine. "In that case, congratulations! You've solved your first forensic case."

She lightly touched her glass to his. "Thanks. Now can we talk about something else?"

"Sure. Would you like to hear about the poodle I took care of today? There was a parrot, too, although that didn't go so well."

"As much as I enjoy your animal stories, I was thinking we could talk about something romantic."

"You mean something not job-related?" He grinned, brown eyes shining. "We've been together too long for that. Now all that's left is our jobs and household-related conversation. Did you notice how many times in the past two weeks I've made dinner?"

"Is that a hint?"

"You could say so. I think, barring any emergency, we should leave dinner to you tomorrow night."

"Okay. I can always get day-old croissants from the Kozy Kettle."

"I'm afraid that doesn't qualify as real food. Maybe we need some guidelines here."

Peggy got up and walked around the table, leaning over to kiss him. "What kind of guidelines did you have in mind?"

"That wasn't fair. I was talking about food." He got up and pulled her close. "But forget the food for now. You've reminded me of other things we could be doing. I can't believe we're actually alone tonight."

"I know what you mean. And if you'll notice, Shakespeare is still outside chasing fireflies. It's really just me and you."

Steve kissed her a moment before his cell phone rang. "It's Mrs. Malone's cat. I was afraid this was going to happen. She was having a hard time with the insulin shots at the office today."

"Cats can be diabetic?"

"I'm afraid so. Let me take this call. Maybe I can talk her through it."

Peggy went down into the basement and worked with her underwater potato plants while Steve talked to his patient's owner. When he came down after her, she could tell by the look on his face that it wasn't good news.

"Sorry, Peggy. I'm going to have to go over there. The cat has to have his shot. They live over on Monroe Road. I'll get back as soon as I can. Unless you'd like to ride over there with me."

"That's okay. I think I'll take a bath and catch up on some email."

He raised one brow. "Not at the same time I hope."

"Probably not. But if the lights flicker . . ."

"Don't even say that!" He held her close and kissed her. "You're kind of important to me."

"Even though we've reached the stage of only talking about our jobs?"

"As long as I'm talking to you, I don't care what we talk about." He kissed her again. "Hold that thought. I'll be back soon."

Peggy smiled as he went back upstairs.

She hummed little fragments of songs she remembered as she finished up in the basement and called Shakespeare in for the night. There was a cicada singing from one of the old oak trees behind the house. With the warm, humid weather she could almost close her eyes and imagine standing on her front porch when she was a child.

It was odd how much she'd thought about her childhood lately. It probably came from seeing her parents recently and realizing if she ever saw her home again, it would belong to someone else.

She wasn't particularly a sentimental person in that way, but that cicada sounded sweet to her ears. How many times had she stood and listened to the same sound when she was growing up? It was funny how things happened. If she'd never met John, she would never have come to Charlotte. She might have spent her entire life in Charleston as her parents and grandparents had before her. And if she'd never come to Charlotte, she would never have met Steve.

Peggy shook her head. She needed to take a shower instead of a bath and get out of her head and into the cyber world. She'd been so busy the last few days she hadn't had time to converse with her friends and colleagues around the world.

Shakespeare barely opened one eye from his place on the bed as she walked past him from the shower still clad in her terry robe. She sat down at her computer and began sorting her email into various folders, except for the ones she decided to answer right away.

There were plenty of spam emails offering banking services and chances to win the lottery. There was even a cleverly disguised virus in an email that said she wouldn't receive a package from UPS unless she clicked on the link. She laughed at that one. How dumb did spammers think people were?

There were several older emails from Nightflyer that she opened with a guilty conscience. She hadn't meant to ignore him. He'd been there for her too many times. She hated to think of him out there somewhere, alone and hunted. She wished there was something she could do to help him, but she didn't even know where he was. Or who he was, for that matter.

She wasn't willing to give up Steve or her life as she knew it to go away with him as he'd suggested. It wasn't a difficult decision to make. She loved her life, the Potting Shed, and her botanical work, and she loved Steve. There was never any real competition between the two men.

Putting that aspect of her life out of her mind, Peggy searched through all the botanical journals she could find to document other cases of aconite poisoning. If the package Marsha sent to Gerald was compromised in any way, they both could have been affected by the poison, especially if it was a particularly virulent strain created by the bio lab. They could have been rendered unconscious fairly quickly after exposure.

But that didn't account for the placement of the bodies. If they were affected by the aconite, they should have been wherever that happened, not miles apart. Even if it was fast-acting, Marsha should have been at the UPS store and Gerald should have been wherever he received the package. Of course in that case, a string of UPS carriers would have been affected, too.

Shakespeare barked his friendly warning. Peggy knew Steve was back from his emergency.

"Are you still up?" Steve asked unnecessarily since she was sitting at her desk. "You couldn't sleep without me, could you?"

"You know me." She shrugged as she turned off her computer. "I have a hard time sleeping with or without you."

He frowned. "My pride is slightly

wounded."

She got up and put her arms around him. "Anything I can do, besides talking about either one of our jobs, that would make it better?"

"We could work on that for a while." He smiled. "It's not *that* late yet."

Peggy heard about Ruth's arrest when she turned on TV the next morning. She put two bagels in the toaster as she watched her friend leave her apartment escorted by Charlotte police and Stanly County deputies. "I can't believe it."

"What?" Steve asked as he poured both of them a glass of grape juice. He looked at the TV screen. "Is that your forensic friend?"

"I'm afraid so." Peggy took out her cell phone and dialed Hunter's phone number. "Ruth may have a lawyer, but if not, Hunter might be able to help."

"Why are you so sure she's innocent?"

"I think the whole thing is circumstance." Peggy closed her phone after being forced to leave voice mail for Hunter. "She pulled up the body. She'd dated him for a while. She knows about underwater forensics. But none of those things make her a killer."

"You have to admit, it makes the beginning of a case against her." Steve took the bagels out of the toaster.

Peggy rummaged through the refrigerator and finally found some cream cheese. "Then it could make a case against me, too. I was there when she brought the body out. I know about aconite poisoning."

"But you didn't date the man," he reminded her. "Unless there's something you want to tell me."

She focused on him, wrenching her brain away from the police arresting Ruth, and laughed. "No. Even if I *had* slept with Gerald, that would be something between me and John, since it would've been before I knew you."

"Okay. I'm officially straight on that now. But you still have to admit there's something fishy, if you'll pardon the pun, about the circumstances. I'd arrest her, too, if I were a cop."

Peggy tapped her foot impatiently on the hardwood floor. "You wouldn't be a very good cop then. It's a good thing you're a vet and you don't have to figure these things out."

Steve looked at her across the table. "Ouch. I'm sorry your friend looks guilty. But I get to have an opinion, too, right?"

She picked up her bagel then put it back on the plate, too anxious to eat. "I'm sorry.

Of course you get to have an opinion. I know it looks bad for Ruth, but I've been right about these things a time or two before. I think I'm right now."

Steve ate his bagel and drank the rest of his juice as Peggy tried to reach Hunter again on her cell phone. "I hope you're right. I know you like her. I'm sure it's all coincidence."

Peggy left another voice mail for Hunter then smiled at Steve. "Are you patronizing me by any chance?"

"No! Not at all. I don't have enough time for that this morning." He put his plate and glass in the dishwasher. "Are we having dinner tonight?"

"I suppose that all depends," she replied tartly. "You don't have to agree with me, but you don't have to sound like you're humoring me by not agreeing with me."

He kissed the top of her head. "I'm ten minutes late for a Siamese tubal ligation or I swear I'd either stay and argue with you or totally agree with everything you just said."

She laughed. "Get out of here while you still can! That Siamese won't wait forever."

"I'll call you later. Love you."

"I love you, too. Have a better day."

Peggy put her bagel in a zippy bag and stuck it in the refrigerator. She couldn't sit around and do nothing. There had to be some way to prove Ruth was innocent. She took Shakespeare out for his walk then pulled out her bike and got ready to ride into Charlotte traffic.

"Yoo-hoo!" Her neighbor, Clarice, seemed to be waiting for her by the fence that divided their properties. "I've been looking for you, Peggy. With John gone, bless his soul, I don't have anyone to ask gardening questions, but I was thinking you might know this anyway."

Peggy's teeth were already on edge, but she swallowed the angry retort that sprang to her lips and leaned her bike against the garage. Clarice and her dog had been a thorn in her side since they moved next door. "What is it?"

"It's this big hydrangea. I just despair of it ever blooming again. I mean, it has a few blooms on it, but look at it, Peggy. I think it must be sick."

The two women walked behind the garage and looked at the large panicle hydrangea. Its leaves were green and healthy, but Clarice was right: there were very few of the lacy white clusters of flowers that should have been there.

Peggy ignored her leopard skin-clad neighbor and walked around the bush. It was easily six feet tall and about that far around. "I think your problem is the shade. Hydrangeas will tolerate some shade, but this bush may be in complete shade most of the day."

Clarice wrung her hands together and made a tortured face that almost made Peggy laugh. "Well, what can I do? I mean, I can't let it sit here and not bloom."

"That's true, I suppose. It seems to me you have one of two choices."

"Oh no! I've never been good at multiple choice. Help me, Peggy. Just tell me what to do."

Peggy considered the matter. Clarice was right. She wasn't John. John would have offered to dig the bush up and replant it in a sunnier spot. She wasn't so good-hearted or ready to break her back to save Clarice's flowers. "I can have a couple of people from the Potting Shed move it for you. Maybe over there by the birdbath."

"That would be heavenly! When can they do it?"

"I'll have to check with them and see what their schedule is. It shouldn't take more than a couple of hours. They work pretty fast."

"Wonderful! Do you think they can come today?"

"Clarice, it's midsummer. They can't move the hydrangea right now. You'll have to wait for cooler weather. It will die if you try to move it now."

"But it's not flowering. And if you move it this fall, it will be too late for it to bloom until next year."

Peggy prayed for strength and patience. "That's true. But think how much happier you'll be next year when it blooms again."

Clarice thought about it. "You're right! Just let me know when they can do it. I'm sure it will be fine."

"I'll do that."

"John would've moved the hydrangea himself."

"I know. See you later, Clarice."

Finally on Queens Road heading for Center City with the rest of the traffic, Peggy considered if Clarice realized the Potting Shed would also send her a bill for Sam and Keeley's services. Oh well. If she didn't like it, maybe she wouldn't ask them to do any yard work again, and that would be fine with her.

Sam wouldn't like that attitude. She smiled thinking about him and Jasper. There was something going on there. She hoped it would be something good. Sam was such a great person. He deserved someone really special.

Peggy arrived at the police lab almost choked by exhaust held down close to the ground by the hot, muggy weather. It was like this every summer. No cool ocean breezes to chase away the doldrums like in Charleston. Charlotte had too many cars and not enough wind to clean up the city. That's why it had so many bad air quality days during the summer. And buses! Diesel engines shouldn't have been allowed in the South!

She hurried into the air-conditioned building, flashing her ID badge. Harold and Mai were in the conference room going over some notes. "They arrested Ruth Sargent."

Harold nodded slowly. "Yes. They did. Did you miss your cup of tea this morning? I think you might be a little behind."

"The evidence is fairly solid against her, Peggy," Mai said.

"Except for those potholes the size of the ones on Sharon Amity Road!" Peggy sat down at the long table with them. "I don't see how the police could arrest her on the little bit they have."

"Because we can probably get her to confess." Jonas Rimer joined them with Al at his side. "You've done a good job, Peggy. Let us do the rest."

"But you aren't doing it," she argued. "There's more to this story. Have you interviewed the team who worked with Marsha Hatley? Any of them had access to the aconite and could have used it on Marsha and Gerald."

"There's this little thing I like to call motive," Jonas taunted. "We all know Dr. Sargent was insanely jealous of Gerald Capshaw's other women. When she saw him with Marsha Hatley, she went insane."

"And Marsha let her have some of the aconite she'd obviously smuggled out of the lab so Ruth would have something to poison her with." Peggy stared at him, waiting for his answer.

"The aconite material was something she lucked out on," Al said. "When she realized what was going on, she took advantage of it. She poisoned them enough that they couldn't fight back then loaded them up in her van and dropped them in a lake somewhere."

"That doesn't make any sense," Peggy said. "There are too many variables in that equation. We wouldn't have half of the modern conveniences we have today if scientists had theories like that."

"Just for kicks," Jonas said, "what do *you* think happened?"

"I don't know." Peggy looked at Mai and Harold, but they were not playing on the same side. "But that's just the point. The little bit of forensic evidence we have doesn't tell us who's responsible. It could be anyone from Marsha's husband to Gerald's wife. Or what about another of Gerald's lovers?"

"For all the years you were married to John," Al shook his head, "you'd think you'd know how a police investigation works. Believe me, Dr. Sargent will confess. She doesn't want to live with this burden any longer than she has to. We'll know in a few hours exactly what happened and where the victims were drowned."

There wasn't much Peggy could say to that. She couldn't continue to argue that Ruth was innocent without some proof of her own. Jonas and Al would only listen at that point.

Her cell phone rang, and she excused herself from the room. It was Hunter finally calling her back. "I hope Dr. Sargent has some money," Hunter complained. "I don't mind taking these lost causes if I get paid."

"I think you got paid pretty well on my last lost cause," Peggy reminded her. "I'm sure Ruth has some money. The main thing right now is to get her legal counsel before she says something she doesn't want to say. The police plan to coerce a confession from her."

The outrage in Hunter's voice was obvious as she said, "You mean with the rubber hoses and shock treatments? That's inhuman!"

"That's not what I meant." Peggy wondered where Hunter got her outrageous imagination. "But Ruth *does* need help. She may already have an attorney. I'm not sure."

"Don't worry, Peggy! I'll take care of her."

Peggy closed her cell phone, not sure if she was more worried about Ruth or Hunter.

"Whose side are you on anyway?" Jonas's voice boomed from behind her.

19

Potato

Botanical: *Solanum tuberosum*

No matter how you spell it, the potato has had a colorful past. As a member of the famed nightshade family, it was distrusted by Europeans, who would rather starve than eat it. The plant originated in South America, where the natives liked its tough, durable growth. It was cultivated there more than 7,000 years ago. It was brought to Europe in the late fifteen hundreds and fed to the poor and hospital patients until its usage caught on with the upper classes as well.

Peggy raised her chin high. "I didn't say anything that isn't true. Ruth is entitled to the best defense possible. There's that little thing called the Constitution. Maybe you remember it."

Jonas squared off with her. "If you're go-

339

ing to work with us, you can't give out advice to the legally challenged about ongoing investigations. That's part of the job."

"I wasn't talking to Ruth," she defended. "I was talking to a friend about the situation. That friend happens to be an attorney."

"Not that it's necessary," Al added. "Dr. Sargent's lawyer was there five minutes after we brought her in."

"Then justice is served, isn't it?" Peggy refused to back down from her belief that what she did was right.

"I think we may be finished with your services for now, Peggy." Jonas nodded to Harold who nodded in return. "Dr. Ramsey will show you how to put in for your pay voucher from the department. Thanks for your work."

"Thank you. I'm glad it's over."

Mai sat with her while Jonas and Al stayed in the conference room waiting for Harold to dismiss her. "It's okay. They'll want you back again. The forensics on this case are mostly done anyway, at least your part."

Peggy patted the younger woman's hand. "You don't have to worry, sweetie. My feelings aren't hurt. I knew the job would be like this. In fact, I counted on it. I didn't want to be here full-time."

"Well, I'm glad you didn't let them push

you around anyway." Mai glanced up at Harold, who was focused on his paperwork. "Don't worry about your friend. If she's innocent, she won't have anything to hide."

"I wish it were that simple." Peggy stopped speaking as Harold came up to hand her a piece of paper.

"Drop this off at the main office. They'll mail you a check." He adjusted his glasses and looked away from the conference room as though Jonas could read his lips. "Good work, Dr. Lee. They wouldn't even have known about the aconite without you. I'm sorry I can't give you more recognition than that."

"I wasn't even expecting that." Peggy smiled as she put her pay voucher into her pocketbook. "Thank you, Dr. Ramsey. It was . . . different . . . working with you."

"I'll see you next time then. Until later, Dr. Lee."

Mai walked with Peggy to the front entrance. "I'm sorry. I have to ask for your ID badge, since you're only a contract worker. I'm embarrassed, but they told me to do it."

Peggy took the badge off and handed it to her. "Not at all. I expected as much. So tell me, while you're feeling bad, how's it going with Paul?"

"I can't believe you'd take advantage of me feeling guilty." Mai shook her head, but she was smiling. "But as far as Paul is concerned, I think we've both grown up a little. We'll see."

"Obviously you weren't feeling bad enough," Peggy joked. "I guess I should've taken it a little harder, and maybe you would've given me a little more information."

"You should ask Paul," Mai retorted. "I'm sure he'll be glad to give you all the details."

"Yeah. Right." Peggy waved. "I'll talk to you later. Thank you."

Not wanting to go home, not wanting to admit how much it really hurt her feelings to be turned out on the street when she didn't feel the investigation was over, Peggy rode to the Potting Shed. She'd hoped to find some solace there but forgot that it was not her sanctuary right now.

Jasper was working on the repairs and remodeling in the shop. Everything that wasn't damaged by water was covered in tarps to keep it from getting dusty. Peggy could tell he'd started work on the pond area, but that was it. Even her rocker was in storage until the work was finished. She didn't want to bother Jasper; he seemed very intent on what he was doing. She went back out through the back door and sat on the steps.

She sat there for a few minutes watching the traffic go by on College Street. The smell of frying onions and peppers wafted out from the restaurants around her as well as from the venders on Tryon Street getting ready for the lunch crowd.

Her cell phone rang. It was Hunter, complaining that Ruth already had an attorney. "You should've called me sooner," she said. "I bet that guy will get a fat paycheck out of this."

"Sorry," Peggy replied. "I called you as soon as I knew she'd been arrested. Maybe next time."

"That's okay," Hunter reassured her. "I gave out some cards while I was at the jail and the police station. Maybe it will bring in some business."

"I hope so, dear."

"Are you okay, Peggy? I didn't mean to go off on you. It's not your fault. You try to have friends with legal problems as often as you can."

Peggy laughed. "I'm fine. Just a little out of sorts, I suppose. They laid me off this morning. It's not like I didn't expect it. I guess I was surprised anyway. And the Potting Shed is a mess. I don't have any place to hide out for a few hours before I go home."

"You're in luck," Hunter announced. "I'm looking for someone to hide out with for a few hours. Let's hide out together."

"That sounds good. Thanks. Where shall we hide?"

Hunter suggested Founders Hall, but Peggy wasn't in the mood to see Smith & Hawken. Peggy suggested the library, but Hunter didn't want to go there because she owed fines on a book.

They compromised on going to the botanical garden at UNCC. Hunter was close by and told Peggy she would pick her up for the trip that would take more than an hour on the bike.

Peggy waited at the Potting Shed after chaining her bike to the Dumpster behind the building. She would have put it inside, but she didn't want to bother Jasper. She was anxious to get the shop back up and running. It felt like a part of her was missing with it closed. It represented a sort of independent security to her, even though the business was far from feeling secure at the moment.

She made up her mind to begin designing the invitations she planned to send out for the shop's grand reopening. Maybe she could hold it in the evening and use candles to illuminate the new pond. She felt sure the water feature would be a hit with her customers and hoped it would lead her in another direction that would keep the shop successful.

Hunter swung by, and Peggy climbed in her car. They made small talk as they traveled down congested North Tryon Street, past whatever festival was being celebrated on the streets that day, to Highway 49. Peggy was glad of the company and the chance to talk about inconsequential things like new summer dresses and nightclubs in the city. Hunter talked nonstop about her new boyfriend (she'd dumped the jock from UNCC) and about her parents' upcoming fortieth anniversary.

"Sam didn't say a word to me about that."

"That's not surprising. He's having some issues with them right now." Hunter looked at her after negotiating a turn. "You must know he wants to work full-time for the Potting Shed and give up the idea of being a doctor."

"I know he's been having problems with school." Peggy was excited for a moment, then clamped down on that feeling. It wasn't what was best for Sam. He was too bright to work as a landscaper his whole life. "Maybe I should fire him."

Hunter laughed. "That might help. Or he might go out and start his own company. Honestly, I don't know what the big deal is. We need brilliant landscapers as much as we need brilliant surgeons. And from my point of view, with all of my credit cards maxed out and one box of Oodles of Noodles in my cabinet, he might be better off doing something where he can make some money."

"Eventually, you'll make money, too," Peggy reassured her. "I know your parents must be upset. Maybe I could talk to him."

"If you want to." Hunter shrugged as she pulled the car into the UNCC parking lot. "What's going on out here?"

There was a large group of students standing around a man at a podium. Peggy saw the Clean Water America sign and recognized it from emails she'd received. "It's a group of environmentalists who are trying to get the government to pass stricter legislation to protect waterways."

"It must be popular." Hunter got out and locked the car doors. "Nothing could have brought me on campus over the summer unless it was popular."

"Fortunately, I think clean water is very trendy right now." Peggy smiled at her. "I hope it catches on all over."

"That's because you worry about things like that. As long as you buy bottled water, you don't have to think about it."

Peggy saw Stephanie in the crowd and urged Hunter to the left of the group to avoid meeting the girl again. "I didn't know there was anyone you didn't like," Hunter remarked. "She must really be terrible."

"I've only met her a few times." Peggy shuddered. "It was enough for me."

Luck wasn't with her. Stephanie saw her, yelled her name, and ran after her. "Peggy! I'm surprised to see you out here! Well, maybe not. I guess Ruth would've been here if she could. I hope she's okay."

"I hope so, too." Peggy saw Stephanie look at Hunter expectantly and realized she was falling behind on her good manners. "Excuse me. Stephanie, this is Hunter Ollson. Hunter, this is Stephanie Nichols."

"Glad to meet you." Stephanie kept staring at Hunter.

"You, too." Hunter smiled. "Peggy and I came out here for some quiet time in the arboretum. Maybe you'd like to join us."

Peggy was making as many unhappy expressions as she could, trying to tell Hunter she didn't want the other girl with them. But it was too late. Stephanie accepted the invitation and fell in step beside them.

"What kind of quiet time are you looking for?" Stephanie walked between them.

"You know," Hunter shrugged, "the kind that can get really quiet."

Stephanie giggled. "You are super funny, Hunter! You should do stand-up. You don't, do you?"

"In a way. I'm a lawyer."

"That's cool. Some of my best friends are prelaw."

"What are you studying?" Hunter asked as they walked into the arboretum.

"I was prelaw for a while," Stephanie explained. "I'm taking some forensic classes now. I'm not sure where I'm going to end up."

Peggy listened to them talk as she studied a delicate anthurium. The arboretum was as beautiful as ever, but she remembered it being a little quieter. Maybe she was wrong to sit and brood over what had happened. That was part of the reason she didn't want to go home.

She had to find some way to prove Ruth was innocent. She had previous experience in solving investigations working from outside the police department. There was no reason to think she couldn't do the same thing again.

The one thing about solving problems outside the box was not having to prove someone was guilty. Maybe she was equally as fettered trying to prove someone was innocent, but it didn't seem that way to her.

"Have you heard from Dr. Sargent today?" Peggy asked Stephanie.

"No. I saw she was arrested. We're having a bail raising party for her later. Otherwise, I don't know anything more about it. I hope she's okay."

"She has legal counsel," Hunter added. "I've never heard of him, but that doesn't mean he's not good. I know the police still haven't finished figuring out what all they're going to charge her with. It's going to be a tough fight. Multiple homicides are really bad."

"What about that old heat of passion defense?" Stephanie walked through a display of *Phormium* and dwarf buddleja.

"That isn't used much in this country anymore." Hunter smelled some lavender plants. "Even when it was, it was used more for husbands coming home and finding their wives in bed with other men."

"Yeah. I guess that's the way I've seen it in old movies." Stephanie shrugged and continued down the path between plants.

"I think we have to focus on some irregularities in the case," Peggy said. "We still aren't sure where they died or how, besides the fact that they both drowned. There's no hard evidence to convict Ruth of anything besides being in Badin when they found Gerald's body, and considering he didn't drown in Badin Lake, that hardly seems to matter."

"She *was* at the scene of both homicides," Hunter reminded her.

"Yes," Peggy agreed. "But I called her to Marsha Hatley's house, and the EMS asked her to help out with Gerald's body. That's not exactly the same as finding either body."

"You need to tell Dr. Sargent's lawyer this stuff," Stephanie said. "He should know about the weak spots in the case so he can help her."

"I'm not able to communicate with him because I worked on the case." Peggy looked at a display of potatoes growing with vegetables. "I know the forensic work is sound. I don't want to mess that up."

Stephanie shrugged. "I could tell him."

Hunter shook her head, the sunlight from the roof gilding her golden tresses. "That would be hearsay. It wouldn't be admissible."

"Like I said," Stephanie breezed by, "I only had a little prelaw."

350

"I think I need to focus on how Marsha met Gerald in the first place," Peggy said more to herself than to them. "They may have been lovers. Goodness knows he had plenty of them. That would be more difficult to discover. But if the people Marsha worked with are right, and she wasn't having an affair with Gerald, how did they meet?"

"I don't know," Hunter replied. "I'm not sure how you'd find out."

"Not from Gerald's wife." Stephanie stepped around some garden hoses on the floor. "She's a witch. I'm sure she wants to see them string up Dr. Sargent."

Peggy didn't comment. She'd been married too long not to sympathize with Benita. No woman would want to find out her husband was always looking for his next lover.

But she was sure the answer to her questions was there, possibly in the past. She walked through the rest of the arboretum with the two young women, not changing the conversation again. She half listened to them talk about the next American Idol and a new shoe guru who was capturing attention in New York.

Stephanie seemed to be a little less erratic today, maybe because there were no men around to impress. Peggy and Hunter left her on campus after picking up information from Clean Water America.

They went to the Melting Pot for lunch, which took much longer than Peggy had anticipated. She didn't get back to the Potting Shed until three p.m. Sam and Keeley were there talking to Jasper when they drove up. Hunter parked her car and came inside to see what the improvements were going to look like.

Sam seemed almost as excited about the project as Jasper. Already there was an indentation in the floor where the water feature would be. Sam explained about all the water plants they could use while Jasper told them all about the waterfall and circular base of the pond area.

Peggy listened, excited by their enthusiasm as well as her own. Keeley had questions about what would be entailed in putting water features into their landscaping projects. Jasper and Sam tried to reassure her at the same time, laughing like old friends as they disentangled their words.

"It sounds wonderful," Peggy said when they all looked at her.

"I'm sorry." Sam grinned. "I didn't mean to leave you out."

"You didn't," she replied. "You know

exactly what I want. I'm very impressed."

"I finished your living plant shelves today." Jasper moved toward the new shelves to the right. "See? They're water resistant in case of spills or leaks. And every upper shelf has a plant light underneath it for the plants on the next shelf. I figured you wouldn't want plants on the floor where no one would notice them, so I was thinking you could use the bottom shelves for plant stuff."

"Like fertilizer, those cute little plant stakes, that kind of stuff," Keeley filled in. She shrugged self-consciously when everyone looked at her. "What? Sam works outside, too, and he's getting to help plan stuff."

"That's fine." Peggy laughed. "What you said is exactly what I was thinking."

"I think it's going to be fabulous!" Hunter enthused. "I'll bet Smith & Hawken will have to fold up and move to Matthews once people see this."

"I've decided it doesn't matter," Peggy told her. "We're a very different kind of store, and we aren't competing with them on the same playing field."

"That's very lofty of you," Sam said. "Where's the real Peggy who wanted to kick the S & H manager's butt?"

Everyone laughed, including Peggy, even

353

as she informed them, "I mean it. There won't be any more badmouthing those people from me, bless their hearts."

"And you know what that means," Keeley said. "My mom told me years ago that you have to pity the people who deserve 'bless their heart' after their names. It's probably the way genteel southern women learned to swear when they were babies."

"I'll keep that in mind," Sam said. "I think Mrs. Ernest blessed my heart the other day after I planted asters instead of zinnias in her garden."

"You're doomed now," Hunter told him. "Maybe that's why Mom and Dad have given up on you."

Her words sobered the moment. Sam looked angry, and Hunter, realizing what she'd said, squirmed. "You know I didn't mean it like that."

"It doesn't matter." Sam glanced at Peggy. "It's not really a secret. You know I've been having some second thoughts about the whole medical thing. I'm thinking about not going back this fall."

"Sam, are you sure that's what you want to do?" Peggy asked.

"I like to work with the plants and design," he said. "Maybe I'm not cut out to be a doctor. Not everyone is. I'm a pretty good landscaper. I think I could be a better one with some training."

"I think you're good right now," Keeley told him. "But this could be a long-term decision. Are you sure you're going to want to do this in twenty years?"

"Who knows?" Sam asked. "I can always go back to school. Look at Peggy. She taught all those years. Now she has the shop and dead people to figure out. Most people don't spend a lifetime doing the same thing anymore. Right now, this is what I want to do."

Peggy didn't know what to say. She kept her own counsel. On one hand, she was as thrilled that Sam wanted to stay with the Potting Shed as if Paul would have decided to be part of it. He was important to her. Not just as a landscaping partner but as a friend.

On the other hand, she wasn't pleased when Paul decided to forgo all the schooling he'd had to become an architect and take on the responsibilities of a police officer. She'd been devastated, feeling he was too talented, too good at what he did to walk a beat or drive a police cruiser. She could understand and appreciate what Sam's parents must be feeling. She didn't want to encourage the rift that would surely come between them. She and Paul had problems for a long time after he dropped out of school to wear a badge. She didn't wish that on anyone.

"Well, I better go," Hunter said. "Do you need a ride home, Peggy?"

"No. I have my bike. Thanks anyway."

Keeley had already walked outside. The mood that had begun with so much festivity was dark and uncomfortable. Jasper had gone back to work. Sam was staring out the front window looking at Brevard Court.

Peggy didn't know what to say, if anything, to lighten the mood again. She tactfully thanked Jasper again for his hard work, told Sam she would see him later, and escaped out the back door with Hunter.

"Wow. I really know how to kill a good time." Hunter put on her sunglasses and took out her car keys. "Next time, tell me not to come inside if Sam's here."

"It's a difficult time." Peggy glanced at the back door, not wanting Sam to overhear them. "I know it's hard for him. But I know it's hard for your parents, too. I don't want to be in the middle of this."

"In the middle might be better than Sam thinking you're on the side of the opposition like he does with me. I never asked Mom and Dad to compare us. I love Sam the way he is. I don't care what he does. It's wrong for them to keep acting like I'm some kind of poster child for doing well and always telling him he's coming up short."

Peggy hugged her. "He'll sort it all out. You'll see. He loves you, too."

Hunter got in her car and drove away while Peggy unchained her bike from the Dumpster. She stowed her pocketbook and bike lock in the carrying case behind the seat.

"I think that back tire looks a little flat," Keeley observed.

"You might be right." Peggy looked at the tire. "I'll check it out when I get home. I think it should be fine until then."

"You know, Sam has been coming to this decision for a long time," Keeley blurted out. "It's all he talks about. He wants everybody to think he's wonderful, which he is. I don't know why we all can't just be happy for him."

"I suppose when it's all said and done, we will be. Until then, these deciding times are always uncomfortable."

"I guess." Keeley squinted at the back door to the Potting Shed as though she was wondering if Sam would come out while they were talking. "You know, I wish every day of my life that he wasn't gay. Sam is the greatest guy I've ever known. I envy Jasper or whoever he's going to be with."

Peggy smiled and hugged her awkwardly across the bike. "There'll be someone for you, too. You're one of the most special people I've ever known."

As though thinking about Sam had conjured his image, he stuck his head out the back door. "Peggy! They just said on the radio that there is new evidence, and your friend has been formally charged with two counts of kidnapping and murder."

20

Crape Myrtle
Botanical: *Lagerstroemia indica*
While called a myrtle, this small tree is not a member of the myrtle family at all. It was brought to Europe from China in the late seventeen hundreds, and its purple and pink blossoms were an immediate hit. It migrated to America in the eighteen hundreds, where it was one of the first ornamentals planted at the Governor's Palace in Williamsburg, Virginia.

Peggy was depressed by the time she got home. Ruth actually being charged for the two murders made it so much worse. If she could find some real evidence to contradict the charges, everything would be all right. If not, Ruth could go to prison or worse.

She wondered what happened to change the status of the case. Had Ruth confessed?

What was the new evidence? She wasn't privy to anything else from the police. Whatever she was going to do, she'd have to do it alone.

It didn't help that it was raining on her way back. It was warm, summer rain, but it still made traffic worse, and she was soaked by the time she got home. To make matters worse, the slightly flat tire Keeley warned her about was completely flat when she put her bike away. There was a large gouge in it. She'd have to drive her truck to the bicycle store for a new tire.

Steve left her a message to let her know he'd be running late that night. It took her off the hook for dinner that evening but left her in a foul mood in the big empty house. She threw off her wet clothes, took a hot shower, then stormed downstairs to check on her plants.

Even her normally soothing routine didn't make her feel better. She felt helpless. With the other cases she'd helped solve, she'd had Nightflyer's help. Maybe she wouldn't have been able to solve them without his input. What if she couldn't help Ruth? What if those other cases had been a fluke on her part?

Not that she regretted her decision. If she never solved another case, she would still have Steve and the Potting Shed. Nightflyer had been a temptation that was difficult to pass up in some ways. But she was sure this was the right direction for her.

With a sigh, she went back upstairs to her bedroom. The rain continued, making puddles where potholes graced the streets, snarling traffic on Queens Road outside her bedroom window. She listened to the symphony of squealing brakes and honking horns for a few minutes. Why didn't people understand that sometimes you have to slow down?

She answered a few emails from friends. One of her colleagues in Tokyo was having some success with hydroponic potatoes. He was very excited about his almost-one-pound spuds. Peggy congratulated him and told him about her pumpkins and other vegetables. There was no doubt hydroponics could be the answer to the question of how to feed an ever-increasing population on the planet.

Thinking of water, she picked up the damp flyer she'd taken from the group at UNCC.

Protecting the Earth's natural resources. A large group of trustees supporting the efforts. Scientists. Educators. Divers.

Divers?

Her fingers flew over the keyboard, typing in Gerald's name followed by Badin, NC. Google quickly picked up on the key words and returned over one hundred responses. It seemed Gerald was very active in several of the more radical water protection groups.

She typed in Marsha's name and Charlotte, NC. No such luck. So much for her sudden insight that could have linked the two outside of a romance.

Peggy stared at the few pages with Marsha's name. One was her obituary. Another was from an award she won while working as a nurse. The third page was a MySpace page. Peggy clicked on that link.

Marsha's image, a smiling, living image, came up with lists of what she liked to do, eat, and what movies she enjoyed. She liked to read, spend time with her children.

Hold it!

Her personal statement was: *"I believe we should save the earth and all its resources for our children and our children's children."*

Peggy scanned the rest of the page quickly. There it was! Marsha belonged to one of the radical protection groups, the Water Revolution, that Gerald belonged to. *There was the connection!*

Not that the information alone would help

Ruth. She could imagine a good DA arguing that Ruth thought there was a romantic connection between Marsha and Gerald and acted out of jealousy, whether it was true or not. Peggy needed a lot more evidence, but this might be a start.

What if sending the aconite to Gerald was part of some kind of radical protest involving the group they both belonged to? Maybe there was something more here she could expand on.

She considered the box Marsha sent to Gerald. It could've been the aconite. If it *was*, Peggy knew Marsha wouldn't have brought the aconite anywhere near her children. She may have sent that box, but she didn't take it home first. Considering she'd worked the day before but hadn't gone into the lab that morning, that meant there was something else.

Peggy took off her gardening clothes, her mind racing a hundred miles per minute, faster than any NASCAR victory. She put on a dark blue sundress with tiny white polka dots and white sandals. She never had to worry about wearing stockings in the summer. Being outside as much as she was made her naturally tan most of the year.

She absently patted Shakespeare's head as she picked up her keys and pocketbook, stopped long enough to look at what size her bike tire was, then pulled out of her drive and into the rain-clogged road.

Traffic was much worse than when she'd come home. She glanced at her watch. She only had an hour to make it across town to the bio lab.

Peggy thanked her lucky stars she didn't encounter any accidents going through Charlotte. It had to be some kind of miracle. Usually traffic was hopelessly snarled with fender benders when it rained. From the road report on the radio, the accidents were contained to the interstates that looped around and through the city.

She pulled up into the lab parking lot at four forty-five. Not much time to spare. Without her ID badge from the police lab, she was going to have to wing it and hope no one called to confirm she should be there.

Sarah James was surprised to see her when Peggy had her paged to the front desk. "I'd hoped we were able to answer all your questions, Dr. Lee. I heard Dr. Sargent was formally charged with Mrs. Hatley's death. What else can we do for you?"

Peggy smiled. "I hate to admit this, but I lost the names of Mrs. Hatley's coworkers. My boss expects the team members' names on his desk by tomorrow morning. We have to get all the paperwork in line."

Sarah seemed to understand. Or maybe it was a relief that she wouldn't have to tell her boss that Peggy needed further access to the lab. "Of course. I'll get those for you."

Peggy waited a little nervously as Sarah disappeared down the long hall for a few moments. If she called the lab, Peggy could expect to be escorted to the door. Hopefully, she wouldn't call.

Sarah's heels clicked on the tile as she came back to the front desk where Peggy waited. "Here you go." She handed her the list of names. "Is there anything else I can do for you?"

"No, thanks. That's it. I appreciate your help. Have a nice day."

The tall redhead smiled. "You, too, Dr. Lee. Good work on catching Mrs. Hatley's killer."

Peggy didn't waste any time getting back out to her truck. She didn't want to hang around waiting to be caught as a fraud. She could look up Marsha's coworkers' names and find their phone numbers and addresses. This might not be the important link she believed it to be, but there were no other avenues to follow without it. She had to hope one of Marsha's team members had the answers.

Peggy stopped by the bicycle shop on Kings Drive and parked in the tiny lot. It was much easier when she was riding her bike. The owner was starting to close up for the day but was happy to help her since she stopped there frequently. He tried to talk her into buying a new bike instead of just a new tire as he always did. She laughed, told him her old bike was fine, and went home with a new tire. It was a ritual of sorts between them. And who knew? Maybe one day, she'd need a new bike. Hers probably wouldn't last forever. Until then, she was satisfied with it.

She hurried home and got on the computer to Google Mary Von Cannon, the team member who saw Marsha outside the UPS office. John always said he watched people who volunteered information. Many times they were the ones who knew what was going on. Mary might not have wanted to commit to knowing any more information at the lab in front of her fellow workers, but she might own up to more if Peggy talked to her alone.

Lucky for Peggy, Mary was a proud PTSO president who was in charge of last year's ice cream and cake fundraiser at her school. Her name, address, and phone number were listed as contact information on the school Web site. Peggy wrote down her address on Providence Road and decided to go there rather than risk being ignored on the phone. It was always harder to ignore people standing on your doorstep.

She was about to go out again when she opened the kitchen door to Paul's and Mai's smiling faces. Any other time, she would have been thrilled to see them together. But she wanted to ask those all-important questions of Mary and wished they'd waited to visit.

"Hey, Mom!" Paul stepped inside. "Are you on your way out?"

"Well, I sort of had something important to do. But it's good to see both of you."

"Steve called me and told me you'd be solo tonight. I thought you might like to go out to dinner with me and Mai."

"That is if you aren't mad at me after this morning." Mai's smile trembled a little at the corners.

How could she say no? If she told them she couldn't go, Mai would think she was angry. "That sounds wonderful." Talking with Mary would have to wait. Right now Peggy had to be a mother who was happy to see her son with someone he really loved. "Where are we going?"

"We thought we'd try a new place, Mama Fu's. I hear their food is great, and they have a vegetarian menu," Paul said. "What do you think?"

Two of the dearest faces in the world smiled hopefully. Peggy sighed and nodded. "All right! I can't wait!"

Dinner was great. The conversation never lagged. Peggy noticed how happy Paul and Mai were being back together again. Funny how seeing Stephanie seemed to change both their perspectives.

Peggy was thrilled to see them laughing and touching hands, but she was eager to get on with her own work. She waited patiently through dinner and the ride back to her house. Paul glanced up at the dark windows and asked if she wanted him to walk inside with her. "I'm fine. The alarm's set, and Shakespeare's inside. I'm not worried about it."

"I was wondering how serious this thing between you and Steve has become." Paul glanced at Mai, who strategically sat in the car as Peggy got out. "I mean, he was worried about you being alone without him for one night. I hope you know what you're doing."

Peggy had to keep her jaw from dropping.

Was this from the same son who'd once dated a stripper? And the whole time she'd kept her mouth closed. Her mother was right. It was better to say what needed to be said and let the chips fall where they may. "I don't think it's a big deal," she said with an earnest smile. "Steve and I have an understanding. And he checks in on me regularly."

"He's a great guy," Paul assured her. "Don't get me wrong. I hope you'd tell me if something was happening between you. I don't want to wake up one morning and read about your marriage in the paper."

"That won't happen." She hugged him to keep from hitting him. "I'll let you know in plenty of time if there's anything you should know."

Paul laughed as he got back in the car. "I'm not too worried about it. Grama and Grampa will be up here next month. With them living here, you won't be able to hide anything."

Peggy waved as the car pulled out into Queens Road. It was totally amazing to her how life could turn around on itself. It hadn't been that long ago that she caught Paul making out with a girl he knew in the basement. Now it seemed, he wanted to catch her and Steve in the act.

She marched all the way up to the house and put her hand on the doorknob before she realized in her anger she'd almost forgotten her mission. She had to go to Mary Von Cannon's house and find out what else she knew about Marsha's day off. Never mind Paul trying to squeeze information from her. She would tell him about her and Steve when she felt he was ready to know.

Bolstered by her small rebellion against her son's curiosity, Peggy got in her truck and headed toward Providence Road. Mary lived in Myers Park in one of the nice, older homes from the turn of the last century. Peggy recognized the address, since many of her friends lived in that area. The houses were smaller than the estates on Queens Road, but they were mellow red brick with lovely hardwood floors and nice yards with mature shrubs and trees. Nothing to complain about.

She found Mary's home easily enough but sat in her truck on the street for a few minutes trying to decide how to best approach the woman. Mary probably wouldn't simply volunteer everything she knew. Peggy might have to find some way to trick her into telling her what she needed to know.

With that settled, Peggy got out of the

truck, locked the door, and walked up the drive. There was an unusually large white crape myrtle next to the concrete driveway. Millions of white single flowers had fallen, almost appearing like snow in the hot, humid weather. She admired a tasteful circle of red geraniums around a sundial in the front yard. Everything was very laid back, as were most of the neighbors' gardens.

She knocked on the front door then waited, going over in her mind what she planned to say. Mary answered, and when Peggy saw her face, she knew she was right.

There was an odd look of dread on the other woman's features. Her eyes were worried, and the hand that held the door open trembled. "Hello. I wasn't expecting to see you again."

"I know. And I apologize for having to look you up at home." Peggy smiled brightly as though nothing was really wrong. "I forgot to have you sign the statement you gave Mai Sato and me."

Relief flooded Mary's face. "Is *that* all?" She pushed the door open wider. "Come in and let's take care of that. Dr. Lee, wasn't it?"

"Oh just call me Peggy; everyone does."

"Okay, Peggy. We can go in the kitchen

and talk. My husband is working with our son on some math problems in the den. Would you like some coffee?"

"Tea would be nice, if you have it." Peggy followed her down the hall covered with baby pictures to the kitchen.

"I'd rather have tea, too." Mary smiled. "What's your favorite?"

"Probably peach. But I like almost anything."

"I have some orange spice and some lemon. Will one of those do?"

"Thank you, dear. Lemon will be fine."

"It's been terrible thinking about Marsha being killed by that crazy woman." Mary shuddered as she put water in the kettle. "You think that kind of thing can't happen to people who lead normal lives."

"I know exactly how you feel," Peggy empathized. "My husband was killed. He was a homicide detective, but I never really imagined life without him."

"That's terrible." Mary put out cups with tea bags, a cute bear with honey, and a little bottle of creamer. "That's much worse than losing my friend."

"Thank you. I've made my peace with it. It hasn't been easy." Peggy took out a small notebook and pen. "I'm afraid I have to ask for your statement all over again. Rules and regulations. You know how it is. Then all you have to do is sign."

"Okay." Mary sat down, a little wary.

"So you saw Mrs. Hatley at the UPS store on Highway Two-eighteen in Mint Hill on the day she'd called in sick from work. Is that right?"

"Yes. I was running late myself, and I saw her. She didn't see me; at least I don't think she did. And she was driving an older truck, not the car she drives to work."

"But you didn't notice the license plate."

"No. I was surprised to see her. I knew she should be at work."

"But you didn't stop or try to call her cell phone. Nothing like that."

Mary got up to answer the whistling summons of the teapot. "I didn't think about that. I just drove on to work."

"After you gave her the box she'd planned to send to Gerald Capshaw," Peggy surmised in a calm voice. "The box that contained the aconite you'd been working on at the lab."

"I never said that —"

"But it's true, isn't it? I know Marsha loved her children too much to take that box home with her. She wouldn't risk poisoning them."

"I wouldn't do that either," Mary argued.

"That stuff could kill people."

"So how did Marsha come from home and have that box to send to Gerald?" Peggy raised one cinnamon-colored brow and waited for an answer.

"I was only trying to help." Mary squirmed and glanced at the kitchen door. "They had a good cause. I don't know what went wrong."

"She and Gerald were overcome by the aconite you brought to her. I'm guessing they meant to use it in some kind of protest to bring attention to the dirty water in the rivers. Is that about right?"

Mary nodded. "Marsha knew not to handle or inhale the aconite. She knew it could be deadly. She asked me to bring it to her. It sounded easy and important. I felt like I could make a difference."

"So you went to work that morning and made plans to sneak some of the aconite out of the lab. You took it to Marsha, who sent it to Gerald in Badin."

"*No!* Marsha wouldn't have done anything so irresponsible. Imagine the consequences if anyone had opened that box. Hundreds of people could've died."

Peggy leaned forward. "The UPS box was a ruse?"

"It was a double blind in case she and Mr.

Capshaw got caught. They were terrified someone was watching them. They never planned to poison the river. They just wanted to show people how easy it could be and play up the damage already done to everyone's drinking water."

"So how did she plan to get the package to Gerald?"

"That's why she was driving his truck," Mary explained. "She put the box in the back and drove somewhere to meet him. She wanted to be sure the box was as protected as it could be."

"But you don't know where they were supposed to meet?" Peggy looked at the other woman's drawn face. Mary was close to tears. "Do you know what river they'd planned to pretend to poison?"

"I think they planned to use the Yadkin River, because it's remote and easily accessible. It provides drinking water for thousands of people. Marsha wasn't a bad person. She got a little carried away with trying to save the planet."

Peggy thought about whether Gerald could have planned to use the poison ruse during his dive in Badin Lake. He never got that far.

She studied Mary's sorrowful face. "I'll have to tell the police you were an accessory to the theft of the aconite from the lab. I'm sorry."

Mary wiped tears from her eyes. "In comparison to Marsha's death, it doesn't seem like much. I'll have to live the rest of my life knowing I helped kill her. If I hadn't given her that package, the crazy woman wouldn't have been able to kill her. It's all my fault."

Peggy patted Mary's back as she sobbed. Her husband glanced in the door with their young son at his side. "Is everything all right?"

"It's fine, Richard. Please take Barnell into the other room, and I'll explain everything later."

Richard glanced at Peggy but did as his wife asked. When he was gone, Mary questioned, "Will I have to go to jail?"

"I can't say. That will be between your lawyer and the DA. But I'd definitely find a lawyer with this kind of experience." Peggy took one of Hunter's business cards out of her pocketbook. "You might give her a call. She's had plenty of experience."

"Thank you, Peggy." Mary sniffed. "You don't know what a relief it is to finally say it out loud. I hope that woman rots in jail for killing Marsha."

Peggy's cell phone rang. It was Mai. She

excused herself and took the call on the porch. "Have I got something to tell you."

"Not before you hear what I have to tell *you*."

21

Moonflower

Botanical: *Datura inoxia*

In November 2002, the Cincinnati Drug and Poison Information Center notified residents that they had treated fourteen adolescents in the Akron/Cleveland, Ohio, area who became ill after intentional exposure to toxic seeds that were identified as moonflower. All became ill shortly after eating the seeds or drinking tea brewed using the seeds. All patients recovered fully after treatment. The plant (a cousin to the angel's trumpet) has large, showy white flowers that bloom at dusk producing a beautiful — and always toxic — effect.

Mai was waiting for Peggy when she got back home. "I got the word from Dr. Ramsey and I thought you'd like to know."

"Come inside." Peggy opened the door.

"Those mosquitoes are crazy tonight."

When they were in the kitchen with the door closed and Shakespeare had finished barking, Peggy convinced Mai to have a cup of tea as they talked. "I can't imagine that Harold wants you to tell me what's happening, so I appreciate you thinking about me."

"I don't think you should be left out of the rest of the investigation," Mai said. "And your part may not be over with after all. If it isn't, Dr. Ramsey deserves to have you refuse to help them out again."

"I appreciate your thoughtfulness. It's not a big deal." Peggy made some peach tea for both of them. "So what's happened now?"

Mai leaned forward over her cup. "There is *no* DNA evidence or any other kind of evidence they can find in Dr. Sargent's van or her apartment. And believe me, they looked. I think the Charlotte police checked it out first and then the Stanly County Sheriff followed. Is it just me, or is that guy gross?"

"So there's no real evidence to link Ruth with either crime." Peggy considered what Mai told her in light of her new discovery. "Everything is circumstantial. I wonder if they'll have to let her go?"

"Not on your life!" Mai sipped her tea. "She's the closest they have to a suspect.

Unless you can prove someone else killed those two, she's not going anywhere."

"I take it she doesn't have a credible alibi for the time they were killed."

"I think she said she was at home alone working on papers."

"That's not much of an alibi," Peggy reflected.

"What about you? You said you had something to tell me."

Peggy told her about Mary delivering the aconite to Marsha. "She had a basic idea of what was going on. I told her she'd have to talk to the police."

"That's interesting, but it doesn't help your friend. Even if Marsha Hatley and Gerald Capshaw *weren't* lovers, Dr. Sargent could've seen them together and assumed they were."

"I thought the same thing," Peggy agreed. "But it does give us a different chain of circumstances to consider. If Marsha mailed a decoy package, where's the real package? It may be possible someone found out about their little scheme to save the world and decided to take their own drastic measures."

"That's a good point about the real package. That aconite stuff is still out there somewhere. The sheriff couldn't find anything at the Badin address where the box was sent, including the box."

"Do you know if they've searched Gerald's home?"

Mai shrugged. "I'm sure the hazmat people have been thorough. I mean this could be a public health threat, right? I think I would've heard if they'd found anything."

"I don't know where that leaves us. I thought if I could get to Mary, it would make it all come together, but I was wrong."

"But you *did* find a piece of the puzzle," Mai consoled. "You just need the eyes."

Peggy glanced up at her. "The eyes?"

"You know. When you put jigsaw puzzles together, you can find everything except the eyes. That's what you need right now."

"You're right." Peggy chuckled. "I need the eyes. Any suggestions?"

"I'm all tapped out." Mai sat back in her chair with a yawn. "I think I'm going home. Will you be all right?"

"I'll be fine."

Mai got up and started toward the door. "You know, I didn't say anything to Paul, and I won't say it, but the last time I was here and you let me use your bathroom, there were two toothbrushes and a man's razor on the cabinet."

"You're very observant."

"I guess it goes with the job. I'm assuming you don't want Paul to know Steve is sleeping over. Don't you think he can handle it?"

"What do you think?"

Mai considered the question. "I don't know. He has this vision of you in his mind. I suppose we all feel like our mothers are perfect, even if we argue with them sometimes. I think he has suspicions, but he can't bring himself to believe you'd abandon his father's memory that way. You know?"

"I do. I'm not ready to broach that subject with him yet. I appreciate your tact."

"I understand. Don't forget; my parents are divorced, and both of them are seeing other people. Probably sleeping with them, too." Mai shuddered. "I *really* don't want to think about it."

Peggy watched the headlights of Mai's car as it left the driveway. She wished she was tired enough to go to sleep. Then she could wake up and Steve would be back and it would be a new day. But it was only ten p.m., and she wasn't a bit sleepy.

She ran upstairs and changed clothes then went out to repair her bike tire. Shakespeare stayed with her. The sounds from the street became less and less as it got later. She could hear the TV from Clarice's house next door; she was watching some game show. There was applause every few minutes.

Peggy put her bike away when she was done and remembered to plug in her truck batteries. She walked around in the yard, appreciating the moonlight and the sweet smell of angel's trumpet from another neighbor's yard. Peggy had dug up her angel's trumpet when she started letting Shakespeare out in the backyard. The poison from rubbing up against the plant could, at the very least, make him sick.

There were moonflowers blooming on the side of the house, pale white against the dark of the brick wall. The vine was more than ten feet tall with flowers the size of saucers. It was one of the few flowering plants she didn't put in after she and John were married. Most of the plants put in by the previous owners were sedate boxwoods and roses. This moonflower was a flight of fancy for some gardener who may have lived and died in the house. She would never know. But it was someone's legacy to the house.

Her cell phone rang in her pocket, and she jumped. It was silly to be spooked by the sound, but that's what came of thinking about departed spirits still walking the grounds. Peggy was a scientist at heart, but in her Low Country upbringing lingered ghost stories and superstitions she'd heard from the time she was a small child.

"Hello?"

"Hi, beautiful. I understand your boyfriend is out of town."

She laughed. It was Steve. "I don't know that I'd call him a boy, but he's out of town. What did you have in mind?"

"I thought I might drop by for a while. A woman like you shouldn't be left alone for too long."

"What about my boyfriend?"

"What about him? I heard he's a big dumb sap who'd rather take care of sick animals than be there with you."

"You have a good point. If you'd like to drop by for a while, I'll open a new bottle of wine." She shivered as she felt his arms go around her in the dark.

"Here I am. Where's the wine?"

Peggy took Steve down to the Potting Shed the next morning to show him the progress Jasper was making. Sam was placing a black rubber lining into the pool area while Jasper unloaded the rocks that would create the waterfall.

"I'm surprised to see you here," Peggy said to Sam. "I thought you and Keeley

384

were putting in that rock garden for the Iversons today."

"We were until the rocks Mrs. Iverson got were white instead of pink granite. We have to wait until the next delivery from the stone works out in Landis. Keeley wanted to do something with her mom today, so we decided to take the day off."

Steve helped Sam when it looked like the black rubber was going to eat him. "This is much bigger than I'd anticipated," Peggy told them as they struggled with the liner.

"Does that mean you're unhappy with it?" Jasper stopped working and stared at her. "I can change it. It can be however you want it to be."

Sam laughed from somewhere on the other side of the black liner. "Don't pay any attention to her. She's working up to how she's going to get it all in. I know there are at least a dozen water plants dancing in her head right now."

Peggy agreed. "You're right. Don't take it the wrong way, Jasper. It's wonderful! Much better than I'd imagined. I'm thinking we could have a stone path around it. I don't want to close it in. I want people to see all sides of it so we can have as many plants and garden art as we can."

"See?" Sam grinned. "I told you."

Jasper looked relieved as he started back to work. "You two have a great working relationship. You seem like you've known each other forever. I'd like to be part of that one day."

"Best thing you can do is learn to ignore her," Sam told him. "That's why we have such a great relationship, right Peggy?"

"I thought it was because you're out in the field most of the time," she answered tartly. "But it might be because you do what I tell you to do."

Steve poked his head out from under the black liner. "Is it just me or should we all have worn our waders this morning?"

"Ignore him, too," Sam counseled. "He's like Peggy. He doesn't know what's good for him."

The four of them were so intent on one-upping each other, they didn't notice the woman who came in the front door. "Are you closed?" she asked.

"I'm afraid so." Peggy went to greet her. "We're remodeling. But I'll be glad to put you on my mailing list so you get an invitation to my grand reopening."

"Thanks." The woman looked over Peggy's shoulder. "Are you putting in a pond? Right in the store?"

"That's right. It will be a whole new Potting Shed."

"I'm Lizzie Maxwell." The woman shook Peggy's hand. "I'm checking out garden shops for a special feature in *Southern Living* magazine. My photographer will be back with me in a month or so. Do you think you'll be ready for company?"

"I think we can manage that." Peggy winked at Sam and Jasper. "We might be able to schedule our grand reopening event when you're going to be here."

Lizzie gave Peggy her card. "Let's keep in touch. I've heard good things about the Potting Shed everywhere I go in Charlotte. I really want you to be part of the feature. And wait until everyone sees what you've done here. It's amazing!"

Peggy thanked her and pocketed her card. "We'll look forward to seeing you in a month or so." Lizzie turned to leave, but Peggy called her back. "Just out of curiosity, who told you about the Potting Shed?"

"Who *didn't* tell me about you? They call you the plant lady, you know. I'll talk to you later."

When Lizzie was gone through the courtyard toward Latta Arcade, Peggy turned to Sam, Steve, and Jasper. "You can't ask for a better surprise than that. Can everything be done by then?"

Steve looked at Sam who looked at Jasper who said, "I think so. I might have to hire someone to help out."

"Money is no object," Sam assured him. "Whatever it takes. You can't buy publicity like being part of a feature in *Southern Living*. It will push our sales through the roof. What's the name of that woman on News 14 who always jets around here?"

"I don't remember," Peggy said. "But I bet we could look her up. It would make a nice community story."

"I can pass the word to all my patients," Steve volunteered as his cell phone rang. "Maybe they could bring in their owners." The phone call was one of those owners calling him, and he had to go. "I should be back early," he told Peggy. "Maybe we can have dinner."

"Maybe." She kissed him good-bye. "I'll see what I can do about that."

Peggy sat talking with Sam and Jasper after Steve was gone. They talked about all the possibilities, all the wonderful things that could happen from the changes they were making.

She called her supplier and ordered some herbs and small house plants for her lighted shelving units. Everything was moving along nicely. The only thing that refused to fall in line was evidence that would clear Ruth's murder charge. Peggy thought about it while she waited for bagel sandwiches and sweet tea at the Kozy Kettle.

"Your shop is looking good," Emil told her, curling one end of his heavy black mustache. "You must be feeling good, too."

Sofia shuffled past him. "You talk stupid! How can she be feeling good when her man won't marry her? She's a scarlet woman. An outcast. No man will ever want her again."

Emil's jovial face immediately sobered. "I am so sorry, Peggy. Sofia's right. When is Steve going to take care of this? My uncle is a priest. He would be glad to marry you for a fraction of the cost he would normally charge."

Peggy smiled a little, careful not to appear as though she was ignoring them. That could have disastrous results. "I'll have to talk to Steve about it."

Sofia crossed herself. "I would take him out and kick his behind myself if I wasn't so busy. We thought he would do right by you. Instead he is like my cousin Guido. We all thought Guido would go far. Instead he shacked up with some woman he met in the city. We tried to talk him out of it, tried to get him to make her an honest woman. Then he left her there, God forbid, and we had to support her until she died."

"That's a terrible story." Peggy took her bagels from Emil. "I hope we can do better than that."

Emil leaned closer to her. "If not, you tell me. We will pay him a little visit one night. He will either do the right thing, or you know what."

Peggy was afraid to admit she didn't know what. She was fairly sure she didn't *want* to know. "Thank you both. You're such good friends."

Sofia kissed Emil's cheek. "That's why we're here."

Emil brushed off Sofia's red lipstick, and Peggy escaped through the door with lunch.

While she, Sam, and Jasper ate, she told them what she'd learned about Marsha and Gerald's plan to make people aware of what was happening to their water supply. "I think they meant well. They got so caught up in their passion to save everyone, they may have killed themselves."

"Is that what you *think* happened?" Sam asked. "Or do you know for sure?"

"Not at all. It's a theory I can't support right now. I talked with Mai last night. There's no real proof against Ruth, but she's the only suspect they have. Until there's some other plausible explanation, she's going to stay where she is."

"Have you talked to someone in this group they were in?" Jasper asked.

"No. I tried looking a few of them up, but they stay pretty well hidden, I guess." She sipped her sweet tea. "There's still the issue of the aconite being out there somewhere. Someone else from the group may decide to use it."

Jasper finished his bagel and thanked Peggy for lunch. "What if I could put you in touch with someone who might be able to help?"

"You mean someone in the Water Revolution?"

"Yeah. Would you have to tell the police? I know she might be willing to help, but not if she has to talk to the police."

"I think I could work that out. Do you know someone from the group?"

"My sister." Jasper nodded. "I don't know if she's been involved with any of this, but I could give her a call and see if she'd be willing to talk to you."

"That would be great," Peggy enthused. "I'd really appreciate that."

"I'll see what I can do."

Peggy's cell phone rang. It was Mai. "They want you to come back on the case, just like I thought. It's up to you, but now

391

might be a good time to make a statement."

"What kind of statement?" Peggy wondered.

"I don't know. Something like 'I'll come back this time, you rotten pigs, but don't ever throw me off an unfinished case again.' Something like that."

"That would be quite a statement." Peggy laughed. "I think I can accomplish more knowing what they know, even if we aren't quite working the case in the same direction. My grandma always used to say, you get more ants with sugar than with baking soda."

"Isn't that supposed to be flies with honey instead of vinegar?"

"Not where I come from. I'll see you in a few minutes." Peggy closed her cell phone. "Looks like I'm back on the case. They must be desperate."

Sam laughed, but Jasper frowned. "Should I still have my sister call you? You won't have to take an oath or something that makes you turn her in?"

"Heavens no! Please have her call me." Peggy gave him a scrap of paper with her home and cell phone numbers. "Assure her that everything she tells me will be confidential."

"Okay. I can't promise anything. But I'll

talk to her."

"Thanks. I have to go. You two are doing a fantastic job! And if you need to hire someone to help out so we can be open next month, let me know."

Jasper nodded. "Yes, ma'am."

Sam followed Peggy out of the Potting Shed. "Are you sure you want to get mixed up with these rads?"

"These rads probably have the right idea." She unlocked her bike. "Our water is very important. People don't seem to realize we can't live without clean water."

"Right. I forgot. You're the one who got arrested in Philadelphia helping the rads there."

"Don't worry. I can take care of myself."

"Now I'm *really* worried." Sam looked up into the ozone-hazed sky. "There's something important I want to talk to you about. Not now. I need some time."

Peggy knew what he wanted to say. Part of her was doing a little dance, but another probably more responsible part wished they wouldn't have that conversation. "I'll call you when this meeting is over. Maybe we can talk then."

She looked into his handsome face and wondered if she was doing the same thing his parents were doing. No one could overlay another person's life with their personal demands or expectations. She knew people did it anyway, but it was wrong. She'd almost learned that at the expense of her and Paul's relationship.

She wasn't Sam's mother even though she felt like it sometimes. She wanted what was best for him and wanted him to be happy. She wasn't sure what that would mean, but if he asked to become her partner in the business, she was going to say yes. She realized it might still only be a temporary arrangement despite his belief that it was the only path for him.

Peggy had seen enough of life to know it never stood still. She felt selfish having Sam for even a little while longer. She never said anything to him about wishing he could stay, since she knew his goal was to be a surgeon. But she wouldn't turn down what fate offered her.

Traffic was light on her ride to the police lab. She parked her bike and chained it to the new rack in front. Mai was at the door, smiling and holding out her ID badge. It was almost like coming home in a weird way.

Harold was waiting in the lab. He rocked back on his heels when he saw her. "I hope you're here to work this time, Dr. Lee. It seems Sato has put us all in a terrible mess."

22

Bladderwort
Botanical: *Utricularia spp.*
Free-floating bladderworts are actually annuals with no roots and flowers on erect stems above the water. The plant is barely eight inches tall. The underwater leaf branches or petioles are inflated with air, which allows them to float. Leaves of the bladderwort trap and digest small aquatic creatures, making them carnivorous.

"What did *I* do?" Mai demanded with a flash of temper that Peggy found very attractive.

"You should have insisted on following through with more protocol," Dr. Ramsey chastised. "The rules of evidence are very clear."

Mai's pretty face turned bright red before she stalked out the lab door. Peggy turned to Dr. Ramsey, "You know, you're going to lose her one day, and it will be your loss, because she can go anywhere."

Harold shrugged. "That's why she's the assistant ME and I'm the chief medical officer for this county. Let's not forget that, Dr. Lee. Enough about Sato's feelings being hurt. Tell me you have some idea from the botanical evidence of what is going on."

"I don't have a clue." She sat down on one of the tall stools near the desk. "I suggest you start from the beginning to find what you missed."

"*I* didn't miss anything. Either you or Sato failed to report something that may have been important to the case. The police aren't sure where to go from here. They're looking to us to provide those clues."

Peggy frowned. "You are one of the most egotistical men I have ever met. You can't even admit you made a mistake. We all make them, Harold. You aren't any better than the rest of us."

The other lab assistants stopped working and listened as Peggy spoke. They looked away quickly when Harold stared at them. "I don't think you understand the proper protocol. It's important to maintain the chain of responsibility around here. If I'm blamed for every little thing, what will happen to the respect this office deserves?"

"Never mind." She sighed. "I don't know what to tell you. You probably know more than I do." She didn't plan to tell him about Jasper's sister. She might not even hear from the girl.

"Let's revise," he suggested. "We'll sit down at the conference table and sort this out."

Peggy was about to agree with him when her cell phone rang. "Excuse me, Harold. Let me take this, and then we'll talk."

He bowed his head and held open the lab door for her. "Of course. Excuse me for taking up your private time. We're only trying to solve a double homicide here. I wouldn't want to interrupt your social schedule."

"Watch it, Harold," she warned as she walked through the door. "I'm not Mai. This is a sideline for me, not the whole enchilada."

Peggy enjoyed seeing the look of disbelief on his face. She closed the lab door behind her and answered her phone. "Hello?"

"Dr. Lee? Dr. Peggy Lee?" A young woman's voice sounded unsure and a little frightened. "I'm Jasper Wheeler's sister, Christi. I told Jasper I'd give you a call. I don't know what I can say to you about everything that's happened."

"Just take a deep breath and start at the

beginning," Peggy suggested.

"I can't. Not on the phone. Someone might be listening."

Peggy wanted to reassure the girl that, so far as she knew, there were no listening devices for cell phones yet. But the kind of fear she heard in Christi's voice wouldn't be reasoned with. "All right. Let's meet somewhere. What about my house?"

"No. People would expect that."

"What about someplace like Starbucks or a restaurant?"

"That's too visible."

"What about my garden shop, the one where Jasper's working?" Peggy was about to give up on suggestions. "We can meet there whenever you like. It's closed, so no one else will be there."

There was a deep breath and a moment of hesitation. "Okay. I'll meet you there tonight, six p.m. Don't tell Jasper. I don't want him involved in this."

"I'll be there." Peggy didn't debate the fact that people would be as likely to look for her there as at her house. "Thank you."

But the line was dead. Peggy closed her cell phone and went back into the lab. Harold was already in the conference room. Mai had joined him there. Al and Jonas were walking down the hall in her direction.

It looked like it was going to be a long session.

Peggy took her chair with renewed hope that she might be able to exonerate Ruth. She might be on the wrong track, but something was putting fear into Christi's voice. She could imagine if the girl knew about the deaths and the aconite, she could be afraid.

How much of her new knowledge would Peggy share with the people gathered around the conference table? Some of the information, the part she'd already told Mai about, was a given. But Mai didn't know about her conversation with Jasper or Christi. That part, she decided, might be better kept to herself. After all, she didn't really have anything but a contact right now. She was far from having the answers they were looking for.

Al smiled at her and nodded. Jonas's lean, usually frustrated face was blank. Harold shuffled his paperwork, and Mai wrote notes on a yellow legal pad.

Jonas was the first to speak. "We're in a mess here, ladies and gentlemen. We have a very good suspect, but our evidence won't hold up in court according to the DA in our county and in Stanly County. What are we going to do about that?"

Harold cleared his throat. "I might suggest that we take a look at the forensic evidence from the beginning again. Maybe we missed something."

"Dr. Sargent has no alibi for the time you people believe our two victims died. She had a strong motive to kill both of them and, according to Mrs. Capshaw, she threatened to do exactly that if he didn't leave his wife and daughter. So we have motive and opportunity. But I need your help to put her at the scene."

"And that's a big part of the problem," Peggy added. "You thought your evidence was strong enough to ignore the fact that we don't know where the two victims died. We know they drowned in the same place, at the same time. But knowing where that is could make all the difference."

Jonas shook his head. "Nice to have you back, Peggy. What do you suggest?"

"We have to find the water they drowned in."

"Which could be anywhere between here and Badin," Harold reminded them. "We could be testing water for weeks."

"Do you have something better to do?" Peggy lifted a cinnamon-colored brow in his direction.

"I'm not saying I do," Harold argued.

"But we don't have that kind of manpower."

"There has to be some way to pinpoint our crime scene without testing every swimming hole in three counties," Al said.

"That might be possible if we could find the box Mrs. Hatley sent to Gerald Capshaw," Mai suggested.

"You might as well look in all those swimming holes," Al replied. "That box is out there somewhere. There are several hazmat units, K-9 units down from Raleigh, as well as a few CDC teams up here from Atlanta. So far, nothing."

"Maybe there wasn't a package," Harold theorized. "Maybe the whole thing was a joke of some kind."

Mai looked at Peggy in that tell-them-what-you-know kind of way. When Peggy didn't respond, Mai added, "Peggy might know something about that."

"I have some information on that score," Peggy said finally. She explained about Mary Von Cannon giving the package to Marsha and the decoy package Marsha sent through UPS. She briefly went into her limited knowledge of Marsha and Gerald belonging to the Water Revolution.

"Why didn't someone tell us this earlier?" Jonas looked directly at Harold.

The ME was at a loss for words. "I didn't

have this information until now. This was something Dr. Lee was investigating independently."

"Independently?" Jonas fixed his stare on Peggy. "What does that mean? I thought you were working for the department."

"Harold means I was working on assignment trying to find this information," Peggy clarified even if she *was* stretching the truth. "I haven't had a chance to brief him on my findings as yet."

"We'll want to talk to Mrs. Von Cannon about this." Jonas scribbled in his notebook. "Technically, she stole the package from the lab and was responsible for transporting dangerous toxins to Hatley."

"I expect she'd be willing to testify, if you need her, in exchange for some kind of deal," Peggy suggested. "She's a PTSO president and probably has never done anything like this in her life."

"She should've thought about that before she went off the deep end," Jonas said. "Does she have any idea of what happened to the package? We might be willing to bargain for that information."

"I don't know. I suppose you'll have to ask her when you talk to her."

"Leave me her contact information." Jonas was ready to move on. "I want you guys to go over Dr. Sargent's apartment and van again. Make sure we haven't missed anything else. We need something to connect her to the crime. If we can find out where this took place, great. But I want something substantial soon."

"What if we're looking in the wrong direction?" Peggy asked. "What if she's not responsible, and the real killer is getting away?"

Everyone around the table groaned. "Peggy, we have a lock on this woman," Al told her. "You're on our team. We're looking for information to finish the job. Stay focused. We can't go around accusing half the city because you don't think your friend was responsible."

That statement prevented Peggy from sharing the rest of her information about Christi Wheeler. Not that she had any warm fuzzies about working with Jonas, Al, and Harold anyway. But if they weren't open to new evidence that might prove Ruth wasn't the killer, there was no point in telling them about her meeting with Christi until she had more solid information.

Besides, they'd only want to come along and spoil things. She glanced at Mai and realized she couldn't say anything to her either. Mai was too worried about impressing everyone. She wouldn't be able to keep it to herself. Peggy knew it was going to have to be another "independent" project that she told them about after it was over. Of course, something would have to come of it to bother doing that.

Jonas and Al were getting ready to go, and Harold was walking them out the door. Mai came over to Peggy's side of the table. "I don't think there's anything to find in that van or Dr. Sargent's apartment. We've gone over it three times already. Either she didn't use the van to transport the bodies, or she was very thorough in cleaning up."

"She's in the same basic business, Ms. Sato," Harold chided her. "She knew what we'd be looking for. So let's get out there and outsmart her. Perhaps Dr. Lee could assist you in case she finds any other botanical discoveries."

Peggy nodded. "That's fine, although I think you're wasting your time."

"Be that as it may," Harold said, "it's our time to waste."

"Not exactly. It's the taxpayers' time to waste." Peggy picked up her pocketbook. "But you're the boss."

Peggy and Mai went over the van with a crime scene tech for the next three hours.

There were plenty of fingerprints, but they all belonged to the sample group of students and Dr. Sargent. There were plenty of plant samples brought in by careless feet and equipment coming right out of the lake or river the group visited. But none of them matched anything they were looking for.

Peggy held up some drooping bladderwort, a carnivorous water plant common to the area. She put it in a bag, but knew it probably had no bearing on the case, which was why it was still there. She almost felt sorry for the poor thing.

"In short," Mai spoke into her tape recorder, "we can't find anything we haven't found before. Nothing appears to be incriminating as far as Dr. Sargent is concerned."

Peggy sighed. "I don't think Gerald or Marsha were ever in this van."

"Could the suspect have another vehicle she used or a vehicle she rented?" the tech asked.

Mai shook her head. "We checked into that. If she rented a vehicle, we can't find any record of it. If she used another vehicle, we have no idea where it could be."

The tech shrugged. "I guess you're out of luck."

Mai checked in with the crime scene team

who'd been assigned to go over Dr. Sargent's apartment. They came up empty-handed as well. "I don't know where to go from here," she confessed. "Dr. Ramsey isn't going to like it."

"What about Marsha Hatley's car or Gerald's truck?" Peggy considered. "Has anyone looked at those?"

"Doc Williamson has Mr. Capshaw's truck. We went over Mrs. Hatley's car. As far as I know, there wasn't anything unusual in either one. If Dr. Sargent was in either vehicle, she didn't leave any trace behind."

"What about aconite?" Peggy was more interested in trying to locate the poison Mary had given to Marsha than trying to incriminate Ruth. That package had to be found.

Mai checked her notebook. "I don't see any record of that. Everything we've looked at has been tested for it since you made your discovery. I don't think it was transported in any of these vehicles."

Peggy's cell phone rang. It was Sam. "Got any free time? We've got something to show you."

She glanced at her watch. It was almost five p.m. Heavens! She had to get Sam and Jasper out of the Potting Shed before Christi showed up. "I think we're done here for now. I'll be there in about twenty minutes."

Sam was enthusiastic. "Great! You won't believe it!"

Peggy closed her cell phone and turned to Mai. "I have to go. If you need me to, I can come back after I'm finished at the Potting Shed."

"I don't know. Let me give this report to Dr. Ramsey, and I'll give you a call." Mai closed her notebook. "I thought the Potting Shed was closed right now?"

"It is, but Sam and a new guy, Jasper, are working on the remodeling. They've really come a long way already." Peggy told her about the visit from *Southern Living* magazine's editor. "I hope we can be ready for it."

"That sounds awesome! I can't wait to see it."

"Are you seeing Paul again tonight?" Peggy asked. "If I'm not being too nosy."

"You are." Mai laughed. "But I don't mind. We aren't going out tonight. Before you ask, nothing's wrong. We just decided not to push it. Paul is working afternoons right now, and it's kind of hard."

"I know what you mean." Peggy smiled at her and squeezed her arm. "But I'm so happy you're back together."

"Me, too," Mai confessed. "It's like being

with an old friend again. Except better."

Peggy would have liked to talk about it more, but she was pressed for time. She left her lab coat and picked up her pocketbook. Harold tried to get her to tell him what they found or didn't find. She deferred to Mai to give him her report and hurried out of the building.

Traffic was hot and smelly, already backing up with people getting out of work. A young man in a red Mercedes yelled out his window at her, telling her to get off the road. Peggy pedaled on, ignoring him. Charlotte drivers weren't the best at sharing the road. Once she'd been doused with a soft drink thrown out a window, but that hadn't deterred her.

It would be easier driving her truck everywhere, but batteries wore out and were expensive to replace. Besides, she needed the exercise, and she liked riding her bike. Maybe someday, drivers would get used to being on roads with bikers. It would help a lot if Charlotte would add some bike lanes so she didn't have to ride right in traffic, but she wasn't looking for that anytime soon.

There was an accident on College Street she had to swerve around. A car coming from behind her blew his horn and swore at her. Peggy kept her head down as she turned into the area behind the Potting Shed. She had an air horn she could have used to make a return gesture, but she wasn't looking for road rage. All she wanted to do was get from one place to another.

Selena's car was parked behind the shop with Sam's truck. Good grief! That's all she needed was a crowd to get rid of before Christi got there in thirty minutes or so. She hoped she could manage to get all of them out of there in time, or she might lose the only real lead they had to what happened to Marsha and Gerald.

There was loud music coming from inside as Peggy opened the back door. Sam was right. She was amazed to find the entire water feature in place and working with water in it. The small waterfall trickled down the rocks Jasper had set. The pond was almost kidney-shaped with water moving steadily in the area below the fall and a calm water area in the other end.

Sam and Jasper had brought in some flagstone to put around the edge of the pond to create the walkway she had asked for. It wasn't set in place yet, but she could tell it was going to be fantastic.

"What do you think?" Sam asked. "Jasper has an idea about putting in some lighting under the water and maybe something from the ceiling to shine on it during those gray days and early dusk."

"Isn't it amazing?" Selena yelled over the loud music. "How much longer until we open up again? You know, I could come in and help out getting things set up."

"I love it!" Peggy shouted. "I can't believe how fast you got it finished."

Jasper turned down REO Speedwagon. "I'm really glad you like it. It isn't completely finished yet, but you can see how it'll be."

Selena went to the front door and walked in like a customer. "Oh my God! I'm so impressed! It dominates the shop. People are going to flip out."

"Well, let's hope it's not *that* amazing." Peggy laughed. "I'll settle for more customers who come in all the time."

"I think this will do it," Sam said. "Jasper is a genius. We're going to make a fortune on water features and fertilizer, if you ever decide to market it."

"Let's wait and see," Peggy decided. "This is enough change for right now. You boys did such a wonderful job. I insist on buying you both dinner."

"Excellent!" Sam yelled. "We already ordered pizza. It should be here any minute."

"Can I stay?" Selena wanted to know.

Peggy put her pocketbook down. She wasn't sure what to say. She knew Christi was coming, but how could she ask them to leave after they'd worked so hard? She was going to have to find some way around it. "That's fine. I'll be glad to pay for the pizza. Maybe we should eat outside in the court-yard. It's such a lovely evening."

"Good idea," Selena backed her up. "I know Emil won't mind us borrowing one of his tables, especially since he closes at six."

"There are a few things I wanted to finish yet tonight," Jasper said.

Peggy assured him he'd done enough for the day. "I insist you take the rest of the night off. We're way ahead of schedule now. You can come back tomorrow."

The pizza got there at five forty-five. Peggy got drinks for all of them from Emil before the Kozy Kettle shut down. Sofia was sitting out at the table with Sam, Jasper, and Selena already, probably telling ghoulish Sicilian stories about her relatives.

Peggy put the drinks on the table then told the group she would be right back. None of them looked up; they were too busy talking about their plans for the future. That suited her purpose. No one would miss her for a few minutes.

She sneaked into the Potting Shed, deciding if anyone asked that she needed to use the restroom. It was straight up six p.m. when she walked into the shop. She glanced around but didn't see any sign of Christi. She looked in the back parking area and saw the girl waiting by the Dumpster with her bike.

"Peggy?" she called her name. "I'm Christi."

Peggy went down the stairs, glancing behind her. As far as she could tell, they were alone. "I'm glad you came. I know this is hard for you, but we have to find out what happened to the package Marsha and Gerald had before they died."

"The aconite." Christi nodded. Her long, straight hair fell slightly in her face. She was a thin, waiflike figure wearing old jeans and a worn Doors T-shirt. "I know where it is. I think I know what happened to Gerald and Marsha. I don't think they were killed. At least not by the woman the police are holding."

"Can you tell me about it?" Peggy hoped she wouldn't spook the girl. Christi was nervous, her hands shaking. "It's not only important to get to the truth about what happened to Marsha and Gerald. The aconite could be deadly."

"I can tell you, but it might be better if I take you there. Do you have a car or something? It's a long way on a bike."

"I have a truck, but it's at home," Peggy said. "When do you want to go?"

Christi looked around. "How soon could you get back here? There's a meeting at eight tonight."

"We could go in my truck." Sam jumped down from the dock behind the Potting Shed. "We could go right now."

23

Juniper

Botanical: *Juniperus communis*

Juniper is a small shrub that grows throughout the Northern Hemisphere. Essential oil has been made from the green yellow berries for centuries, only recently being replaced with synthetic oil of juniper. The shrub has a sharp, fragrant scent that is immediately recognizable. It has been used by the Chinese for centuries as the perfect bonsai.

"I thought we were alone." Christi backed away from Peggy.

"I thought so, too. I'll get rid of him." Peggy met Sam before he could reach Christi. "What are you doing out here? I'm trying to have a private meeting."

Sam glanced at Christi over Peggy's shoulder. "You're trying to get yourself in trouble. Let me come with you."

"She doesn't trust either one of us," Peggy argued. "Go away and let me take care of this."

"Sam?" Jasper called from the dock. "Christi? What's going on back here?"

Christi started to get on her bike. "Nothing. I'm out of here."

"Wait!" Peggy tried to stop her. "They don't know anything. You're doing the right thing trying to help me with this. Please don't let them scare you away."

Jasper came down the stairs. "Christi, I think you can trust her."

"What are you doing here?" his sister demanded. "She was supposed to meet me out here alone. Not with a pack of helpers."

"This is all a misunderstanding," Peggy said. "I'm sure Jasper and Sam will go away so we can talk."

"Sam?" Christi looked at him. "So you're Sam, huh?"

"Yeah. Hi. You're Jasper's sister." Sam held his hand out to her. "If it makes any difference at this point, Peggy didn't tell me anything about your meeting. I'm just nosy."

"Sam's a good friend," Jasper said. "And I've told you Peggy has made me feel right at home. You can take off, Christi, but I know you feel guilty about everything that's happened. There's nothing wrong here but

415

a little mix-up. Don't let that stop you from doing what's right."

Christi sighed and put down the kick stand on her bike. "I'm sorry, Peggy. I should've realized Sam was like Jasper. He can't mind his own business. But if Jasper says both of you are okay, I know I can trust his judgment. I'll take you out to the meeting."

"Just a minute." Sam pulled Peggy to one side. "Are you sure you want to get mixed up in this? Jasper has told me a little bit about this group his sister belongs to. They sound like a bunch of whackos."

"Whackos or not," Peggy whispered back, "they may be the key to everything that's happened. I have to take the chance. It might not come again. They certainly aren't going to trust the police."

Sam shrugged. "Okay. I'm going with you."

"Hey! What's going on out here?" Selena's voice preceded her appearance on the dock. "I thought you guys went to check on something. Peggy, what are you doing back here?"

"Would it hurt if Sam comes along?" Peggy asked Christi, ignoring Selena.

"I suppose it won't matter, if he can keep his mouth shut." Christi glared at her brother. "Jasper's been to a meeting."

"If Sam's going, I want to go, too," Jasper added. "It'll be better in case there's any trouble."

"There won't be any trouble unless you say something stupid," Christi clarified. "I guess it won't matter if the four of us go. It's not unusual for groups to sit in at meetings."

"Great!" Selena joined them. "Then I can go, too."

"Who's she?" Christi asked.

"I'll fill you in on the way," Jasper promised. "It'll be okay."

"These people aren't stupid," Christi said. "If any of you say *anything* about why you're really there, it could be bad for all of us."

"That's what I like," Sam mumbled, "a group of people who'll kill for clean water."

Peggy was relieved when it seemed to be decided. She rode in the truck with Sam while Selena, Christi, and Jasper rode in back.

Lights were starting to come on around Charlotte as they left the city headed toward Cabarrus County where Christi said the group was meeting. Heavy clouds had rolled in, making the evening darker than it should have been. Peggy hoped the rain would stay away long enough for them to reach shelter before the three in the back of the truck got soaked.

"Turn on Highway Forty-nine," Christi yelled through the opening in the back window. "We're heading toward Mount Pleasant."

"Okay." Sam shifted lanes to make the turn. "This is crazy," he said to Peggy after Christi closed the window. "I know you want to get to the truth, but this might be the wrong way to do it."

"If I could've thought of a better way," Peggy answered, "I would've. You see how nervous Christi is. If Jasper hadn't been there when you came out, she would've been gone, possibly taking the answers to what really happened to Marsha and Gerald with her."

"How do I let myself get into these situations with you?"

"I don't know." She smiled. "Maybe I'm a bad influence. I'm sure your parents are thinking that about now."

Sam glanced at her as he turned on Highway 49. "Hunter has a big mouth."

"What else is new?" Peggy sobered. "I know how your parents feel. I wasn't happy about Paul becoming a police officer either. I thought it was a waste of his talent. I'm sure your parents feel the same way. You're very smart and a hard worker. You'd make a wonderful doctor just like Paul would've made a wonderful architect."

"Does that mean you're considering taking me on as a partner?"

"There's no thought involved with that, if you're sure that's what you want. You know I'd love to have you stay with the Potting Shed. I can't imagine working with anyone else. But you're giving up a lot to be a landscaper. I'm sure you've heard all the arguments from your parents."

Sam snorted. "You can say that again. Mom sobbed and Dad threatened to cut me off. He said they'd leave everything to Hunter if I didn't finish college and become a doctor. I always thought it was *my* idea to go into the medical profession. I realized they've been telling me I *had* to do this since I was a kid. But *you* know I've had my doubts for a while."

"I know you have. I've tried to stay out of it. I know your parents are disappointed right now, but they'll come around. You'll see."

"Thanks, new partner. Maybe you *are* a bad influence. I don't know if I would've realized how much I love doing this work if I hadn't answered your ad that day. And I think I'm good at what I do. I drive past houses and businesses we landscape all the time, and I'm proud of our work. I think that's important, too."

Peggy wished she could hug him. She brushed tears from her eyes and squeezed his big hand on the steering wheel. "I agree. Besides, you can always change your mind. There are plenty of older people in college now. If you decide landscaping isn't for you, you can go back to the original plan."

"Thanks." He flashed her a brilliant white smile. "We're going to take the botanical world by storm! By this time next year, we'll be the award-winning Potting Shed Landscaping."

She laughed. "You have lofty ambitions."

"Of course. I'm sure you wouldn't want it any other way."

"You're right. Do you want to come up with some kind of name that signifies the difference between the shop and the landscaping?"

"I don't know yet. Let me think about that." He stuck his hand out to her when he stopped at a traffic light. "Partner."

Peggy put her hand in his. "Partner."

The back glass slid open again. "Turn left up here," Christi said. "Hurry up. I think it's starting to rain."

It was raining hard by the time they

reached the old house on the outskirts of Mount Pleasant. There were about a dozen cars pulled into the yard and the driveway. Huge old oaks stood guard on the hill where the house sat. Stone pillars, mostly falling down, marked the drive.

It was easy to tell that this wood frame house was once a home. A rusted swing set sat in the yard. Cultivated roses and huge junipers full of developing berries grew wild by the porch. The house needed paint and a new roof. From the look of it, it was doubtful anyone still lived there.

Christi told them all to wait in the truck. Her long hair was plastered to her head and neck, her T-shirt revealingly wet. Peggy watched the girl walk up to a group of young men who stood in the shelter of the spreading oak trees that kept them dry.

"Do you think they'll go for it?" Selena whispered through the back window. "I hope so. It's drier up there under the trees, and I'm soaked. And I'm thirsty."

Sam glanced back at her. "How can you be wet *and* thirsty? You should've held your mouth open on the way here."

"Ugh!" Selena shivered and wrapped her arms around herself. "Bugs!"

"I've never been out here," Jasper told them. "I went to one of the meetings in

Charlotte. This looks more like a group of nervous businessmen to me. I don't like it. Christi's crazy to be part of this."

"Don't say that too loud," Sam warned. "They might be clean water activists *and* gun-toting nervous businessmen."

Christi came back to the truck. "Okay. They said you can stay for the meeting. But remember not to say *anything* about why you're really here."

"That will be easy," Selena whispered. "I don't have any idea why we're here."

Peggy got out of the truck. The group of men was watching all of them closely. She wasn't sure if she was going to be able to find out anything new. If she couldn't appeal to the members to hand over the aconite package, how would she move forward in the investigation?

They went inside the old house, carefully stepping around holes in the floors. Apparently there was no electricity, since there were several kerosene lamps on the fireplace mantel in the front room.

There were as many holes in the walls as there were in the floor. Peggy wondered why the group was meeting there. If they'd had meetings in Charlotte before, why come out all this way to meet? It made her uneasy as she looked into the faces of the members of the radical group.

"Beer?"

"No, thanks." Peggy smiled and tucked her hands into her pockets.

Sam stood beside her, glowering like Thor before a storm. "This is a bad idea."

"Hush," she warned. "I know you can mind your manners."

He glanced at her with one golden eyebrow raised but didn't say a word. Selena and Jasper stood behind them, almost pressed into the large fireplace.

Christi hadn't accompanied them into the house, but Peggy saw her come in through the back door. She approached them carefully with a quick nod at the man with the beer. "Peggy, come with me."

"She's not going anywhere without me." Sam crossed his arms over his chest, biceps bulging in his green Potting Shed T-shirt.

"Relax, Iron Giant. She'll be fine, but I need the rest of you to stay here and mingle," Christi said. "Talk about dirty water and how it affects us all. And quit looking like huddled mice. No one's going to eat you. Most of us are vegetarian."

Peggy patted Sam's arm. "It's okay. Let's not come this far to end up with nothing."

Sam didn't answer, but he didn't try to stop her again. Peggy looked back once as she followed Christi out the back door. Selena took one of the bottles of beer and started up a conversation with the man who was passing them out. Jasper stepped out of the corner and smiled at Sam.

"It's out here," Christi said as they walked out into the rain. "They were afraid to keep it anywhere else. No one except Marsha knew how to handle what was in it, and I guess she didn't do a very good job."

"So that's why you're out here." Peggy pushed her wet hair out of her face.

"We had to decide what to do with it. I convinced Stan, our president, it was safe to give it to you. We're lucky. He was arrested with you in Philadelphia last year. He believed the whole song and dance. Besides, I think he was scared to try to do something with it himself. Good timing for you."

"Do you know what Marsha and Gerald had planned to do with it?" Peggy stood outside a dilapidated shed beside a dripping magnolia.

"They planned to put it in the reservoir. Everyone thought people might pay more attention if they found an obvious poison in the water instead of the usual toxins." Christi smiled at her. "Sick, right? I guess we get desperate sometimes."

"I don't think anyone from your group

424

has anything to worry about at this point. Even if the police get involved, Marsha and Gerald are both dead. It was *their* plan. By turning the package over to me, the group shouldn't be involved. This time anyway. I hope for all our sakes you never get this desperate again."

Christi shrugged. "I gotta go back in for the meeting. Do whatever you have to do. The package is in there."

Peggy watched the girl walk back to the house in frustration. There was nothing she *could* do. She couldn't move the package out of the shed. There was no way of knowing if it was safe. She needed a hazmat unit to handle it, but she couldn't call for one without giving the location away. She didn't want to see Christi arrested, which could be a possibility despite her denials. They would have never found the package without her.

She blinked her eyes as she tried to think what she should do. Mist and fog were gathering about one hundred yards from where she was standing beside the shed. She walked past the old magnolia and felt her stomach drop.

There was a small pond behind the shed. It couldn't have been more than twenty feet around and didn't look very deep. Cattails and bulrushes grew on one side. An old pier was partially sticking out of the water.

Peggy felt certain this was the scene of Gerald's and Marsha's deaths. The pond was crusted with duckweed and other plant growth that covered the water in slimy green. She had to get a sample of the water, even though she hadn't come prepared.

She rummaged around in her pocketbook until she found an old aspirin bottle she kept for emergencies. She dumped the aspirins into the pocketbook then bent down to scoop some of the pond water into the bottle. If she was right, the same phytoplankton would be in the pond water as was in Gerald's and Marsha's lungs.

The problem was how to get the police and hazmat out there without ruining Christi's relationship with the group. It could be dangerous for the girl if they suspected she'd brought the police into the situation.

On the other hand, if Peggy's hunch was right and the pond was the crime scene, between that and the aconite package, she couldn't leave without telling someone. She had to think of some way to take care of the problem without implicating Christi.

She knew what to do. It was going to take some building up of her confidence to do it. She felt like she had no choice. She hoped

Sam, Jasper, and Selena agreed with her.

With a sigh she took out her cell phone and hunched over it in the pouring rain to keep it dry. When she was finished, she closed it and walked back to the house.

There was a heated debate taking place in the front room where the twenty or so group members had gathered. Thankfully, it didn't involve the Potting Shed group being there. Instead, it was about the level of natural arsenic found in local wells. Apparently, one source said the level was safe, but the group disagreed.

"Just because the EPA says the levels are safe doesn't mean anything," a young, intense man with a coal black beard argued. "They've lied to us before."

"But we don't have people dying from arsenic poisoning," a young woman disagreed. "If the levels were as high as you're saying they are, why wouldn't it be showing up in autopsies?"

"It is. The state is withholding that information." The young man slapped a folder on the floor. "This is proof that the levels are too high."

"Let's say they *are* too high," another man offered. "What can we do about it?"

"We have to send water samples out of state. We can give them to independent labs for testing and not tell them where the samples came from. Then we can go public when we get the results. Let's see them try to argue *that* away."

Everyone in the group added their comments to the discussion. The sound coming from outside was slight at first, sliding past the frogs and crickets, covered by the steady rain on the tin roof. The men and women, many of whom appeared to be college students and business owners, were talking so loudly they barely noticed.

Peggy took a deep breath. She stood in the corner of the room with Sam, Selena, Jasper, and Christi close by. There was no way to warn them about what was coming without ruining the whole thing. This way, Christi would be safe from suspicion. She hoped Sam would still be speaking to her by the time the night was over.

One man near the front door saw the first Cabarrus County sheriff's car pull into the drive. It was rapidly followed by several more brown cars, gray highway patrol cars, and a large hazmat unit. "Oh my God! They're here for us!" he yelled to the group.

It wasn't until that moment that Peggy realized her plan could have created a stand-off. If the group in the house was armed and willing to do anything not to be arrested, the scene could have turned ugly.

Barcly able to breathe, she said a prayer of thanks when the police called out for everyone to exit the house, and one by one, the group put up their hands and walked out.

"What's going on?" Sam askcd, putting up his hands.

As the group filtered outside, the law enforcement officers pushed them down into the runny red mud and handcuffed them.

"It won't take long," Peggy said undcr her breath. "Don't struggle. It'll be all right. Trust me."

"Peggy," Sam growled before he was pushed into the mud.

The group was divided in two so they would fit into the buses brought to transport them to Concord, where they would be processed. Peggy couldn't see whether or not Sam, Selena, or Jasper was in hcr group. Her face was covered with mud, and the handcuffs chafed her wrists. She hoped she'd made it plain on the phone about the toxin they would find in the shed. Out of the corner of her eye, she saw the suited hazmat team walking behind the house.

It was certainly not a good way to end the evening. They led her back to the bus, and she was instructed to stay facing forward.

She couldn't see because of the muddy hair in her eyes. She was worried about the others, but she'd made her choice.

Since everyone was being arrested, the group wouldn't be suspicious of the newcomers. If Christi was right and the group members hadn't done anything wrong, they'd be fine once Peggy explained the situation to the Cabarrus County sheriff. But if they were involved in what happened to Marsha and Gerald, they'd have to pay the price. It was a small one to pay to ensure the aconite was in safe hands and the possible crime scene would be preserved.

Peggy had seen something like this on *Law and Order* once — or it may have been in some detective movie. She was fairly sure John wouldn't have encouraged her to take this action, but he wouldn't have wanted her to go out there in the first place. She could imagine Steve would feel the same way.

There was going to be a little hell to pay for everyone until the truth could be safely told. They would all have to be bailed out to make it look good for Christi. She'd done the best she could in the situation. She only hoped it was the right thing to do.

Once the buses reached the county jail, the prisoners were escorted into the building. They were all a soaking, muddy mess dripping on the clean tile floors. Peggy couldn't tell where she was being taken. They divided everyone up again, and each person was sent to a small detention room. She tried to see someone she knew but could barely make out where she was supposed to walk.

The deputy beside her opened one of the doors, told her to step inside the room, and said someone would be with her shortly. She did as she was told, her heart pounding fiercely, even though she knew she wasn't really in any trouble. At least she hoped not.

Someone was already in the room. She could see shoes as she heard the door close behind her. A hand moved her hair out of her face as a key unlocked her handcuffs. "Bad night to play detective, Peggy," Jonas said.

24

Arrow Arum

Botanical: *Peltandra virginica*

Arrow arum is a freshwater plant always spotted growing along the water's edge. It is also known as duck corn because ducks love to eat it, making it a staple of their diets. The seeds contain calcium oxalate, making them unappetizing to most other birds. The seeds grow in a spike-shaped pod whose leaves can grow as high as three feet. The flower is thin and tapering with a narrow spadix. The plant also grows black green berries. It has become a popular water plant for gardeners in recent years.

The other shoes in the room turned out to belong to Al. They'd both come out to answer her summons left on Al's answering machine. "We don't know anything yet except that the package in the shed was the one from the biotech lab," Al told her. "Looks like you did a good job, Peggy. But you could've identified yourself to the sheriff and avoided all this for you and your friends."

Peggy explained her thinking about keeping Christi's name clean with the group. "I don't think they're as bad as people make them out to be, but I didn't want them thinking she ratted them out."

Jonas chuckled. "Well, that was your call. Are you prepared to go through the whole thing?"

She was and told him so. She told Hunter and Steve the same thing when she called them a few hours later.

Hunter was glad to come and bail out the Potting Shed group. She did it with emergency funding Steve provided and around two a.m. they arrived to pick up the tired, damp jailbirds.

Some members of the Water Revolution group had already been bailed out. Peggy was worried about them, but the police had nothing substantial to hold most of them on, except one man who had an outstanding warrant for DUI against him.

Christi and a friend with a car were waiting for her brother outside and offered to drive him home. Peggy was glad the girl didn't suspect she'd called the sheriff. Christi thought it was a freak accident that caught them all there, and there were no hard feelings. Peggy didn't tell her any different.

Sam and Selena were another story. They drove back from the courthouse to Sam's truck with Peggy and Steve, the two young people taking turns yelling at Peggy. She reminded them briskly it was their idea to come along with her. She didn't tell them she was the one who called the sheriff either. What was the point of throwing oil on *that* fire?

Steve pulled out of the drive after making sure Sam's truck was running. He headed back toward Charlotte. Peggy noticed he hadn't said a word the entire time. Had she finally committed the fatal error that would end their relationship?

"I appreciate you coming out for us," she said. "And getting the money together for the bail."

"Al told me I'd get it back after this is over," Steve responded. "Otherwise I would've let all of you rot in jail for your crimes."

It was dark. Peggy had to look carefully at his face in the pale dash light to see if he was joking. His voice sounded serious, and she couldn't make out a smile on his lips. "Well, thank you."

They drove along in silence for several miles. Peggy didn't know what to say. She wanted to tell him everything but was afraid she'd have to get through the last part of bailing her out of jail in the middle of the night first.

"I'm sorry —"

"I can't believe the lengths to which you'll go not to organize dinner," he began. "You'd rather go out with your radical friends and get arrested than break out a box of macaroni and cheese. I'm not sure about this relationship. Where do we go from here?"

Peggy threw herself against him, kissing him over and over again while his SUV swerved from one side of the road to another. "I thought you were *really* angry. I thought we might break up or something."

He laughed. "Because I had to drive out to Concord in the middle of the night and get you out of jail? *Please!* I always expect that from you."

When the car was steady on the road again and Peggy was back in her seat wiping tears from her grimy face, she told him the story from the beginning. "I gave the pond sample to Jonas. He'll probably get Harold up and make him analyze it. I could be wrong, but I have this gut feeling that Marsha and Gerald died there."

"I hope you're right. Maybe this will wrap it up." Steve glanced at her. "You know, I'm not mad about bailing you out. I *am* angry that you didn't call me and let me know what was going on. I know it's not the same, but when I'm waiting for a foal to be born and it's going to take longer than I thought, I call and tell you. The next time you have to infiltrate some strange group of people who might kill you or get you arrested, I'd at least appreciate a phone call."

"You would've tried to talk me out of it. I only had a minute to decide I was going to do this."

"You had a long ride from the Potting Shed to that old house. You could've called me anywhere along the way. True, I might've argued the point about your safety, although I would've felt better knowing you were with Sam. I can't see too many people messing with him."

"I'm sorry. You're right. I should've called. But we couldn't fit you and Shakespeare into the truck as well, and I *know* that's what you would've wanted to do."

"That's a good point. And you *did* save the world and get the aconite off the street.

436

Next time, call me and make something up. You can always say you're working late. I won't know the difference, but at least I won't look for you at both our houses and find your bike still at the Potting Shed with no one there."

Peggy caught her breath. "I didn't think about you doing that. Is there some way I can make it up to you?"

"I think if you take a shower when we get back and you kiss me good night — not around Shakespeare either, a *real* kiss — I might find it in my heart to get over it. *This* time."

Peggy met Steve's rigid requirements for forgiveness and then was up early the next morning, heading for the police lab before eight a.m. Harold and Mai were already there with Doc Williamson on speakerphone as they compared notes.

"If it isn't the heroine of the hour," Harold greeted her. "Come in. Sit down. Maybe you can do some real work before you get arrested again."

Doc Williamson laughed. "That's right. Does she get to work on this case anymore, considering she's a convicted water rights activist?"

Mai added, "You know Peggy. She always

dives in headfirst."

Peggy was ready to move on. "If everyone is finished giving me a hard time because I found the aconite, could someone take a moment to check my water sample for phytoplanktons?"

"No need, Dr. Lee," Doc Williamson informed her. "Harold had some of the water brought out here so we could both check it. It matches what we found in Marsha's and Gerald's lungs. We have a crime scene."

"Except, according to Sheriff Barbee, we don't actually have a crime scene except by virtue of the stolen aconite," Harold told her.

"What do you mean?" Peggy asked. "Marsha and Gerald are still dead."

"Apparently when Sheriff Barbee went out to tell Mrs. Capshaw what happened, she and her daughter broke down and confessed to moving both bodies." Mai ignored Harold's frown at having her steal his thunder. "They told him the daughter, Mandy, followed her father to the old house in Mount Pleasant. She thought he was having an affair with Marsha and planned to confront him. She found them dead in the pond."

"Why did she move the bodies?" Peggy

couldn't believe the two had kept quiet through the investigation.

"Mandy called her mother. The two of them moved the bodies so they wouldn't be found together," Mai explained. "They still didn't get it. They didn't realize aconite was involved. They just thought Gerald was having another affair, and they didn't want everyone to find them dead together. They put Gerald where he was supposed to be at the dam. Then they found Marsha's address in her wallet. I guess they thought she was wet anyway, why not leave her in the pool?"

Peggy was astonished. "So Marsha and Gerald weren't murdered after all?"

"The sheriff and Captain Rimer will hold a joint press conference this afternoon to announce the deaths are being ruled accidental," Harold answered. "The evidence backs up the theory that both of them were overcome by the aconite and accidentally drowned in the pond when the old pier gave way beneath them. We believe they were planning on testing their scheme to poison the water and lost control of the experiment."

Doc Williamson added, "The daughter didn't know what was in the box. She found it on an old dock or pier and put it in the shed where hazmat picked it up last night.

She's being tested for aconite poisoning right now. We won't be releasing that information until the area has been thoroughly evaluated. No need to start a panic."

"Will Benita and Mandy be charged with anything?" Peggy tried to take it all in. When the answers finally came, they rushed in.

"There could be some charges against the mother," Mai said. "I think everyone is still considering that. But it's over for the most part."

"Your friend is going to be released this afternoon," Doc Williamson told Peggy. "Good job, Dr. Lee. This was a tough one."

"It's amazing." Peggy smiled. "I wouldn't have guessed it, but I'm glad it worked out this way."

"I think you should receive a commendation for your work, Dr. Lee." Harold smirked. "Or perhaps you could get a reduced sentence. Or a Get Out of Jail Free card for your next visit."

Peggy ignored him. It was over. That was all that mattered. Ruth would go free. Marsha's and Gerald's tragic deaths were a terrible mistake. Now maybe she could get on with planning her grand reopening for the Potting Shed.

Peggy and more than fifty newspaper and

TV reporters met Ruth as she was released from the Stanly County jail. The release took some coverage away from Sheriff Barbee and Jonas as they explained what had happened to Marsha Hatley and Gerald Capshaw and how they'd solved the case.

"Thank you for meeting me," Ruth said to Peggy as they pushed their way through the crowd. "I tried calling Stephanie, but I couldn't get in touch with her."

"Don't be silly. I was glad to come out and get you. It was the least I could do since I feel like I had a part in putting you in there in the first place." Peggy opened the truck doors, and they got in despite the reporters screaming questions at them.

"That's better." Ruth shut the truck door, sat back in her seat, and closed her eyes. "This has been the worst week of my life."

Peggy started the truck. "I hope things pick up from here. It was a terrible thing that happened, but now that we know the truth, we can all get on with our lives."

They drove out of the jail parking lot, the press finally giving up and wandering over to hear what the sheriff had to say. Peggy had thought for one moment that one of the reporters was going to try to climb on the truck. He must've changed his mind at the last minute. She supposed even a great scoop wasn't worth his life.

"I really appreciate you getting me out of this." Ruth opened her eyes and watched the passing scenery along the highway. "I don't know what I would've done without you."

"I was only trying to find out what really happened. Who knew it would turn out to be an accident? It looked bad for a while. You can never tell until it's over."

"That's true." Ruth smiled at her. "Do you think we could stop at that Sonic place and get one of those frozen yogurt fruity drinks? I don't know why, but I've been craving one of them. But I know it's a little out of the way."

"Sure thing. One frozen yogurt fruity drink coming up." Peggy turned right to head toward Sonic and through the shopping district of Albemarle.

They pulled into one of the parking spaces at Sonic. "I want the peach and strawberry one," Ruth said. "I'd offer to buy you one, but I don't have any money. They wouldn't let me bring any with me when they arrested me."

"You can buy me one later," Peggy said. "You know, you still owe me scuba lessons."

"That's right. But I'm surprised you want

to get in the water after this. Who knows what's in it?"

Peggy ordered the two drinks, and they waited, listening to the sounds of a band both women recognized but couldn't name. A young, fresh-faced girl brought them their drinks. Peggy paid for them and told the girl to keep the change.

"Mmm," Ruth said as she slurped. "This is what I was craving. Thanks."

"This is good!" Peggy sipped more of her drink. "I think the Water Revolution means well. We seem to have trouble keeping the air and water clean."

"But putting poison into the water doesn't seem to be the answer to me," Ruth said. "I can see protesting, writing letters, that kind of thing. But if someone would've fallen into that pond after it was poisoned, they'd be dead, too. It was a bad idea. The police were lucky the package didn't fall into the pond when Marsha and Gerald fell in. That pier was pretty rickety."

Peggy stopped sucking her fruit drink. "What did you say?"

Ruth looked up. "What did I say?"

"You said something about the pier at the pond being rickety. I thought hazmat had that off limits in case of contamination from the package. What intrepid reporter managed to sneak in and report that?"

Ruth stirred her drink with her straw. "I don't know. I heard it somewhere. This is good, isn't it? I think the summer got hotter while I was in jail. I guess it must be global warming. I suppose there's a rad group for that, too."

Peggy stared at her old friend. "I can't believe anyone would endanger their life to take a picture of an old pier."

Ruth stared back for a long moment, then her gaze dropped away. "It doesn't matter. People do things. They might regret them later, but it's too late."

It was as though the world began to move in slow motion, but everything was startlingly clear. The last swallow of frozen yogurt stuck in Peggy's throat when she tried to speak. She *knew*. "What happened?"

"It doesn't matter." Ruth smiled. "It's all over now."

"No. It isn't. We got it all wrong anyway, didn't we?" Peggy put her drink down in the cup holder. "At least *I* got it all wrong. The police were right, weren't they?"

Ruth wiped the condensation from the sides of her cup with a napkin. "You know I didn't mean it to happen. I saw them together, and I followed them out there. Gerald wouldn't answer my phone calls anymore. I wanted to know what was going on."

"And then, when you found them together?"

"They were unconscious on the pier. They may have already been dead. I'm not sure."

"You put them in the water."

Ruth sipped more of her drink. "It just happened. I tried to help Gerald up, and the pier broke under him. He slid into the water. I didn't know about the poison, but it felt right to leave him there in that slimy green pond. Once he was in there, it was easy to put her in, too."

"They were alive," Peggy told her. "There was water in their lungs."

"I know now. It happened so fast. It wasn't real at all. Afterward, I left." Ruth stared out the window. "Imagine my surprise to find out he was at the bottom of Badin Lake. I didn't know what to think after that. I guess his sweet little wife and wonderful daughter couldn't handle the truth about that two-timing scum."

Peggy drew in a deep breath. "It can't stay this way. You have to tell somebody."

"Why? It's all settled now. There's no point in going back over it. I might've saved a few lives, too. Look what they were planning on doing. I don't feel bad about this. I

445

don't think you should either."

"We can't look the other way. You have to tell the truth," Peggy insisted.

"There's no reason to ruin the rest of my life over this. I know you wouldn't expect me to do it. Let's let sleeping dogs lie. Everything is settled. We can go on with our lives like you said."

Peggy stared at her friend, realizing she didn't know her as well as she'd thought. "We can't go on, Ruth. You have to tell the truth."

"Or what? You won't be my friend anymore?" She laughed. "I know you, Peggy. You can't bring yourself to kill a spider that climbs in your bathtub. Give yourself a few days. You'll feel better about this, and we'll have lunch and plan that scuba date."

Peggy didn't answer. She felt cold despite the heat of the day. She drove Ruth to her house on Lake Tillery without saying another word. Ruth got out of the truck and thanked her again for picking her up. "I'll call you in the morning. Everything that's happened has been for the best. You'll see. Things will be fine."

Ruth smiled and waved before she disappeared into the tall pine trees that surrounded her lakefront house. Peggy picked up her cell phone and dialed the number for the Stanly County Sheriff's Office. "I want to report a perfect murder."

The renovations to the Potting Shed were finished in the early morning hours before the grand reopening party. Emil and Sofia had to fight Jasper and Sam for space as they delivered food while the two young men finished helping Selena, Peggy, and Keeley stock the shop.

It didn't look like it was going to come together for the party, but by the time the first guest showed up, the Potting Shed group was all smiles, sporting their new T-shirts and ready to show off all of the changes.

Peggy couldn't be sure, but it looked as though everyone she'd sent invitations to showed up plus a few more. Steve came with Shakespeare right behind Mai and Paul. Even Harold wandered in, confessing that he'd wondered what the shop looked like.

By the time Lizzie Maxwell and her photographer from *Southern Living* made their way through the crowded door area, the party was in full swing. Customers and reporters were impressed by the water feature and plants that caught their attention.

Peggy spent most of her time in the center of the room, giving away bulbs for planting in the coming fall months and answering questions about gardening and the shop.

One reporter asked her about her work on the Capshaw-Hatley murder case. "You're a friend of the accused, right?"

"We were friends for a long time," Peggy answered carefully since her testimony would be used during Ruth's trial. "That's all I can say."

"Did your knowledge of plants help with that case?" The reporter pushed forward.

"My love of plants influences all of my life," Peggy responded. "Excuse me. I see someone I have to talk to."

Christi had just entered the shop. She looked a little lost in the large crowd. Peggy picked up a cup of punch and went to greet her. "Hello! I was hoping you'd come."

"Thanks." Christi took the punch and looked around the shop. "This place is really cool. I don't know much about gardening, but I can imagine hanging around here."

"Well, if you're ever looking for a job, I'd be happy to talk to you. Jasper tells me you're an art student."

She nodded. "That's right. I wish I could paint this."

"I have just the person you need to meet."

Peggy took her arm and guided her toward Nathan, who was sitting beside the pond sketching the arrow arum they had such a hard time getting started. "Nathan, this is Christi. Christi, Nathan. You two seem to have a lot in common. Excuse me, I think I see someone I've neglected."

Peggy left the two young people and walked over to pat Shakespeare's head. "I'm glad you two could make it. What do you think?"

"Compared to what it looked like at midnight when I saw it the last time, it looks pretty good," Steve said. "You *were* talking to me, right?"

"I think so." She looked around the room at the large number of people who were eating and talking. "I have something I want to show you when this is over."

He smiled. "I hope it involves something more than punch and cookies."

"My suggestion would be to take Shakespeare home and come back in about an hour." She stood close to him and whispered in his ear, "I've heard there's a spot beside the pool that's a romantic dinnertime favorite for some couples who might enjoy that kind of thing."

"I'll be back in an hour." He kissed her and laughed. "And as long as *you're* here waiting, I really don't care if there's anything to eat or not."

PEGGY'S GARDEN JOURNAL

Summer

During the summer months, gardening takes on a less active role for most folks. The flurry of spring planting is over, and the role of the gardener is more about maintenance. This is the time to sit back and enjoy what your hard work has brought forth from the earth.

Well, almost, except for the maintenance part. Maintenance can be a lot of work, even in a small garden. Between getting rid of slugs, keeping roses from getting too leggy, and watering, there is still plenty to do.

I recommend you take out that hammock for rests between jobs. After all, there is nothing like the scents and sounds of a summer garden. I hope you planted something for the butterflies and hummingbirds that add so much richness to our summer outdoor experience.

It's an old belief that you shouldn't plant

during the hot summer months. The only time not to plant is during a drought. Summer planting can be even better than late fall planting, since the ground is much warmer and more open to root growth. Results will be sensational! Water daily after planting as roots are forming.

Peggy

Summer Garden Q & A

Summer can be difficult because so much is going on all over your yard. As gardeners, we can't wait for this season, but it can be hectic with kids home for the summer, extra company, and vacations, all things that can lead you to spend less time in the yard. Try to take a few minutes to look around your garden and see what needs to be done. It might be hot, but a little time now will be a very welcome respite for your plants.

Q: How do I dry hydrangeas?
A: You can do it naturally by letting the flowers stay on the plant until the end of summer. Cut the blooms with as much stem length as you want before the first frost. Remove leaves and place the stems in a vase or bucket without water. Keep in a dry place, because damp can encourage mold. At one time people believed you had to

hang them upside down, but it's not really necessary.

You can also dry the flowers in silica gel. It takes longer and is more expensive, but if you need to get the flowers inside, it can be the answer for you. Silica gel is available at craft shops.

Q: I have a yellow jasmine vine that is not blooming. What should I do?
A: You might have to move the plant. Yellow jasmine likes early morning sun and should be planted facing the southeast for best results.

Q: I have several hosta plants that have developed small holes in the leaves. What should I do?
A: It's probably slugs. You can put sand or ash from your fireplace around the plant, and slugs won't cross it.

Q: How do I make my water lilies bloom?
A: Ponds should be located where they receive lots of sunshine. This is the most common reason for water lilies not to bloom. Also, don't place water lilies where water sprays on the tops of their pads. They don't like to have their pads wet. Keep water lilies well-fertilized. Try two Pondtabbs per

water lily each month during growing season.

Q: *What is deadheading, and should I be doing it in my garden?*
A: Deadheading is the term for removing the faded or dead flower heads from a plant. Deadheading is beneficial and necessary to the plant. It lengthens the blooming time of some plants, increases the amount of blooms for others, and keeps the garden looking neat. Perennials as well as annuals benefit from deadheading.

Q: *What can I do for my leggy roses?*
A: You should probably consider pruning your roses. Before you ask if summer is a bad time for this, the answer is that you can do it at any time of the year. Prune out the interior branches first as this will create more circulation and prevent fungal diseases. Prune the branches at the node of the leaf branches or stems where two branches meet or where a leaf meets a stem, about one quarter inch up from the node.

Your rosebush probably needs fertilizer, too. Find an all-purpose fertilizer that is higher in phosphorus. Use organic fertilizers like bone meal, dried blood, and Epsom salts to increase the micronutrients in the soil. Work it into the soil at the base of the plant.

Starting a Moongarden

People are so busy nowadays, it's hard to find time to enjoy your garden during daylight hours. Even with the long summer days, most people are strapped for time with jobs and other activities. There is a way around this problem by planting a moon garden. Night-blooming gardens are designed for evening enjoyment. They are attractive during the day, but they take on a whole new look and feel at dusk. Pale-colored, silver plants and white flowers reflect light from the setting sun and the rising moon. They shine luminously and give the garden a wonderful glow. Fragrance is stronger after dark in these gardens and becomes even more important.

A small moon garden is a good way to find out how you feel about this type of planting. It can be enjoyed during the late evening and early night hours, even later if you enhance with lights or view during a full moon. Be sure to pick a space that is best seen in moonlight as your white flowers will be breathtaking in the silver, pale light.

Before we talk about plants, there are

other ways to enhance your moon garden. Fountains and birdbaths are nice. The water shimmers in the moon's glow. Pick white, silver, or pale-colored accessories. Add white rocks for more appeal. If you plant near a tree, hang clear glass ornaments on the branches or silver wind chimes.

Your moon garden doesn't have to be planted in the ground either. You can find a pretty outdoor table or decorative plant stand to hold your plants on decks or stairs. Use white or pale-colored pots. Don't forget: you can always paint them if you can't find what you want. The idea is to create a space that will be best seen in the moonlight.

Some flowers only bloom at night, and others will stay open at night even though they are day bloomers. Bear in mind the space you have for your garden and how it will look in moonlight and shadow. Take your time, and view the area during the next full moon, if need be, before planting.

Some good plants for this type of garden include:

- Giant moonflower is a fast-growing vine related to the morning glory. It is an annual and could climb to as high as ten feet. The flowers remain closed during the day, opening at dusk to release a sweet fragrance. The large flowers can be seen very clearly in the moonlight.

- Pink evening primrose is a nice border plant that grows to about twelve inches. It has pretty, silky, rose-colored flowers that have a pale yellow center. They will open in the evening with a gentle perfume.

- Jasmine tobacco is a sweet-scented, flowering tobacco with white, trumpet-shaped flowers. The plant will flower at night and during the day, but flower heads must be constantly picked off to keep brown ends away that would ruin the effect.

- White angel's trumpet is a wonderful moon garden plant with large, showy white trumpet-shaped flowers that droop down about eight inches along a sturdy stalk. These can be extremely fragrant, especially at night.

- White spider plant will grow about three feet tall. It boasts almost shiny white flowers that grow in profusion. This is planted from seed.

- Queen Anne's lace is a weed to most of us but is highly cultivated in other parts of the world. The play of moon and shadow on the soft, lacy flowers makes its own statement about the value of this plant in a moon garden. Just remember that it grows tall.

- Dusty miller has a very silver look in the moon's light. It will be about six inches tall and grows quickly.
- Pure white petunias are a knockout in a moon garden. They smell wonderful at dusk and are easy to grow.

If you like your summer moon garden, remember: the moon shines all year long. Plan for the seasons. Choose a variety of white annuals and perennials, shrubs, and trees that flower at different times. White hyacinth and jonquils in the spring; dogwood, spirea, and rhododendrons for late nights. Magnolia and gardenia will truly enhance a large moon garden. Consider white mums and shasta daisies for fall. If you want to put a pond in your moonlight area, you can include white water lilies and water irises. In winter, your garden can gleam with paperwhite birch and white holly.

There are many possibilities. Try blending scents and shapes, textures, and design. Remember to use your taller plants as backdrops and shorter plants with large blooms in front. Enjoy your night blooms in the moonlight with the music of the breezes in your wind chimes and the song of crickets and frogs. This is the time to relax and let the enchantment and beauty of the night take you away.

Encourage Native Plants

The importance of encouraging native plants in your yard can't be overstated. Native plants are ones that have been living in your area for more than fifty years. Anywhere you live is home to beautiful native plants that make excellent garden plants.

Native plants have adapted to local conditions down through the years. They are easier to grow and maintain, which saves you time and money. These plants can withstand droughts, freezes, and other severe weather better than exotics. Native wildflowers are also perennials or self-sowing biennials that will take care of replanting for you. They will not invade natural habitats the way exotic, invasive plants do. Native plants also promote biodiversity, offering the food, nectar, cover, and nesting areas that local birds, butterflies, and mammals need.

If you are unsure about the native plants in your area, check out these websites to get started or contact a local nursery. Be sure to purchase your native plants, don't tear them out of the ground so that none are lost in our haste to propagate more.

www.epa.gov/greenacres/
www.abnativeplants.com
www.npsbc.org
www.rirdc.gov.au/programs/wnp.html
http://wildflower.utexas.edu/organizations/ affiliates.php

Sarah P. Duke Memorial Garden

There are some beautiful botanical gardens in North Carolina. Each is slightly different in form and design, some more formal than others. Each is a treasure to be savored and appreciated.

For gardeners, they can also be a source of inspiration and ideas. You might not be able to have the same elaborate design or quantity that you see in a public garden, but you can copy them on a smaller scale. A walk through a garden like this can inspire some ideas on what you'd like to see in your garden. The plants you see in a local garden are likely to do well in yours, since master gardeners have scrutinized what will grow in their area.

One of the best gardens in the state is the

Sarah P. Duke Gardens in Chapel Hill. Built on fifty-five acres in the heart of Duke University, most of the garden is located in a valley that the planners of Duke University hoped to turn into a lake in the 1920s. Fortunately for all of us, funds ran short. The idea of a lake with elegant fountains was abandoned, and the first plantings were made in the early 1930s.

The garden is a result of the vision and enthusiasm of Dr. Frederic M. Hanes, an early member of the original faculty of the Duke Medical School. Dr. Hanes possessed a special love for gardening. He walked by the debris-filled ravine and determined he would turn it into a garden of his favorite flower, the iris.

He persuaded his friend, Sarah P. Duke, widow of one of the founders of the university, Benjamin N. Duke, to give twenty thousand dollars to finance a garden that would bear her name.

By 1935, more than one hundred flower beds were in glorious bloom with forty thousand irises, twenty-five thousand daffodils, ten thousand small bulbs and assorted annuals. Sadly, all of the plants were washed away in heavy summer rains and a flooding stream. By the time of Sarah P. Duke's death in 1936, the original gardens were destroyed.

Dr. Hanes would not be defeated. He convinced Sarah's daughter, Mary Duke Biddle, to construct a new garden on higher ground as a memorial to her mother. Ellen Shipman (1869–1950), a pioneer in American landscape design, was selected to engineer both the construction and the planting of the new garden.

Duke Gardens is considered Shipman's greatest work and a national architectural treasure. Most of the 650 other gardens she designed are gone today. This masterpiece lives on with her delicate touch showing in every flower bloom and twist in the path that leads you through the garden.

The Sarah P. Duke Gardens consists of four major parts: the original Terraces and their immediate surroundings, the H. L. Blomquist Garden of Native Plants (this contains flora specific to the Southeast United States), and the Culberson Asiatic Arboretum (devoted to plants of eastern Asia). There are five miles of allées, walks, and pathways throughout the Doris Duke Center and surrounding gardens.

The garden charges no admission and receives no tax money. Half of its operating budget comes from Duke University. It depends on donor gifts for additional support. It provides a fantastic background for weddings and other events as well as a wealth of horticultural information and education. It is a place that provides inspiration for those who come and spend time here.

A few words of caution: Wear your good walking shoes. The garden is huge, and though there is something delightful at every turn, it will take a couple of hours to walk through it. Consider bringing snacks and something to drink. You won't want to stop and go back for something at the entrance to the garden. There are plants for sale in a small shop as you come in, but wait to purchase them until you are ready to leave.

To visit or for more information:
Sarah P. Duke Gardens
426 Anderson Street
Box 90341
Duke University
Durham, NC 27708-0341
919-684-3698

Happy Gardening!

We hope you have enjoyed this Large Print book. Other Thorndike, Wheeler, and Chivers Press Large Print books are available at your library or directly from the publishers.

For information about current and upcoming titles, please call or write, without obligation, to:

Publisher
Thorndike Press
295 Kennedy Memorial Drive
Waterville, ME 04901
Tel. (800) 223-1244

or visit our Web site at:

http://gale.cengage.com/thorndike

OR

Chivers Large Print
published by BBC Audiobooks Ltd
St James House, The Square
Lower Bristol Road
Bath BA2 3SB
England
Tel. +44(0) 800 136919
email: bbcaudiobooks@bbc.co.uk
www.bbcaudiobooks.co.uk

All our Large Print titles are designed for easy reading, and all our books are made to last.